War Machines

Gregory Peterson

War Machines by Gregory Peterson

Published by Six String Press

Cover by ebooklaunch.com

ISBN: 978-0-578-28191-9

To Amber.
My lifeguard in the storm.

ACKNOWLEDGMENTS

Lots of people to thank here, particularly my family for not telling me that I'm crazy and to knock it off: Dr. Steven Finkelstein of the University of Texas, Austin for answering my ridiculous physics questions without laughing his ass off—any mistakes are mine, not his; Brandy and Miles Penner for letting me trash their beautiful homes in my book; my Beta Team of Neil, Steve, and Reagan, you all rock in my book.

Most of all—my humble thanks go to you, Reader. Without you, none of this can happen. By the way, if you enjoy my book, please don't forget to leave a review at your favorite outlet for that sort of thing. Cheers.

AN UNEXPECTED BEATING 5

WE ARE FAMILY 15

TIGHT WAD HILL 28

BREAKING THE RULES 44

YOU DROPPED A BOMB ON ME 51

FIRE AND ICE 61

HERE COMES REVENGE 68

THE REAPER 76

DON'T ASK ME NO QUESTIONS 79

WOULD I LIE TO YOU? 88

INSIDE INFORMATION 97

VIDEO GAMES 103

THE DEVIL WEARS A SUIT AND TIE 110

WHO DO YOU WANT TO BE 120

ON THE DOORSTEP 133

SKIN 138

SEMPER GUMBY 145

DEATH DON'T HAVE NO MERCY 151

BURNIN FOR YOU 163

BRAIN DAMAGE 174

ONLY SOLUTIONS 186

CRAZY TRAIN 198

THUNDERSTRUCK 211

RUNNIN WITH THE DEVIL 219

HIGHWAY TO HELL 227

END OF THE WORLD AS WE KNOW IT 234

IT SERVES YOU RIGHT TO SUFFER 242

FLIES AND SPIDERS 251

BATTLE WITHOUT HONOR OR HUMANITY 267

THE SOUND OF SILENCE 287

SUGAR MOUNTAIN 295

MASTER OF PUPPETS 307

NOT DEAD YET 314

DELETER 325

YOU WANT IT DARKER 327

COPY OF A 338

ONE MAN ARMY 352

LOST IN TIME AND SPACE 362

AN UNEXPECTED BEATING

The back of my head throbbed from where they sucker punched me coming into the alley.

Always know when to leave the party: that's one of my main rules. Rules keep you safe. Rules also keep you out of jail. And they definitely keep you from being held up against a brick wall by a couple of well-dressed walking mountains of muscle while a third little weasel of a guy with halitosis holds a knife to your throat. To add insult to injury, it happened to be my knife he's holding.

Always know when to leave the party.

The shimmering mist, one of the fifty different kinds of rain in Portland, Oregon, washed the night air. That clean October mingling of the scents of cold rain, the evergreens, and wet pavement that I loved was being ruined by weasel-boy deciding to get up close and personal while he made his point—with my knife.

"Where were you headed to in such a hurry, Al?" he wheezed in a thick Russian accent.

"You know, just taking in a breath of air before you decided to make that a bad idea. Have you considered breath mints, Mort?"

Thing Number One punctuated my wit with a solid rabbit punch to my breadbox, forcing my neck down harder on the inward-bent edge of my kukri. Believe it or not, one of my other rules is to keep my mouth shut as much as I can. It's one of those rules that I seem determined to ignore.

I really gotta start following my own advice.

I looked up at Thing One. He had a dirty-brown mustache that stretched across his face to his sideburns, and his hair was pulled back in a ridiculous man-bun. "I love what you've done with your hair. How do you get it to grow out of your nostrils that way?" I gasped.

Thing One let loose another shot to my gut, doubling me over again.

See?

Mortimer Madievsky—aka weasel-boy—shook his head as he looked down to his left, where my loaded black duffel bag sat in a widening puddle. "You always pack for your walks, Al?"

"I needed to go to the laundromat."

"The laundromat?" Mort nudged my bag with his foot. "Lotta laundry."

"Yeah, I'm a dirty boy. Hey, you know what? Why don't you come with me?"

Mort snorted. "Why would I want to do that?"

"I think there is a dentist across the street from the cleaners. Maybe you could stop in for an emergency oral detox while I wash my underwear. That way, they'd both stop smelling like ass."

Mort glared as Thing Number Two decided it was his turn. The blow came in low and fast, but this time I was ready for it, tightening my abs while exhaling when he connected: it makes it hurt less. That's what I told myself anyway as I sucked wind afterward.

Mort used his free hand to reach inside my Columbia Titanium jacket and pull out the long rectangle of paper stuck in the inside pocket. "Looks like a boarding pass to me…a flight tonight to San Francisco. Hmm, I thought you hated flying." He flicked the pass against my face. "It looks like you are skipping town, Leigh."

"Aww, it's just so fucking adorable when you pretend you know how to read," my mouth said before it checked in with my brain.

Mort moves quickly for a little weasel. The hand holding my knife dropped down and to the side as his elbow came across my jaw whip-fast, drawing blood and ringing my bell. I spun and bounced off both the Things as they shoved me between them like a pinball for a few moments while I hunched my body and made the most of the distraction. It ended with a final shove into Mort who grabbed me by the throat and pulled me close to him.

"Anything else you want to say?" Mort inquired.

My brain sent down a rapid response team to lock up my mouth while I shook my head in what I hoped was the negative.

He shoved me back into the waiting arms of the Things. "Good. You're not entirely stupid." Mort smiled and I got a good look at the reason why no breath mint was ever going to help, as well as why my little comment about the dentist had made Mort snap— the half-dozen teeth that remained in his head were jagged and yellowed. They looked like they hadn't seen a toothbrush since Amazon was a startup. A little more *Eau de Mort* wafted into my face, causing me to retch a mouthful of blood. "Mr. S. always says what a smart little thief you are. I was starting to wonder."

Mort nodded to his muscle, and I dropped to the ground— soaking my knees and scouring my palms with the rough sidewalk while rain and blood dripped down my face. "Now, before you go back to your Chink-infested pad by the Bay, Mr. S. would like a word." He gave an exaggerated shrug. "Maybe your fingers…maybe more, but that's up to him. Let's go."

In addition to his many other charms, Mort is also a racist shitheel.

I pushed myself up to a mostly vertical position as one of Mort's well-heeled goons scooped up my duffel while his buddy grabbed the back of my collar, heaving me all the way back up. We headed out of the alley onto Burnside, where a black limo idled by the curb. Despite Mort's comment, I am not a small man or a lightweight, but the goon had me up on my toes and off-balance while he escorted me to the car. He knew enough about me to know that letting me have solid footing could be bad for him. I had already decided to take the meeting—albeit under duress—but it was good to know that despite being outnumbered, disarmed, and recently pummeled, they knew I was still dangerous.

Well, it helped my ego to think that anyhow.

Mort followed us to the car, tapping my kukri against his thigh as he walked. He stared up at me (did I mention he's short?) as he passed by our not-so-little group, keeping eye contact with me and happily not noticing the new bulges in my coat. We got to the curb, and he opened the limo's rear door.

As the door swung open, I caught a brief glimpse of my reflection in the rain-streaked window. My very Irish pug nose was as crooked as Lombard Street, but in fairness, it had looked that way before they beat on me. Water dripped from my shaved head, and the bruise on my jaw was blooming like a mutated rose against the paleness of my graveyard-tan skin—courtesy of the past year in Oregon.

Mort leaned down and said something I couldn't hear to the occupant of the limo. He stepped back and nodded his head in the direction of the open door. "Get in."

I thought about fight and flight for a brief moment. We were out in the open and not in the cramped confines of the alley where the fight had been in their favor. I was pretty sure I could outrun the lumbering Things One and Two, all that muscle would slow them down. Mort was a heavy smoker, so he was no problem in a footrace. But there was nowhere in the Pacific Northwest I would be able to hide from the owner of the limo. Like I said, I was taking the meeting whether I wanted to or not.

I got in.

The smell of leather washed over me as I climbed into the back of the dimly lit limo. Across from me sat a tall, powerfully built man in an immaculate Savile Row suit. He kept his long salt and pepper hair pulled back into a ponytail—which lent him a certain elegance. Anyone else trying to pull that would have looked like a douche. His ink-black eyes regarded me with a look that could have been amusement but knowing his reputation, it was probably the same look he would give a bunch of puppies before drowning them one by one as their littermates were forced to watch.

There was another man in the seat next to me, but his upper body remained in shadow. All I saw were blue jeans and expensive leather shoes. As he said nothing, I directed my attention toward the boss.

Josef Sabitov, Pakhan of the Pacific Northwest Bratva, reached behind him and pulled out a towel. He handed it to me with one pale, long-fingered hand. A knotted cord was wrapped around his wrist: it was a chotki, an Eastern Orthodox prayer rope. I knew he wore a three-bar crucifix under his shirt as well. Sabitov was a devout believer, but I wasn't exactly sure how all that squared with his business.

I nodded as I accepted the towel, drying my dripping scalp with the soft Egyptian cotton and thinking carefully. Sabitov was my current employer, and I had done my research on him before leaving the Bay to come north to work for him.

He was former Spetsnaz—Russian special forces—a commander with their naval detachment. He came to America after the fall of the former Soviet Union, bringing with him a small fleet of midget submarines and a group of fanatically loyal former Spetsnaz and KGB operators. He put his little fleet to good use running marijuana from British Columbia to the States while having his crew infiltrate the local outlaw motorcycle gangs and using them as his distribution network. He branched out over the years with a simple business model: join forces with him or die…usually in the most gruesome way possible.

Local gang leaders who had opposed him disappeared, only to have their body parts mailed to their loved ones. Suffice it to say, the opposition to his operation faded away, and he became known for richly rewarding those who joined without the need for him to engage in bloodshed. The motorcycle gangs, Oregon's so-called "Big Five," assimilated under his umbrella and worked for him from the street to the prisons. Anything they touched—he got a piece of. It wasn't long before pretty much everything—prostitution, protection rackets, gambling—all of it was controlled by Sabitov and his Russian wolfpack. Meanwhile, his legal ventures in construction, real estate, and logging made him a very wealthy man.

Seeing the legalization of marijuana on the horizon, he retooled his operation to produce high-grade crystal meth and reversed the direction of his subs to bring his product from America to Canada. Lately though, he and his Bratva—or Brotherhood—had been trying their hand at complex computer crimes like fraud and identity theft. To protect his operation, he depended on bribery and sophisticated countersurveillance techniques to thwart any law enforcement agency that became interested in his operation.

That's where I came in.

I had served in the Corps as a Marine Raider, as well as for a special division of counterterrorism known as "Section" during the war. After close to fifteen years, I had left the military due to a slight case of major insubordination. My sociopathic CO got a bunch of civvies killed in what was supposed to be a non-violent snatch and grab mission outside of Kabul. Fed up, I lost my shit and called him a half-witted, cousin-humping, knuckle-dragging, useless bag of-dicks…and then dropped him with a right hook.

Not my finest hour.

Even though everyone agreed with my assessment of said bag of dicks, you don't strike a superior officer. The dishonorable discharge included extras like contempt toward officials and committing conduct unbecoming of an officer. That lost me my security clearance and closed the door to any hope of gainful employment in the real world of post-military life that most of my comrades went on to.

I was already struggling to adjust to civvie life; being pissed off and broke didn't help matters. Frustrated, I fell back on my youthful talent for theft and combined it with the skill set I learned in the Marines to create a niche market for myself. I became a tech pirate: a cyber-Blackbeard flying my digital Jolly Roger across the net and the world. I would work for anyone if the money was right—and it didn't directly involve drugs. Even foreign governments I used to hunt down wouldn't get more than a batted eyelash of dissent from me. You got the cash; I got the skills. My country had turned its back on me, so I returned the favor.

It wasn't long before Sabitov heard of me through my relatives in Vancouver and contracted my services. His mandate was three-fold: bolster his real-world and cyber security, set up countersurveillance, and utilize my ability to get past any security system in the physical world or the digital one to procure whatever Sabitov needed. You know… stealing.

Usually, I work for myself and by myself: it's less of a headache and better security if no one is a party to what I do. However, certain financial obligations on the home front led me to accept Sabitov's offer to come north. But it had been a year now, and my contract was up. I had the money I needed and I was itchy to get out from under Sabitov's thumb. I wanted out. Sabitov had other ideas though, and he was a man used to getting what he wanted. Even under the best of circumstances, dealing with Sabitov directly reminded me of the times I negotiated through fields of landmines in Kandahar. I had better watch my step, or I would be short an appendage.

"Mr. Leigh—I hope my associate wasn't too rough with you?" His voice was rich and cultured, with only a hint of a Russian accent.

I rubbed my jaw. "He was insistent."

"One of his better qualities, I assure you. Persistence and zeal for his work. I like that in a man."

"I thought you were in Taiwan."

"Our negotiations there were complete. In celebration, my wife and our two boys are in Hong Kong. I believe she intends to buy out the entire Fendi store. As of next week, we will be taking over Mr. King's operation in Astoria—thanks to you."

It had taken me the better part of a month to find out how King and his crew had been smuggling their product into the Pacific Northwest. He had refused Sabitov's overtures, so before Sabitov did what he usually did to the competition before I arrived (body parts in the mail), I asked for time to uncover the source and make a better deal with them than King could offer. It cost me no small amount of effort and a bunch of time both on and in the water just off the coast of Astoria, but I had cracked it. Now Sabitov would control the supply, and King and his boys would be cut out. But for once, no one got hurt.

"Mortimer was convinced you would not succeed," he continued.

"And this is how I get thanked? You need to get him on your dental plan or get him a better one, Mr. Sabitov."

"Please, it has been a year. Call me Josef, or just Joe, if you prefer. Again, I apologize for Mort. May I call you Aloysius?"

I winced, and it had nothing to do with the pain in my jaw and gut and everything to do with the moniker my mom had saddled me with. "Just Al, thanks."

"Al, then. Yes, I have tried to convince Mort of the need for better hygiene, but he has an overwhelming love of sweets and a terrible fear of pain—rather strange considering how good he is at dispensing it." The Russian gave an elegant shrug. "However, he is family. What can one do? You and he are similar in some ways. His mother was British, and my cousin, his father, was Russian. It made his childhood, shall we say, difficult. A foot in either world, belonging to neither but wanting to be accepted by both."

I leaned forward. "We are nothing alike," I spat out.

Sabitov gave me a thin smile. "So. But you understand family. Your brother has caused you no small amount of grief over the years." He reached over to the leather case on the seat next to him, opening it to the warm glow of a tablet that illuminated his face. "Not to mention the problems he has caused for his daughter: your niece."

He turned the screen in my direction, showing me a photo that wrenched at my heartstrings: a five-year-old girl in a hospital smock clutching a stuffed red monkey smiled at the camera. Her face was far too thin, and her jet-black hair hung limply from her head and was coming out in patches, making her look old before her time. Her smile in the photo was radiant and showed none of the constant pain she suffered—pain no child should endure.

Sabitov spoke, but I only had eyes for the photo of little Jeni. "Her mother contracted the virus from a dirty needle, I believe—an addiction she did not have before she met your brother. Heroin is a cruel mistress."

I glanced up at Sabitov. The friendly demeanor was gone, and his eyes looked like the black eyes of a shark I had seen at the Monterey Bay Aquarium as a child—flat, emotionless, alien.

The photo must have been recent. I had just sent the monkey to her last week. I hadn't seen this picture yet, but it was on this scumbag's tablet. My throat closed up with grief and pain at seeing her body so wasted away. The anger at my brother came boiling up from my gut, and I cleared my throat. "You know she is why I will not assist you with your drugs or the money associated with it. I have gotten you valuable intel on your competition; I have set up your computer security, acquired the tech you have requested, both legally and not so legally, and trained your hand-picked soldiers in the latest countersurveillance. I have fulfilled our contract to the letter in every way you have asked. That contract was for one year, ending today. We are done, Mr. Sabitov."

The Russian ignored me as though I had not spoken. "Your financial compensation has been going to her treatment and her mother's rehabilitation, I understand. Quite commendable. However, very little has remained in your pocket. I can remedy that with a new contract."

There was a dripping noise in the expensive limo, and I looked down to see my hands were clenched white from wringing the towel. I was thinking about my brother and wishing it was his throat in my hands.

"You already have my answer. I have a flight to catch and a little girl to see." I reached for the door handle.

"Two million dollars. One job. No drug involvement."

I paused. Two million for one job? I looked over at Sabitov. The corner of his mouth turned up in a grin.

"I am not—how do you say—yanking your chain? Three hundred thousand in advance deposited to your overseas account right now, and the rest upon completion." He was a fisherman and knew how irresistible his bait was to me. That thought alone gave me pause. I wasn't some fish to be landed...but two million?

"Your niece's immune system is compromised. As much as it pains me to point this out, this treatment will probably not be her last."

I thought about the cushion that money would give me. I could afford her bills and hire a full-time nurse. Best of all, I wouldn't have to be constantly skirting the edge of the law, risking jail and losing what time I had left to be with her.

Sabitov's hook dug into my cheek.

It was a slippery slope, however. The problem with having a price tag is that the higher the price on your personal tag, the more likely you will have to give up something you value to merit that price. For most people, that might mean a job that keeps you away from family or maybe moving to a place you don't want to be. In my line of work, the things you gave up usually left you with gouged-out bloody chunks of your soul and portions of your anatomy on the ground. What if the Russian demanded more of me? How long before my rules of no drugs or murder were left by the wayside? How long before I became something I despised?

"If I refuse?"

Sabitov's grin remained in place, but his voice was the icy emptiness of the steppes in winter. "Then I reach out to my contacts in San Quentin, and your niece is minus her biological father. Not long after that, she will wake one day with her mother's arms surrounding her while her mother's head rests on her shoulder...." He paused before continuing. "However, the rest of her mother's body will be missing, I fear."

I clenched my fists and met his gaze.

"You forget whom you work for, Mr. Leigh. Perhaps my learned associate here can educate you." He leaned forward and flicked a recessed switch. A small light came on and illuminated the upper half of his mystery guest.

He looked late-middle-aged, reasonably tall, and heavyset. He'd been enjoying his meals. His hair wasn't just receding, it was in full retreat, but I doubted he was worried about that anymore.

I had never seen him before, but I was sure he had looked better without the garroting wire cutting deeply into his neck. His eyes bulged from his heavily bearded face, which was purple with trapped blood, and his blackened tongue stuck out of the corner of his mouth. I'd seen plenty of corpses in my time—he'd only been dead a couple of hours. Not long enough to smell…yet.

Sabitov leaned back, removed a silver samovar from a walnut cabinet set into the side of the limo, poured a steaming, pale yellow liquid into a china cup, and offered it to me.

"Come, it doesn't have to be that way. You know me; you know my reputation—I keep my word and reward generously." He motioned the cup toward me again. "Lung Ching, your favorite."

I accepted the cup and tried to ignore the fresh corpse next to me. I brought the liquid up to my face, inhaling the aroma. It was Dragon Well, all right: Imperial grade. The vegetal bouquet of the tea calmed me, and I sipped the velvet soft liquid—letting the buttery flavor linger while I thought about his offer.

His threat.

The Russian poured another cup for himself and waited with that fisherman's patience while the fish swam closer to the boat. "I wonder, though…you let Mort and the boys get so close to you; perhaps you are not up to the rigors of the job?"

I flexed my sore jaw a little. "They paid for that privilege."

Sabitov raised an eyebrow as he took in my condition. "They did? What happened? Did you bleed on their suits?"

I stared him in the eye as I put the cup into a holder in the door. I reached into the voluminous inner pockets I had sewn into my jacket, pulled out the contents one by one, and let them fall at Sabitov's feet: three expensive and bulging leather wallets, an iPhone, and two wristwatches lay next to Sabitov's shining, black loafers. As each one hit the floor of the limo, his smile widened.

"Mort doesn't wear a wristwatch," I sighed.

Sabitov tilted his head. "No, he has a beautiful pocket watch— a treasured heirloom from his father."

I pulled a glittering gold pocket watch out from my jacket and twirled it on its long chain while maintaining eye contact with the Pakhan. My pulse was elevated, and my stomach was clenched, but I kept it hidden under a mask of cocky arrogance. He needed to see the professional.

This wasn't the kind of guy you showed weakness to.

Ever.

If he even suspected how unsettled I was sitting next to a fresh corpse and directly across from his cold-blooded killer, I'd be joining our mystery guest on his final trip to the landfill. So, I squashed all that fear into a ball and locked it up in the box with the rest of the terrors in my life I don't think about, all while smiling at the psycho across from me. "What's the job?"

He guffawed and raised the cup to his lips, confident the fish was landed.

"Technology: you steal it, and then you bring it to me. Not so different from our previous arrangement."

I tossed the watch into the pile on the floor of the car.

"Why now? Why me?"

"I have only recently become aware of its existence. Otherwise, I would have had you procure it while still under contract. As for why you? You are the only one in my organization capable enough and, if I may pay a compliment, trustworthy enough. Despite your profession, you are one of the most honorable men I have met." He paused and took a sip from his tea.

"As of now, I believe I am the only person outside of the creators of this technology to know about it. That will not last long, though. The technology is to be revealed to a government panel at the end of this week, after which, I have no doubt, it will be moved to a more secure location—beyond even your abilities. Hence, the large reward."

I thought a moment more and took another sip. Heaven. He may be a scumbag, but he enjoys exquisite tea. I tried to figure out a way to wriggle off this hook. Maybe I could get out of this if the job was far enough away. "Where is it?"

"Here in Portland."

Ah, crap. Break out the filet knife and tartar sauce: he had me.

"What is it?"

"A key."

My brow furrowed. "A key to what?"

His grin widened into a shark's smile.

"To everything."

WE ARE FAMILY

I got out of the limo with all of my digits and limbs still attached, no wire around my neck, and a host of unanswered questions I hadn't had an hour ago. Security, building schematics, and intel would all be sent to my dropbox on a secure server in Southeast Asia, but as to the actual nature of the tech I was being paid to acquire, Sabitov remained mum about it. He said it was a need to know, and I didn't need to know. I just needed to get it for him.

I didn't like that. In my business, information was everything. Hell, when you got right down to it, information was my business.

I reclaimed my knife and duffel from the Things along with a sealed bag I was told contained the biometrics I would need to enter the lab. Mort was already seated in the front of the car, munching out of an industrial-sized bag of Skittles while looking at a large book of Hindu art and blatantly ignoring me.

Hopefully for him, there were lots of pictures and not too many wordy-words.

I watched the limo and its grim cargo pull away from the curb as my brain volleyed reservations and questions back and forth for a few sets. I caught myself unconsciously brushing off my coat with my free hand; dealing with Sabitov always made me feel dirty. But *damn* he paid well. The rain had stopped but the chill wind was still blowing, so I pulled a dark knit cap out of my jacket pocket, tugged it on, and trudged my way up Burnside to NE 23rd and hung a right.

I used the walk to clear my head and tried without success to be present in the moment. I was supposed to be on a plane tonight, back to the warmth of family and friends.

Of course, the part of me that hated flying was, to be honest, more than a little relieved. Regardless, I should be walking down Mason Street with Chen-chen to the Pinecrest Diner tomorrow morning for some serious ham, eggs, and Belgian waffle action. Instead, another job weighed on my thoughts. Dark clouds scudded across the waxing quarter moon, and damp leaves spun in miniature cyclones across the tree-lined sidewalk as I hoofed it the first two blocks of the street, then turned left onto NE Flanders before hitting the trendy part of 23rd.

Restaurants and shops lined the main drag. The wet streets were covered in fallen leaves and lit by the ebb and flow of evening traffic. I usually loved to walk the streets here in this weather. I always enjoyed the feel of nature on my face and the smells from all the incredible eateries as I wandered faceless and anonymous. But not tonight. Tonight, I watched my feet as they moved with the solid rhythm of a metronome counting time, my head down in the drizzle, trying to shake off the grisly image of the dead guy in the limo who I was sure would be visiting me in full IMAX and Dolby surround sound in my dreams at some point. I got to the corner and came to a three-story building painted a cool sky blue. I jogged up the steps to the polished black doors with a large swinging sign above them that read, *Ogami.*

Ogami was a family-owned Japanese sushi bar and robata that was popular with…well, pretty much everyone in Portland who liked good Japanese food. They accepted no reservations; it was first-come, first-served, and the wait for a table in the evenings was easily an hour or more. However, no one seemed to mind, and they had a steady crowd of regulars.

I pulled open the heavy door and walked into the comforting warmth of the foyer. The decor was traditional, with lots of cedar planking and soft lighting. Against the left wall was a clear glass case containing a 16th-century suit of Japanese armor, and above it on the wall, hung a long dōtanūki katana in a cobalt blue sharkskin sheath. On the right wall was an actual rock waterfall that gurgled happily into a small pond with live koi swimming in it. An ancient-looking wooden baby cart stood incongruously to the side of the pond, and the whole thing was bracketed by a pair of live boxwoods.

There was no one at the hostess stand, so I stuck my head through the moon gate entrance to the dining room and inhaled deeply as I looked around. The intoxicating aroma of fresh fish along with the meats and vegetables roasting on the robata greeted my senses, and I could feel a smile tugging at the corners of my mouth. The dining room held about twenty-five tables that were only sparsely populated this early in the evening. To the left was a sake bar done in white marble where customers could sample sake or wait for tables. To the right, the sushi bar stretched against the wall of blue-threaded marble, and beyond that were two tatami rooms for private dining.

The Taniguchi family or clan (there were that many of them) were the employees and owners of the restaurant. Akihiro and his brother Daisuke were working the sushi bar and yelled out the traditional greeting when they saw my head. *"Irrashaimase*! Al-san!"

I grinned and waved and was about to respond when I was tackled from behind by what felt like a munchkin-sized linebacker.

I looked down to see eleven-year-old Akiko, Akihiro's youngest daughter, hugging me from behind. She had the same long, dark hair as her willowy mother, who was working the sake bar. It was a lustrous black so deep that it had blue highlights and was held back with a Hello Kitty barrette. She was still in her school uniform skirt but was rocking a Billie Eilish concert t-shirt from this past summer at the Gorge Amphitheatre.

She beamed up at me. "Uncle Al! You're back; you're back!"

I nodded and was about to speak, but she ran right over me in typical fashion.

"Did you forget something? Did you leave it upstairs? Some guys were here looking for you. One of them reeked, and I didn't like them, so I told them you went to Boise. I think they knew I was capping. Who goes to Boise, anyhow? Hey! What happened to your face?" I was about to respond when the perceptive little thing continued, "Oh, they found you."

"Yep," I answered. Hah! A whole syllable. With Akiko, that was a triumph.

She asked in a much quieter voice, "Are you okay?"

I gave her a thumbs up and a smile, and she revved her motor back up to warp speed. "Does this mean you are staying? Oh, you have to see my new sketchbook. I did some cool manga art! I'm getting really good! Can we go back to our kicking-butt lessons? Oh! A new *Attack on Titan* starts this week; we could watch it together to see who dies horribly this season. You still owe me five bucks from last season, by the way."

I put my fingers over her lips to stop the inevitable torrent. "Akiko-*chan*, cool the jets a sec. Yes, I am staying if your *obaasan* will give me my room back. Just for another week, though."

She gave a muffled squeal and mini-bounced up and down. Jeez. Did I have this much energy as a kid?

I continued in a single breath, "And yes, we can squeeze in at least one more lesson—they are called self-defense, not kicking-butt lessons—I think you are an outstanding artist and would love to see your new sketches. We can watch *Titan* if your folks say it is okay, but I need to find your Grams right now. Where is she at?" And…inhale again.

I took my fingers off her smiling lips long enough for her to blurt, "You say everything is outstanding…." I covered her lips again and raised an eyebrow. I pulled my fingers back slowly.

Her grin widened, and she jerked her thumb over her shoulder. "Kitchen."

I returned her hug with my other arm. "Good to see you too, kid."

She broke away and held my hand in both of hers as she looked up at me with sparkling brown eyes and said, "You can put the five bucks you owe me in the Jeni fund."

"I can? Outstanding!"

She laughed as she bounced up and down some more. "You're back; you're back!" She squealed the way only a pre-teen girl can and sped off toward her mother. I half expected to see a Road Runner-like dust plume in her wake.

The kid needs to cut back on the *matcha*.

I walked under the moon gate and weaved my way through the tables to the back of the house. Akihiro was pulling double duty on the robata, and I wondered idly where his oldest son Hitoshi was, as he usually worked the grill on Tuesdays.

I nodded to a couple of servers as I entered the kitchen. Long counters of stainless steel gleamed as steam rose from the giant woks and hung around the ceiling like clouds in a Daoist painting. Mrs. Taniguchi was at the line, closing out checks next to a POS. Mrs. T. was a short woman who had once been plump and had cheerfully passed that stage on her way to becoming round. She wore a traditional blue kimono and had her long silver hair swirled upon her head, secured with onyx chopsticks. A pair of reading glasses were perched on her nose as she added up totals on her iPhone. I can be as quiet as a ghost on the water when I want to be, but there was no sneaking up on Mrs. T.

"I could hear my granddaughter's shriek from here. I am sure there were dogs down by the river and perhaps some dolphins in the Pacific who heard her as well. You are back?"

"Yes, ma'am."

"What happened to your face?"

Okay, that was just creepy. She hadn't even looked up or turned her head to look at me. Before I could ask how she did it, she pointed to my reflection in the microwave next to her. I grinned and leaned against the counter beside her.

"I ran into a co-worker."

"Watch where you are going next time."

"Yes, ma'am."

Other than some family and a few close friends, Mrs. T. was one of the few people outside of the shadow world who knew what I did for a living and why. She and her family had taken me in when I arrived in Portland over a year ago. I had originally planned on using this place as cover, but over time I was adopted by the Taniguchi family as one of their own. Mrs. T. became the closest thing to a mother I had known since my own had died when I was a year younger than Akiko. She may have a soft exterior appearance but inside was a core of steel hammered and folded ten thousand times over like the legendary katana of her ancestors.

"Why are you staying?"

I sighed. "They made me an offer I couldn't refuse."

She took her glasses off and peered up at me. "If it is about money, I will do what I can to help you and Jeni."

I shook my head. "They threatened her parents if I don't come through. I just need my room back for a week. I can give you the whole month upfront."

She cocked her thumb back over her shoulder to a rack hung with blue serving aprons.

"Hitoshi broke his arm down at Burnside Skatepark this afternoon. Can you cover?"

"Does this mean I get my old room back?"

She gave me a warm hug and said, "You don't need to ask, *musuko*."

I walked over to the rack, pulled off my hat and jacket, tossed my duffel up on a shelf, and pulled an apron over my head.

Black-clad servers arrived for their shifts, most of them college-aged with a sprinkling of old-school, lifelong waiters. They amassed on the opposite side of the kitchen as they clocked in, many writing down the night's specials on their pads and grabbing their station assignments. I reached behind me to tie on the jewel-blue apron and gave head nods to a few of the servers I worked with regularly.

"Aloysius."

She was the only person other than my deceased mother who could use that name and not make me cringe. I turned to her as I smoothed the apron and grabbed a clean cloth from the shelf.

She nodded toward the bruise on my face and asked quietly, "Are you in danger?"

I thought about Sabitov and the questions he wouldn't answer, as well as the ridiculously high price tag of the job. I squirmed a bit. "Maybe."

She crossed the floor and tilted my cheek with one finger to look at her.

"As long as you know it. Watch your ass, Marine."

"Aye-aye, skipper."

She gave me a fierce smile. "Jeni's parents have always been too selfish…always putting their needs before hers. You are all she has; she needs you alive."

"That, Mrs. T., is a two-way street."

"Then don't fuck it up."

With those sage words, she went back to her checks, and I threaded my way through the crowd of servers out onto the restaurant floor.

I left the kitchen and crossed the floor to the sushi bar and robata. I gave Akihiro a casual hip-check off the grill. He gave me a fist bump and a grin that said "welcome back" better than any words, and I settled into cooking.

After my mom died, my brother and I fostered with Chen-chen and his family in San Francisco's Chinatown. When he brought me to his home, I asked him why he would want two white boys in his Chinese family. He told me, "You're a Leigh; I'm a Li. Somewhere we are related." I am forever humbled by that man who took me in and raised me as his own. He never saw my Irish heritage as being something so different from his Chinese heritage as to be something foreign. Chen-chen believes people are just people, and our humanity is what binds us, not what makes us different.

Growing up, there had never been someone that genuinely believed in me before. Dad was gone, Mom was busy swimming her way down to the bottom of a bottle, and my brother and I grew up without boundaries of any kind. We deserved the hopeless assessments of the teachers, the police, and the courts as we careened out of control. I had no guidance, only a big bucket of growing rage at my parents for being useless and a world that didn't seem to have a place for me. Chen-chen changed all that for me. He taught me the value of hard work and to cherish the family and friends I had. He tried to tame my wild temper with something no one else had done before—patience and love. Not that I made it easy on him, but rather than dismiss my anger and frustration, he tried to understand where it came from and how to harness it. He was and is such a contradiction to me, a dynamo of energy and purpose crossed with a deep well of calm and peace, and his acceptance of me into his family meant the world to me.

That being said, Chen-chen had no use for boys who didn't pull their weight. Chen-chen had been the first in his family to go to college, while his old man had supported him and the rest of the family with his *dim sum* restaurant. After graduating from Stanford, Chen-chen had made his bones as a software engineer and eventually bought his old man's restaurant as well as three others in Chinatown. A real-life story of a local boy makes good. Suffice it to say; the man had a work ethic he thought we should share. I started washing dishes in his restaurant off Grant Street and then worked my way up to prep. By high school, I was working on the line with the cooks. Chen-chen taught me many things, but cooking is the skill I was always the most grateful for. I discovered early that cooking was something special to me. It was more than just adding this to that or heat and prepare something in a particular fashion: it was a Way or path. It allowed me to impose order on the chaos in my life; it was my first true love. Unfortunately, the pay sucks, and the hours are worse. Crime may have been riskier, and I definitely would be seeing fewer corpses in my evenings as a cook, but anything was worth it for Jeni.

The restaurant filled quickly, as it always did, and I lost myself for a while in the work—marinated strips of beef-wrapped asparagus on skewers, baby lobster tails in cream sauce, roasted scallops, and vegetables. Mrs. T. stopped by with a large chawan filled with *matcha,* just the way I liked it: the green tea whipped into a foamy mass that floated on the surface of the liquid. Hours passed while everything else faded from my mind but the flames, the food, and the seemingly never-ending string of orders.

The next thing I knew, the restaurant had emptied out, and I closed up the grill for the night. The brothers teased me about being unable to stay away but never questioned my return or the condition of my jaw…only accepted it and me, as they always had—with grace. Akihiro handed me a cardboard box filled with poke: a Hawaiian dish of rice and chunks of raw Ahi tuna, salmon, snow crab, masago, cucumbers, and cherry tomatoes, drizzled with fresh shoyu and sesame oil, all covered with strips of fresh avocado. I walked back through the kitchen and headed up the stairs in the back of the building to the third floor. Someone had left my duffel outside the door. I took down the key to the apartment from its hiding spot on the lintel and let myself in.

The apartment was a small one-bedroom with simple furnishings and a tiny kitchen that faced out toward the street. I put my duffel on the faded red couch in the main room and put my dinner on the low oak coffee table. I walked to the kitchen, grabbed a lone sparkling water from the fridge and a pair of chopsticks from a plain cylindrical stoneware stand on the counter, then headed back to the main room and plopped down on the couch. I was hungry and ate quickly. Then I pulled my custom-made laptop out of my duffel and got to work.

First, I sent an email to my sister-in-law letting her know I would be delayed and would not be in to see Jeni on Wednesday morning as I had hoped. I asked her to reassure Jeni that we would FaceTime later in the day as we had every day, her condition permitting, for a year now.

Second, I checked on my Swiss account. Sure enough, I was flush three hundred thousand dollars with a notation that an additional 1.7 million was in escrow, to be deposited in my account at the end of the week unless otherwise ordered by the depositor. Sabitov was as good as his word. The three hundred was mine, free and clear.

Alright, alright, alright.

I mentally put on my tech-pirate, tricorn hat—hoisted my digital Jolly Roger, and hit the cyber seven seas.

I logged onto a secure server, and after working through the multiple passwords and encryptions, downloaded the files Sabitov had sent me. I gave them a once-over to make sure everything I needed was there. While clicking through the schematics, the contractor's name popped up at the bottom: Belaya Ruka, one of Sabitov's companies. It explained how he had stumbled onto this job and how fast he was able to procure what I needed. He wouldn't tell me how he got the biometrics I was going to need, but he had assured me they were legit. His usual methods for that sort of thing were bribery and extortion. Dead-limo-guy was an example of what happened when the first two didn't work.

Next, I dug on the net for info on Vegrandis, the company that the Russian had aimed me at. I struck out on the first try. The company had no webpage and no listing of its products or purpose. There wasn't even a phone number. Vegrandis was a null entity.

Rather than let this frustrate me, I picked up the pace. What were they hiding? And why? When I was a wild child, the cheap thrill of petty theft motivated me more than getting whatever trinket I was stealing. It was the act, not the acquiring, that lured me back time and time again. They were keeping something from me, and I relished the challenge of taking it. I rediscovered the same thrill when I hacked my first network. I felt like a bloodhound sniffing out data, squirreling into the dark corners of the internet. You can't keep secrets from me. I'll find them. I don't really care what your secret is; I just know you don't want me to find it, and that's enough for me.

It took me several hours of hacking and sifting through dummy corporations and false fronts before I found two names that gave me a hint of what Vegrandis did and a clue to what I was being paid so much to acquire. The first one meant zilch to me...a Dr.

Franco Persici out of Cornell—Ph.D. in organic chemistry and a specialist in Interface and Colloid Science. Huh. No photos of him, but plenty of references to his research. However, I'd heard of the second name and recognized him from the pictures. He was out of my alma mater, U.C. Berkeley...Dr. Adam Zinn: Ph.D. in Condensed Matter Physics, and former fellow at Lawrence Berkeley National Laboratory.

Why were they here in Portland? This was pretty much the boondocks for both men with regard to their fields. There were no federally supported high-tech labs or devoted research campuses here for them to work out of. Intel and Hewlett-Packard were up here, but not with the gear these guys would be playing with. The Bay Area would have been the optimal place to set up shop.

Perhaps they hit on something together? Something big that they needed privacy to develop away from prying eyes and potential tech pirates. Enter, Vegrandis. So, what were they doing over there?

Considering their respective fields, I could only come up with one wild answer, one word flashing in my head repeatedly.

Nanotechnology.

But they couldn't have done that—could they? It was possible, but it should still be decades away. If they had come up with a breakthrough, however.... Well, shit.

I leaned back and considered the implications.

If it was what I thought it was, Sabitov's two million was chump change compared to what this kind of tech would fetch on the open market. The applications would cross every field: medical, industrial, and most definitely military. There was no end to the list of buyers who would want access to this, who would quite literally kill to acquire it if they knew about it.

And he wanted me to steal it.

A grin stretched across my face that was at odds with the tightening of my gut. That weird heady cocktail of fear and excitement combined with the thrill of the hunt that I couldn't ever walk away from had just been slapped down on the bar in front of me. My face flushed warm with blood, and the coppery taste of adrenaline was at the back of my throat, and though I would never admit it to anyone—it was my addiction as surely as my brother's love of the smack. I thought about what Mrs. T had asked me earlier.

Was I in danger?

Oh, yeah.

And that just made it more fun.

TIGHT WAD HILL

I went over Vegrandis security and building layouts. Each job is a bit of a riddle that I have to solve. First, you have to assess what kind of riddle it is, and then how many questions are there? Most of the security—the type of riddle, if you will—was of the automated biometric variety that had become so popular, coupled with a lightly staffed security unit. As usual, people are the weakest link in a secure network, so I ran down the company handling the physical security, and sure enough, it was almost exclusively ex-military.

That made things much more manageable.

For me.

The U.S. military has been collecting biometric data on everyone that came through since 2009. Fingerprints, faces, irises, and DNA are all collected and stored in one place in a system known as the DoD Automated Biometric Information System. That system was managed by the DFBA, the Defense Forensics and Biometrics Agency. I'd spent months hacking their system years ago for a previous job, and it was only a matter of minutes before I had what I needed on the security guards at Vegrandis. First question dealt with.

As for the interior lab itself, that had a two-step biometric identification system that was far more difficult, but Sabitov had come through with the recording I needed and a vial full of the necessary DNA. Provided it was all the real deal, I had everything I needed for questions two and three.

The beeping of the alarm on my watch told me it was 5:30 am. Too wired to sleep, I pulled my sweats out of my duffel and headed out for my pre-dawn run.

I did some warmup stretches in the postage-stamp-sized parking lot behind the restaurant, enjoying the icy darkness, and set out. I immediately picked out my tail as I headed out onto NW Flanders. The exhaust plume wasn't as visible to me in the pre-dawn gloom as much as the smell of the fumes wafting across the street. Someone decided to leave the motor running to ward off the chill. He should have brought a blanket.

I kept an ear out as I pounded pavement up to NW 24th and heard the car pull onto Flanders in my wake. I picked up the pace as I turned left onto 24th and made for Washington Park. I caught a glimpse of the guys in the car and was only a little surprised to see one of the Things driving, with Mort riding shotgun.

So, Sabitov wanted to keep tabs on me? Protecting his interest, or making sure I didn't welsh on the deal and ghost myself out of Portland? And why put his pet psycho on me when he had soldiers I had trained myself who were far better at keeping tabs on me than Mort? Unclear.

Mort was having to go under the speed limit to match me. Putz. My muscles loosened up as my body temperature rose, so I poured on the gas as I passed Burnside, hoping to leave Mort at the light, but Mort ran it. So did the car behind him. That's when I caught tail number two. I'm observant that way.

What the hell? Backup? The car that I was sure was following the Mortmobile went under a streetlight at Burnside, and I got a solid look. Standard government issue sedan: not Sabitov.

Not good.

The sedan slid back into the light morning traffic a few cars behind Mort. I didn't think Thing or Mort had made the tail. They were too focused on me.

A wave of icy sweat that had less to do with my chilly morning cardio and more to do with the unknown second car poured down my spine. What was this?

I was sure Sabitov didn't want the law anywhere near me or my business, but then again, they may be sniffing after Mort. An unconscious snarl lifted my upper lip in anger that Mort and whatever chickenshit detail he was on would get me noticed.

I decided to lose them both as I double-timed it up to NW Stearns and then as they followed, I juked hard onto Sherwood—which runs only one way—against Mort and the mystery law machine. I cut across the park, staying off the street and out of sight as my feet carried me toward the Portland Japanese Garden. I cut around the fence and came out of the trees in Washington Park.

Take that, asshats.

I may not have liked Mort much, but I had a much more profound distrust and dislike of the government and anyone who worked for them. I'd put my life on the line for my country, and for what? I was reduced to either barely getting by or having to break the law to get what I needed and seeing as how the government made up those laws and likes to enforce them; I liked to break them. I reflected, not for the first time, that perhaps an anger management course might be helpful for me.

Who was I kidding? It would just piss me off.

I walked on toward the Chiming Fountain at the center of the park. I was curious to see if Mort would continue to stay on my six once he discovered his own shadow or if he would tuck tail and ghost. Mort would know where to find me. Some of my habits were cultivated specifically to allow for a public venue for meetings that needed to seem inconspicuous. This was one of them.

I waved to the small group of people practicing t'ai chi on the grass, took up my usual spot next to the large fountain, and joined them. I needed to think, and this always helped. Time did its little mind trick as I exercised and stretched out until I found myself in closing posture, in the full light of morning.

I looked toward the nearby parking lot and saw no sign of the Mortmobile, but I saw the bland sedan with a lone silhouette behind the wheel.

Shitballs.

Well, that answers two questions. I considered waiting and using my usual covert means to find out who was following me and why, and then I thought about my timetable. No time.... Fine—a frontal assault then.

I pulled the hood down off my head and walked toward the newest member of my fan club. I came upon the passenger side and rapped on the window. The lock popped; I opened the door and got in. The driver was a middle-aged guy in a dark blue suit, sporting a thick shock of unruly black hair peppered with grey. He radiated Fed, not local. Huh. All kinds of questions swirled around in my head.

"Good morning," he said with a pronounced New Jersey accent.

I nodded and gave him a polite, "Morning."

He tilted his chin toward the Chiming Fountain. "You all done there?"

"Yep," I smiled sunnily at him. Feds all have a stick up their ass—the trick is finding out if it is a twig or a baseball bat. Being a hard ass with them gets you nowhere. Happy people, though? Happy people make them uncomfortable.

He stared hard at my idiotic grin, giving me cop face. I kept smiling.

He shifted in his seat and watched an older couple power-walk by us. I thought of Jeni, of good food, and caffeinated things. Between that and my fading endorphins, I positively radiated good cheer.

"You dizzy from all that dancing around? You need to lie down or something?"

I showed him my teeth.

"Should I introduce myself?" he asked. I said nothing and continued to smile at him. He sighed.

"Would coffee help?"

Okay, so not a Louisville Slugger.

I put one finger to my nose and pointed at him with the other hand. He grunted and started the car. "Yeah, me too. Buckle up." He backed the sedan up and aimed for the exit. "And for Chrissake, stop smiling…. Creeps me out." He pulled out of the lot, and we made our way sedately out of the park.

Special Agent Willy Moscato didn't disappoint me on one front: he was cheap. We sat in a local Starbucks. I had a black coffee, and he had something complex sounding that ended in ino.

"So, there I am, keeping an eye on one of my favorite douchebags, and I see your beaten ass being hauled into and then let out of said douchebag's limo." He stirred his thing that looked more like a hot milkshake than a cup of joe and tilted his head at me. "The thing that bothers me is, I don't know you. I know everyone—well almost everyone—on his crew and anyone they deal with. You? I don't know you."

I gave him a small shrug and made like a rock.

"So, I decide to look into who is this guy that takes private meetings with the Shark." Moscato pulled an oversized smartphone out of his pocket and swiped it open.

"Interesting stuff—what I was allowed to read, that is." He leaned forward, elbows on the table. "Want to tell me what a former Marine Raider is doing chatting with Josef Sabitov?"

A year of being invisible, of keeping to the shadows, and I get blown now? Damnit! I can't have this guy on my case. Our Lady of Improvisation, don't fail me now.

"I don't really want to talk about it." Hah! Take that.

"Considering your service record and what you were, I was hoping to do this casually."

Yeah, I'll bet you were.

"But we can do it formally down at the office if you want."

Moscato hadn't been able to dig deep enough to uncover my work with MARSOC—the United States Marine Corps Special Operations Command—and certainly not its Special Operations Command evil stepbrother, the black-ops unit known only as Section. My job then and now was scrounging for intel, and not just in the cyber world. I spent a good chunk of my time in Section doing HUMINT: human intelligence undercover work. The key to selling it when I was undercover was acting…. Tell a story; make 'em believers. I connected some dots, wove a bit of truth into the mix, and hit the stage.

My shoulders slumped a little, my gaze dropped, and I did my best embarrassed, down on his luck shmoe.

"We owed Mr. Sabitov some money."

"Who is we?" he asked. There was a hint of puzzlement in the back of his mind. This wasn't going how he thought it would.

"Me and Hitoshi from work."

"How much and why?"

"A lot. If you read my file, you'll know why I was discharged.*"
You don't know it all because it's been redacted: I've seen it.* The thought of my discharge brought back the shame and anger at the military, who turned their backs on me for one stupid mistake after more than a decade of service. And let's face it, not a little of that anger was at myself for letting the rage beast out of its carefully constructed prison in the first place. I let the discomfort and shame show on my face. It would serve a purpose here.

"Only the discharge for insubordination, no details…" he leaned back and crossed his arms.

"Gambling," I lied. He blinked.

"You must be in deep for Sabitov to see you personally." He still sounded skeptical.

"They broke Hitoshi's arm yesterday at Burnside Skatepark, so I decided to skip town," I whined. "Mr. Madievsky found me before I could go." I pointed to my face. "He wasn't happy about that." I sensed a wave of revulsion from him that had nothing to do with me being beaten. No, he doesn't like addicts. Okay, I can work with that.

Moscato took a long pull from his spiced milk thingy and eyeballed me.

"You came to Portland last year?" he asked.

I nodded.

"See, my problem is, about a year ago, Sabitov's operation changed. The security of his organization got a major upgrade. His soldiers are harder to find, their illegal operations harder to pin down. One theory is that he brought in an expert—someone we haven't seen who has been helping. An outside contractor, one might say."

I looked blank.

"What brought you to Portland?"

"I came to apprentice with the Taniguchis. I want to open my own place; theirs is one of the best in the Northwest." The lie rolled off my tongue with ease. It had been the perfect cover at the time.

"You gonna tell me the restaurants in San Francisco aren't good enough for you? Lots of places in the Bay Area you could have done an apprenticeship."

I shifted in my seat and ducked my head. "I have a, umm, reputation there."

"For gambling?"

I nodded and mumbled, "And some drinking at work." I looked up, hopefully. "Hey, you got anything I could put in this coffee? It's kind of weak. You guys drink like fish, I hear."

This time he didn't bother to hide his disgust. I'd sold it.

"C'mon man; they took all my money last night. Just a little snort.... I thought a run and some meditation would help, but it didn't—not as much as a vodka would." I showed him my right hand, which I gave some tremors for added effect. "I seen some stuff...maybe not important stuff, but worth a drink or two at least." I reached out to touch his sleeve, and he all but recoiled. He didn't see me as an operative with over a decade of wartime experience who might sell out to the highest bidder. He saw me as an addict and a loser.

Special Agent Moscato stood up and gazed down at me while I shrunk in my chair.

"I know the war was a bitch but pull yourself together. I'm sorry I wasted your time. It's four blocks back to your pad. Need a lift?"

I shook my head and watched his narrow back as he left the shop.

People see what they want to see; my story would keep him off my back for a while. It would take him some time to find anyone in the Corps who would talk to him, but sooner or later, someone would let him know that I might like to gamble, but not with money, and that I had never drank in my life. Yeah, he would be back on me like white on rice soon. I needed to be Casper before that happened.

Time to gear up.

I walked back to my apartment, void of any tails I could spot. The cool morning air was crisp and smelled of autumn. While other trees had already lost their leaves, their bony limbs reaching skyward, the Japanese maples lining the sidewalk were riots of oranges, yellows, and reds. Pumpkins and hay bales populated storefronts. Witches leaned over cauldrons of colored smoke that bubbled away, ghosts were taped to windows, and every cafe and restaurant had an organic, pumpkin-flavored something on their daily menu.

I took my time and finished my coffee, mentally going over the security and schematics I had downloaded while I enjoyed the fall weather. I took the exterior wooden stairs up to my apartment two at a time, got inside, and showered off. Jeans, Pink Floyd *Dark Side of the Moon* t-shirt, hiking boots, an old, olive-green field jacket, and a dark ball-cap, and I was ready to go.

I went downstairs to the kitchen and begged a few onigiri rice balls from the prep guys, then shouldered my way out the back door, popping a rice ball into my mouth with one hand and putting on a pair of Wayfarers with the other.

I stood in the shadows of the side of the building finishing the onigiri and watching the street for twenty minutes until I was sure it was clear—no sign of Mort or the law.

I walked down the street, glancing in storefront windows to keep an eye on my six. When I was positive I was clean, I got on the commuter bus to the downtown station and transferred to the Hood River bus. I found a window seat in the back, pulled my cap down low as I put in my earbuds, and listened to the digital recording Sabitov had provided me; the second question in this riddle game began here. The first step (no pun intended) of the interior lab biometric security was a behavioral system. This particular one was keyed to the physical gait of the keyholder. The security could 'hear' the walking style peculiar to the keyholder. These behavioral biometrics are unique to each person, but to quote Thufir Hawat, the mentat-assassin of Frank Herbert's *Dune*, those sounds can be imitated.

If you're good.

I'd encountered this kind of system before with moderate success but would have preferred a video assessment to match up with what I was hearing. It was going to make it harder, but not impossible. I watched the deep blue Columbia flowing outside my window as I listened to the shuffling gait repeat over my earbuds.

We headed east along the river, passing Troutdale and the outlet malls. The overt signs of civilization had dwindled, and I pushed my cap up to look out the whole of the window. The day was unseasonably free of clouds, and both Mt. Hood to the southeast and Mt. St. Helens to the north were visible against the cold, royal-blue October skies.

Towering majestically above the gorge, Mt. Hood is a dormant volcano popular with Portland locals for its skiing and hiking. Just across the river in Washington State, Mt. St. Helens had been puffing steam from its decapitated top for the past several weeks, but locals reassured me that it did that from time to time, and while it meant an eruption could happen, it probably wouldn't. Probably.

I was still trying to figure out if I was reassured or just glad I was getting out of town. I thought about getting out of this burg and back to caring for Jeni. She had been doing so well last year before her relapse. Her smile was infectious, and her laugh had been the carefree one of a child not feeling the pain that had plagued her first years. Out of all the things in my life I missed the most, it was the simple one of rocking her to sleep at night that I ached for. I would spend hours rocking her, huddled around her warmth, and listening to her gentle breaths. I resented the lost time I had been away from her, but I hadn't had much choice. Two active tours, most of another decade working in the shadows, and now—nothing, not even my reputation. I had no other way to get the outrageous sums of money I needed for her care. Healthcare in America is a ridiculous fucking joke whose punchline was always the same—more money.

After an hour's drive, the bus pulled into Hood River, and I got off. The town rose from the riverbanks, climbing the gentle, tree-lined hills that rose to the south. Long orange banners hung across the main street, marking the Hops Fest and Harvest Festivals to be celebrated later that month.

I walked a few blocks, then grabbed a cab near the Full Sail Brewery. I had the driver take me out of the postcard-perfect river town, and into the surrounding farm country to the south.

The local land outside of town was filled with farms rich in volcanic soil provided by the lonely, snow-capped volcano further south. A few miles out of town and I had the driver turn onto an unused dirt road. It wound through a dense evergreen forest layered with moss for a couple more miles, eventually leading to a small cherry farm surrounded by a sturdy wooden fence. In the distance, through the acres of now-dormant cherry trees, a large hill rose at the back of the property with the red and white roof of a barn running perpendicular to the just-visible hill.

I paid the driver in cash and watched him drive back down the dirt road. I walked to the sturdily locked gate. A large postbox stood next to the gate with a small redwood sign swinging from its base. It read: *BAG END FARM.* I unlocked the heavy-duty lock and chain and let myself in.

I had come to Hood River right after moving to Portland and instantly fell in love. I found the farm and quickly bought it under a false identity I kept in reserve for just such an opportunity. With the exception of my lawyer in San Francisco, who had helped me purchase the property, no one knew I owned Bag End. I grinned again at the name. I had been a fan of the books since I was a child and couldn't wait to introduce Jeni to them when she was ready. I had hoped that this could be our home when she was better, back when I was still optimistic about her recovery. I wanted to bring her up here when the cherry trees were blossoming in the spring and tell her that this would be where we would build our new home—that this would be where she was going to grow up.

Now, I had doubts. I worried that I was running out of time with her. I needed to be done with the Bratva and get my ass back down to the Bay.

I walked faster up the winding dirt driveway to the doors of the big red and white barn nestled at the base of the large hill. I opened a false panel in the barn's exterior, disarmed the alarm, unlocked the triple bolted lock, and went in.

As I hit the overhead floods and they flickered into life, isolated islands of light were created in the great pool of darkness. A machine shop ran along the right wall, everything covered and put away neatly. Farm equipment was stacked against the back wall, and off to the left was an enclosed room with a locked door. Suspended from the ceiling were my surfboard and wind sail, and in the middle of the floor was a tarp-covered car, much longer than a contemporary vehicle. "Baby" was waiting where I had left her twenty-four hours before, thinking I would not see her again until the spring. I stroked her covered hood as I walked past on my way to the office.

I unlocked the door to the office, the light from the barn behind me illuminating my way. There was a couch that folded out to a bed and a bare metal desk. My skis and poles leaned against the wall in the far corner while a large wooden bookcase loaded with well-thumbed paperbacks dominated the area at the back. I slid the bookcase aside on its hidden track, exposing what looked like an armored, watertight hatch in a submarine. The hatch was painted a bright green while the wheel-latch was done in gold paint. It looked like the door to a certain other house under a hill…just more heavily armored and better concealed.

I typed in the eight-digit code on the pad next to the door and was tempted to hum the *Get Smart* theme as I opened the final door to the bunker.

In 1942, Japan had sent a submarine with a specially attached seaplane to the Pacific Northwest on a secret mission. The plan was to drop incendiary bombs that would start massive wildfires, forcing the Pacific Fleet to patrol the coast, thereby drawing support away from the Pacific theatre. What most people don't know is that the mission was a partial success. Two such bombs were dropped in southern Oregon, just outside of Brookings on the coast. Unfortunately for the Japanese, the bombs were dropped after a particularly wet, early autumn, and only one of them caused a fire. The blaze was relatively small and extinguished without too much trouble. It was the only time during the war that the continental United States was attacked, and the last until 9/11.

The attack did, however, light a fire under Bag End Farm's previous owner: a paranoid and wealthy family man who immediately moved from Brookings to Hood River and built this bunker. Constructed using thousands of tons of steel and concrete covered over by additional tons of dirt, the bunker's existence had made selling the farm after the market crash in 2008 difficult. None of the granola-munching prospective buyers who could afford the property wanted a giant bunker as part of their farm, and the cost of trying to remove it would have been exorbitant.

Tightwads.

I didn't want it removed. I renovated it.

Put that one on HGTV.... *Bombass Bunkers*, perhaps?

The bunker and the barn had been my project for the past year. I would tell anyone interested that I was heading up to the Meadows on Hood to ski or was going out to the gorge hiking or windsurfing, but I was actually coming here. I flipped the lights on, exposing a long and wide, tastefully lit room complete with polished hardwood floors. Along the right wall was a rich brown leather couch with a gleaming hickory coffee table in front of it. Above the couch was an enormous photo of a shore break by Clark Little, the giant wave crashing in turquoise, indigo, and white foam onto the sandy-hued shore.

Set into the wall to one side were two guitar cases that held a pair of genuine D'Angelico archtops from the hand of master luthier John D'Angelico himself. The hard case with my Blues Queen—a more contemporary, semi-hollow guitar built by Chuck Thornton of Maine—reclined in the corner. Next to the guitars stood a trio of amps: a Carr Rambler, a Two-Rock Bloomfield, and a mint, '63 Fender Deluxe Reverb. Dominating the left wall were lit shelves that held my collection of rare teaware. I had started the collection when I was stationed at Okinawa with 3rd Recon and had continued for the past decade-plus: it represented both an investment and one of my passions. I had resigned myself to the collection's eventual sale, but Sabitov's latest offer might make that move unnecessary.

I continued to where two broadly carpeted corridors formed a T with the main room. To the right was an industrial-grade kitchen, a dining room, the head, and a trio of bedrooms, but I turned left and made my way to the end of the other corridor where two heavy, locked oak doors faced each other on either side of the passageway.

The room to my left housed my gun safe, which also contained several false identities and some run-like-hell cash, along with the weaponry; however, I ignored this room for now. Hopefully, this wasn't going to be that kind of party. The kukri would be enough.

During my time in Okinawa with the 3rd, I'd had the occasion to train with a Gurkha regiment in a series of joint exercises. I had been impressed with their ferocity and tenaciousness as fighters. Osama bin Laden was reported as saying he would "eat Americans alive" if he had Gurkhas on his side. Adolf Hitler had held them in such high regard that he had claimed, "If I had Gurkhas, no army in the world would defeat me." The kukri was the weapon of the Gurkhas. Its recurved blade made it effective for chopping, as well as slashing. It was as much a tool as it was an efficient weapon for close combat. I had specialized in edged-weapon combat and had adopted the kukri as my personal weapon ever since.

I pulled out my keys and unlocked the right-hand door. Shelves and wire baskets held the tools of my sneaky trade. I grabbed a couple of heavy-duty, ballistic nylon backpacks from a shelf and loaded up what I would need for the next few nights. I locked up the bunker and office, walked across the polished concrete floor of the barn, and pulled the tarp off of Baby.

She gleamed darkly under the floods, and I admired her a moment. Baby was a 1968 Dodge Charger R/T 440 Magnum and looked as new as the day she came off the assembly line. She was the same model the bad guys had driven in *Bullitt,* and I loved her fiercely. I reflected that despite the cost of the barn and bunker renovation, keeping her here was still cheaper than parking her in San Francisco.

Sigh.

I opened the main barn doors, exposing the fading sunlight and swiftly encroaching night. The long rows of cherry trees stood like sentries with their bare arms raised in the sunset. I put the backpack full of goodies in the deep trunk of the Dodge, got in, and fired Baby up.

The Dodge gave a gut-shuddering rumble as she coughed to life, and I turned on the headlights concealed by her grill. I eased her out of the barn and secured everything. I drove down the driveway through the gate, locking it behind me before driving off.

I left the farm behind me, cruising like a growling wraith through the shadowed emerald forest until I hit asphalt. I fiddled with the radio until I heard the opening bars of Led Zeppelin's 'Ramble On.' I opened up Baby's throttle, and she roared her challenge, tires spitting gravel and dust behind her as we flew down the road back to town.

BREAKING THE RULES

I passed back through town, heading for the Columbia River. I drove over the Hood River Bridge to the Washington side of the river. I followed State Route 14 back west alongside the Columbia toward Vancouver, a bedroom community just across the river from Portland. The sun was heading down, and the cloudless skies promised me a chilly night of surveillance. Vegrandis had set up shop just east of Vancouver outside the neighboring town of Camas, or as the locals referred to it, Cam-ass.

Baby ate up the miles back along the river toward the reason for the unfortunate nickname: a paper mill that blanketed the surrounding area in a stench—like, well…. You get it. I passed the gag mill and drove out of town toward the mostly undeveloped timberland to the north.

Fifteen minutes later, I parked Baby off a small logging road about a mile from Vegrandis, got out and pulled fallen tree limbs and brush over into a pile to keep Baby unseen while I was gone. I opened the trunk and stripped down as fast as possible, grabbed my base layer long johns from the first backpack, and skivvied into those. I got back into my street clothes, added a black pullover sweater, a knit cap, and gloves from the backpack, then transferred my supplies into it. Once Baby was shut up tight, I camouflaged her with the pile of brush.

My nose had gone dead to the smell of the mill, and with that cheery observation, I took a heading with the compass on my Suunto. Oriented, I pulled a pair of Integrated Augmented Vision

System goggles from my backpack over my head, slung the pack over my shoulder, and hoofed it north through the chilled forest—my breath steaming in the green-tinted light of the darkness-penetrating goggles.

The building that housed Vegrandis was a two-story deal set off from the main road and locked up behind a perimeter fence. Two guards worked the exterior, trading front gate duty and perimeter checks. I knew another guard was inside the building itself. The remaining security was of the electronic variety.

I'd set up on a knoll at the southwest corner of the property where I could watch the guards and the front entrance. Security was done by a private firm in Portland with a solid rep, but I had extracted items for Sabitov from far more difficult places. I sat on a small plastic tarp, watching the guards as I tore into a bite of jerky and tried to look at this job from all angles. I knew that Sabitov had a couple of guys who were up to handling the security here, but he was going out of his way to push me on this job. He'd said I was honorable, and in many ways, I was. In criminal parlance, that meant once I had been bought, I stayed bought. He didn't trust his boys with this job, yet he still had Mort and Thing—his hitter and his muscle—on my tail. Did he put them there to remind me of his other methods of dealing with people should I decide to ghost myself out of town? Or was he worried that I might choose to take the prize for myself?

As for the prize, no matter how I approached it, I kept coming back to the same answer: nanotechnology—self-replicating, microscopic, biological/mechanical machines. I didn't know for sure what stage the good doctors of Vegrandis were at or even what flavor of nano they had come up with, but if their work was going to be presented to a panel for government funding, they must be close to operational.

I thought about the lifestyle I could live if I successfully got the nanotech out on the open market myself.... Cars, travel, the best cuisines, and the best care for Jeni would be within my reach. It all spun in my imagination like the sparkling facets of a brilliant jewel: the things I could do if, just this once, I didn't keep my word and kept the prize.

I chuckled to myself. I may have some pricey needs, but the things I wanted most in the world were Bag End Farm and raising Jeni in a safe, loving place. All the things that might have caught me with their glamour in my youth had changed when I took on the role of a father.

I decided to dismiss Mort and Sabitov's threat. Mort was an amateur at what I did, and I knew I could lose him at the drop of a hat. I was going to do the job and take the money. Taking the tech for myself just wasn't something I would do. No amount of money was worth looking over my shoulder for the rest of my life because as sure as shit, Sabitov would spend the rest of his life hunting me down.

Now, I might be an honest thief, but I wasn't going to be stupid. My dealings were shady enough that I needed to take certain precautions. For starters, delivery would be on my terms in case Sabitov decided this was the one time to be a welsher himself. I mentally checked off a few other items on my "to do" list to ensure everything would go as smoothly as possible.

Do the job; get the tech to Sabitov; conclude our business. Then, get my ass gone south as fast as possible.

That decided I leaned back against the tree trunk behind me, settled in, and kept watch.

I got back to Portland not long before dawn. Using one of my false identities, I checked in as a guest at one of the pricey hotels by the Willamette, saw Baby safely put away, and placed my backpacks in the room. I went downstairs, caught a Lyft back up to NW 23rd, and walked the last block to Ogami.

Mort was sitting in his car across the street eating a doughnut, and I cheerfully gave him the finger. Dick. Mort chose the high road, opting not to return my greeting, and kept eating. Double dick. I pointed to the Suunto on my wrist, giving it a frustrated shake, and then gave a brief shrug of my shoulders. Got the time, bro? He reflexively grabbed at his waist to check his pocket, and I laughed loudly. I went up the back stairs and in the rear door to my apartment. I stripped off, showered, and promptly racked out on the bed.

I awoke four hours later to someone beating a gong next to my ear and realized it was my phone. I remembered that I had promised to FaceTime with Jeni this morning.

I swiped open the app and saw my face in the video. I tilted my head and moved the phone, so the bruise on my jaw was shadowed and hard to see, and waited for the video to come in. Her mom murmured in the background, then the picture sprang to life. My face dropped to the bottom corner of the screen, and there was my little girl.

When Jeni was born, her father was already behind bars for his role as the leader of a commune that was a cover for his heroin business. He kept the commune members hooked on the junk, forcing them to be his labor in the factory or mules on the street. Jeni's mother was not his only "wife," just the only legal one. The commune was a cult with my brother and his "tears of the poppy"—as opium is known in China—as its leaders. It was slavery of the worst sort.

Eloise, Jeni's mother, was three months pregnant when she managed to break free of my brother and come to me for help. I helped her get to the police and to try and get clean. She had plea-bargained a reduced sentence for testifying against my brother, but the courts had denied her custody of her newborn child.

I did everything I legally could to get custody of baby Jeni, as well as a few not-so-legal things. She was not going to go to a foster home—no way. My experience was not the norm, and I knew it. This was how I became a father.

Mind you; I knew very little of fathering at the time. My useless excuse for a father left after I was born, but an enormous Chinese family had surrounded me since I was a preteen, and I knew how to care for kids. I had never told Jeni that her birth father was my brother. She was so small, and she had enough on her plate to deal with. I had always been her Daddy.

Eloise had done her time and had gotten out last year, around the time Jeni's condition declined. The bills were mounting beyond what I could handle, and I realized I needed a full-time gig to help cover the bills. It was hard to be away, and I had to put more trust in Eloise than I would put in anyone, but you don't often get a choice in life.

Seeing Jeni on my phone screen made my heart swell with happiness, and my eyes fill with tears at how thin and wasted away she looked. She wore an oxygen mask and a smile and hugged her new, giant red monkey.

"Daddy!"

"Hi, baby!"

She tried to say something else but had a coughing fit. Eloise came to hold her hand until she could catch her breath. Jeni pointed at the monkey and gave me a thumbs up.

"You like the monkey! Awesomesauce, sweetie."

We chatted for a couple more minutes before it was apparent she was tiring, and we ended the call with me promising to be back on Monday at the latest. Eloise pulled the phone away after Jeni had planted a dry kiss on the screen. She made sure Jeni's mask was back in place before looking down at the phone. "Al, don't go. I need a minute."

I waited a moment while Jeni's mother stepped out of the hospital room into the hallway. Eloise's face came into view on camera; she was in her late 20s and wore her thick brown hair short and spiked. She looked miles better than when she had appeared on my doorstep almost five years ago, begging for help. She had discovered weightlifting during her time in jail and looked fit, but the stress and lack of sleep showed around her eyes.

"Al, she's getting worse. I'm scared. When are you coming back?"

"As fast as I can, I promise. How you holding up?"

"Still clean."

I shook my head. "That's not what I meant."

"I know, but it's what's most important…. Staying that way for Jeni."

"You got heart, lady. You're going to do fine. I will be home soonest. We'll all have dinner at Chen-chen's."

She gave me a very adult look—not one I'd seen on her before.

"If you say so. Just hurry. And be careful up there. I can see that bruise." She arched an eyebrow at me and hung up. Look at her, acting like a parent.

Now that no one was looking, I let my emotions out. I put my head in my hands and tried to control my breathing. Jeni! I wanted to rage at my brother, the cause of so much of my childhood misery and now the author of so much more.

I needed to get home; I needed to be by Jeni's side—I had to finish this job and get my ass out of here. I could move up the timetable. It was a straightforward sneak and grab; there was no need to overthink this. All sorts of excellent logical reasons to wait clamored for my attention; I shoved them into a dark hole and slammed down the lid.

I can get this done tonight and be there tomorrow morning.

I paced the apartment, unable to slow down. I couldn't focus on any of this right now. I needed space and movement. I glanced at my front door and went downstairs to the kitchen. The lunch crowd was flooding in, and Mrs. T. was expediting orders.

I caught her eye through the bustle of servers. "Need a hand?"

She saw the expression on my face and nodded at the aprons on the wall without asking. I grabbed one and went out onto the floor. As I walked toward the grill, I passed a large window overlooking the tree-lined street. I paused to look for the Mortmobile, but there was no sign of it. I rolled my eyes, glad to have somewhere to direct my worry and anger. Watching the building when I'm not here, gone when I am.

Some watchdog!

I would have occasion later to curse myself for not thinking that one through. I want to say that my only excuse is that I was out of my mind with worry for Jeni. But it wasn't just that. I was arrogant.

It would cost me.

Dearly.

YOU DROPPED A BOMB ON ME

I stared in semi-confusion at the blinking, pale green light.

Huh.

It was on an unfamiliar detonator plunged into the equally foreign gray mass of C-4 attached to the bottom of the wall in the hallway of Vegrandis.

That wasn't here when I came in, I thought stupidly, still trying to catch up. I shrugged my backpack—laden with the case of nanos—more securely over my shoulder and took a closer look. I only had a few minutes and change until the device detonated. As I straightened up, I peered down the darkened hallway and saw more blinking lights.

Lots more.

Correction, I thought. *I only have a few minutes until this building blows itself into orbit.* My mind went into overdrive, and all the pieces I had failed to put together fell into place.

I was well and truly screwed.

Rewind.

After my shift at the restaurant, I ditched my apron and went upstairs. I quickly changed and was out the back door five minutes later. I wanted to say goodbye to Mrs. T. and tell Akiko we would have to delay her self-defense lesson indefinitely, but it was better for them if I stayed away until all this was over.

With no sign of Johnny Law or Mort on the street, I slid down NW Flanders and caught a cab to the windy riverside, walking to the pricey hotel where I had left my gear and Baby. I went over my plans, uploaded my biometric data into the Vegrandis security company's network, gathered my things, and took Baby across the river to Washington, where I parked at a movie theatre in Salmon Creek. I spent the next couple of hours at a nearby park practicing the shuffling gait on the recording until I was sure I had it. I waited until dark fell and took Baby back out to the woods, concealed her again, geared up, and hiked in to wait 'til just before the witching hour.

The break-in later that night had been smooth and textbook. I entered through a slit I cut in the southwest fence, waited for the hourly patrol to pass by the back loading dock, and then walked right up to the back door. While biometric security is very reliable, it can be hacked. I stared up the camera next to the door where the security program read the details of my face and found them to be a match for the guard who had just passed by—and the door unlocked with a muted click.

I had hidden my biometric data within the files for all the guards in their network. Whether the camera saw one of the guards or me, the face was recognized by the system as legitimate. It was a reverse Deep Fake with the system seeing the fake rather than a physical viewer. The code with my data would delete from their server along with any digital record that the cameras captured of me automatically, and they would be none the wiser.

I was in.

It was the work of moments to find an office and terminal to plug my custom laptop in, and after that, their building security, excluding the lab, was mine to do with as I wished. Cameras leading to the lab would be looped, doors would unlock when I approached, and it would never register at the front security desk. The interior lab was on a separate system and would still have to be dealt with, but I now owned the rest.

I hid and waited again for the guards to perform their interior security sweep, then walked through the building from memory to the hallway leading to the central lab with the final two biometric locks. The riddles in the dark required their answers now. I plugged in my earbuds and listened once more to the shuffling gait. The owner was overweight and favoring his left leg a little, or perhaps that leg was shorter than the right one. I was nervous about not seeing a video to match the gait, but I didn't have much choice. I exhaled slowly and matched the slight drag/shuffle of the recording as I moved down the sensored hallway. As I walked, I kept my eye locked on the green sensor light above the large steel security door to the lab, alert to any changes in its color.

Drag/shuffle. Drag/shuffle.

A divot in the otherwise smooth carpet nearly ruined everything as it caused me to stumble slightly. The sensor light flashed yellow as I caught myself and continued the drag/shuffle walk to the black steel door. The light seemed to hesitate before deciding I was someone it recognized and switched back to green. I approached the final biometric lock, a small pin pad with a tube to the right of the heavy metal door. A few more steps, and I was there.

A DNA key opened the last lock, and there was no getting around it. I typed in the code Sabitov had provided and then poured the clear liquid from the vial he had given me into the tube.

Saliva.

I wasn't sure I wanted to know whom it belonged to because then I would have to ask the follow-up questions; were they still breathing, or were they enjoying a dirt nap underneath a landfill next to Sabitov's mystery limo corpse? I shuddered a little and was glad I could still feel at least that much. The war and this job had worn away so much of my humanity I was grateful for what little I had left.

The spit worked, the lights flashed green, and the heavy black steel door swung quietly open, followed by a billow of cold air as I stepped into the sub-zero lab. Clouds of icy fog obscured much of the lab, and turning on the lights wasn't an option. I pulled out my IAVS goggles, and the room jumped into clarity. There were half a dozen large glass cylinders set into the far wall containing what looked like a liquid suspension that was unaffected by the cold. The liquid had a greenish cast, but other than that, it looked like nothing more than liquified lime Jell-O. I went to the cylinders, pulled off my backpack, and removed a fitted black case. I carefully lifted a cylinder off the icy shelf, placed it snugly into the case, and then struggled to return the case of green slime to my backpack. My laptop blocked it, and for a moment, I thought it wouldn't fit back in, but I shifted things around, and it finally did. Which goes to show you, there's always room for Jell-O.

Once I had the case with the suspended nanotech safely in my backpack. I had closed up, made my way out of the lab, and had been making my exit—my now abruptly abbreviated exit—when I found the final hall full of explosive surprises.

There was a scuffle from a hallway on my right that led toward the front entrance; I loosened the kukri tucked into my lower back and activated the IAVS goggles, pulling them down from my forehead. I went from the balls of my feet to my knees and slithered myself flat on the plush carpet, hugging the wall as I slowly peeked around the corner.

The parking lot light shone through the glass front doors of the entrance: it silhouetted a prone pair of legs jutting out from behind the security desk. The legs belonged to an adult male. I silently prayed it was a guard, not what I feared, hating myself for the prayer.

"I can see you, Leigh," the voice whispered from speakers overhead.

I tilted my head and saw what should have been a defunct security camera high on the wall. I say 'should have been' because I was the one who supposedly defuncted it. A small red button of light at the bottom winked merrily as if to say, *Guess again, asshole.*

I sighed. "Hi, Mort."

"Do you understand it all now?" his voice seemed to ooze from the darkness above me.

My stomach flopped over inside me, and I wanted to scream. Outside I was frosty. "Don't do this, Mort."

"It is done."

"Sabitov will figure it out, Mort. You know he will come for you. You can only run so long before the shark sniffs you out and tears you apart. We can all still walk away."

"You'd let me walk away?"

If he had done what I thought, fuck no. I would put him down like the rabid dog he was.

"It doesn't matter. Sabitov is a condescending prick; I will deal with him one day. I may stick his prick in a jar and keep it on my dresser. As you have no doubt noticed, we are running out of time, so do like that song by the band Parliament—and give up the funk."

I spent agonizing seconds rising to my knees.

"Who is it, Mort?"

He gloated over the speakers, "You don't know?"

I shook my head and pushed myself to my feet, trying to control my beating heart and slow down my rapid breathing. "Which one?" I asked.

There was the sound of heavy tape ripped away from skin, followed by a choked sob, and my heart tore in my chest as she cried out.

"Uncle Al, help!"

Akiko.

I didn't hesitate; there was never any question in my mind. He had Akiko.

Game over.

I slung the large backpack off my shoulders and held it in front of me as I came slowly around the corner.

"I read it wrong. You were the douchebag Moscato was following. He was sniffing after you, hoping to get something on Sabitov. You sicced him on me."

"I needed you to be too busy to think, and here we are. Come all the way out. That's it."

I kept the backpack extended in front of me, obscuring as much of my head and vitals as possible, and I stepped out into the hallway. Thing One was holding a shaking Akiko against his body as he pressed a long, double-edged dagger across her throat, its razor-sharp edge gleaming in the half-light of the hallway.

I thought of the body armor and arsenal of weapons back at Bag End Farm that I had ignored. I had brought a fucking knife to a gunfight.

"Let her go, Mort."

Mort slowly stepped out from the guard's station, the faint but unmistakable outline of a Glock held in a two-handed grip in front of him. "When I am sure."

"You win. Here are the nanos. You have me. Let her go," I motioned the bag toward him.

"Closer. I need to be sure."

I edged closer, unzipping the backpack a little and showing the edge of the canister case. "They're right here. I have them. They're yours; let her go." I got closer and hoped I might get into striking distance of the twisted little shit. The clock in my head ticked down.

Mort shook his head. "Still not sure."

"Sure of what, Mort?"

Twin cracks from his Glock lit the hallway, the glare magnified by the IAVS goggles, blinding me as the bullets punched into my chest. Akiko screamed. I fell onto my back, banging my head against the floor, knocking the goggles off my face. The heavy backpack landed on top of me, making the bullet wounds howl in harmony with Akiko.

"My aim. This light is so dim."

My chest was a blaze of heat being washed with a spreading layer of cold. My hands traveled up the bag and felt the holes in the backpack that Mort had shot through.

"The nanos," I wheezed.

The upper half of Mort's face appeared out of the shadows— the way his cheeks were uplifted told me he was smiling. "Your other bungle, I am not here to take the nanos. There are interested parties who would like them never to be born. I am doing this like, how you say…? An abortion." He gestured to Thing. "Bring her closer. I want him to see."

Thing simply straightened his back, and Akiko's struggling feet were lifted off the floor as he walked toward us, sheathing his knife with his other hand.

"Sabitov," I gasped. It was getting hard to breathe and there was a liquid heaviness in my chest. One of Mort's bullets must have punctured a lung.

"Oh, Sabitov. The Shark and his associates will think you are the one who sold out to other interests but flubbed your escape. That's if there is enough left of you to identify," Mort shrugged. "Or they might think it was Dr. Zinn, as he will have disappeared after the grisly murder of his colleague, Dr. Persici, earlier. I guarantee you they will never find Zinn's body." He gave a dry chuckle and tucked his gun into his pants. "But they will not be thinking of me. And if Sabitov or his friends do come after me after all I've done for them? I'll cut their nuts off and put them in a jar; I'll burn them all."

The man had a serious fixation with Sabitov's genitals in a jar.

He gazed down at me. "But for tonight, I'll start with you."

Thing arrived to stand next to Mort and effortlessly plopped Akiko's feet to the floor in front of him. Mort pulled a pair of plastic bottles from his pocket and popped the tops off with his thumbs, and immediately sprayed their contents down on me. The smell hit me the second he removed the tops.

Gasoline.

"What are you doing, you crazy fuck?" I rasped.

"You know what they say. All work and no play." The sadistic light twinkled in his eyes as he emptied the bottles onto me.

Akiko had stopped struggling and had shut her eyes. Thing gazed on with a face that looked like he'd hit it when he fell off that rung of the evolutionary ladder. His eyes were vacant and bored: he had seen this before. Mort was the head. He was just the muscle.

My breath bubbled in my chest.

I turned my head toward Akiko. "Akiko-*chan*. Be strong. You have to be strong now, for all of us." Mort tossed the empty bottles out to either side of himself with a little flourish and reached into his pants pocket.

"Remember your lessons, sweetie. Be strong. Remember, what goes up must come down." The cold had spread from the top of my chest to my core. My insides were icy blocks grinding against each other. "Up and down."

She opened her eyes, and the spirit of her grandmother peeked out at me. Mort brought out a Zippo lighter and flicked open the lid.

"Up and down." So cold, so very cold.

Akiko went limp, and Thing leaned forward instinctively to stop her fall. She lifted her patent leather school shoe and drove her raised heel down onto Thing's instep. Thing gasped, and his hold on her loosened. His head came down in reflexive pain as Akiko's right elbow raced straight upward into his larynx. Thing gagged, arching backward and holding both hands to his throat.

Mort stumbled back as Akiko pushed the off-balanced Thing at him. Thing dropped to one knee, coughing and retching next to me.

Close enough.

I pulled the kukri out from underneath me, my chest blazing in frozen fire, and sliced through the meaty hamstring at the back of his leg. Thing screamed as he fell all the way down, blood spraying and pumping in heavy spurts—I'd hit his femoral artery.

Akiko sprinted into the darkness of the building, away from the exit. Mort switched the lighter to his other hand and pulled at the gun in his waistband. Akiko was almost to the corner as Mort brought his gun up.

"Little bitch," he snarled.

I heaved the dripping backpack at his outstretched arm as he shot, my chest screaming at the continued abuse. My aim wasn't great, but it knocked the gun out of his hand as it went off. I heard Akiko shriek and the Glock clatter away into the shadows. Mort turned to me as I came to my knees, reversing the direction of the kukri toward his mid-section. Pain arced through my body like an electric current as I got close, and Mort leaped back, weasel-quick, but not before my blade passed through something more than fabric, and hot drops of blood spattered on my cheek.

Mort swore something in Russian as he clutched at his stomach. He flicked at the wheel of the lighter in his left hand, and in its flickering glow, a spreading stain of damp scarlet glistened on his shirt. Heavy purple loops of intestine poked out wetly from between his fingers. A smell far riper than Mort's characteristic odor filled the air.

"Burn," he hissed.

He tossed the lighter at me.

It spun in a lazy arc toward me. I tried to bat it away but missed as agony shot through my lungs, freezing my arm as the lighter hit me in the chest. A jagged icicle stabbed up into my skull, and my body was a glacier of pain. The last thing I saw was Mort lurching for the exit.

Then, the world caught fire.

FIRE AND ICE

Have you ever been burned? We have all touched a hot toaster or pot on the stove and felt our body's instinctive reflex to pull away before our brain even realizes we have come too close to the heat source. But have you ever had a real burn?

When I was twelve, there was a grease fire in Chen-chen's kitchen, and my right hand was splashed in flaming oil. I remember those first moments of searing agony where your surface nerves scream as they roast, but that initial pain fades and recedes a little as your body marshals its endorphin army, and shock sets in. But with a severe burn, that moment of respite is brief due to the deep, relentless tide of throbbing pain that swallows you. It is the kind of pain from which nothing can distract you, the kind where all you want is for it to end. I had taken beatings from my brother and neighborhood kids, careened off my bike going down California Street, resulting in broken bones and stretches of my skin left across the asphalt. I even had a spinal tap when I was nine. But nothing else in my young life had compared to that oil burn for its malevolent tenacity.

This was a whole other beast.

I was incapable of thought, time compressed to a never-ending, charred moment. The smell of the gas and my skin roasting in the heat were the only things that made it through the paroxysm of agony. I gasped for a breath inward that scorched my mouth and blocked my scream. I tried to remember to roll, but my body was just an organism responding to the searing kiss of the flames. My legs tattooed a violent drum beat on the carpeted floor. A horrible ripping carved deep into my chest. It was too much.

My heart stopped.

For a moment, there were only the flames and the silence.

A crackling whoosh broke the silence, and there was a dry blast followed by the blessed relief of cool air. The whoosh cracked the air a few more times. I could feel the delightful coldness that is the simple absence of heat.

"Uncle Al?"

Her voice echoed in the distance, and for a timeless dark moment, I knew I could just stay with the silence. No more pain…. Just drift out of the rest of forever on the quiet.

Is that what you want? The silence whispered.

"Uncle Al, I need you! Wake up!"

No.

My heart stuttered, then kicked back to life, and I gave a deep heave for breath. I opened my eyes, and there was Akiko's tear-streaked face with a fire extinguisher clutched in her hands.

I groaned and gazed down at myself.

My body was covered in white retardant with a pair of maroon spots on my chest where I was shot.

"Uncle Al, are you okay?"

I groaned louder.

I thought young people had good hearing.

"Uncle Al, we need to go. Those clocks on the silly putty…."

I forced myself to sit as Akiko dropped the extinguisher and helped pull me all the way up, covering herself in soot and retardant. Every breath was a screaming exercise in pain, but each one was easier than the last. Akiko slung my left arm over her shoulder, and we hobbled to the exit. The body of Thing lay motionless on the floor. Akiko kicked it as we hobbled past it.

I looked down at my right hand—it was clenched and burned around the handle of my kukri. The skin was cracked and oozing blood and clear fluid.

I wheezed, "How much time?"

"One minute or less by now."

"Shit. Faster, kid, faster." We broke into a staggering lope. "You didn't hear me say that word," I gasped.

"I love you, Uncle Al, but I have more to worry about tonight than your Marine mouth."

My body was shaking in aftershocks of agony, my burned clothes and skin sent a stink up my nose, making me want to throw up everything I had ever eaten, but I forced myself forward.

We pushed out the front doors, and off to the left, taillights weaving down the road past the front gate: Mort.

The rest of the parking lot was empty except for a long, dark shape that swallowed the light and made an even darker patch.

Baby?

Akiko pulled me along faster. "He touched my car?" I panted.

Akiko looked up at me. "It was how they got me. The car pulled up after the dinner rush, and I thought it was you."

A new surge of rage scoured away some of the pain, or the pain was getting less, which couldn't possibly be happening unless I was closer to dying than I thought.

Focus! Get the kid out of here!

I crashed into the side of Baby, a fresh wave of misery washing over me. Colors swirled wildly out of the corners of my eyes as Akiko opened the door and helped push me inside. I sat in the driver's seat and looked stupidly at the knife stuck to my hand as Akiko rushed to the other side. I slammed the palm of my left hand down on the back of the blade and felt the handle tear away from my right hand, taking a massive patch of unburned skin with it. Stars exploded across my vision, and I roared.

"Uncle Al!" Akiko shook my shoulder.

My spare hide-a-key was in the ignition, and I turned it left-handed. Baby growled to life as I punched the gas pedal to the floor, her rear tires screaming as her back end fishtailed. I popped the clutch, and she leaped forward, tires eating asphalt. I wrapped my raw right hand around the Hurst gearstick and shifted her, my mouth gaping open in anguish.

The lights of the building grew suddenly brighter in my rearview as we roared past the empty guard booth whose windows were splattered in gore—more of Mort's handiwork.

The light mushroomed as Baby tore down the road. It became a sun going nova: a blossom of orange and yellow that wanted to devour us like some carnivorous flower. The shockwave from the explosion was right behind the light, and it blew in the rear window, glass shattering as it lifted Baby's back end and shoved her violently to the right.

I spun the wheel into the turn, and someone screamed a high-pitched shriek. It had to be Akiko because I couldn't reach that particular pitch even if I had a ladder.

As far as you know.

The rear wheels bit back into the ground, and we rocketed forward in the darkness toward Highway 14, burning trees at our backs and charred leaves twirling in our wake.

I looked over at Akiko who was curled into a ball on the passenger seat. "Kid—you, okay?" I had to raise my voice over the cold wind whipping in from the lack of a rear window. She peeked out from between her fingers.

"Define okay," she squeaked.

"You in one piece?"

She lifted her soot-covered face, her long hair flying in the chilly breeze, and gave me a thumbs up. She reached out to touch the burned remains of my sweater, which crumbled off at her touch. I was expecting worse, but the skin didn't look half as bad as my hand. The multi-colored flicker happened at the corner of my eye again, but nothing was there. I wondered if the fire had damaged my cornea.

"You need a doctor, Al! He shot you and you look like something that got left on the robata!" Concern and fear were printed on her face; she was barely holding it together.

She wasn't wrong, I still didn't understand how I was even functioning, but I just told myself I was a tougher bastard than I thought. Or I was going to drop dead soon, I had no idea which, and I was legitimately scared for the second option. I'd never taken this much damage before. I couldn't let her see that fear; she needed a grownup. Unfortunately, that was never my best look, so I gave her what grin I could muster and topped it with my bad, British-accented Black Knight.

"I've had worse."

It coaxed a smile, and an equally bad Cockney accented, "You liar." Nothing like a little Monty Python to cut through the terror. The tension in her face eased a little. She took a few deep breaths and nodded to me.

Flashing red and blue lights appeared, but this time when I looked, it was a pair of Staties that zipped past, sirens wailing, as they headed back toward the smoking crater where Vegrandis used to be. The Camas off-ramp was approaching, and I gunned Baby up the ramp; every movement of my body sent another shockwave of electric agony from my skin to bones.

"Akiko, open the glove box and see if my phone is still in there." I rasped.

She uncurled herself, opening the compartment and pulling out my phone as I came to the top of the ramp. I turned Baby hard at the corner and skidded to a stop in front of a Chevron station.

"Akiko-*chan*, I am so sorry for what happened to you." I grabbed the phone with my left hand, unlocked it, and handed it back to her, wincing. "Call your *baa baa* first. Tell her what happened and where you are. If she wants to go to the cops, it's her decision. Tell her I'm sorry."

I leaned past her and opened the door, the pain of the movement registering on my personal Richter scale. "Out, kid," I gasped.

Akiko stuck one leg out onto the ground. She looked back at me.

"Where are you going?"

"Gonna catch up to Mort. There's only one direction he can head."

"Are you going to try to kill him?"

I paused while the world swam before my eyes, giving me a moment to consider how to respond while I waited for my eyes to refocus. I could have given her the easy answer, the one she may have wanted to hear or maybe expected to hear after a lifelong diet of sitcoms and police procedurals where everything was wrapped up neatly—the good guys were always good, and the bad guys always had justice served up at the end.

The only problem is, I don't think of myself as one of the good guys. Don't get me wrong, I am not a black hat either, but there is a gray no-man's land in between where I live. I exist in both worlds, neither belonging to one nor laying claim to the other. There are few absolutes in my world, and I'd spent more time hiding in the shadows lately than I had basking in the light.

I could have told her some frivolous lie that would shield what remained of her innocence a while longer and maintain her good opinion of me. And her good opinion of me did matter. But there were other things that mattered more.

She was still just a kid, but after tonight I owed her one of those aforementioned absolutes in my world, one I held for my family, my closest friends, and my comrades-in-arms. Tonight, she had been all three.

I owed her honesty.

I met her gaze and tried to keep the anger out of my voice. "Yeah, kid. I'm gonna try my hardest to bury him."

She threw her arms into the air. "You can barely drive!"

"I'm feeling better, I swear." There was a strange metallic taste in my mouth—I spat outside my window and turned back to the kid who hadn't shut the door yet.

She looked at me quietly for a second and then said, "I think Grams would be quoting Confucius at you right now." I knew the quote she meant, and yeah, it would be something Mrs. T would say.

I nodded.

She stepped out of the car and then leaned her head back in.

"Be careful."

I grimaced and shrugged, causing some soot and fire-retardant to puff off of me. "Aren't I always?"

She was close to tears. "Try harder."

She slammed the door closed and stepped back. Ouch. Shut down by the eleven-year-old. I'd done what I could to get her to safety, but now Mort had to pay.

With Akiko out of danger, my rage rose inside me like Godzilla on the beach, just getting bigger and bigger with every beat of my heart until I thought I would never see its tail. I tightened my grip on the wheel, the pain focusing my will, as I unleashed Baby on the road.

Mort had taken his best shot at me.

My turn.

HERE COMES REVENGE

Before you embark on a journey of revenge, dig two graves.

Fucking Confucius.

Chen-chen had insisted on Chinese school when my brother and I moved in with him, and there was plenty of Confucius and his followers' commentaries to bore me to tears for years. We had been loosely raised Roman Catholic by our mom, but Chen-chen made himself clear. We may not be Chinese, but we were in a Chinese home, and learning about another culture would broaden us. Or we could spend that time cleaning the grease traps at the restaurant. You ever clean a grease trap? Gag. Classes had been in the backroom of an herbalist's shop off Powell. To this day, even the smell of dried herbs can induce narcolepsy on the spot for me.

It wasn't all bad. Some of the studies had been rather enjoyable. The language and history had been fascinating, Lao-Tzu and Chuang-tzu mystical and exciting, and Buddhism a balm for my thoughts. But Confucius was dry, prosaic, and moralizing, and I would rather have surgery on my junk with a sharpened spoon and no anesthetic than have to re-study *The Analects*. Chen-chen likes to point out that my disregard for Confucius is probably why I have such "adaptable" morals.

I wasn't really on a journey, anyhow; I was just headed a short way up the road. The way I figured, Mort was injured and in the open. He certainly couldn't go to anyone in the Bratva. When word got to Sabitov, it wouldn't take him long to mobilize everyone he had to find Mort. No, Mort needed medical attention and a ticket out of town, pronto.

There was nothing to the east down the SR 14 except for the gorge. No help for him there. PeaceHealth Southwest Medical Center to the east and north was less than fifteen minutes away in Vancouver, but I was betting Mort would want to lay low and avoid the hospitals to keep the Shark from sniffing him out. That meant south—to Portland.

Two bridges connect to Portland in that part of Washington: the Interstate Bridge on I-5 and the Glenn L. Jackson on I-205. The I-5 bridge was further west, down SR 14. In contrast, the I-205 connector was only a few miles away and went right past Portland International Airport—lots of hotels and parking structures along that route to lay up in, get a sawbones on the shady side of the street to patch him back together, and then catch a plane as far from Oregon as he could run.

I put my money on the 205 and played catch up.

Traffic was light, and Baby sprinted and danced between the few cars I saw. The radio carried dimly over the wind from my broken window. It was still on the oldies station; Jim Morrison urged me to break on through somewhere. My anger and rage kept me warm as the pain started to recede from my awareness. I felt a little giddy but wasn't sure if that was from blood loss or the fumes coming off my clothes. I couldn't get that metallic taste out of my mouth; it wasn't blood, it was…it was like when I touched my tongue to both connectors of a 9-volt battery as a kid. It was a buzzy-coppery tingle. I spat outside the window again, trying to get the flavor out of my mouth.

I wondered exactly how much blood I had lost and how much longer shock and endorphins would let me go before it all came crashing down on me. I came upon the half-cloverleaf ramp that led from the 14 to the 205 south across the Glenn Jackson Bridge when the Mortmobile passed under the halogen streetlight at the top of the ramp.

I snarled to myself and flexed my right hand around the gearstick as I down-shifted Baby onto the ramp. I didn't notice how easily my hand was moving and flexing. The music on the radio went from The Doors to Duane Eddy's version of 'Peter Gunn.' As I shifted up, my right hand was illuminated in the faint green light from the console. There was no bleeding or lymph fluid. The skin was dirty and bloodstained but looked dry and almost pink.

I turned my hand over in the console light, confused. I looked up and saw the taillights up ahead of me put on a sudden burst of speed. Mort had seen Baby and dropped the hammer. I forgot all about my hand that gripped the Hurst shifter loose and easy and punched the gas pedal to the floor.

The 205 bridge is a segmented highway that runs north and south, four lanes each way, across the Columbia River. It connects Portland, Oregon, with Vancouver, Washington. Below, a mile or so away and a little over halfway out, was Government Island. On the other side of the island on the far shore was Oregon, and to the right, bordering the river, was PDX. The bridge takes a downward slope leaving Washington as you approach the island, and I had a clear view ahead of me. Mort was the only car for a mile.

One of my favorite courses I took after Section had plucked me from MARSOC was the combat driving course. I heard endless humor about my California driving skills, but at the end of the course, I had been the one with the highest marks.

I mentally apologized to my car, opened Baby's throttle, and came up fast on Mort's tail, ramming his sedan. The back of his head, with its bad combover, rocked violently back and forth in my headlights as I dropped back. The back end of the sedan wiggled left and right from the collision; I timed the next hit and sped up to give the back end of his sedan a hearty smack to the right, putting him into a spin.

I eased off the gas and watched the Mortmobile spin across the highway, smashing the passenger side against the middle median—with its protected bicycle path—before continuing its spin back across the highway, only to smash again against the western riverside of the bridge not far from the edge of the island. The vehicle came to a shuddering halt, smoke billowing into the air.

I hit the brakes and stopped just past the wreckage of his car. I reached down to the car's floor until I found the handle of the kukri, my blood still tacky on the handle against my smooth palm. Too distracted by bloodlust to notice anything but my prey, I muscled my way out of Baby's driver's seat.

The sedan's front windshield was a spiderweb of glass behind the jet of steam coming from his engine. The head and taillights had gone out, leaving the car a steaming shadow, but Mort's airbag had deployed, and I knew he was hidden somewhere behind it. We were alone on this side of the highway except for the distant headlights of a car just leaving the Washington side and headed down toward us. Plenty of time.

Lightning flashed off to my right, illuminating the bottom half of Mt. Hood in the distance, its upper half cloaked in dark clouds. I limped toward the wreckage of Mort's car, knife in hand, as a frigid wind plucked at my burned clothes, causing pieces of fabric to tumble away in the icy breeze. The smell of the freshwater from the river below wafted up while the sharp, ozone crackle of lightning on the air drifted down. The gentle lapping of the river on the shore of the nearby island pounded as clearly in my ear as the beating of my own heart. All of my senses were keener, sharper. My chest was tender where I got shot, but my left arm swung free and easy. Anger clouded my thoughts; I wanted only one thing: my knife in Mort's heart.

Thunder rolled down the gorge as I got close to Mort's door. Cordite and gun oil trickled through the air—Mort was packing. I hunkered down next to the driver's side front wheel and banged the back of my kukri against the door.

Five tiny cracks echoed like Taiko drums in my ears as I came smoothly to my feet and reached in the smashed window to grab Mort's gun hand around the wrist. I spun his forearm counterclockwise as I stepped forward, bracing his twisted elbow against the doorframe and applied pressure.

Hard.

His arm snapped, the elbow bending out the opposite way anatomy had intended, and a .32 revolver dropped to the ground. He screamed, and it sounded like sweet music. I dropped his useless arm and kicked the gun under the car. I opened the door, punched my kukri through the airbag, and pulled him out of the car like a rag doll, slamming him up against the mostly undamaged rear door of the sedan. I put the razor-edged blade against his neck and used it to tilt his head back.

Now it was my knife against his throat. What a difference forty-eight hours makes.

He had a jacket on, but he had taken off his shirt and used it as a makeshift bandage around his waist. It was soaked in blood and was bulging unnaturally. His narrow chest heaved in agony and terror as his body quaked. He refused to look at me—turning his head away and sobbing in Russian.

I grabbed the back of his thinning hair, giving me a clear view of his protruding Adam's apple. His rancid breath made my stomach heave, and I could smell his bowels. I looked down at his weasel face as my blood sang and told me to take what was mine to take. He had gone against me and his boss; he had murdered almost a half-dozen people today, he had nearly killed me and would have certainly killed Akiko, and I didn't want to even think about what he would have done to her before she died.

"Do it!" he sobbed. "What are you waiting for?"

What was I waiting for?

"You don't do it, I go to San Francisco, and I kill your bitch niece!"

Akiko, and now Jeni? I nearly put my weight into the knife as I thought for a brief moment of those girls. I thought of how they looked to me. Killing changes you. I had to do it before in wartime; death then had been in mortal combat, and I had accepted that. I hadn't killed like this—never like this: rage and the sweet-sick taste of violence at the back of my tongue with my opponent helpless and unarmed.

There's killing, and there was murder. I'd had to do the former as a soldier, but I had never done the latter. Ever. Was this the kind of death I wanted on my conscience, no matter how badly I thought he deserved it? Would I even be able to look at myself?

I looked again at Mort and saw a shriveled excuse for a man, probably one the world and I would be better off without. For a moment, I saw the lank hair, the narrow chest, and bad teeth, and I was reminded of Tolkien's Gollum. I remembered how Gandalf had said it was pity that stayed Bilbo's hand when Gollum was at his mercy, with Sting ready to end the miserable wretch's life. I understood why Mort wanted to provoke me now, but I wasn't going to be the one to take out the trash.

I dropped the knife from his throat and let go of his hair.

"No. It's not pity that's gonna stay my hand, Mort. It's that there's nothing I can do to you that Sabitov won't do so much better. And by better, I mean worse. You're not my problem."

Mort clutched his broken arm and continued to sob.

The colored flicker happened again, and I batted at my eyes. I sheathed my knife as I looked in the rear door window to check my eyes and saw my reflection. I was dirty as hell, but my face looked fine. Unburned. I leaned closer and turned my head. The bruise on my face from Mort was gone.

"What the hell?" I muttered.

Mort opened his tearing eyes and looked at me. "*Shto?*"

I peered closer at my reflection in the glass: my pale green eyes had become vivid swirling whirlpools of lime, without a hint of white or pupil.

Things became quiet for a moment as there was a slight pinching on my chest, followed by a tiny *plink!* a second later. I looked down at the ground and saw a 9mm slug lying at my feet. Mort looked down at the slug and then back up at my chest as another pinch followed the first. The second slug slowly pushed out of my chest as the skin closed behind it like it was never there. The slug fell to the ground next to the first with another *plink*! Mort looked from my chest to my glowing eyes.

"*Bozhe moi!*"

I stepped away from Mort with my back to the guardrail as he scuttled alongside the car away from me.

I tilted my head back, and the light of the stars pierced the clouds, not faint and twinkling as I had always seen them but as fierce cauldrons ablaze with colors I had no name for. My ears picked up the susurrus of the water as it flowed across the Dalles Dam forty miles distant and the frantic beating of Mort's heart as he stared slack-jawed at me from a few feet away. My skin and the muscles beneath moved and shifted as the damage done to my body tonight was knitted up, reinforced, and strengthened. Drunk on sensation—I tried to pick out individual threads from the liquid cacophony enveloping me.

That was when the headlights lit up Mort.

I turned swirling eyes to the left and, with crystal clear vision, saw my doom. A white Volkswagen Rabbit was plowing toward us, its whiskered, flannel-wearing hipster driver illuminated by the glow of his smartphone as he was—texting? Checking the time? Was he late? Whatever he was doing, he wasn't watching the road where Mort's darkened car had stopped.

There was only a moment before a solid THUNK hit me with what felt more like *resistance* rather than force and hurled me high into the air over the river. The crash and scream of tortured metal ripped through the air a second later, and I saw another, far shorter form follow me over the side.

I only got a brief glimpse of Mort's legless torso falling after me, his mouth gaping open and closed like a fish while his intestines flapped helplessly below him.

The dark waters rushed up to meet us like a bottomless black pit, and I had my last clear thought.

Fucking Confucius.

THE REAPER

Silence. Darkness.

Awareness of their existence increased by degrees. How do you hear or see what isn't there?

Who is it that hears?

The pivotal moment came when I realized their nature: that they were silence and darkness, and what their continued presence implied.

Silence. Darkness.

At first glance, they are simply the absence of sound and light. Silence and darkness are what happens when we stop making noise and close our eyes. But of course, we don't see the world the way it is. We can only try to conceptualize and model in order to understand our surroundings, our reality. For example, we all agree that tall thingy over there with the scary arms and rustling green hair is called a "tree."

Chen-chen raised me to believe that many things that at first glance seem to be opposites are complementary. The model of my youth was yin-yang—the split half-circle of the Taijitu: the symbol of the complementary opposites of nature. There can be no light without darkness, and silence is only the beat between the notes.

Life has taught me otherwise.

My reality—my model, if you will—is that silence and darkness are absolutes. They are states of existence only momentarily interrupted by a child's laughter or the reflection of the sun as it dances on the waves. Silence and darkness: they were there before; they will be there after, forever and ever. Amen, and chunky peanut butter.

We are just a flicker in the endless night.

Am I dead?

Who is it that hears?

The Zen riddle percolated up into my thoughts again, and I was aware I had thoughts.

Not dead—I don't think.

I struggled in the emptiness to find an answer. In chaotic flashes, I relived my evening…the break-in, Mort and the explosives, Akiko, and getting Memphis-style barbecued. I remembered the crazy on the bridge and the thunder of light and sound.

The faintest of echoes clopped rhythmically from off in the distance: slow, muffled footsteps, it seemed. Relentless and even, the steps grew louder as I reasoned they must be growing closer. The soft footsteps became resonant—pounding, moving faster— as if they knew I had become aware of them and might flee. A gentle roaring filled my hearing. Fear gripped me as I remembered the stories of Yángwáng Chen-chen had told me when I was a rebellious pre-adolescent: King Yan come to judge me and drag me to Diyu—hell.

And boy, did I deserve it. My time in Section alone guaranteed that.

The footsteps sounded like they were running toward me now, thudding and vibrating faster. Bearded Yan was rushing at me, long fingers outstretched like claws as his dark robes swirled in his wake, and I had nowhere to hide.

Remembering Section snapped me back to myself. I stopped trying to impose my subconscious model of what I thought I was hearing.

No judging, no preconceptions.

Perceive.

Not footsteps: not the dreaded Yan come to bring my soul to the Ten Courts of Hell.

Perceive.

Comprehension dawned as I realized I was hearing the panicked beating of my heart. The gentle roaring was the blood flowing past my ear canals. The rapid beat slowed as I calmed my mind, and the image of Yángwáng finally retreated into the clammy darkness of my memory. Filled with resolve, I swam upward through the endless night, struggling to find the light. I howled, and I raged, but there was no sound.

Voices from far away whispered gentle ripples across my mind.

Secondary target reached—linkage ten to the seventh power.

What?

There was a crackle of static.

"Someone tell Moscato his perp is waking up."

I opened my eyes.

DON'T ASK ME NO QUESTIONS

The dim lights of the room blinded me for a moment, and I blinked to clear my watering eyes. I tried to wipe them, but my hands wouldn't move. The momentary panic threatened to come back, but I calmed myself.

Perceive.

There was the rough edge of nylon at my elbow cutting into my skin, and the cool metal of a handcuff encircled my wrist.

I was restrained.

My nose told me what my eyes were too busy readjusting to see. Sterile air flavored with ammonia informed me I was in an infirmary of some kind, and even without the dim radio chatter, the tang of leather from a Sam Brown belt, coupled with too much Axe body spray and stale coffee, told me five-oh was in the room.

Where am I?

I struggled to think back. I had been on the southbound 205 when all the weird went down on the bridge. If Johnny Law showed up and pulled me out of the drink, it would be Washington's jurisdiction. I was either a guest in Vancouver Police lockup or one of the secure rooms in the wing off the ER in PeaceHealth Southwest Medical Center. I was betting on the latter, as there would be no need to have a personal babysitter if I was in Vancouver jail.

Early on in my extended stay in the Pacific Northwest, I made it a point to visit every major hospital in the area that had a Level One Trauma Center—both in case I ever needed their expertise or if I just happened to become an unintended guest. I was never a Boy Scout, but my time in Section had taught me the value of being prepared for as many eventualities as possible.

Like Mort pulling the double-cross? Where did that come from?

The potential for the nanotech was too great; I should have anticipated there might be other interested parties. But how did they get to Mort so fast?

I didn't see that one coming, but I bet neither did Sabitov. That wouldn't make it easier on me when he found out that his top lieutenant crossed him. He'll want to know how his intel and security guy, his *very* expensive intel and security guy, missed that. Then again, it's what he gets for springing this job on me without giving me time to vet it thoroughly.

To which he will rightly ask why you jumped the gun like a nervous virgin and didn't take more time to, you know…vet it thoroughly.

I exhaled—one thing at a time.

I pulled gently on the restraints to see how tight they were. Nice and secure.

As weird as the rest of the night had been, being bound and detained was at least something I had some experience with.

No, not like that.

It had been a part of my Marine training, as well as my time in Section. Staying on the down-low was my bread and butter but getting caught was always a risk—one I had mostly prepared for. One that I had kept tight control of before tonight's fuckaree.

Question was, how much trouble was I in?

I thought about that for about a split second before the wiseass in the back of my head cheerfully informed me: probably a lot.

Forensics on my car will put it at Vegrandis. So, theft, arson, and possibly murder are all on the table. Most, if not all of it, I could legitimately pin on Mort.

Maybe.

I couldn't afford to tell the whole truth, but I was pretty sure Mort wasn't in another room waiting to contradict the story I was rapidly building in my head.

Well, maybe the lower half of him was over in the morgue, but it wasn't going to say shit.

Question two—how blown was my cover? Assume all the way. So how long before they started backtracking my various travels and linking them to my other jobs?

A brief surge of adrenaline coursed through me at the thought, and again I slowed my breathing to clear it. No need to activate the escape hatch to go underground for the next decade or so. Not yet. I needed more data.

I blinked my eyes as the room came slowly into focus. I looked down at my body, half expecting to see it bandaged from the toes on up from the burns that, by all rights, should be covering my body. I was in one of those embarrassing hospital johnnies that flash ass from the back, but my legs were bare against the sheets.

No bandages.

I remembered ripping the kukri from the oozing, melted skin of my palm and how the same patch of skin had been dry and unmarked by the time I stopped Baby on the bridge. I flexed my right hand easily into a fist and then spread my fingers wide— nothing...not even a twinge. I bent my fingers and ran them against my palm. It felt smooth and undamaged.

Huh.

I ran my thumb along the top of my palm below my fingers. Even the calluses from years of weight training and weapon practice were gone; my entire palm was fresh and soft.

A sense of doubt crept up on me—I should be a mass of weeping tissue. The fire was real, damnit. Even if I had imagined it all, it didn't explain the disappearance of my calluses. Shit like that doesn't just go away.

In my memory, I heard PLINK!

That fucknuts Mort shot me. Yeah, and then we watched the slugs get ejected from my chest á la Wolverine. Plink! Something isn't right. Either I am imagining that the shoot-up and barbecue happened, or everything that happened afterward is a dream.

Or....

Or what? Mort shot me! That happened: I felt it. I could still feel how the slugs punched through the case and into my chest....

Oh, shit.

The case. He shot me through the fucking case.

The case full of nanos.

Before I had time to process that little tidbit, the door to the room opened, and in walked Special Agent Willy Moscato, his spiky black hair in disarray and his face set in a scowl just for me.

Here we go.

Moscato glanced at me briefly before talking quietly with the uni. He finished murmuring and gave an unmistakable toss of his head toward the door. The uniform picked up a paper cup with the PeaceHealth logo on it and stomped out the door, closing it none too gently behind him.

"You seem to rub people the wrong way, Agent Moscato," I opined.

Moscato looked confused for a moment, then glanced at the now-closed door. "Our friend there? The boys in blue are a little bit jumpy tonight. All kinds of odd goings-on."

He pulled the chair the uniform had been sitting in over toward the side of the bed and plopped his lean frame down in it. He placed a closed, industrial-looking tablet on his lap and stared at me.

"So..." he began and then just trailed off and smiled at me.

I smiled back and admired his demeanor. He was seemingly chill and ready to play, but I could tell he was unsettled.

His left finger tapped the cover of his tablet in a quiet but quick manner; his breathing wasn't the long, deep breaths of a man at ease but short and shallow. His spiky black hair was more disheveled than I had seen in the past, and I could easily imagine him running his hands through it when upset or distracted. He was covering it well, but the minutiae said Special Agent Man was spooked.

Made for two of us.

"We're still dragging the river for the other half of your playmate and, judging by the condition of the rear of your car, I'm betting the tire tracks we lift in Camas will match that beauty of yours."

"Camas?" I asked innocently.

"The fireworks show. You know, the one with the dead people?"

"If someone was injured tonight, I am genuinely concerned for them, but I didn't kill anyone."

Moscato leaned forward with his elbows on his knees. "What about Mortimer? You concerned about him? Or you going to play dumb on that one too? Because I can most definitely put you at the scene."

"I didn't kill him."

Moscato shrugged. "Maybe not directly, but I bet you can tell me all about how you both happened to be stopped on the bridge in the middle of the night."

"Car trouble?" I threw out nonchalantly.

"Try again."

I pulled on the restraints covering my arms. "Do we really need these?"

Moscato nodded his head. "I really think we do."

"Wow, didn't take you for the bondage type—being around handcuffs all the time must keep you pretty worked up."

I pulled on the restraints again, but he just shook his head. "Let's talk first."

"Oh, I enjoy our conversations, agent, but perhaps I should have a lawyer here this time."

Moscato's easy smile turned grim as he nodded. "Yeah, I'll bet you do. But first, I want to show you something." He opened the metal cover of his tablet and booted it up. He typed a few commands and then braced the tablet with the cover so it would stand on its own. He then put it on my chest so that I had a clear view of the screen.

"Netflix and chill, agent? I don't put out on the first date…at least not without dinner first. The coffee doesn't count, by the way. I'm not cheap, but I am easy."

He said nothing but reached out and tapped the enter key. A warm spot appeared on my chest underneath the tablet.

Contact.

What? There was no volume on the screen, and Moscato's lips were sealed tight in a white line. Who said that?

The window on the screen opened up and caught my eye as a grainy video played. The camera must have been up near the lights on the bridge because the picture had that orange halogen tinge, and it looked downward onto the southbound 205. The video was time-stamped at the bottom, and the two pairs of headlights raced toward the camera. As they flashed by, the first could have been the Mortmobile, but the second was clearly Baby. The picture jumped as another camera took over the footage just as Baby surgically knocked Mort's car out of position. There was me getting out of the car with a knife, the gunfire, and me breaking Mort's arm before putting the knife to his throat.

All on camera; all of it looking like I was attacking Mort without provocation, and he was shooting in self-defense. Without context, there wasn't a rational person in the world who wouldn't watch that and not think that I was some kind of murderous thug.

Moscato reached out and hit pause on the tablet. "Here's where the rubber hits the road, so to speak." He held my gaze as he reached out again and hit play.

The pale Rabbit sped into view. Mort and I turned our heads to look, and the Volkswagen exploded…at least, that's what it looked like. A violent blur was followed by a white flash.

The video began again, except in slow motion this time. The white car clicked into sight, frame by frame, the driver looking up from his phone as his headlights lit up the pair of us by the car. I had sheathed my knife and was staring up at the sky. I turned my head as Mort raised his uninjured arm in front of his face, either from the glare or from the realization of what was about to happen.

Or what should have happened.

What happened was that the front of the VW rippled like a wave across the hood as the entire front end collapsed like an accordion.

Before it got within a full meter of us.

I had a brief glimpse of the bearded driver's head before the front seat became part of the rear bumper. There was a flash, and the recording ended.

The warmth on my chest had become an itch.

Moscato leaned forward.

"I'm not going to pretend I understand what I just saw there. Or how you ended up in the river where we fished you out, and why you are sitting here in one piece when your pal had to split. As soon as you went airborne, it seems Mort lost whatever protection had been available to you both moments before. I want you to think very carefully about what you say to me in the next few moments. You get one chance to come clean with me."

He stood up and tapped the tablet screen so that the video looped repeatedly. "You take a moment and think hard."

He strode over to the door, pulled out his cellphone, and started tapping away.

Think hard.

Shit.

Think fast.

Too much had happened, was happening. I had to get out of here, but force wasn't an option right now. I needed to seek the lower road: water flowing down toward the path of least resistance. My only option was to try and talk my way out of this, but I didn't have enough information. I didn't know how closely hewn to the truth my story had to be to weave my lie successfully. I needed to know what he knew and how.

The video on the tablet slowed and then halted. The window was quickly replaced by a file marked ACTIVE.

I glanced over at Moscato—was he doing this with his phone? He had the phone to his ear and was murmuring into it.

The window flickered and showed the logged forensic items listed from my car. Fingerprints, dust from the explosion, and mud from Baby's tires: everything the cops needed to put me at Vegrandis when the shit went down. It was just a matter of time until their forensic labs were done.

Another file had a list of names and addresses of Vegrandis employees and their families. A notation at the bottom had a short list of two nameless former employees. There were employee ID numbers but no Social Security or addresses. Both were cross-referenced with the file of a drug dealer in Astoria. Someone got canned for doing drugs? In the PNW? Had to be hard stuff.

The itch on my chest was edging toward burning, but my attention remained focused on the screen. Not enough. I needed more.

Moscato finished his call and pocketed his phone.

Another window flickered open: WITNESS STATEMENTS. Names flicked across the screen, and one of them was Akiko's name. The file immediately opened, and there was her statement, given two hours earlier. You go, kid.

Moscato came to the bedside and grabbed the tablet. I looked up at his face, looking so sure of himself. "Seen enough?"

I glanced back at the tablet as he took it away and saw the video from the bridge flashback onto the screen. I looked down at my chest and saw a small, perfectly circular hole in the top of my smock where the tablet had rested a moment before. My skin underneath the hole faded from an angry red to my normal, graveyard-tan skin tone.

The flash of color happened again at the bottom of my sight. I blinked my eyes, and a bright dot appeared at the bottom of my left eye's vision. It resolved itself into a tiny image of a dragonfly, flashing white.

An icon.

Seen enough?

"Apparently not," I muttered.

WOULD I LIE TO YOU?

Moscato sat back down in the chair, leaned back, and locked gazes with me—one of those mucho-macho, let's-see-who's-more-alpha, first-one-to-twitch-loses things contests, which worked in my favor at the moment because I had reflexively gone motionless with shock.

The little white dragonfly icon sat there impossibly in my field of view. I wanted to see if this thing was floating around in space, or was it just me? But Willy and I were locked in our manly gaze. I was pretty sure he didn't see the dragonfly, and it was all me, though. I certainly would have said something if I was in his shoes. The best idea for me was to keep my mouth shut about it.

But could I keep it shut? C'mon.

"What do you tell the other boys when you stare like this? This really works for you?"

Got a mild elevation of his left eyebrow on that one, but the stare-off persisted. The dragonfly pulsed and glowed at the bottom of my eye.

Oh, fuck this.

These things were never my style. They reminded me of nothing more than my teenage years. Back then, these kinds of stare-offs were just a great chance for me to get close enough to you to lift your wallet, phone, or watch. When the ole up-close-eyeball happened in the Corps, I resorted to what my DI used to call tactical escalation, aka…knee to the balls. That usually ended those particular encounters.

I like to think I've outgrown those things. Mostly.

"Can I have some water? Please?" Politeness costs you nothing.

Moscato paused, nodded, and broke our tough guy stare-off. As he reached for a nearby super-50-ounce hospital sippy cup, I turned my head to the right a few degrees and looked out of the furthest part of my right-hand field of view.

The icon (eye-con?) stayed down in the lower left part of my eye. It had stopped blinking but just sat impossibly in my vision like a Heads-Up Display.

As I thought furiously, Moscato held the barrel-sized plastic cup, swiveling the bendy straw my way.

What did I know about nanotechnology? Theory-wise, it involved microscopic, self-replicating machines. Okay, what else? What could these tiny machines do? When I had needed to get more information to take on Moscato, it popped up like I had asked for it. The little hole—it required contact. The burns; my skin: repaired like new. Cellular manipulation?

So, fast healing of severe trauma and the ability to physically hack a secure device just by touch? That alone told me the nano's probable application and likely target audience.

All of it military.

Imagine what a spy or a soldier could do with this? My mind reeled. I slowly slurped down the cold water. Okay—it was (or they are) a machine of some sort. That means there has to be a means of control. Something was driving it/them. If there was hardware, there must be software, and if there was software, there must be....

Moscato tugged on the cup; I glanced up at him. The dragonfly eye-con glowed gently against my field of view.

An interface.

It's an interface icon.

Okay, so where's the fucking mouse on this thing?

Moscato pulled the cup away and put it on the table. He turned back to face me. First things first.

"Got anything you'd like to say?" Moscato probed.

A lawyer wasn't going to be able to help me with this. I needed out—now. That meant doing it my way.

I sighed and muttered, "Yeah."

Moscato held his silence and patiently waited for the truth—or the lie. Truth's a funny thing: bend it the right way, and even it can become part of a lie that can work. You just need enough truth. Sometimes, just a sliver.

As for the rest, deny like a motherfucker.

"I don't know about any of that stuff on the bridge. I have zero explanation. I mean, what the fuck was that crazy-ass shit? Maybe something in Mort's car? Maybe he stole something from that lab?" *Sniff down that trail*. I shook my head. "I can tell you why I was at that place out in the woods in Camas." He'll already know I was there. The forensics will confirm that. "Mort and me…."

Moscato leaned forward.

"I owed Mr. Sabitov. He gave me twenty-four hours to come up with twenty large. I was short. Mort told me to meet him. I didn't want to go there. I wanted to meet somewhere public. I don't know what the fuck he was doing out at that place." I sniffed a little. "He made me come out there."

Moscato's eyebrow's shot up. "He made you?"

I nodded.

"How?"

I had an idea of what Moscato knew, but I was pretty sure he didn't know how it all fit together. I needed to know his intent. Was he dead set that I was a bad guy who needed to be locked up? Was it possible he knew it was me who was there to rob the place? Could I wiggle out of this?

Miyamoto Musashi was considered one of the greatest swordsmen ever to live. His treatise on combat, *The Book of Five Rings*, is a masterpiece on strategy. In the Fire chapter, he discusses a strategy he refers to as "Moving the Shadow." When in doubt of the mind of your enemy, feint with a vigorous attack to force him to reveal his intent. Musashi's chosen weapon was the sword, but his advice transcends the katana. Like all good strategies, it transcends even the arena of combat. From the general moving his armies to the mortal combat between individuals, down to the dialogue between opponents—there are many kinds of arenas and different sorts of combat. Most importantly, there are many kinds of weapons.

A section of truth will be my katana.

"He kidnapped Akiko."

Moscato gave me cop-face.

"I was short, and he took her, and he told me to show up there, or else he was going to hurt her."

Moscato took one of his folded hands from his tablet and lifted it palm up toward me.

"Why didn't you go to the police?"

I gave a very honest snort of derision at that idea. "You chase the Bratva. You know how well connected they are here. You know what they do to rats? You think there's a cop in this city they can't buy if they don't have something on him already? These guys invented *kompromat*."

Li'l Willy shifted a bit uncomfortably at this.

"He said no cops, no guns, but I wasn't going empty-handed. I don't trust that weasel, so I brought a knife."

"You…literally brought a knife to a gunfight?"

"The Corps was a long time ago. I'm a cook these days, Special Agent, not a gangster. So yeah, a knife."

"On that bridge, you took out an armed man from a secure location like you do it for breakfast. Not too shabby for an ex-Marine."

"There's no such thing as an ex-Marine. Some things die hard."

Traces of doubt crept into his eyes.

"What happened then?"

"Could I have some more water?"

"In a moment. Let's go on a bit here."

I paused and stared down at the sheets, letting my voice drop into a monotone. I let my imagination lead me. "I got there, and the guards in the booth, they...I didn't look too closely." I let my voice drop further. "There was a lot of blood. I got to the parking lot and came in the front. The door was unlocked, and the lights were off. There was another dead guard on the floor, and Mort was there with his Russian BFF and Akiko."

Moscato opened his tablet and fingered his way around the screen. "Pavel Ivanov of Battle Ground, Washington, 43 years of age. Go on."

I nodded.

"I told them to let her go. He made me get on my knees. I knew then he would kill us both, maybe leave my body there to take the fall for whatever he did. It wouldn't make sense to leave her body there, but I knew Akiko would die by Mort's hand after he was done with me."

I stopped. I glanced over and caught Moscato's eye and said with utter honesty, "It was worse than that. He wanted to burn us alive. It's how he gets his kicks."

The tightening around Moscato's eyes was all I needed to know that he was aware of Mort's little obsession.

"Akiko...that kid is a fighter. She saw what was happening to me and distracted the big guy by stomping his instep. It knocked him enough that I could cut him and bring him down. Mort chickened out and hightailed it out the door. The kid told me about the explosives, and we scrammed."

Moscato leaned back into the chair.

"You say you brought down Ivanov? Did you kill him?"

I shook my head and lied like a rug. "I sliced his hammy—he was alive when we ran out. We only had seconds between Akiko telling me about the explosives and getting out the door. He didn't even occur to me until after the blast. But he helped kidnap that little girl. Who knows how many of the deaths at the lab are his handiwork? And to top it off, he was going to sit there and watch me get barbecued alive. So, I'm not feeling too fucking guilty about leaving him behind."

Moscato came out with the one I had been waiting for: "Why didn't you take the girl and go to the cops right away?"

I exhaled. "You ever been truly, righteously furious, agent?"

Moscato said nothing at first but then gave a small nod.

"He took that little girl from her family because of me. He killed those people and was going to leave my corpse as the fall guy—after he burned that innocent kid and me alive, of course." My voice had dropped into a dangerous growl, and I mentally pulled back. He needed to see the lamb, not the tiger. "I dropped the kid off and went after Mort. I shouldn't have, but I was beyond furious. So, I went after him, and I had him on the bridge."

I stopped and shrugged honestly.

"I couldn't do it. It's not who I am."

Not anymore.

"You saw the rest."

Moscato was tapping his fingers against his tablet. The hook was set. "Why should I believe you?" he asked.

I looked him dead in the eye, the picture of innocence. "Ask the kid."

His expression didn't change, but his posture shifted ever so slightly. He had asked Akiko, and she had told him the bare bones of the lie. Mort put something over her mouth, knocked her out, and took her. When she woke up, she was at Vegrandis, and I came and saved her. No elaboration…just that. Over and over.

"I want to bring someone in to take a detailed statement from you."

Score!

"I spoke to the young lady. Her grandmother reported her missing earlier and then called us after you dropped her at the gas station." He paused and shrugged. "She confirms most of your story. I want you to stay here for observation, the statement, and another loose end. Hopefully, forensics can get some of this cleared up, and we can confirm the rest of your story in the next couple of days."

"I have to stay? Am I under arrest?"

"No, but you are a material witness to multiple homicides. Best case you could be charged with a justifiable homicide, even if it was in self-defense. We can hold you for 48 hours if you want to make a stink."

"Can we do the statement in the morning? I'm wiped."

Moscato looked at his watch and nodded. "We can get started at 9 a.m. Good for you?"

I gave him a weak smile. "Happy to help."

Moscato stood up and walked to the door.

"Special Agent Moscato?"

He looked back at me.

I pulled gently on my restraints. "Are these still necessary?" I nodded to the locked door. "I'm not going anywhere. I'm safer here than out there if Sabitov wants me." That wouldn't last, though. The Russian's reach was long. I needed to talk to him to get things straight before he made the wrong kind of assumption.

He pursed his lips and walked back to me, fishing keys from his pocket. A quick snap, and my hands were free.

Moscato walked back to the door. "If you need anything, just speak up." He pointed to cameras housed in heavy-duty metal mesh in the corners of the room, near the ceiling. "We'll hear you. If you need to use the john, wait for someone to unplug your chest electrodes. Doctors want you under surveillance for the night."

I smiled at his retreating back. "Thanks. Say, Special Agent? If I could ask, what about that other loose end you mentioned?"

Moscato slid a passkey across the lock and opened the heavy metal reinforced door.

"I ran your name through the Pentagon, and it sent up a flag. Some full-bird Army colonel wants to talk to you. Says back in the day, he was your CO. Also said you skipped out on a debrief after your court-martial and disappeared. He wants a quick word with you. In-person. Thought you were a jarhead. What's with the Army?"

"Marine Raiders are part of the United States Special Operations Command, SOCOM. We worked with operators from other branches," I replied. A chill had set in my gut.

"What exactly did you do—if I may ask? Most of your file is…above my pay grade, I've been told."

I thought about it a moment. Another big truth that would come out soon, sprinkled with a little lie that could paint me a little more harmless, couldn't hurt.

"I was nothing special; the unit I was assigned to handled counterterrorism for Southeast Asia and the Pacific Rim: tracking pipelines for Afghan and Chinese opium, intercepting technology headed to North Korea, breaking up human trafficking rings. We were everywhere."

I looked at him with a rueful grin. "I was just the IT guy."

Moscato snorted and nodded.

Show him what he wants to see: a passive threat. Dangerous? Who, me?

"Why'd you split on your debrief and ghost out?"

I thought about one of my friends and co-workers at Section, a Navy lieutenant named Sam—the real IT guy. I used to talk shop with him. I remembered what he used to tell me and repeated it back to Moscato, "I may not have been a front-line operator, but I saw all the intel that crossed our path, what the people we went after did. I read reports. I saw the photos. You see enough of that, and it wears away at you...your spirit, your soul, whatever. It withers. Navy docs say it's PTSD, but by the end, I just wanted out and away. I just wanted to be left alone. Start something new."

Liar.

Moscato nodded again quietly and turned to leave.

"What's his name? The colonel?" I asked.

Moscato paused and shook his head. "Some Irish or Scottish, Mac-something."

"Micawber?"

"Yeah. That's it. Your old boss?"

I nodded.

"Be talking to you soon, Mr. Leigh." Moscato left.

Micawber.

Fuuuuck.

INSIDE INFORMATION

Micawber.

Not now. Not after all this time. He'd been waiting for me to stick my neck out and do something stupid. Now he knew precisely where said neck was.

Micawber had just sent me a message through Moscato. I had never skipped anything. 'Skipped' indicated a code word was coming and that word was *debrief*. Debrief in Section jargon meant *peaceful talk, no violence.*

Interesting thing to lead with, but considering our history, not too surprising. Whose toes did I step on tonight?

I spoke out. "Ummm, hi. I need to use the head—bad."

There was a squawk above my head. "One moment."

In moments, the passkey lock flashed from red to green, and there was a loud click! The door opened, and a beefy local PD uniform assigned to the hospital walked in with his hand on his piece.

"Moscato says to treat you like a civvie for now, but this is my beat, and I expect you to be respectful while you are here. I have a full house tonight, and I don't need any monkey business. We had a fight down at the real jail, and four boys who need the professional help are here, being stitched up." He spoke clearly, making constant eye contact with me. I got the sense that my healthy condition disagreed with him.

"I just need to pee, man. Then I want to rack out. I'm no trouble."

"As long as we understand each other." He walked over, disconnected the electrode wires from the monitor, and undid my finger monitor as well. He motioned for me to stand up as he slung the loose wires over my shoulder and pointed toward the door.

I looked at the name tag attached to his tactical vest: *HOPKINS, GIL.*

I walked out the door into a hallway. There were two doors to my right and a bathroom door directly across from my room with the round blue image for universal usage on it.

As I walked across the hall, I looked further to my left and saw that it was a short walk to another security door with a small wire-mesh-lined window. Beyond that, there was another hallway and what looked to be a glass-sealed nursing or security desk near the double-swinging doors that led outside.

There was no way to get out except right past Gil and whoever else was down there.

I walked into the head and let loose. After washing up, I looked at my reflection in the grimy piece of metal on the wall that served as a mirror. My eyes looked like their usual selves; I was unsurprised by that as the doctors and Moscato would have mentioned the swirling green pools that had replaced my eyes on the bridge if they had been visible. I squinted and looked closer; I couldn't see the dragonfly icon in the reflection either. I went back out into the hall where Gil the Guard was waiting and then back into my room/cell. Gil wired me back to the monitor with his purple-gloved hands and re-attached my finger monitor. My readouts flashed to life on the screen, and he walked out without another word.

Not sure I liked Gil, but he probably didn't like seemingly healthy people cluttering up his ward or the extra work that came with said healthy people.

I blew air through my pursed lips.

The Feds had me in custody. How long before their investigation trips up someone who gives away that I worked for Sabitov instead of owing him money? And lets out what kind of work I did for him? How long before Sabitov decides that my time as a guest of the law, coupled with the Mort/Vegrandis disaster, has made me suspect, and he puts out the quiet word for a hit? And most especially, how long before Colonel Kurt 'Blackguard' Micawber and his Not-So-Merry Band of mercs and murderers from Section got here?

Tick-tock, tick-tock.

All this, and I've got some honked-up tech in my body that I don't know what it does or how to get it out.... Or if I can get it out.

It occurred to me at that moment that of all the people in the world who might be interested in getting said tech out of me, the most ruthless of the bunch was headed my way. This shit would be straight up the boss-man's alley.

And he wouldn't care how he got it out of me.

The chill that had set in my gut took the bullet train up my spine.

Micawber showing up right as this crazy shit goes down?

Coincidence, right? Had to be.

He can't know about Vegrandis; they were private. The possibility of the military being brought on board was what had spurred Sabitov to go for the grab. This sort of thing wouldn't have even filtered down to Micawber's layer yet.

No, he was here for me—old business.

But boy, he sure would be interested in the new toy that's been shoved into me...and how to keep it for himself.

I gotta get out of here.

I closed my eyes to clear my mind, and the icon glowed against my closed lids. Fuck meditation. How in the hell was I going to sleep with that thing on?

There had to be a way to interact with the interface if that's what the thing was. A phrase from college anatomy class bubbled up: function determines form.

Okay.

Say this thing was made with the military in mind. If the operator needed to interact with the tech, the process of initiating it would need to be silent and preferably, hands-free.

Is it possible it was thought-controlled? The very idea stunned me momentarily. It made the most sense, however.

Nano-power, activate! I thought. Nothing.

Had to try.

Probably something more conventional.

Login. Nothing.

Access. Nada.

Entry. Nope.

And so, I spent the next fifteen minutes going through every command I could think of, including a few choice ones I was sure would not have been included in any kind of programming outside of Grand Theft Auto.

No reaction.

Maybe an anatomical trigger?

I double tapped each of my fingers; I clenched my fists. I snapped, touched thumbs, and did the Spidey web-shooter; I even wiggled my toes in every sequence I could think of. The little dragonfly just sat there like a glowing piece of white shit against my closed eyes.

White shit. Wait a sec. Maybe my sphincter? What, like flex it?

I'm not going into detail on that one. You can guess how it went.

I finished the experiment feeling frustrated yet legitimately relieved that my last idea hadn't been the trigger. I could just hear some drill sergeant yelling at a newly nano-infected recruit: "How do you think you control it, maggot? Put your ass into it!" The bad jokes piled up after that.

My stomach growled.

I opened my eyes and sighed with frustration.

If I was some dipshit programmer, what would I do?

Kill myself.

No, before that.

Function determines form. Yeah, I would do that—except our guy or gal didn't. Probably some genius software engineer who got contracted to come to the PNW and became a stoner. Every good programmer I know up here is a stoner. I didn't particularly care. I think, out of all the things you can do to yourself, the herb is pretty benign. But it does start affecting things upstairs after a while.

Function determines form.

I looked at the eye-con.

Huh, it's not that simple…is it?

I blinked once. I blinked twice. I blinked three times.

Again, nothing.

I rested my head against the pillow and tried to control my rising frustration levels. I was ravenous; it wasn't helping me think.

I thought about being back at the restaurant. I wanted a ginormous bowl of poke and a bathtub-sized mug of *matcha*. I pictured Akiko laughing and Hitoshi with his skateboard in one hand and his ever-present vape pen in the other. Although, with his arm in a cast, I imagined he could only hold one of the two at a time now. I wondered which one got precedence? Probably the pen.

A mental image of Hitoshi's metallic grey pen with its glowing white button suddenly struck me. I thought about the cannabis vaporizer pens that were now ubiquitous in Portland. Technically, you were supposed to keep that stuff in the house, but the pens were discreet, and most of Portland didn't care. The image of the power button hit me again, glowing white just like the dragonfly icon. You had to press the button five times to turn it on or off.

I blinked five times.

The menu spread open across my eyes like a glowing HUD at the fifth blink.

Stoners.

VIDEO GAMES

The menu hung in space across my vision, glowing a gentle green. Again, I wished I had a mirror to see how visible it would be to an observer. As it was, the menu itself was relatively simple.

*Interface

*LightCam

*SoundWve

Next to each option was a small image of an hourglass. The 'Interface' line's hourglass icon was full of glowing white. The 'LightCam' hourglass icon was half full of a glowing yellow, and the SoundWve hourglass was empty. The little dragonfly icon had shrunk smaller but remained down in the lower left quadrant.

I had no idea what any of this meant, but this was some cool-ass shit!

On the surface, a part of me was able to lose myself in the sheer fun of new technology, but underneath that thin, brittle layer of fun was a deepening well of unease. This wasn't a new Xbox or weapon targeting system. *This...thing was inside me. What had happened to me? What was I becoming? Is it going to hurt me? Can I undo it?* The questions sloshed around against the walls of my mind, drowning my initial excitement at finding the menu. The well of unease had opened to a dark cavern with powerful currents that could pull my mind down into the depths of fear, and I couldn't afford that now. I compartmentalized it for later, took a deep breath, and turned my attention back to the problem in front of me.

Okay, how do I click on these files?

Now that I had the essential clue, I was able to work out in minutes how to move around by blinking. Four blinks with both eyes was enter, three blinks with both eyes was back, three blinks with the right eye would move the cursor down, three blinks with the left eye moved it up.

Okay, now that is just fucking outstanding.

I scrolled down to Interface, and quad blinked. The file opened to a submenu that read:

*Progress Meter ON/OFF

*Remote Access

The Progress Meter was currently toggled to 'off.' I flipped it on.

The bottom of the little dragonfly glowed yellow like the LightCam hourglass icon. They mirrored one another. So, the dragonfly icon gives me the current update of LightCam? What happens when it fills? I become a flashlight and can take pictures?

I scrolled down to Remote Access, but there was only a single menu item:

*Infiltrate YES/NO

The toggle was set to YES as a default. Infiltrate and Remote Access sounded like what had just happened to Moscato's tablet.

I scrolled back to the main menu and flipped down to LightCam. When I tried to access it though, the hourglass flashed, but nothing opened. Same thing on SoundWve. No opening the file until the Progress Meter is filled? The setup of this was distinctly video game-like if that was true. Until I had enough Experience/Progress, the next level's abilities were inaccessible. But then again, what better interface for a generation of young soldiers bred on video games? It would be the most intuitive system.

How did I accrue Progress then? Or was it out of my hands?

Perhaps it was a measurement of the nano's progress in facilitating the next level?

Not helping me now.

I went back to Remote Access and saw only binary choices: YES/NO, ON/OFF.

Is that the only level of control the operator gets or is more offered later? I reasoned that this was an early, beta-like version, so perhaps commands were limited. I could understand restricting a soldier's choices to keep it simple, but then the rest of the process must be automatic.

I blinked five times and exited the menu. The dragonfly stayed half yellow, or had the level of color gone up a hair? It was so tiny; it was hard to tell.

I looked around the room: it was a standard, windowless hospital jail room with only one door and two ceiling cameras: no closet and no bathroom; nowhere to hide or ambush. I looked at the passkey lock on the door and felt certain my new little friends could get it open, but... How to do it without being seen? I looked up at the cameras.

If I can only access devices by touch, it will be a ball-buster with all that mesh. Then I have to get out onto the main hospital floor and outside without my ass hanging out, literally begging to be noticed. Then, I'd be out in the street in October with no clothes or money, and a list of federal alphabet soup agencies—probably local PD, one violent, angry Russian mob, and Micawber (I didn't even want to think about that)—on the lookout for me.

One thing at a time.

Was there any way to get to those cameras? I looked around the room without much hope. This was precisely the kind of room they don't leave the sharp objects in.

I looked over at the wheeled monitor next to my bed that kept an eye on my vitals via the electrodes. Smash it or the wheeled stand it was on to get to the camera? Kinda loud and likely to bring some unwanted visitors. Working cross-purpose there, not to mention I didn't even know how I activated the nanos to get into Moscato's tablet in the first place.

What had I been doing?

Nothing. Lying there stunned and panicked and desperate for intel. Panic as a motivator? If it was only meant to be used in extreme emergencies, perhaps, but this technology was like a spy's wet dream. It demanded cooler conditions to operate, as I suspected it was meant to. Okay, then. Need? I had needed to know what Moscato had.

What I needed now was a way to turn those cameras off or loop them, like at Vegrandis. Something that would let me get to the passkey and pop that lock to get out of this room. I focused on that need.

A tickle on my chest itched again, except this time, under the electrodes.

I blinked open the menu and scrolled to Remote Access. The Infiltrate line was gone. In its place was one of those countdown pies, like when you are downloading an app.

The tickle under the electrodes became a warm tide that flowed out of me. I rode it up the wires, into the monitor, and down to the power cord into the wall. The tide became a blinding rush through a maze of lightning until I saw a video image of me lying in my bed as a timestamp at the bottom kept track. I closed my eyes but could still see the video transmission.

Loop it.

The timestamp continued its count, and I continued to lie, seemingly asleep in the video. I raised my right arm from the bed, but the image of my sleeping form remained unchanged.

Holy shitballs. I had never done drugs, but I imagined this is what it was like.

I sat up and felt the warm tide race back to me through the wall and up the monitor.

My vitals.

The tide paused, swirled, and then continued its rush back to me. The pie on my menu HUD was full. In a moment, the Infiltrate line returned.

I blinked out of the menu and looked at the readout on the monitors, pulling the electrodes from my chest and the clip-on one from my finger. They hung unattached as the monitor continued to read my heartbeat and measure my O2 levels.

I glanced down at the electrodes and back up at the cameras. Had the nanos been able to access the video feed by following the power source? I looked over at the door and the electronic keypad next to the door. If so, that thing is going to be a piece of cake.

There was a *click*.

The light on the passkey lock had changed from red to green.

I waited a moment, but no one came in.

I got out of the bed and padded to the door. I silently turned the knob and opened the door a crack. I saw down the hallway to the connecting security door, but no one was around.

Who unlocked the door then?

I looked right and saw closed doors—every one of them locked up.

Had the nanos anticipated or read the nuances of my need and opened the door remotely while also looping the cameras? As no one approached and no one was politely asking over the intercom why I was out of bed and if I wanted anything, I had to assume that was the case and that the looping had worked. How? What was the process? So many questions.

My inner soldier slapped down my inner nerd. Fuck off, hippie; we don't have time for this. I needed to get out of here and find a way to get these things out of me. As nifty as all this was, I normally didn't put anything stronger than ibuprofen in me, and the idea of these machines, however remarkable, swimming around inside of me still creeped me the hell out. God alone knew what they're fucking with in there, and I was positive they hadn't been FDA approved yet.

That's it; stick to the humor. It's always been your armor and shield, but only to cover for your fear and uncertainty.

I wasn't sure I had enough humor to cover the uncertainty right now. I mean, there was a whole lot of my uncertainty just hanging out in the open where anyone could see it.

I shook my head at myself as I peeked down the hallway. See, in a movie, this is where you conveniently find a janitor's outfit or a covered cart of laundry. Real-life, no such luck.

Gonna have to balls it.

Easy to say, how you going to do it?

I glanced at the door to the bathroom across from me. A spot of red on the wall next to the door caught my eye. I considered it briefly.

Hardly subtle.

I wasn't worried about the rest of the hospital. I was sure a secure ward would be compartmentalized from the ER and the main building.

Well, pretty sure.

Maybe.

I mean shit, it *should* be. Great, more uncertainty.

I remembered that the uni, Gil, had mentioned his four other wards and his admonition to be a proper guest. I had just managed to bypass their cameras and locks like a ghost; it would be almost unprofessional of me to take that route.

No. I'm better than that. I ignored the easy red temptation on the wall and padded out quietly into the empty hallway. *Cocky and arrogant much?* I asked myself.

Whatever. I will float out of here as quiet as a snowflake on the wind.

I am stealth.

THE DEVIL WEARS A SUIT AND TIE

The lights overhead flashed, and ear-splitting sirens honked and wailed while a cop strobe-light spun in its clear cover from the ceiling, painting the hall in garish yellow flashes that reflected the water streaming from the ceiling sprinklers.

A frightened-looking Gil and a male nurse I didn't recognize were rushing two of the injured cons from the hallway back into the last room. Someone else was screaming in a strangled voice from my room; smoke was pouring from the bathroom, the stench of charred flesh rode the air like a witch on a broom, and Satan himself was standing in the doorway leading to the hall in front of me.

Yeah, I am stealth.

It hadn't started out this way.

I'd stepped out into the hall, watching the interconnecting security door to the left that led to the passageway, when two surprising things happened.

The first was that my leftward gaze showed me that the little dragonfly was now two-thirds full of glowing yellow. When had that happened? Since the video hack?

The second was a hairy, muscular forearm covered in tattoos coming in sideways from the right, straight for my neck. My right hand flashed clockwise upward in a lightning parry but only managed to deflect the lethal blow enough to keep me alive. The rest of a smock-covered wall of tattooed muscle and hair slammed me into my room and down onto my back.

We skidded back across the floor, my attacker on top of me, and collided with the monitor cart, which fell over with a crash next to us, wires trailing on the ground. Another tattooed, smock-wearing goon, this one shaved bald, followed us in, and closed the door behind him.

I'd seen enough of the tattoos on that forearm to know what was up.

Russians.

Sabitov had either decided to take me out over the fiasco at Vegrandis or because I was sitting pretty here under federal custody while Mort was dead. These guys pick a fight at the jail and get put in the infirmary right next to me.

Just business.

I fired a series of rabbit punches to the bottom of my attacker's rib cage, right at the tip of his short ribs. A muffled *crack* erupted on the last hit, and his breath exploded out of him. I snaked my left arm between us and spun him off of me, onto his back. I used the returning momentum of my arm to send it back his way, powering my forearm straight out and down across his trachea.

He made a strangled, gakking noise and clutched at his neck as I did a kip-up to face the skinhead Russian, who was already headed toward me in a classic boxer's crouch.

The lock hadn't been me, and either Gil or his co-worker had taken Bratva money to let these guys in. I was betting on Gil. They'd waited to see if I made a break and then came for me. No amount of noise was bringing reinforcements my way. They were here to kill me.

Gil was going to let them.

Baldy feinted and came in low with his left. I parried and went for an eye strike that he ducked, which set him up for my solid right uppercut to his left cheekbone. His head snapped back, and blood flew from his split orbital, but he lowered his head back down and charged me. I was blocked between the bed and his fallen pal; I had no room to maneuver. He hit me like a linebacker, and I dropped a left elbow to the back of his neck as we went down, but I didn't have the leverage to give it more than a glancing blow.

As I went down, the back of my head slammed against the floor, stunning me. Viper-quick, his hands were around my throat as he straddled my chest. There was a bandage going up his left forearm. He had really needed stitches to get in here. I slammed my fist against his bandaged forearm again and again and saw his bloodied face go white with pain, but the vise on my throat got tighter.

He pulled me up off the ground by my neck and slammed the back of my head violently onto the floor. I stopped the hitting and started the blacking out.

NO!

My hands grasped at his baseball-bat-sized wrists, but it was like trying to move a pair of tree trunks. He lifted me again and slammed my head to the ground while he tightened his grip on my neck.

Again.

Stars exploded as the blackness at the outer edges of my personal galaxy grew larger, and my vision got smaller. The slamming must have made me blink enough to open the HUD menu. The LightCam hourglass was almost full.

My hands fell away from his wrists and dropped to the ground.

I looked up at the cameras—the ones I'd looped weren't recording this. I'd inadvertently given Gil an excuse: the cameras couldn't see this.

I was slipping away. My feet were drumming on the ground, and my hands had fallen weakly to the ground. The fallen electrode wires pressed under the back of my hand.

My old DI screamed in my head. *Improvise! Adapt! Overcome, maggot!*

I blinked four times.

Remote Access.

As the blackness closed in on the room, my attacker's face flashed in and out as if it was being lit by…

Lightning.

Pie wheel.

I liked pie.

A powerful surge ripped through me, followed by a piercing, agonized scream. The mingled smell of burning plastic and skin floated past my nose as the pressure on my throat immediately eased, and I gasped for breath. The screaming stopped, and the weight fell off my chest. I rolled to my knees, wheezing, as smoke from the charred remains of Baldy—who now lay in a fetal position at my side across the either unconscious or dead form of his pal—filled the room.

I exhaled my own cloud of smoke. I was pretty sure if I had had hair, it would have been standing straight up.

Fuck me sideways.

Keep moving. Question later. Move now!

As my vision cleared and the pain in my head receded, I lurched to my feet and stumbled into the hall. There was smoke coming from underneath the bathroom door along with wisps from a power outlet in the wall. I'd started an electrical fire.

I stumbled to the fire alarm, feeling better by the second as the nanos repaired me, and pulled the handle, setting off the alarm. Gil may have ignored the cries for help, but no one would ignore a fire alarm in a hospital.

The menu was still active against my eyes, and the LightCam hourglass was now full and glowing.

Gil and a male nurse rushed through the security door. Either my room or the bathroom contained an active fire because the sprinklers kicked in.

Gil saw me still standing up…obviously not the position he'd expected to find me in, and stood stock still as the water plastered his hair and clothes to his body. I stared at Gil; whatever expression was on my face (perhaps a faint glow from my eyes?) made him blanch, and he took a step back.

I pointed to the other two rooms and snarled, "Get the injured guys out of here."

Gil nodded hastily, running past me with the nurse right behind him.

And happy day, they left the connecting security door open behind them.

I moved for the exit when the double-swinging doors leading to the ER beyond it opened, and an incredibly tall, thin figure flanked by thirteen shorter figures swept into the hall. The shorter figures fanned out with practiced grace behind the leader in a protective V, the grim outlines of guns in their hands.

I knew that gangly-ass silhouette anywhere.

Micawber.

A chill ran through me, and I took a reflexive step back as my hands clutched into fists, my fingertips digging into my palms. Few people can give me the heebie-jeebies, and he was one of them, for an excellent reason.

He was insane.

Just then, the strangled screaming erupted from my room. I guess the hairy Russian goon wasn't dead and had discovered his crispy-critter pal lying on top of him.

The lights flickered out. Smoke and falling water filled the darkness, along with the sirens and the hoarse screams of pain and terror. The only light came from the dim, pulsing flashes of the strobe that struggled to illuminate the darkened, smoke-filled hallway. The door was open, freedom beckoned from beyond, and the scariest motherfucker I knew was standing in my way.

I stepped behind the smoke billowing out of the bathroom and deeper into the wet shadows. The armed figures checked the security room and swept down the hall, weapons up.

Yeah, sure. Debrief.

I was trapped. I was not going quietly, not with that asshat.

I scrolled down the menu to LightCam. It was now followed by the familiar binary, YES/NO. The default for this was NO, so I was hoping there was an offensive nature to it.

Voices called for fire extinguishers and lights. Within moments, flashlights appeared held in Morro-style grips; the gun braced across the hand holding the tactical light allowing the shooter to point the light and shoot simultaneously.

I toggled the switch to YES and waited for what I was sure would be a light show of some sort. The pie wheel spun, but much faster than before, almost like it had undergone an upgrade.

Four shadowed figures rushed the interconnecting door, the lights below their gun barrels slicing the darkness. I moved back deeper into the hallway. They split up into pairs. One opened the bathroom door while the other covered him, and the other team did the same to my room.

Textbook sweep and clear.

The spray of a fire extinguisher echoed from the bathroom, and the braying of the sirens stopped.

The pie wheel stopped as well, and the LightCam line returned with the toggle set to YES.

Nothing.

Shit.

I crouched down below the clouds of smoke as the flashlight beams pierced the dark above me. I was wet and cold all over, from head to toe—like, freezing. Lying practically naked in the water was probably not helping.

I lay flat and close to the wall, hugging the cave-like darkness of the hallway around me.

The teams cleared the two rooms opposite and returned. Again, their beams passed above me as I stayed flat. I wasn't sure why I bothered. As soon as the lights came up, my lone hiding spot would disappear. Instinct; my training perhaps. To never give up and to stay hidden in the shadows, waiting to strike, had been drummed into my very bones, first by the Marines and later, in Section— coincidentally, by the same man walking toward the doorway.

Micawber entered, practically dipping his head to come through the door. Through the smoke and water, he looked like a praying mantis that had learned to walk on its hind legs.

One of the squad reported to him. "One casualty and one injury in the target's room. It looks like an attempted hit gone wrong for the hitters. There are four others in the last room: guard, nurse, and two patients."

"Any of them Leigh?" His voice was smooth and textured. He always enunciated with great care.

"No, sir."

The screaming, which had dropped off, picked up steam again.

Micawber said nothing, just motioned with his head to my room. One of the squad peeled off and went into my room. There was a wet-sounding snap, and the screaming stopped.

Cold-blooded.

"Sir, it's possible he was already gone before we got here. The security door was open. The guard in the last room there said he had seen Leigh in the hall."

Micawber snapped. "Get some men onto the floor of the hospital. Lose the tactical gear and check the ER. If he's out there, find him. Two of you check the cameras in the security booth; the rest of you get the lights on and search again. Call the fire department and cancel the call. No one comes in here until we have cleared the wing. Be sure."

The lights flickered on, and Micawber was illuminated. Tall and scarecrow-like, he had a head of rich silver hair, a handsome face, and eyes like chips of the palest blue ice. It made him look like one of those dogs you see in Alaska, except with an insect body.

He looked up at the lights and smiled like a child. "Ask, and ye shall receive."

Lights were on. The jig was up.

I stood up slowly with my hands raised, standing close to the wall, never taking my eyes off the head of Section.

Micawber's head turned toward me, the angelic grin still on his face, and he called out, "Leigh!"

Fuck you, asshole, I'm not saying shit. I stood there with my hands raised and waited for the rush of the squad—possibly a tackle to the ground—and the handcuffs. An unwelcome sense of defeat bubbled up, Micawber would win again, and I'd have to suck it.

Stupid LightCam.

I shivered from the cold. Even my face and scalp were icy.

"Lieutenant Leigh!" Micawber shook his head. "Leigh, you can come out now. No need to hide."

Umm…what?

Micawber's eyes tracked right past me and back to his squad leader. "Search those rooms again and bring out the others from the back."

I looked down at myself and didn't see shit. There was nothing there. Nada, nothing, squat, shit, fuck-all. No feet or legs. I just saw wall and floor.

I nearly gasped out loud and screwed up everything.

Soldiers rushed past me, and I held my breath as I made myself flat against the wall.

I'm in-fucking-visible.

LightCam.

Cam isn't camera. It's camouflage…. Light Camouflage. If they can heal and manipulate my skin at the cellular level, are the nanos able to…what? Use my skin to bend the light around me?

A pair of armed soldiers brought out Gutless Gil and company from the back room.

Micawber walked over on his stork legs and peered closely at each of the prisoners, along with Gil and the nurse.

"Get them out of here. Put them in the hall. I want to question them myself. Rip this place apart and make sure Leigh hasn't found a place to squirrel himself away. He was always good at that."

"Yes, sir."

Micawber walked into my room. I slipped in behind the nurse at the end of the line and walked through the security door right past all of Micawber's Section boys, and not one of them knew I was there.

Giddy, I looked over my shoulder as Micawber's gawky frame came out of my room. He seemed puzzled. Two dead Russians and no Leigh. I liked that he looked confused.

It made me happy.

I cheerfully turned backward and gave him the finger as I walked. Both barrels.

You evil prick.

His head swiveled my way, and his eyes squinted like he had heard me.

A superstitious shiver went through me.

Mógui!

Calm down. He's not the devil.

I can't see me; he can't see me.

I checked behind me. The row of cons, the nurse, and Gil had peeled off and were standing against the security window in the wall. Gil was looking down at the floor near me, right where Micawber was looking, and I peered down.

There were my wet footprints, plain as daylight. Before, they had been hidden by the line of men in front of me.

Not anymore.

My footprints had created their own trail across the floor to the exit.

Oh shit.

I am stealth.

The swinging doors were open behind me, and I sprinted out onto the emergency room floor.

WHO DO YOU WANT TO BE

The floor in the ER was dry, so I was right—the fire alarm and sprinklers had been compartmentalized to the secure wing. Nurses, doctors, and orderlies all went about their business, but they kept stealing frightened glances at the doors to the secure wing.

I didn't wait to see if Micawber was on my tail. I ran as carefully as I could with wet feet on linoleum, past the central nurses' station as I tried not to skid into anyone. I hung a left and made for the exit to the hospital floor. A Section operative I didn't know but could easily recognize as the type—close-cropped hair and a black suit bulging at the shoulders and arms— stood near the exit staring at his phone and then at any passerby.

I was willing to bet dinner and drinks he was staring at a picture of me.

I timed my exit and followed a volunteer pushing an elderly gentleman in a wheelchair with a new cast on his leg out the door. The Section guy mostly ignored them, but his nostrils flared as I walked past, and I wondered how much I smelled like smoke.

I kept moving out onto the floor. There were couches and chairs dotted with people. Even this early, it was busy with others checking in for procedures, waiting for care, or for loved ones already inside. A kiosk that sold snacks, stuffed animals, shirts, books, and drinks were just rolling up their security gate. There was the smell of fresh bread cooking and coffee brewing from the cafe next to it. My stomach tried to eat itself.

The bottoms of my feet were warm, and I looked down with relief as I was now on a rug, and my wet footprints had disappeared.

I looked behind me, but no one was following me or on my trail. Yet.

The little dragonfly pulsed black and yellow. A small notification appeared and flashed across my eyes:

WARNING—1 MINUTE TO UPGRADE

That was it.

Hell, the last upgrade had made me invisible. What was next? SoundWve, whatever that is.

It didn't give that warning last time, however.

The smell of fresh pastry pulled my attention away from that issue to the more pressing one of starvation. I was light-headed. I couldn't remember ever being this hungry before.

I walked silently through the lobby, passing by a young couple asleep with their heads on each other's shoulders. A fresh blueberry muffin from the cafe sat next to them. They must have grabbed a snack on the way in and collapsed. Neither of them looked injured, just exhausted. They were probably here for someone else.

The smell of the fresh muffin had my stomach trying to crawl out of my mouth. I looked around.

Four Vancouver PD uniforms walked in together from the front door. They joked and laughed amongst themselves. They had probably shown up for the alarm and just received the stand-down order. Not here for me, or even looking this way.

I looked at the muffin.

I can't just pick it up…. Someone's bound to notice a muffin floating in mid-air.

I knocked it gently onto the floor and got down on my hands and knees, peering about. Looked to be all clear. I bit the frosted top of the muffin off and horked it down. The sugar hit me in seconds. It tasted like blueberry-flavored heaven.

UPGRADE STARTING

You go; I'm eating. I took another bite of blueberry bliss and looked around. The HUD menu blinked out, and the dragonfly icon went dark against my eye.

What?

The cold that had gripped me since I'd been in the hallway disappeared, and warmth returned. I was kinda damp, but not a shivering mess anymore.

I looked down.

My hands were flat on the ground, fingers splayed and obviously visible.

I popped my legs up under me, and as I stood up, I glanced behind me, between my legs.

Micawber was staring straight at me, or rather, at my now exposed ass-crack, as I was completely bent over.

I wondered if this was how Isildur felt that day in the river.

Micawber didn't see my face, but he had a typical human reaction at coming across an unclothed person's ass in public, and he looked away—for a moment.

My heart pounded as I thought furiously. I kept my hair short back when he knew me and not shaved. It's been six years. He didn't see my face, just my ass.

I didn't hesitate. I chewed and swallowed the remaining muffin as I walked straight to the police officers gathered near the door, wearing an authentic, panicked expression on my face.

"Officers!" I hissed. "That man has a gun. He was back in the emergency room, threatening people with it! That's why the doctors pulled the alarm. Please, he followed a bunch of us out! There is a gun in the back of his pants and a little one on his left leg." I was betting Micawber hadn't changed his carry habits or where he stashed his hideaway.

I pointed to Micawber, who was now trying to get a better look at me.

The officers swarmed toward him as I made for the now-open gift shop. I grabbed a dark pair of sweatpants and a hooded sweatshirt in my size—with the hospital logo on them—and went to the twenty-something hipster counting out his till.

"Dude, the cops are about to totally drop that guy in the lobby. It's going to be epic!"

The clerk's eyes lit up.

I pointed, and sure enough, the cops were bracing Micawber, who appeared to be his usual asshole self when dealing with people he considered below him. One of the cops pointed to Micawber's backside and the gun that must have been printing against his jacket. It went downhill for Micawber from there.

The clerk saw the cops dogpiling on Micawber and let out a delighted, "Dude!" He slammed the till shut and rushed out to watch.

I pulled the top of the register back, exposing the base, and reached underneath for the manual release, which popped the drawer. I grabbed the cash, rolled it up in the sweats, and slid out behind the clerk and the now-gathering crowd. Section guys raced from their posts outside the front door to the aid of their boss. I used the distraction to walk casually out of the now-unguarded sliding doors and to the line of cars waiting at the curb.

I looked back. A crowd had gathered, and I couldn't see Micawber or the Section goons through the glass doors. I ignored the Ubers and got into a cab, and we pulled away from the hospital, driving off into the early morning darkness.

I pulled the sweatpants on in the cab's backseat and ripped off the hospital johnny. I pulled the thick heavy hoodie over my head and shoved the cash into its front pouch.

The cabbie looked back at me. "Not an escapee, are you?"

I looked at him, sizing him up. I needed a temporary ally, not a witness. Older guy, Carhart jacket, heavyset with a T'Wolves hat. Guy's guy.

I pulled the wad of bills back out and held them up. "If I was, would you not want any of this?" The cabbie held up his hand, but I laughed and said, "I'm just kidding man. I had too much fun on one of those party barges down on the Columbia and went in the drink. Lost my clothes. My wallet is shot, but I still have my greenbacks."

The cabbie snorted. "I've had a few of those nights. Where to?"

I thought a moment, then gave him an address just down Mill Plain.

It was a quick drive, and the fare was barely ten bucks. I pulled out five twenties from my wad. "So, between you and me, I went in the drink because my fiancée didn't like the attention I was giving her bridesmaid at our engagement party if you know what I mean?"

The cabbie roared with mirth. "Oh, you had one of those nights."

I nodded sheepishly.

"Anyhow, her old man who paid for all this is pretty uptight, and he's going to be looking for me to find out what I did to his little girl on her night. So..." The cabbie glanced back and saw the twenties.

"Just don't mention where you dropped me off. He's well connected, so they may try to call you back to talk to you. But if you could just shut off your radio for an hour, that would let me get cleaned up before I deal with him."

He reached back and swiped the twenties. "Buddy, I ain't never seen you. I been on coffee break at the 'Bux."

I gave him a fist bump. "My man."

He squinted a moment. "Wait, don't tell her old man where I dropped you? This ain't yer house?"

I opened the door and winked at him. "Bridesmaid."

The cabbie's howls of laughter followed me as I got out into a quiet neighborhood set back from Mill Plain and waved goodbye.

I felt fairly confident my new friend would unknowingly buy me some time before Micawber or Moscato got to him, and he'd realized he'd been had. I needed to make the most of it.

Once he was out of sight, I pulled my hood up over my head as I cut back and over five blocks to come out at Muchas Gracias, a local Mexican drive-through. A legitimate hole-in-the-wall, customers had to drive through a sketchy old tunnel in a wall to get their food. It was also open twenty-four hours. And they had great bean and cheese burritos.

Trust me; it's making the most of it.

Ten minutes later, I was headed barefoot as a hobbit across Mill Plain with my bag of burritos and a jumbo coffee. I got to my destination and wolfed down three burritos in as many minutes. A well-crafted bean and cheese is divine...one where the beans are made with lard (yes, lard—you can't make good beans without it; nothing else has that salty, creamy goodness), and you have those little pockets of melted cheese that are a bit of ecstasy. They are my ultimate comfort food choice. My stomach screamed for the other two in the bag, but I held on to them for later. By the time I finished my coffee, the stores were opening, and I walked into Fred Meyer.

Twenty minutes later, I walked out of Freddy's in a pair of sturdy, dark trainers and a pair of sunglasses. I used the burner phone I'd purchased and the last of my money, for a cab to take me back across the river and drop me in downtown Portland. I made one more call to Hitoshi at the restaurant and then dumped the phone in a trash bin.

It was seven blocks to Burnside. I ate the last two burritos and walked. It was with a full stomach and a moment of breathing room that I finally reflected on the night before. It hit me as I trekked down the street that I had taken not one but two lives (three, if you count Mort, but I notched that one to the Rabbit) last night.

Such an innocent activity—walking down the street—to realize something of such magnitude: that you have taken everything from someone; that your soul is lost again.

I stumbled a bit but kept walking.

I'd managed to avoid the killing since I'd left Section. There had been violence, and some close calls (Mort, for one), but I'd sworn I would never go back to being the person I was in Section. Chen-chen had spent many years with me, working on my anger. It was such a foundational piece of who I was—it never really died, and it never truly went away. We buried it in a shallow grave where it lay uneasy until the Marines unearthed it, dusted it off, and then Section hooked that sucker up to their lightning rods where it roared back to life.

And now here I am again, in the same goddamn place. Six years after I thought I had put it behind me. I had wanted to put it behind me, damnit!

The road to hell is paved with good intentions, isn't it? In the end, it had been as simple as flipping a switch. Threaten the survival of an organism, and it will respond. Consciously or not; in fight or flight. Everything wants to survive.

And speaking of survival—since I had—exactly why had Sabitov sicced his prison hitters on me when I had been in custody scant hours? It was unlike him to be vindictive or give in to anger, certainly not with an ally. Did he think I was responsible for the fuck-up at Vegrandis? That I was responsible for Mort? The man I had come to know the past year would have wanted a full debrief. He would've wanted to know why the job had gone sideways.

If my answers weren't to his liking, then he would have had me strangled. Not before.

Considering how explosive the potential for the nanos was, perhaps he just decided to eliminate any potential trails to him? Or he realized Mort had gone off the reservation on this and, again, decided to get rid of loose ends.

Still didn't add up.

I continued to mull hitmen and gangsters, subjects I was equipped to understand, while I consciously avoided the thing I didn't: the bizarre tech now burrowing into my innards.

I got to the Burnside Bridge, a steel bridge that crossed the Willamette River, and ducked down the path beside the bridge. The sun was rising out beyond Mount Hood, and the sky had lightened to a deep purple. The air was cold, and my breath steamed as I stared at the darkened shape of the dragonfly against my vision while I walked down the path.

A concrete, DIY skatepark was tucked away under the bridge, and I settled down out of the way to wait. I watched the early-bird (or late-night remnant) skaters shred the mini half-pipes, pools, and pyramids as the early sun lit up the park. I didn't have to wait long. He showed up shortly after, nervous, an oversize paper bag from Trader Joe's in one hand, the other arm in a bright blue cast.

Hitoshi.

He was twenty-seven and fit. He was my height, with his hair fashionably faded and he sported an impressive beard. Ornate tattoos stuck out of the leather jacket sleeve of the arm *sans* cast. His lower left leg and black leather engineer's boot were covered in white dust. He peered around, looking for me.

I came over next to him and tapped him gently on the shoulder.

His disgustingly handsome face broke into a worried grin, and he gave me a one-armed hug. "Man, you ok?"

I returned the hug. "Holding up. You get it?"

He raised the paper bag. "*Baa baa* is going to kill me when she sees what I did to her wall, dude."

I looked at his drywall-dusted pant leg as I took the heavy bag from him and clapped him on the shoulder. "I gave your grandma a ridiculously large security deposit for a reason."

He looked at the bag uncomfortably. "I didn't know you were, uh, you know...."

I smiled at him. "Shady?"

He nodded.

"It's just work, man. I'm not a bad person; at least I try not to be. I never meant to get so close to you guys. It was like being part of a family, and I missed that. I should have been more professional." I paused a moment. "How's Akiko?"

His handsome face darkened with anger. "Police brought her home late last night. She was ticked off.... She's such a little pistol, but you could see she was scared. Then it all hit her, and she cried for hours till she fell asleep."

It felt like someone had kicked me in the stomach. *My fault, my fault, my fault*, repeated endlessly in my brain.

He looked me up and down. "The way she told it, you looked like you'd been left on the robata for too long. She made it sound like you were all fucked up. You look fine to me."

Despite the welcoming hug, it was apparent he was seething underneath.

I let my breath out and shook my head. "She, uh...I wouldn't have made it out of there without her. She saved me. She did you all proud, and I am so fucking sorry."

He nodded and looked away from me and, I understood things were different now.

Enough. They were your cover, not your family.

But I owed them. So much.

"Just so you know, the guys who took your sister both paid for it. They won't be coming back."

"Good." His gaze was fixed, and he nodded at the bag. "How long has that been in the wall?"

"Since I moved in."

He shuffled uncomfortably. Despite the decade difference in our ages, he was the closest thing to a casual pal I had in Portland. Hitoshi had been the guy who invited me to ski up at Meadows when I moved up here. He had shown me Hood River and got me into windsurfing. I looked at him and realized that the charade was over.

I wasn't just Al, the line chef, anymore…I was the guy who kept a gun, wads of loose cash, and fake IDs in the wall. The guy who got his little sister kidnapped, and, although he didn't know it now, I was sure the Taniguchis were about to have the Feds crawling up their collective colon with Special Agent Willy Moscato holding the flashlight—all courtesy of yours truly.

Shit.

He reached into his pocket and pulled out a set of keys. "I did what you said. I drove around like you said and made sure. It's parked down by the diner. Your bag from your room is in the trunk. You sure you don't need help?"

I looked at his angry face. "Oh, no. I've put your family through enough trouble. I don't think you will be seeing me again for a while. Tell your *obaasan* I'm sorry and that I can never repay her generosity."

"Yeah, she caught me on the way out. She said you'd say that. She made you a bento box. It's in the bag. And a note too. You know she has to have the last word."

I nodded. "Yeah, I do. I'll get the car back to you, pronto."

He met my gaze, and it was an older Hitoshi who looked back at me. "If it keeps you out of our lives, it's yours."

Stung, I stepped back as he turned and walked away.

I called out, "Hey!"

He stopped and looked over his shoulder at me.

"Tell your little sister I think she's a badass."

He smiled a little, then turned and hiked back up the path, the rising sun glowing down on him through the bridge pylons. I watched his retreating back with regret as he passed from light to shadow and back again and cursed myself roundly.

I never meant to hurt them.

Guilt washed over me like I hadn't felt in a long time. Good old-fashioned Catholic guilt and shame, hand in hand, teaming up and trading kicks to my tender spots.

I went behind a pillar, knelt, and opened the bag. On top was a sealed bento box with a note underneath a rubber band. I pulled the box out and set it aside. Underneath that was my heavy black coat which I immediately pulled on over the hoodie, grateful for the extra warmth. At the bottom was a large, heavy-duty plastic envelope. I casually watched the skateboarders for a few and ensured I was being ignored. I opened the bag without looking down, keeping my gaze on the skaters.

My fingers ignored the soft paper of the wad of cash, moved past the plastic of the alternate driver's license and credit cards, the backup smartphone, and found the loaded magazine. I slid it effortlessly into the receiver of the G38, a compact .45 caliber by Glock. I'd used the G19 in the Corps, but I never felt like the 9mm provided enough stopping power. If I need to shoot at something, it better leave a big goddamn hole. I thumbed the slide release and felt the round chamber as the well-oiled slide slammed home. I slid the gun into a special holster in my jacket, sealing the Velcro flap.

Nothing worse than an unloaded gun when you needed it loaded. I'd swap out the magazine for one whose spring hadn't been under tension for so long when I could.

Next came a long, leather-scabbarded, double edged-dagger called a Tai Pan. It got tucked into its special holder on the jacket's opposite side, hilt down. Unsnap the release, and it would drop into my hand. A box of shells and the spare mags went into the outer pockets. I put the bento box back in the bag on top of the plastic bag containing the cash and identification, put the Trader Joe's bag in my left hand to keep my gun hand free, and stood up.

I left the skatepark and walked back up the path. I watched for a few minutes as morning traffic sped past across the bridge before I left the path, making sure Hitoshi had not brought unwanted visitors with him, then turned onto Burnside and walked the three blocks to the diner. Hitoshi's dark blue Subaru was parked at the far edge of the tiny lot. It had an irradiated-looking-neon-green Ducks sticker on one side of the rear window and a giant cannabis leaf sticker on the other that said KEEP OREGON GREEN along the leaves. Up here, that's called blending in.

Again, I watched and waited.

When I was sure the car was clean, and Hitoshi had followed the basic tradecraft I had dictated to him, making the drop without being followed, I walked to the car, thumbed the alarm fob, and got in. I opened the bag and pulled out the clean, backup smartphone, plugged it into the dash, and waited for it to boot up. I looked down into the bag and saw the note on top of the bento box.

Not now.

The phone lit up, and I punched in the address. I needed a little extra time to think and plan out my next move, so I chose the scenic route. I got back out onto Burnside and then down to the freeway and swung north. I took the Interstate Bridge that crossed over the mist-covered Columbia back into the deep green of Washington. On the opposite side, I passed by downtown Vancouver, ducking down in my seat a little while the sun came up on my right.

Hitoshi had his radio set to the local NPR station, KOPB, and they were doing a Woody Guthrie retrospective, playing his *Columbia River Collection*. The twang of Woody's Gibson guitar and his drawling, lyrical love of the Pacific Northwest filled the car as I headed into the morning light.

I drove for about forty minutes until the turnoff past Kalama and swung west back across the Columbia onto Highway 30 into Oregon again and toward the coast. As I sped along the heavily forested two-lane highway that ran parallel to the river, I passed a green highway sign with reflective white letters that spelled out my destination.

Astoria.

ON THE DOORSTEP

A few hours after I left Portland, I pulled into Astoria. I'd had to spend some time up here at the end of the summer to try and trace the King family's source of supply for their heroin. The weather then had been among the sixty-some-odd days of sunshine that Astoria gets annually, and since I had spent most of my time out on the water, it had been relatively pleasant.

The rest of the year, Astoria got three different kinds of weather. Damp, wet, and soaked.

All of it cold.

Today was no exception. As I closed in on the mouth of the Columbia at the coast, the clouds had gathered and darkened while the rain misted down. The highway emptied out of the river-carved canyon into the flatter river basin and the west coast of America's oldest port city.

I drove through the town, an eclectic mix of old and new buildings, some in better repair than others. I followed the GPS route as it wound through town and back into the steep hills. I drove past the gabled Victorian mansions to a series of older Cape Cod-style homes that had seen better days, and then some mobile homes followed by some dwellings that were one step above shacks. I finally came to the address that had been in Moscato's file. The building for the address was non-existent and looked like it had been torn down. Only a foundation remained with a sign out front bearing the contractor's name and phone number. I hadn't expected Moscato's dealer to still be here—if the address had even been legit, to begin with. The file was six months old, but I needed to be thorough. I called the number on the sign out front, pretending to be a bill collector looking for a delinquent account. The contractor's secretary was helpful but said the property management company had gone out of business and they had no records of the previous tenants.

I pushed the red End button on my phone and blew air from my pursed lips. If he was still local, I knew who would know where to find him. But it was gonna be hella awkward.

I drove back down into town and pulled in at a gas station. I filled up using one of the virgin credit cards, then grabbed my bag from the trunk and went into the bathroom to change. I skivvied out of the sweats and into some of my own clothes: jeans, a dark green, long-sleeved Henley, and a black Columbia pullover, followed by my jacket. I pulled on some warm socks and some worn-in, steel-toed hiking boots. I quickly swapped out the older magazine from the G38 with a freshly loaded one and loaded up the spare mags while I was at it. Knit cap and sunglasses on, and I was back in the car. I hit the bridge going across Youngs Bay and was back out onto the 101, heading past the small airport and south out of town.

I got past the local country club, and the coast opened up on my right. The bruised clouds full of rain hung low over the froth-capped peaks, making their way toward the shore.

The Kings of the Road motorcycle repair shop was about twenty minutes out of town, set in a large, converted barn just off the coast road overlooking the craggy rocks that jutted out of the heaving, steel grey Pacific. A dirt road led off the 101, cutting through the scrub grass for a couple of miles down to the barn. I went a mile or so past it, parked at a turnout, and pulled out the bento box Mrs. T had packed for me.

I looked down at the note, and another wave of guilt racked me. I wasn't ready for that right now. The restaurant seemed like an ideal cover at the time; the hours were flexible, no one really noticed me, and who would believe that a line cook was the intelligence officer for the Russian mob? Truth be told, I had been lonely and more than a little heartsick taking a job so far away from Jeni at such a critical time, and Mrs. T had caught me at a weak moment. I'd been taught that everyone will break during torture; we all have limits. But the military thought I should know what it was like. During my training, I had been beaten, waterboarded, shocked with high voltage, and gassed. Good times.

All it took from Mrs. T was a motherly look of concern, and I cracked like an egg. I gave it all up.

After that, I got pulled in by the unquestioning affection and joy of their family like a moth to a bonfire. I should have left as soon as that happened and found new digs rather than let them become possible collateral damage in my life.

I fucked up.

I had put my own needs ahead of my professional responsibility. *Kinda like what got you got court-martialed and inspired your premature run at Vegrandis, huh?*

Damnit.

I needed a clear mind. I put the note in my inner jacket pocket and gratefully ate the lunch of noodles, Hamachi Kama (grilled yellowtail collar), and pickled veggies while I watched the heavy surf crash and spray against the rocky shore through the low-hanging clouds and windswept rain. I washed it down with a small bottle of iced tea from the gas station and considered my options.

I needed information, allies, and access to weaponry. I was cut off from the Bratva and their resources, and there seemed to be a wet order out on me. The Feds and local law enforcement were sure to be on the lookout for me by now. I had foster-family relatives up north across the border in Vancouver, Canada, I could hunker down with, but it was a short-term solution. Micawber would know about them, and borders didn't mean much to Section. The farm was out for the same reason.... Even though my lawyer was the only one who knew it was mine, Micawber's resources were vast, and a little B&E in a lawyer's office was something he wouldn't think twice about, so I was no longer sure Bag End was safe. Running wouldn't solve my problem anyhow. I only had one place to turn.

The enemy of my enemy is my friend.

Except I was damn sure they weren't going to like me or what I had to tell them. I knew what would be waiting for me in there. If I went in, I might not be walking out.

Tick-tock, tick-tock.

I looked at the darkened dragonfly eye-con. No sign of when it would come out of its slumber, and no amount of blinking was activating anything.

I needed to talk to someone who knew what these things could do and, if possible, how to get them out of me. Moscato's witness list of Vegrandis employees and their families were going to be getting the third degree from the law. I needed to talk to the people who were further down on their list: the two terminated employees who seemed to be linked to this dealer.

Enough.

I started the car and pulled back out onto the 101. I turned onto the dirt road and drove down the pot-holed muddy road to the faded brown, paneled barn at the edge of the cliff. A stiff wind whipped in from the ocean, stinging my face with saltwater and cold rain as I got out of the car and walked to the barn. A wide awning hung over the building's front porch, and at least two dozen Harley Davidson motorcycles were parked out front underneath it, protected from the rain.

Full house.

I paused on the doorstep under the awning that was dripping a solid sheet of cold water from its edge, and opened the Velcro flap on my inner holster, freeing up the Glock. I closed my eyes briefly, exhaled, put on my game face to cover the fear that's always cowering somewhere behind the anger, and stalked through the door.

SKIN

The smell of oil, gasoline, cigarette smoke and the fainter but sweeter odor of pot permeated the building. Underneath all that was the unmistakable smell of saltwater, and damp, rotting wood. Repair bays lined the left wall of the barn, and motorcycles in various states of repair filled that side of the building. To the right was a small desk and filing cabinets; beyond that were some elevated tables with hanging lights above them and motorcycle parts strewn across the surfaces. In the far-right corner were some rickety-looking round tables with chairs and what looked like a small, wooden wet bar.

The sound of air drills, the pound-pound of hammers, shouted obscenities, and hard rock filled the air, although after a moment…that changed. It got quieter and quieter as the twenty to thirty men gathered in the barn noticed my presence. After a minute, the only noise was Metallica on the radio and the sound of the rain beating down on the roof.

I glanced left and saw a bullet-riddled Russian flag against the wall.

Like I said, this was gonna be hella awkward.

A long-haired, walking beer-gut with a ZZ Top beard approached me.

"Help you?" There was a malevolent silence after the 'you' like he wanted to add on something else.

I smiled. "I'm looking for Elmore King."

The tension in the room rose.

ZZ Top tilted his head at me. "If you got a bike that needs working on, we got other guys here that can handle it—less busy, if you know what I mean."

I shook my head. "No, I really need Elmore."

He looked me up and down. "Ain't here," he growled and turned his back on me. Drills started sporadically, and some of the men returned to their work.

I couldn't afford to be blown off, and I could not appear passive. Not here, not in front of this bunch.

"Hey, fucknuts. Tell your boss Sabitov's intelligence officer is here, or get me someone higher up the evolutionary ladder who can."

At the mention of the Russian's name, drills stopped, the radio was turned off, and this time in the resulting silence, the only noise to break the steady hammering of the rain on the roof of the barn was the sound of the door behind me being locked.

Clap! Snap!

Maybe this wasn't such a hot idea.

A drop of sweat snaked down between my shoulder blades, and I forced myself to stay facing forward. I heard my old teacher repeating Sun Tzu in my head—*show strength when you are weak.* I couldn't show a hint of how spooked I was, or this crowd would tear me apart.

ZZ Top turned around with his right hand behind his back, reaching for his waistband.

I raised both my hands. "I have a gun in my inner left pocket and a blade on the right. If you gentlemen would like to hang on to those, I'd still like to have a word with Elmore."

A gravelly voice called out from near the bar. "Sabitov, eh? That Cossack piece of shit would know better than to send an emissary. We are at war. No quarter."

"That's because he doesn't know I'm here," I answered.

"Interesting."

ZZ reached into my jacket and claimed my weapons. He pulled my jacket off me, roughly patted me down, and then shoved me hard on the back toward the bar.

I looked over my shoulder at him. "Thanks, I see the way."

I waited for the follow-up shove I was positive was coming and lightly side-stepped ZZ's sucker push. I cheerfully watched him stumble past me and fall.

"I said I see the way, thanks."

ZZ glared at me from the floor, but I was already past him and halfway to the bar. The bikers had all left their work bays and crowded behind me as I reached the bar.

A short man with the body of a fireplug—all shoulders and no neck—and a white brush cut sat at a scarred wooden table. Elmore J. King. A skinny man with thinning blond hair in a plaid flannel shirt and oil-stained jeans sat next to him.

I nodded politely. "Mr. King."

The blond man leaned over and whispered in King's ear, and he nodded.

"So, you're Sabitov's secret weapon. Heard rumors; didn't think you were actually real. Why're you here?" King growled.

"I'd like to make a deal," I kept my tone even and polite.

"I've told your boss I'm not interested in selling out or kissing his ring."

"I'm not here on behalf of Mr. Sabitov."

King stood up. He stared me in the eye. His enormous head barely came up to my shoulder, but he was twice as wide as me. "So you said."

"I have some information that I think would be of value to you."

"You think so? I can tell you now that there is nothing you can say that is of interest to me, nothing at all. See, you chose to work with those cocksuckers, so as far as I'm concerned, you're a traitor.

To be honest, you're not really a man, you're not even really human, so anything you say just doesn't matter. It's just yammering and bleating."

He nodded, looking behind me—hands grabbed me from all sides.

"Just let me speak for one more minute," I said calmly.

King shook his head. "Nah."

A cloth gag whipped over the top of my head and was pulled roughly into my mouth. NO! I needed to be able to talk to make this work!

I struggled but was tackled to the ground and rolled onto my back. There were too many of them, and I couldn't get up. They beat and battered me while they bound my hands with rope and pulled me to my feet.

The other end of the rope got tossed over a rafter, and a half dozen men pulled me several feet into the air by my arms and then lashed the rope to a support beam.

King wandered over to where I was swinging.

"See, a message went out this morning about a bald asshole with green eyes. Russians are offering 250k for you…. Just proves you're a thing. Men don't have price tags. Things do." He gave a sunny smile. "I'm thinking of sending them your head for free," he proclaimed magnanimously, then shrugged. "I hear Sabitov likes that sort of thing. Might get him off our backs once and for all." There was an accepting murmur from the crowd of bikers gathered around us. King preened under their attention. Self-important prick.

He stared at me. "You will die here and never be found. For an intelligence officer, you don't have much intelligence."

I struggled to talk through the gag. Nothing came out except, "Mmmmfgggmg."

"But the boys here need a little fun and there is nothing you can say that will stop that. So, before I chop your traitor head off to wrap up for Fed-Ex, Mikey here is going to skin you."

The skinny blond stood up and pulled a long, slender filet knife from his belt.

He's going to what?

That…escalated fast. This was not going as planned. I stared at the dragonfly eye-con, but it stayed dark. Shit, shit, shit.

The blond guy walked over to me and grabbed the back of my pullover. He sliced the knife effortlessly up the back of the sweater and through my shirt underneath, exposing my back. That's…a sharp knife.

I struggled, which made me swing from side to side. Blondie stepped back and made a "tsk, tsk" noise. "Y'all keep swinging around like that, and I'm liable to mess this up. What say you hold still?"

I tried to say, "What say you eat shit and choke on the spoon?" but all that came out was, "Aayyyooooeeeiiihhhann?"

King called out, "One of you boys, get your camera phone up here and record this; it's gonna be good." About half the crowd pulled out their phones and started recording.

Bag-biting ass monkeys.

Blondie cut the remnants of my shirt and sweater from the rest of my upper body and motioned to a couple of the bikers. "Hold his legs for me." Two guys rushed forward and grabbed my legs. I stopped swinging. My body was stretched taut, and Blondie licked his lips as he fondled his knife.

Not happening, not happening.

He placed the blade of the knife against my nipple and sliced it down with an icy sting. Warm blood poured down my side and into my waistband. My heart, which had been struggling to remain calm, kicked into overdrive like I was on a treadmill stuck on maximum.

Yep, coming here was *definitely* a bad idea.

I panted through my gag, and despite the chill in the barn, sweat poured freely down my body, mixing with my blood.

Blondie knew I was close to the edge, and he grinned at me. "Here we go."

He leaned forward.

I closed my eyes.

"STOP!"

My eyes flew open. King walked toward me and spun me so that he could see my now-bare arm. "What's that on your arm?"

A tattoo of three Latin words formed a triangle on my upper bicep: *CELER - SILENS - MORTALIS.*

King's eyes widened. "Take that gag off him!"

Blondie got a chair, climbed up, and used his knife to cut the gag off me.

"Why is that on your arm?"

I panted. "You know what it means."

"Swift, silent, deadly. You Corps?"

I nodded, and sweat fell from my head.

"What was your unit?"

"3rd Marine Recon, 1st Division, and then Raiders, 2nd MSOB."

He squinted at me and stepped back. "Bullshit. Prove it."

I hung with my shoulders screaming in fiery agony, and stared straight at him.

"I can speak without saying a word and achieve what others can only imagine."

King's eyes went wider as I recited the end of the Recon Creed, and he lifted his sleeve to show me the Globe and Anchor tattoo on his bicep. He then rolled his arm over to show me the faded but still recognizable parachute, wings, and diver of Recon on his forearm.

"Cut that man down—now!"

SEMPER GUMBY

"That tattoo and your service bought you your life and two minutes. Talk."

We sat by ourselves at one of the small wooden tables near the bar. I silently gave thanks to my stubborn rebelliousness at Chenchen's Confucian upbringing, which forbade disfiguring your body with tattoos, when I had gone in on the ink with the rest of my original Recon unit.

The bikers had all gone back to work, and Blondie—Mikey, who once upon a time had been a Navy corpsman, had been grudgingly apologetic as he expertly bandaged my chest. The healing that the nanos supplied was apparently offline as well. Good to know.

I wore a black, long-sleeve shirt with a picture of a crowned Ghost Rider riding a flaming Harley on it and KINGS OF THE ROAD printed in fiery letters at the bottom. My jacket hung from the chair behind me, and an empty water bottle sat in front of me. I had known about King's service and walked into this pit counting on a saying from the Corps: "We only see shades of green" to keep me alive, but I hadn't been sure. Even the Corps has bad apples.

"I need your help," I said.

"I am not exactly of a mind to help the Bratva."

"In case you hadn't noticed, I think the Bratva and I have parted ways. I can trade information."

"I doubt that there is much you could tell me that would catch my interest."

I looked at him and said two names, "Bob and Betty King."

There wasn't a flicker of response from the older man at the mention of the names. Guy had a hell of a poker face.

"My cousin and his wife.... What of it?"

"I went to their restaurant over the summer."

"Yeah? You fond of fried fish, are you?"

Bob and Betty King owned a small seafood restaurant down the coast that was pretty much a duplicate of the ubiquitous fried fish shacks you could find everywhere up and down the shorelines of America.

"The crab legs were good," I responded.

"Bob and Betty are a couple of holier-than-thou's who don't much approve of me, and we haven't spoken for decades. Pretty common knowledge. You're barking up the wrong tree and running out of time."

You have no idea.

"Back in the spring, Sabitov decided that since you wouldn't give up your heroin trade, he just wanted you all dead. I try to avoid that when possible, so I told him I would trace your supplier instead. He had tried for years and said I couldn't do it." I tilted my head at King. "I love a good challenge."

King said nothing and made like a rock.

I continued, "It wasn't coming overland—Sabitov controls everything around your turf—he would have found out. The quality said Far East, so it was coming by sea or by plane. I discounted the sea right off as this is a Coast Guard town. They patrol the shit out of this area, so I figured the standard of tossing the drugs over a passing ship with a floating buoy and a GPS marker was out, so it had to be air."

King continued to sit there serenely, secure in the belief that his long-running operation was watertight. No pun intended.

"But I kept doing my due diligence on you. Still not sure we weren't missing something by land, but I was ready to bet on an air delivery. Until I decided to check out your cousin and ate at his place, he had this picture on the wall, a statue of a mermaid underwater. I recognized it.... It's sunk offshore of a dive resort in Grand Cayman—Sunset House. I've been there; great place."

King was beginning to look uncomfortable. "Thirty seconds," he growled.

"I guess back in the day, you reached out and paid for them to go there on a late honeymoon. That was very generous of you."

He nodded cautiously. "They're family. I tried to make up to them years ago with that, but they took the vacay and never a word of thanks."

Nice delivery—heartfelt. I'd almost buy it.

"Like I said, I've been on vacation there myself. See, the only thing to do there is dive, eat, drink, and play dominoes. There's no sandy beach to lie out on, just a rocky approach to a fun reef dive. It's a miles-long walk to Seven Mile Beach and all the touristy stuff—definitely off the beaten path. Not exactly a romantic vacay hotspot, but it's fabulous if you like to be away from the crowds and are a diver...or want to learn to dive."

King had gone from leaning back to sitting up straight. I had his attention.

"Your cousin has an old-school setup. Nowadays, most of the fish places just buy from local fishermen, but he still has his own fishing boat and a plot for lobster and crab pots out there. He is proud that he only cooks what he catches. Been doing it for forty years, he says. I imagine the Coasties must be used to seeing him out there. Hell, Coasties eat at his place. He's a fixture around there."

I raised my eyebrows. "How much time do I have left now?"

He leaned forward, elbows resting on the table as he squinted at me. "You just got yourself an extension."

"Your supplier wasn't floating the drugs; they were sinking them out by your cousin's crab pots. He or Betty would go over the side after the drop, get the stash, and bring it up with the pots in the wee hours of the morning. Your family argument and you three not talking to each other is just cover. It's slicker than snot. Who would ever think that a nice, sweet, local old couple are just a couple of fucking, diving drug mules?"

Kings' lips had compressed to a thin line, and his face had gone white with anger.

"Took me a while to catch them in the act and trace the ship back to Taiwan and then use my contacts there to find your pipeline, but I did. As a matter of fact, Sabitov just got back from Taiwan, where he had some successful negotiations with your partners: the 14k Triad. Or former partners, rather. See, when Bob or Betty goes down for the drugs next week, there won't be shit. Or the next month. Or the month after that. It's all going to Sabitov and the Bratva now."

I paused before ramming the knife home. "You're out of business."

King's gravelly voice shook with anger. "Corps or not, gimme one good reason not to string you back up again."

I let him sweat for a few, payback for the butcher shop routine earlier. His jaw worked back and forth as he frantically worked the angles, chasing down the logical conclusions of what would happen when he couldn't deliver the smack. His crew might be loyal to him, but to my eye, they looked loyal to the next payday. They might decide it's better to get a new leader who could work with the Russians. Or hell, they may just straight-up bend the knee to Sabitov. Of course, Sabitov would demand proof of their loyalty and assurance that King wouldn't be causing any more trouble.

A head, perhaps.

That dreaded word, mutiny, had to be crossing his mind. King realized he would be a king no more. I waited another moment, savoring his growing panic and hiding my self-disgust as I played my card—my only card. The card that also happened to be the key to his kingdom. "Because I know when and how Sabitov gets his drug shipments. All of them."

Comprehension dawned on King's face. He leaned back again.

"Giving up your boss isn't going to be good for your business future. Or your future, period," he opined.

"Yeah, well, the boss is already trying to have me killed. Which is also bad for business and my future."

"You can bet your ass on that one."

"It's time to make things worse for his future. I think this is a time us Americans need to stick together—especially us leathernecks."

King looked at me, really looked at me. I recognized the look. I'd given it to the cabbie this morning. He was sizing me up, deciding how much he could trust me. I leaned forward and put my elbows on the table, matching his posture. "So…what do you say, Gunnery Sergeant King—ready to talk turkey?"

King gave me the considering look for a moment more, then smiled broadly and spread his stubby hands wide. "As long as I get the drumsticks, Devil Dog."

Two hours later, I walked out of Kings of the Road slightly worse for wear and my spirit a little dirtier for the experience, but I was alive. I lifted my face to the rain and inhaled the scent of the sea deeply.

I'd gambled and won but at a cost. King would be able to intercept the shipments and take out any of Sabitov's soldiers who came for it. I'd just shifted the balance of power, but trading Sabitov for King was just more of the same.

More importantly, I'd broken my own rule. *Extraordinary circumstances*, I told myself.

Doesn't matter. You have to find a way to make it right.

I will, I promise.

Whatever, you've broken your promise once. I bet you do it again. All your precious values are just for shit. Semper Gumby. Next thing you know, you'll just be a mule for some dealer. Asshole.

That's a bet you will lose. I'll fix this. I promise.

Yeah, how?

Maybe a tip to the law?

Them! Really? You go to the law on this, and your role will come out, and you will just incriminate yourself. How much deeper were you planning to dig us?

I'm not sure, but I have a pretty big goddamn shovel.

That shut me up.

I took a deep breath. I needed to focus on the now. The details of wiping that sin clean I would figure out. Somehow.

The surf continued to pound the shore, the rain fell like a curtain as before, but the familiar giddy high pumped through me, and my senses were magnified. I'd stared death in the face and survived again. The rain tasted sweeter, the cold was invigorating, and the smell of the ocean was a bouquet of sensation.

I walked back to the car with an unlikely new ally, something that felt like hope in my chest, an address, a duffel bag full of guns, and a promise to myself to keep.

DEATH DON'T HAVE NO MERCY

I drove back up the coast until I got to the Columbia and swung around east, heading for the mouth of Youngs River, where it emptied into the Columbia and then the sea. I then turned south and followed the smaller tributary past verdant fields of farmland surrounded by thick forest stands and low steep hills, headed to the address King had given me.

Dodgson, the dealer, lived in a small house tucked into a small box canyon not far from Youngs River Falls. The afternoon light was fading behind the steadily darkening clouds as I drove down the gravel road to an unblocked dirt turnoff that led to the hiking trails to the Falls and parked behind a copse of moss-covered trees.

Getting out of the car, I opened the trunk where the duffel bag of guns and my black clothes duffel sat side by side. I opened the gun bag and pulled out a matte-black Kimber .45 Raptor that I reflexively checked the slide, port, and safety on before I slammed home a magazine and released the slide. I stuffed it into a DeSantis Small of Back Holster that I had threaded into my belt, securing it on the back of my pants. I took a few experimental draws from the S.O.B. with my right hand, but I couldn't clear leather without my sweater getting in the way, so I tucked it into my pants behind the butt of the Kimber.

I had reconfigured my inner jacket holster for a left-handed cross-draw for the G38, and I still had my Tai Pan hanging from its concealed inner sheath. I pulled out a powerful tactical light and a Swarovski Z8i rifle scope that I put in my coat pockets. I locked up the car, pulled my hood over my head with one hand, called up a compass app on my phone with the other, took a heading, and hiked into the darkening woods.

After the wind by the coast, the chilled air in the trees felt still, as though the forest had just taken a deep breath and was waiting to exhale. The rain that had fallen incessantly all afternoon was blocked from overhead as I passed beneath thick stands of Sitka spruce and Douglas fir trees whose heavy, moss-carpeted trunks were surrounded by emerald clusters of sword ferns glistening in the wet gloaming.

About twenty minutes later, I reached the edge of the woods where it intersected with Dodgson's sinuous, gravel driveway. A pasture with a modest red barn and several large cows not yet in for the night were all off to the left. The house—although looking from here more like a log cabin—was set back, kind of homely, and surrounded on three sides by the low walls of the box canyon. The nearest neighbor was well over a mile away, which I was sure came in handy for Dodgson's work, as things could get smelly.

I leaned against the trunk of an enormous bigleaf maple tree, pulled out the Swarovski, popped the lid, and peered through it toward the house. The front door jumped into view with remarkable clarity. The grains in the wood of the door were visible, and it felt like I could reach out and touch the rough-curved and twisted edges of the wrought-iron door handle. The optics on this thing were exceptional. I moved the reticle across the field of view and assured myself Dodgson was home and alone, as King had told me he would be.

"Man won't leave the house except for supplies and to do his monthly duty for me. You're gonna have to go to him. Guy's practically a hermit, but the Cut Chemist is the only one who still whips that shit up proper," King had explained.

Chuckie "Cut Chemist" Dodgson was in charge of two things for King; making sure the monthly supply of Chinese heroin was cut properly, as well as his side business and passion project—"the shit" as King had called it—LSD production.

"He knows you're coming but be careful. He's not dangerous or anything...he's an odd one. He's magic in the lab and knows all kinds of arcane stuff, but he's kinda twitchy." That had been King's last advice on the subject.

I took the illuminated scope from my eye, and the darkness hurtled back into view, enveloping me. The windows were lit squares of light in the falling dark, and the rhythmic thump of music came from inside. I capped the scope, put it in my coat, and walked out of the wet, silent woods up the curved driveway, my feet crunching on the gravel toward the bright lights and music coming from the log house.

I climbed five wooden steps to a wide, covered front porch that wrapped around the front of the home. The musical thumping resolved itself into the final bars of Robert Johnson's 'I Believe I'll Dust My Broom' that softly faded away to be replaced by his 'Cross Road Blues.' I approved, but I was also glad it hadn't rolled into Johnson's 'Hell Hound on My Trail.'

A black, wrought-iron lantern set in the wall cast its light on the door and showed the warm vapor of my breath in the cold air as I raised my hand to knock. The door opened before my knuckles even brushed wood to reveal a medium height, middle-aged guy with unkempt brown hair wearing a bright red shirt that said: *BANRÍON DEARG ALE, ASTORIA*. He also sported a pair of dark sunglasses—at night.

I stepped back from the door to give him space that he immediately stepped into, taking off his shades to reveal bloodshot, watery brown eyes as he brought his face inches from mine.

"You're the traitor?"

I blinked and resisted the urge to shove him back into the house and out of my space. It was his porch, after all.

"I'm a guy who needed the work and didn't care who paid the bills, something I think you would understand."

"I guess."

"That doesn't make me a traitor."

He appeared to give it real thought. "Yeah, you're probably right. It's just the Russians are dangerous fuckers."

I raised an eyebrow. "So am I."

He blanched and stepped back.

"Look, I only have a few questions, then I'm out of your hair. Can I come in? Kinda chilly out here."

"Yeah, man. Yeah. Sorry."

He stepped out of the doorway to let me in.

I've been in my share of dealer dens over the past decade and a half, everything from the hardcore gangs that control entire swathes of countries to street-level weed dealers. They can vary in opulence, but most usually have one thing in common: they are messy, disorganized shitholes that you can't believe someone would willingly live in.

This was not one of those.

The immediate sense I got as I walked onto the polished wooden floors was one of order. Furniture was precisely placed in equidistant relation to other pieces. Low bookshelves filled the space, the books themselves organized by color and height. Framed Boris Vallejo prints lined the walls, each precisely the same height and distance from one another. There were smaller photos on the tables and shelves of the Oregon coast, Multnomah Falls, Mount Hood, and St. Helens in various seasons. There was not a speck of dust, and the wood throughout gleamed with care. The Cut Chemist was either very house-proud or seriously Type-

A, OCD. I guessed the latter…. That need for order and precision would serve him well as a chemist.

"Out of this world don't begin to describe that man's product. Man's a genius: a poet with a beaker and a Bunsen burner," King had boasted.

Robert Johnson faded away to be replaced by Muddy Waters as Dodgson closed the door behind him and stood awkwardly by the door.

I nodded to him. "You have a beautiful home."

"Yeah, I like it here."

He continued to stand there, swaying softly to 'Mannish Boy,' seemingly oblivious of my presence. He looked high, but I sensed more was going on with the Cut Chemist. I'd been around a few people at Cal that I'd known were genius-level intellects. A couple of them used to be this way—moving through the world on autopilot while their minds wrestled with puzzles elsewhere.

Or he was just, you know, really, *really* high.

"Can we sit? I'd like to ask you some questions."

He blinked as though he was surprised I was there.

"Just questions?"

"Yes, I'm looking for someone. I think you can help."

He moved over to a beautiful chair next to the couch I was almost positive was a Stickley and sat down in it. I took off my coat, hung it by a coat rack near the door, and returned to the couch. Dodgson's eyes had gone wide, and he sat back in his chair, looking more than a little terrified.

Damn, the butt of the Kimber was sticking out from under my sweater. I quickly covered it. "I don't mean you any harm, Chuckie. Not at all. No way. But I'm a little nervous about people myself right now. It makes me feel safer."

He seemed to get that and eased back into his chair.

"Do you want to get high?" he asked timidly.

"Uh, no. Not right now, thanks."

"You sure? It always makes me feel safer. Better than carrying a gun around." He pulled a small, clear plastic bag out of his pocket and handed it to me. Curious, I peered closer. The bag was filled with several white paper squares. Printed on each was what looked like an albino Bugs Bunny wearing shades and throwing a middle finger. "It's my best batch ever. I call it: 'What's up, Dick?'"

He laughed uproariously at his joke, and I snorted as I handed it back. He likes Bugs; he can't be all bad.

I raised a hand and shook my head. "I'm good, thanks."

He jerked his thumb in the direction of the cow pasture. "I got 'shrooms too. Li'l magic for your evening?" He waggled his fingers mystically at me.

I shook my head again and leaned back on the couch.

"Okay, man. Your loss." I heard him mutter, "Whatsupdick?" and continued to giggle at his joke as he put the small baggie back in his pocket.

"I'm looking for a couple of former customers of yours."

His eyebrows came together quizzically. "Mine? Not Elmore's? Small group. Who?"

"I don't know their names—that's part of the problem, but I can tell you they probably lived in Portland and worked at a lab across the river in Washington. A place called Vegrandis."

Dodgson's face fell, and it looked like he was about to cry.

"Oh, her. Them."

Not the reaction I was expecting.

"Her? Her who? What's her name?"

"Daphne. Daphne Philips."

"Where does she live? Where can I find her? It's important."

He looked down at his sock-covered feet. "You can't find her. No one can."

"Try me. I'm good at finding people."

"You won't."

"You leave that to me."

He took off his sunglasses and looked at me as a tear fell from one red-rimmed eye. "You won't find her. She's dead."

I looked at him and realized her death genuinely hurt him, and this wasn't an act to throw me off. One avenue of investigation just closed off…. I'd lost fifty percent of my chance to find out how to deal with all this.

"I'm sorry for your loss. Umm…she was a good customer?"

He nodded and sniffed while he wiped his eye. "She bought in big batches. Pretty regular, for more than a year."

"Big ones? Was she dealing?"

He looked up with a shocked expression on his face. "Daphne!? Hell no. She would never. Besides, the strongest thing that girl could handle was a joint every now and then and 'shrooms twice a year. My shit woulda nuked her into forever."

"Why the big batches, then?"

"She said I should never tell anyone."

I looked at his crestfallen face and softened my tone.

"I'm sorry again for your loss, but if she is dead, whatever you tell me isn't going to hurt her now. And I will make sure it never comes back to you."

I can try to make sure, that is.

I was stretching the truth a bit, but I was more than a little desperate. As far as Chuckie's safety, I was counting on King to keep his own crew safe. Not my circus, not my monkey.

He stopped to think.

"Promise?"

I crossed my heart and held my right hand up. "Marine's honor." *As long as it's in my control.*

He looked out the window for a moment and then nodded. "She needed them for her work. I was the only one who could make the potency and quantity they needed."

What?

"Wait, say that again? She was buying them for work?"

"For her boss, Frank. He got her to buy it. They needed it for some kind of experiment."

"Frank? Franco? Dr. Franco Persici?

He sniffed again. "Yeah, him."

"I was led to understand she lost her job because of drugs."

He shook his head hard, and his mop of brown hair went in all directions. "Not true…it's not. That's just some easy excuse for them. She quit because of what she saw; then they said they fired her after she died. Buncha bullshit."

I leaned forward. "What did she see, Chuckie?"

He reached over to the table next to him, opened a small wooden box filled with neatly rolled joints, and pulled one out. "Do you mind?"

"It's your house, brother."

He pulled a match from a small dish next to the box and lit it with his thumb. He put it to the end of the joint and took a deep drag. The room filled immediately with the spicy, sweet smell of cannabis.

"Daphne was in charge of the animals there. She grew up here but moved to Portland about five, six years ago. She wanted to get out of here her whole life. She finally did. She got a job at the Oregon Zoo—vet nurse. She got hired away from the zoo by the lab about two years ago. She was a good, nice person, man. Animals loved her; she loved them." He trailed off for a moment as he took another drag.

I was guessing that it wasn't just the animals that loved Daphne.

"She said they were working on something she just called 'the project.'" He gave air quotes with his fingers as the fragrant smoke drifted up from his right hand.

"They were putting 'the project' into her animals. Although she was a li'l baked one time, and she called it 'EPU.' I asked her about it, and she just laughed and said, 'Ask a dead president.'"

I nodded. "What did it do to them?"

"She wouldn't say, but it scared her. She just said they were able to do things that they shouldn't. Before that, she would just come to me for pot before it was legal and occasionally for 'shrooms after. More than a year ago, she started asking for acid— just a few tabs. A couple of weeks after that, she came back and asked for a full batch: ten sheets. Told me it was for science. I don't care as long as I get paid. This goes on for over a year. 'Bout three months ago, she comes back for an order, and she tells me it's going to be her last; she was going to quit. She saw something that freaked her out."

He took another hard pull on his joint. "Week after that, she died in a house fire."

I raised an eyebrow. "Fire?"

He nodded.

A suspicious death and fire. Mort? The time frame didn't match up, though. Sabitov told me he had just become aware of the nanos. Of course, he could have been lying. Or her death by fire could just be a coincidence. Yeah, like how Micawber just shows up to the hospital accompanied by a Section wet squad with weapons cocked and locked just for little ol' me? I wasn't ready to accept anything to do with this job as a mere coincidence anymore.

"Do you know what she saw?"

He took a few moments and finished his joint. I was trying not to breathe any in, but I was starting to feel a little light-headed and might have been getting a contact high.

"She had a baby monkey and a dog she was close to there. She said those two animals loved each other. They would cry when they were separated but would like cuddle and shit if they were in the cage together. They were kind of like her babies." He gave a soft smile before his face turned grim. "Anyways, time comes for their turn for 'the project.' She said after they put it in them, they changed. They would go nuts when they saw each other, and not in a good way. She said they were like opposite sides of a magnet. They had to be kept in separate rooms and separate cages or they would howl and scream at one another."

He ground out the roach in a small ashtray next to the box and matches.

"So one day, for whatever sciencey reason, they give the dog and monkey my stuff and put them in a room together after it kicks in. She said they went after each other like they were mortal enemies." He fell silent.

I waited and then asked, "Then what, Chuckie?"

"They disappeared."

"Someone took them away?"

"No, man. Like, they went 'poof'—gone."

"Say what?"

"She said it was like a hole opened in space, and they got sucked in. They just flat-out vanished. She said it almost destroyed the lab. Scared the ever-loving shit out of her. She told Frank she was done, but he begged her to do one more run."

He looked over at me with red-rimmed eyes.

"Sounds batshit crazy, right?"

I thought about last night at the hospital and shook my head. "No. No, it definitely sounds weird, but I think I believe her. You do too, don't you, Chuckie?"

He nodded his brown mop up and down.

"What happened after that?"

"It was the last time I saw her. We texted a few more times, and then…" he looked away.

"You were sweet on her, huh?"

He blushed a little and nodded. "We been friends since we were kids. Her family used to take mine to her grandmother's cabin on Mount Hood out at Rhododendron. We would go skiing up there. She never judged me or looked at me weird when I would read her my poetry or tell her what I thought the universe was made of." He paused. "She was nice to me."

He cried softly, his thin shoulders shaking. I didn't really know how to comfort him, but I needed him on track, so I nudged him away from Daphne.

"What's the universe made of Chuckie?"

That question perked him up. Like all Type-A's I'd met, you throw them a puzzle, and they go after it like a dog with a ball. "Energy, man. Everything in the universe, all matter, is just energy vibrating at different frequencies. Tap into that shit, and you're in touch with God, man."

Ahhh, stoner philosophy. A little physics mixed with some philosophy cribbed from China.

"You sound like a Daoist."

"Yeah, man! Those guys were on the right track till they got all wound up with trying to live forever and shit. All that alchemy and putting metal into their bodies ended up killing them, not making 'em live longer."

Back on track.

"Chuckie, you said 'them' when I asked about your customers. You know the other person too, right? Are they still alive?"

He sighed and nodded.

"I need a name."

"Emma. Emma Burr."

"What did she do there?"

"She was a programmer."

Oh, jackpot!

"Chuckie, it is vitally important that I talk to her. Do you know where she is?"

He looked at me with his weepy, red eyes and a surge of pity rose in me for this strange introvert.

"I don't think I should talk anymore."

I decided to take a chance, roll the dice.

"Chuckie, it's a long story, but 'the project' got in me. I'm pretty freaked out, and I need to talk to someone who knows what it can do—maybe how to get it out of me. The doctors who invented it were murdered, the lab was destroyed, and even more people were killed to get it. Right now, Emma could be in danger."

"It's in you?"

I nodded.

His jaw dropped open. "You should know, then."

"Know what?" I asked.

He closed his mouth and stared hard at me with his eyes all glassy and blazing red.

"That you're the one in danger, man."

"Excuse me?"

"Except for the two that did the Houdini bit and disappeared, every one of Daphne's animals that got 'the project' died, man…. Like within days of getting it. She said they died bad, all of them."

Oh, shit.

"You're fucked, man."

BURNIN FOR YOU

I sat stunned for a moment.

They say before you die that, your life flashes before your eyes. Chuckie had laid out a potential death sentence for me, but it wasn't my life that flashed before my eyes; it was Jeni's. I saw everything; the hard nights of infancy as she struggled with her initial symptoms, watching her learn to walk in a hospital corridor, her big eyes gleaming with pride, the way she called apples 'beebeebows,' and her soft breathing as she would sleep on my chest. I saw it all and understood that I might be the first to go and that I hoped it wouldn't hurt her too much. I thought of my dreams and hopes for her and realized that all my dreams were for her future, and not many were of my own. My life might not be much to give up, but I was afraid of the hole it might leave in Jeni's.

The music changed from classic Muddy to the more contemporary Austin 'Walkin' Cane's 'Murder of a Blues Singer.' Out of the frying pan and into the fire, or in my case, out of the fire and into the…shit.

I looked over at Dodgson.

He pointed to the joint box with one hand and his pocket containing the LSD with the other. "Sure you don't want to change your mind?"

Ummm….

I shook my head. "I need to talk to Emma Burr. Now."

Dodgson stood up, walked over to a polished redwood table, and retrieved his iPhone.

"I'll be back. You change your mind man; help yourself."

He walked back to the kitchen, turned down a corridor, and disappeared.

Just like dog and monkey.

Dafuq?

One thing at a time. I was restless; Cane's deep, bluesy baritone and the shuffle of the drum had me wanting to move around. I stood up and walked to the ornate stereo unit against the wall with speakers that looked big enough to rock a small club.

There was a small digital clock on the stereo that read 5:55 p.m. It had been over twelve hours since the nanos had shut down this morning.

All of them died bad. Dodgson's words rang in my head in time with the song's final chords. There had been a small part of me— just a tiny part, you understand—nurturing the hope after seeing how the nanos had repaired me that maybe, just maybe, this tech meant there was a chance for Jeni. That little hope had been burning in me since I had grasped what the nanos could do.

I didn't care if I went; I'd made my peace a long time ago, but for Jeni's sake, I had hoped.

Hope.

Hope can die too, and it can die badly. I let out a choked sob. Grief washed over me in a dark wave, swirling me around. The frustration and fear around her death that I'd held back spilled out. It was too much.

Freakin' blues....

I don't know how much time passed, but the music had shifted to the steady throb of Ben Harper and Charlie Musselwhite's 'When I Go.'

Enough.

Harper's slide guitar cut through my grief like a razor. I took in a deep breath and centered myself.

You survive. You overcome. You do not give in.

Ever.

That cleared the tears out of my eyes and ignited what my mother would have called Irish fire in my belly. Yes. You do not give in. You do what you always do: find a way to win. And you take out any motherfucker that stands in your way.

Big words. You can't do this by yourself this time.

I looked at the clock again—6:01 p.m.

A familiar metallic taste filled my mouth as my tongue tingled like it was touching the connectors to a 9-volt battery. The darkened eye-con at the corner of my vision suddenly ignited with color. The dragonfly now burned with a deep orange, and the HUD flashed across my vision.

UPGRADE COMPLETE

It's up!

I tried blinking to the menu, but nothing happened. Then I heard it.

Welcome, User. A woman's voice with a soft, Southern drawl floated across my mind.

I gave something that might be charitably called a high-pitched yelp and spun around, looking for the voice.

Upgrade is now complete; mental connection established. I am Daphne System; you may address me as Daphne or System. Please use either of these forms of address to activate me or begin your commands. May I know your name, please?

It's Texas…. It's a Texan drawl. Disoriented, I grabbed the stereo cabinet to steady myself,

"Al?" I said with a decided upward pitch at the end.

Vocalization is unnecessary, Al. How may I assist you today, sugar?

Sugar?

"What the-holy-shit-monkey-fuckballs?"

I got a little dizzy, and the room spun a bit.

"How am I hearing you, and why the hell do you have a Texas accent?"

I covered my ears with my hands.

Connection is made through the nerves of your auditory canal. I will respond to your thoughts provided you preface a command with Daphne or System. As for my accent, I was programmed this way, sugar.

Her voice was clear as a bell in my mind. My hands over my ears didn't do a thing. I dropped them down to my sides.

"You can read my mind?"

Only when prefaced with the activation word. You seem to prefer vocalizing, however.

"Yeah, less weird."

"What's weird?"

I spun at the sound of Dodgson's voice as he stood in the room.

"Nothing, nothing. Hey, you said Daphne was from here, right? Not Texas."

Dodgson blinked. "Daphne was born here in Astoria." He held up his phone and wiggled it. "Emma is from Houston. She's got a little accent—kinda cute. How'd you know about Texas?"

I shook my head. "You get ahold of her?"

He walked over to stand next to me by the stereo. "Yeah. She'll meet you, but only in public. Oregon Zoo tomorrow at four by the little train station inside. She said to come alone; she's seriously spooked. She said she would be wearing a red scarf and also to bring this." He handed me a small but thick foil envelope.

"What is it?"

"Twenty sheets worth of 'What's up, Dick?'—everything I have left except for my personal stash. She said you needed it, and you would pay me for it."

"I'm bringing her drugs?" I sputtered.

"She said if you want to live longer than a couple of days, to bring those. I think she wants you to drop. And she said you would pay for it, man."

My conscience demanded its own immediate payment on our bet. Jerk.

I walked over to my coat on the rack by the door and stuffed the envelope into the interior pocket next to Mrs. T's note, sealing it shut. "Whatever I owe you, get it from King. I have an open tab with him at the moment. He's good for it."

Warning.

I pulled on the jacket. "Oh, you're not shutting down again, are you? It was awkward last time."

Dodgson looked confused. "Pardon?"

Warning, perimeter alert.

My hackles rose, and I looked up from zipping my jacket. "What do you mean?"

Dodgson threw up his hands. "I don't know! I asked you first, man."

A few things happened right at that moment in quick succession: the music shifted to Ben and Charlie playing 'Moving On,' as a bright red dot briefly centered on Dodgson's forehead just before his entire head exploded in red gore across the stereo unit, accompanied by the sound of breaking glass and the fading echo of a rifle shot.

Warning: armed targets attacking.

I slapped the light switches on the wall, plunging the room into darkness, and dropped to the floor about a half-second before Dodgson's headless body did the same.

"No shit!" I snarled.

Vocalization is not necessary or recommended right now, sugar.

Charlie Musselwhite wailed on his harp as multiple beams of red target lights shone through the windows and lit up the room. Chuckie's leg was still twitching in the dim light.

I pulled the Kimber out and flicked the safety off— the room shook from the blasting combo of Musselwhite's harp and Harper's vocals and slide guitar.

"Daphne, you sensed their approach. Can you tell how many of them?"

Sensors indicate over a dozen armed intruders, as well as shooters placed in the trees and on the canyon walls.

"Not good." It wasn't the law—they wouldn't have shot Dodgson. No, one of King's men had taken the Russian bounty and ratted my location.

LightCam? Can I Bilbo my way out of here? I looked over at Chuckie's body and felt that righteous anger welling up; my hand tightened on the grip of the Kimber.

Another promise broken.

"I don't want to sneak out. Those Russian asshats killed Chuckie," I muttered.

Shall I activate Combat Mode?

I felt my eyebrows shoot upward. Combat Mode?

"Oh, fuck yes."

Holster your weapon. Your hands need to be free.

"Put away my gun? We're outnumbered! What are we going to use? Snark?"

Now.

I thought about the hospital room and the roasted Russian and slid the gun back into the DeSantis S.O.B., muttering, "What do you have in mind?"

Target beams continued to trace the room, and voices barked in Russian as they surrounded the house.

Activating.

The HUD appeared across my vision, blocked into grids, with red dots showing the approaching Russians. There was a rustling movement as something covered my ears, and the music was immediately muffled but still audible. It just sounded distant. I reached up to my head to find my ears wholly encased in a hard substance that felt like bone.

Combat Mode initiated. Taking control.

What?

A liquid curtain of ice spilled across my skin, and a burning itch seared my palms as I stood up and walked unerringly through the dark to the stereo unit.

I was invisible again.

I cranked the volume to full and then turned to face the front door. There was only one problem: I wasn't doing any of that. I felt as though I had been shoved into the back seat of my mind, and Daphne was driving.

I don't like being restrained as a rule, not my kink. But this was an order of magnitude worse; I had no control. All the things I took for granted, like breathing, speaking, and movement, were taken away. I was a bodiless prisoner with no way to rail against my captivity. My panicked mind kept repeating the title of an old sci-fi short story by Harlan Ellison, "I Have No Mouth, and I Must Scream," over and over. If Daphne felt my panic, she did nothing to assuage it.

The HUD showed three target dots moving onto the porch outside the front door. The music, which had been a distant hum underneath the bone earmuffs, was now an earthquake. I/Daphne could feel the entire house shake.

Daphne raised our burning right hand toward the door.

The music went dim as a drumbeat rush of energy passed through me and focused on the front door, which exploded outwards. The three red target dots that had been outside the door on our HUD vanished.

Windows shattered as bullets slammed into the house.

Low frequency.

Daphne raised our left hand, and this time, the music flowed into and out of us as a low wave beating like a gentle surf knocking against my legs at the beach. The shooting slowed to sporadic bursts and then silence as the target beams disappeared.

What happened?

Daphne didn't hesitate, walking us through the demolished front door while the blues thundered behind us. The outdoors blazed with light like it was high noon and not full night; our enhanced vision made the illumination function on the Swarovski look like candlelight. We saw a dozen armed men, some on their knees vomiting, others clutching at their eyes and crying out, weapons on the ground, forgotten.

Again, Daphne raised our right hand and faced it palm outwards toward the disoriented and sickened men. Once more, we felt the music, the energy, pass through us, but this time as a snare staccato, as though bullets of sound were passing through our hand. Men clutched at their heads as blood spurted from their noses and eyes, all of them screaming in agony before falling to the ground.

For each one that fell, another red light was extinguished on the HUD.

I tried to yell, "They're unarmed! Stop!" but nothing came out. Daphne had control of our vocal cords.

In moments, the yard was filled with unmoving figures. A puff of dirt exploded near our feet. The snipers were taking guesses.

The air around us went glacier cold in an instant, and frost formed around the house and across the fallen bodies. Daphne raised our right hand, and two pine trees burst into flames, followed by the screams of the men in them. Flaming bodies fell to the ground, spasmed uncontrollably, and then were still as the flames continued to hungrily lick their forms, casting demented shadows across the wall of trees.

There was the whoosh of air as bullets whizzed past us, followed by the high crack of rifle reports.

Daphne turned toward the low tops of the box canyon, lifted both our hands, and again, music became death as explosions of dirt and rock flew into the air as though we had launched grenades.

The last two lights from the target dots were extinguished.

The rustling on the sides of our head happened again, and suddenly, a cool breeze caressed our ears, and our sense of sound returned to normal. Ben and Charlie faded out, and the music stopped.

I screamed in my head, a prisoner in my own mind, as Daphne turned us away from the darkened, quiet house and the still bodies that littered the yard, all of it rimed in white frost that sparkled in the illumination of the burning trees. We left fire and death in our wake as we ran more swiftly and silently than I could have ever dreamed into the darkened woods.

What had taken me twenty minutes took Daphne five. We had run at a full-out sprint through the woods, our feet unerring on the uneven terrain. We arrived at the car, and our heartbeat was as steady and calm as if we had been sitting comfortably in a chair, relaxing, instead of having just finished a five-minute mile through the woods at night.

I kept trying to yell, "Stop!" but nothing happened. Daphne also ignored my thoughts. It wasn't till we had opened the car and got inside that I remembered: *Daphne! System, stop!*

Combat Mode ended.

The HUD dropped from my eyes, and warmth washed across my body. I was in control and visible again.

My heartbeat immediately shot upward as my feeling of panic was no longer blocked from my autonomous system.

"Don't ever do that again," I panted.

Combat Mode?

"Take control of me like that."

You are unaware of the capabilities we possess. It was only logical for System to take over.

"Don't fucking do it again."

Your opinion is noted.

Opinion?

"I don't have time to argue," I growled as I pulled out my phone and hit my latest speed dial addition. The gravelly voice answered on the second ring.

"Leigh, I just found out. You ok?"

"Not really."

"It was Mikey. It's been dealt with. Chuckie make it?"

"No."

I waited five seconds before I interrupted King's non-stop cursing.

"I need an evac to Portland. I'm not injured, but I'm hot."

"Slow boat to China suit ya?" he growled.

"Portland."

"Drive to the harbor; leave the keys in the car. One of my boys will move it somewhere. I'll call you back in ten minutes with an intel dump on your new ride."

The signal got sketchy, and the bars on my phone dropped and then rose. But King was gone.

I tried to get a map to the harbor on my phone, but the signal was still intermittent. I was surrounded by low hills, so not too surprising. I turned off the phone, tossed it onto the passenger seat, and started the car.

"Do you have GPS?" I asked aloud.

Of course.

"Astoria Harbor."

BRAIN DAMAGE

I dumped the car a few blocks from the harbor, grabbed my duffels, and walked past the brightly lit Victorian houses lining the hills above the stygian waterfront and down the steep streets to the dock. As I reached the waterfront, I passed a Motel 6 and a KFC, and at the scent of the chicken, my stomach rumbled as though I hadn't eaten in a week. I ran across the street to the harbor entrance, my feet splashing through the growing puddles. The rain continued to fall in an unending sheet, and the wind whipped at my coat as I made my way down the wooden gangplank to the public dock. As Elmore King had promised in his follow-up call, my chariot awaited.

A familiar fishing boat was tied up at the end of the dock.

The Krusty King Krab looked as shipshape as when I had last seen her over the summer. I called out over the drum of the rain beating down on the dock, "Permission to come aboard?" A tall black and silver-bearded man in a knit cap, turtleneck sweater, and peacoat—looking for all the world like the Gorton Fisherman's better-looking brother—stuck his head out of the wheelhouse.

Bob King waved me aboard and pointed to the bow. I nodded, tossed my duffels onto the moving deck, and headed for the bow ropes. I untied the bow and jumped aboard as King pulled the Krab away from the dock and into the channel.

Grabbing my bags, I joined King in the wheelhouse. It was dry, warm, cozy, and smelled powerfully of fish and pipe tobacco. The lights from the console illuminated King's bearded face as I glanced over at the Krab's captain and waited for what I was sure would be the inevitable tongue-lashing about the man's loss of income.

Where Elmore was short and powerful, Bob was tall and long, but they both shared that gravelly voice. "You're the one that found us out, huh? I think I remember you. You were in our place over the summer. We talked about Grand Cayman."

The boat pitched quite a bit as we entered the channel and passed underneath the Astoria-Megler Bridge and the 101 highway that connected Oregon and Washington near the mouth of the river. The top of the four-mile-long bridge was lost to our view in the rainy murk; I could only see the bottom of an enormous, supporting pylon rising Cthulhu-like out of the whitecaps off in the darkness. I casually grabbed the console to steady myself.

"Yep, sorry about that."

Bob King looked over at me.

"Are you kidding? I should thank you. Hell, I am thanking you! Elmore's had us over the barrel for years. We hit hard times in the early '90s at the restaurant, and Elmore was the only one we could turn to for the money. No more tanker deliveries means no more diving for us. Elmore is cutting us loose. I taxi you wherever you want to go, and we are free. Betty and I are getting too damn old to go diving and muling in this frozen bitchbox any longer. We're ready to retire to Arizona. So, you did us a solid."

I was a little stunned; despite how I felt about having to give up Sabitov's drug shipments to King, it seemed to at least have done some short-term good for someone.

"Really?"

Bob nodded. "Too bad about Chuckie. I've known that guy since he was a kid. I liked him." He turned the wheel, pointing the Krab's bow into the chop, and gave her a little more power with the throttle. His coat sleeve rode up as he spun the wheel, and there was a small blue dragon tattoo on his inner wrist. "Mikey—him I won't miss so much."

I took a chance. "Did you know Daphne Philips?"

"Oh, did poor Chuckie bend your ear about his lady love?"

"Sorta. You knew her too?"

"Yessiree, they were pretty much inseparable since they were kids. I used to be friends with her grandmother before she moved to that cabin on Mount Hood."

"What was Daphne like? He spoke highly of her."

King gave a gentle snort. "I'll bet. I always figured Chuckie must have been what they call 'on the spectrum' these days. He was a genius about so many things, but he could be blind as a bat about people."

I was confused.

"She wasn't nice?"

"Oh, no! She was great…smart, whip-smart. If she could have gotten out of here sooner, I think she could have lit the world on fire. Her grandmother was a sharp one, too. Daphne had street smarts to boot, but she had to, of course."

"So, what was the problem?"

"Chuckie gave his heart to that woman when they were still kids, but he never understood: her door didn't swing that way."

Oh. Oh!

"She never told him?"

"No, and people around here weren't exactly nice to her about it back when she was growing up. There was a reason she wanted out of Astoria…well, two reasons. She wanted to go someplace she could be accepted for who she was, as well as be closer to her grandmother."

He paused as a stiff wind pushed the Krab hard to starboard. Once he had the bow back into the wind, he continued, "I'd heard she found someone at her work up there, and they were an item. I thought it would work out for her, but hey, the man upstairs is fickle."

So, that explains why programmer Emma named her creation after Daphne.

I grinned at Captain Bob. "You're not much like your cousin Elmore, are you? You seem a little more…open-minded?"

"Because I'm not a homophobe or a racist? That man and the others with him are in the same boat, and that barge's name is fear. All those boys just fear what they don't know. Most of them have never been farther than Portland."

He was quiet for a few minutes as he negotiated the channel.

"I like to think that if these boys had more of an opportunity to get out and see the world, they might be less afraid of it. Elmore got out with the Corps, but the war just reinforced his fear of anyone who looks different from him. You read Mark Twain?"

"Huckleberry Finn and Tom Sawyer in school."

"He has a great quote that I love—says a lot about human nature: 'Travel is fatal to bigotry.' You get out there enough, and you learn that we are all the same. We are all brothers, no matter what our skin color."

"If you prick us, do we not bleed? If you tickle us, do we not laugh? If you poison us, do we not die?" I quoted.

King gave me a polite golf clap. "A man who can quote the Bard can't be all bad."

I grinned ruefully as I heard my own thoughts about Chuckie an hour earlier repeated back to me. "I hope not."

Across the channel, an orange Coast Guard Cutter appeared through the rain like a ghost off the port bow. I tracked it as it passed.

King watched me watching the cutter.

"Don't worry—he's headed out, and as far as he's concerned, we're doing what any sensible boat captain would do in this shit: head for home. You should get below and stay below, though. It's seventy-two miles to P-town, but as long as there's no rush, I'll have you there by noon tomorrow."

"Works for me."

"Betty threw together a cooler of food and drinks by way of thanking you. She said to say she would have made you a seven-course meal if she had the time."

"That was kind of her; please give her my thanks."

"I will. There's a small cabin down forward with a bunk and an even smaller head with a shower. It's all yours. And if you'll excuse me, this part of the channel is tricky, even in the daytime, and I need to focus."

"Thanks, Mr. King."

He nodded and winked. "I'm going to move somewhere it never rains, so thank you."

I grinned and went below.

Although the holds down below were empty and washed clean, the smell of fish below decks was enough to almost knock a person over. I, however, had spent my teenage years helping Chen-chen get our daily fish order together. The smell reminded me of time spent with my foster-father down at the fish market in the early mornings. Kinda made me feel at home.

A door in the hull separated the hold from the living quarters. Beyond it, there was a small kitchen, head, and a small cabin with its own door. I opened the cabin and dropped my duffels on the floor. Despite their heaviness, I felt no sense of relief at their weight being gone. It hadn't bothered me to begin with. Odd.

There was a small, neatly made bunk built into the starboard hull with a curtained porthole above it and a small, built-in desk filled with charts and manuals. A swing-out chair was bolted underneath, on the port side. In between was a large, blue Yeti cooler. I closed the door.

"Daphne, you still there?"

Always, sugar. Can I help you?

"I have questions."

I will answer what I can.

Kinda cagey answer.

The hull rose and fell in the wind-driven chop. I had to grab onto the edge of the desk for balance.

"What are you?"

My designation is Daphne or System. I am the interface for the EPU System, the technology that has bonded with you.

"Bonded?"

The EPU System has attached itself to your nerve endings and major physiological structures, bonding with them at the cellular level.

"What's EPU stand for?"

E Pluribus Unum.

I had to search my memory for a moment, but I remembered the translation: Out of many, one.

That explained dead Daphne's comment to Chuckie to ask a dead president. I sat on the edge of the bunk, unlaced my boots, kicked them off, and eyeballed the cooler.

"Why am I so fucking hungry?" I muttered.

Use of the EPU System by your body requires caloric expenditure. Those calories must be replaced. The greater the expenditure, the greater your need for sustenance.

"Nothing's free, huh? What does the EPU run on?"

That information is authorization only. You are not authorized.

Yeah. I've heard that line before.

I opened the cooler. There were piles of baked chicken legs and breasts in baggies, a giant container full of mashed potatoes, a smaller one of gravy, what looked like cherry pie, and…I pulled out a clear container full of large, dark blackberries. I opened the top, then grabbed and ate one.

Marionberries…Oregon's finest. Oh, hallelujah.

I grabbed more, hungrily stuffing the berries into my mouth and biting down as the sweet berry nectar exploded in my mouth. I horked it down and grabbed another handful.

"What else is 'authorization only'?"

Unclear. I was not unaware of the designation until you requested the information.

I dug around in the cooler. Covered carafes of what looked like tea and lemonade stood upright in the corner of the cooler, and a few bottles of beer were laid flat on the bottom. I grabbed the lemonade carafe one-handed, popped the lid off with my thumb, and drank a third of it in a single gulp.

The boat gave a violent lurch to starboard before correcting itself; I gave myself a mental high-five as I managed not to drop any berries or spill any lemonade on the bunk.

I wondered, was Daphne high-fiving me back?

"Daphne, are you conscious?" I popped the handful of berries into my mouth and washed it down with more lemonade.

I understand your meaning. Your question is, does EPU System possess self-awareness? We do not.

"You use both I and we to describe yourself. Which is it?"

Both. I am Daphne or System. I am both myself and the EPU. I am our voice. My identity is dualistic in nature.

"E Pluribus Unum, huh?"

Exactly.

I had finished the berries and moved on to the chicken and potatoes. I opened the potatoes, dumped semi-congealed gravy all over them, and then dipped a chicken leg into the potatoes and used it as a spoon.

"Can you tell me what happened on the bridge last night? Everything went crazy. Do you know when I mean?" I asked between bites.

Yes. Initial bonding had just been completed. The gravity of your injuries required an immediate connection. System programming calls for bonding to be done in steps and sequence. As your vitals were deteriorating rapidly, protocol required speed rather than care. EPU could not afford to be gentle, and as such, you experienced a form of overload before your senses could be properly cushioned and prepared for the new input.

I tried to talk with my mouth full of potatoes and chicken, but all that came out was, "Duffffggeegnn?"

Vocalization is not necessary, sugar.

I focused my thoughts. *Daphne, does System mean me harm?*

I felt a sense of surprise spread through me and realized it wasn't my own.

Absolutely not. EPU is bonded to you. We are a part of you now. To harm Al Leigh would be to harm ourselves.

"On the bridge, how did you stop the car from hitting us?" I asked between bites of chicken and creamy mashed potatoes.

I have no data on the actions that impeded the vehicle.

"You don't know how you did it?"

It was an early stage of development with multiple ongoing tasks.

"Lot of moving parts. I get it...but that force field, or whatever it was, would have come in handy against those Russians tonight. I didn't see it in your menu."

The menu you viewed is from an earlier iteration.

I waited for any further explanation, but none came. I swallowed and looked down. The chicken was gone, as were the potatoes. There was still some gravy with bits of thyme leaf floating in it left in the smaller container, and I used two fingers to spoon it out and into my mouth.

"Why did you kill those men back at the farm? They were unarmed. How did you do that, by the way?"

Which question would you like answered first?

"What did you do to them?"

I used focused, high-frequency sonic pulses to take out threats at the front door and later on the canyon walls. I used low-frequency sonic waves to induce nausea and blurred vision among the surrounding targets. Once they were disabled and disarmed, I again used focused, high-frequency sonic pulses to rupture their brains. As for the targets in the trees, I was able to redirect and focus local thermal energy, thus nullifying their threat.

"You set the trees on fire, neat."

No, I set the men on fire. Their combustion ignited the trees.

Oh.

Human torches and ruptured brains...Ewww.

I looked down at the cherry pie and, with the thought of ruptured brains, decided to save it for later.

"Like you said, they were disarmed and disabled. Killing them wasn't necessary. Is that part of your programming?"

No. It was yours.

I blinked. "Pardon?"

The EPU is tapped into your nervous system, your 'hard-wiring,' as it were. What you call your instincts is a form of biological programming. EPU sensed your innate command to end their lives, and it did so.

"I didn't tell you to kill them. I kept trying to tell you to stop. I said 'no.'"

We didn't hear you, and your body said 'yes.'

I felt like I had been kicked straight in the balls.

This thing just used a rape justification on me.

Why not? It had raped me after a fashion: the violent penetration, the unwanted seed that spread through my insides, the way Daphne had taken control of my body against my will while I was helpless to stop it. Pretty much the definition of rape. Rage boiled up in me—I was close to panting in anger as my pulse quickened.

"You trying to tell me I secretly wanted it?"

Yes.

Daphne must have sensed my flaring anger.

Without the EPU, you would have died. We saved your life.

I waited a moment, trying to control my breath.

"Is there a way to get the EPU out of me?"

Unknown.

"Is there a way to turn you off?" I growled.

We have no off switch. If you desire privacy, you may simply command: 'Daphne, disable AV.' This will disable the audio and visual input for the EPU. When you are ready to reactivate the AV, follow the command syntax mentally to enable it. Before you take this step, please check your bandages, sugar, and may I suggest plugging in your phone as it is low on power.

I reached up and felt my left side where Mikey had bandaged me up. No sting.

I pulled off my sweater and shirt and used a pair of scissors on King's desk to cut off the reddened bandages covering my torso. Other than the crusted blood, the long cut was gone, as though it had never existed.

We are a part of you now; we will care for you.

"Daphne, disable AV," I snarled.

Disabling.

The bright orange eye-con went dim, but not dark, as it had before the upgrade. The dragonfly was still glowing orange, but the intensity of color was greatly diminished.

I waited a moment.

"You still there, you piece of shit?"

Nothing.

It didn't mean that she really couldn't hear or see, but I would have to go with her assurance and the empirical evidence of the eye-con's alteration.

Ghost in the *goddamn* machine.

I stripped and walked out of the cabin into the head. Nature called, and then I squeezed myself into the tiny shower, wondering how the much taller Bob King even fit in this thing. There was an extra towel on the sink, and I took it with me to the cabin. Closing the door, I dried off quickly, got into a clean pair of underwear, jeans, and socks, and then crawled under the covers.

I realized I hadn't really slept in two days but doubted I could sleep after the day I had endured. I got out of the rack, reached down into my duffel, grabbed a spare charging cord, and plugged my phone into the jack near King's desk, noting that Daphne was right: the phone battery was almost dead. Weird. I thought I had plugged it in while I was in the car. It shouldn't be dead yet. She was right about that.

At the thought of Daphne, I was hit with the shakes so powerful that I dropped the phone and collapsed back on the bunk. The cabin spun like a merry-go-round on crack, and it was hard to breathe; I was gasping for air while my heart raced out of control. I was overwhelmed with anxiety so potent that I wanted to throw up.

She had taken over me! I couldn't move! I couldn't scream! Fuck, fuck!

I tried to control my breathing; I couldn't; I was shaking so hard my teeth were clattering. I grabbed the blanket on the bed and shoved it in my mouth to keep from screaming. The attack lasted a few minutes that felt like hours before it subsided enough to pull the blanket out of my mouth and take in deep lungsful of air as the shaking turned to short, violent tremors spread out over moments before finally fading away.

I felt as though I had just run an ultramarathon; I was weak and drained. The urge to throw up had passed, and my muscles had that warm, heavy-weighted feeling I would get after a hard session in the gym.

The boat had stopped its tossing and was swaying gently as it moved against the river current. I felt its rhythm and listened to the steady thrum of the rain beating down on the deck above.

I slept.

ONLY SOLUTIONS

The dim autumn sun peeking through the porthole curtain woke me. I pulled the little dark curtain aside, letting the weak light illuminate the cabin. I couldn't see much from my angle, but it looked like mid-morning sun. Anticipating some soreness from the previous couple days of mayhem, I stretched slowly and reached for my phone, thumbing on the display.

9:45 a.m.

It felt like I had been asleep for a week, not twelve hours. I mean, all in all, I felt kinda great. Then I remembered last night's panic attack followed by my conversation with Chuckie and realized that I might not have too many mornings of feeling great left ahead of me—if Daphne let me feel anything at all.

At the thought of the thing in my head that should remain nameless, my heart rate sped up, but I focused on my breathing and got it under control. I'm in charge, damnit.

For how long?

I sat up slowly but realized nothing was aching or strained or in any other way bothering me except for needing to pee, drink coffee, and eat something—preferably in that order.

I did what I had always done on my rack in the Corps and threw my legs over the side and gave a little bounce to help me up....

SLAM!

I bounced off the door to the cabin three feet away from where I had just been sitting a moment ago. My forehead stung a little, but there was now a crater in the wooden door shaped like my head.

Uh, whoops…I think. What had just happened?

Something nano-related, I guessed. Wake Daphne?

Pee first, questions later.

I carefully opened the door and padded down the short, dark, and chilly companionway smelling of fish until I reached the tiny head and let fly. A gallon of lemonade later, I washed up and was about to hang the little hand cloth back on its hook when the boat lurched to port. I instinctively thrust my hand out to steady myself…and found my arm through the thin but sturdy metal door up to my elbow.

Fuck.

I pulled my arm out and carefully walked back to the cabin, closing the door with exaggerated care. I sat down in the swing-out stool under the desk and thought about what I wanted to do and what I *needed* to do. So far, my temper had not been helping—as usual. Yelling at the program, or whatever it is, wasn't going to help. So, wanting was out.

What did I need?

I needed to make sure that shit never happened again. I resolved to find out if there was a way to turn this thing off for good or at least make sure it stayed on its leash. This thing was going to work for me, not the other way around.

I'm in charge.

"Daphne, enable AV."

The little dragonfly eye-con flared bright orange at the base of my vision.

Good morning, sugar. How you feelin' this morning?

"I feel fantastic. I'm also all kinds of curious today. I've been thinking about what you said. The EPU seems to be able to manipulate nearby energy like you did with the music and the tree firebomb thingy at the cabin—that was really cool by the way. How?"

The cumulative activity of the EPU creates a field of energy around us. The EPU can manipulate that field, focusing and redirecting nearby sources of energy.

"Could I ask how it does that?"

That's classified, sugar.

Okay, saw that one coming. But I'd never heard that phrase put quite that way before. Certainly, beat the usual derogatory adjectives that went along with it in the Corps.

"So, you—the EPU—redirect energy. Is it possible that on that night on the bridge, you redirected the kinetic energy of the approaching car and used it to shield us?"

An excellent hypothesis and well within the EPU parameters, but as stated, no data exists to correlate that hypothesis. All recorded data was focused on the bonding and healing of Al Leigh.

"But, if necessary, could you replicate that effect? Could you redirect that much energy and stop that much mass?"

Theoretically, yes.

"Theoretically isn't comforting if a Mack truck is about to flatten you."

Theoretically, sugar, I didn't know if the EPU could fight our way out of the ambush at Chuckie's cabin last night. We had never activated or tested our combat systems until that moment.

"Great, so everything is trial by fire—good to know. So, earlier this morning, I managed to put both my head and arm through our host's doors, and not because I was trying to. Why am I moving so fast?"

A side effect of the EPU bonding with your nerves is that similar to the myelin your body naturally produces, they have increased and magnified the insulation along your axons allowing for decreased electrical resistance, thus resulting in faster signal impulses.

"Okay, anatomy and physiology class was a long time ago. Come again?"

Our reflexes are faster and will continue to get faster. Our muscular and skeletal structures have also increased in density and structural integrity. This means we are also stronger, more resistant to damage, and more capable of inflicting damage. These enhancements will also continue.

"Continue? For how long?"

Until maximum efficiency is attained.

Wow. That sounded like some serious, super-soldier shit. It would be impressive if it weren't for the recent intel dump indicating that I wouldn't live long enough to attain...maximum efficiency. Besides, it also sounded like an ad for a new and improved laxative, now with...you guessed it—maximum efficiency.

I looked down at the cooler and leaned over carefully to open it up. I ignored the beers rolling around the bottom and reached for the carafe of iced tea. Primitive me grunted: 'some-caffeine-better-than-no-caffeine.' I also grabbed the container with the cherry pie and filed it under the mental heading of 'if life is short, then an entire pie is breakfast pastry.' I found a baggie underneath the container with flatware, napkins, and wet naps sealed inside that I had missed during my gorging session the night before. I closed the top of the cooler and set up breakfast on the desk in front of me.

I opened everything up and dug in.

Pie is good. Breakfast pie is even better.

I thought for a moment. "Eventually, I'm going to be moving too fast for me to control by myself, aren't I?"

Yes. Particularly during Combat Mode. The EPU was created as a symbiotic structure to....

"Uh-huh. Not happening."

What?

"Me ceding control to you again. I'm pulling your driver's license, kid. You're a hazard."

You will be unable to control us with the efficiency and speed that I am capable of....

"Not interested. I'm driving; you navigate. I choose the playlist; you can pick every other song."

There was a pause.

What makes you believe you can control me?

A cold sweat broke out across my upper body. What kind of programmer would put that kind of menace into the code? Was it a defensive measure? Or perhaps I was just reading too much into its statement. My heartbeat had jumped, and I took a calming breath.

I bluffed.

"There's no way you were programmed to override your user, associate, host...whatever I am—not unless it's a dire emergency that threatens you both. That's what happened last night: am I right?"

Again, there was a pause.

Yes.

Holy shit, if I'd been wrong on that one.... I thought a moment.

"You need my permission to take over, don't you?"

Pause.

Yes.

My fingers drummed on the desktop; I tried to think like its programmer.

"Activating Combat Mode gave you that option, didn't it?"

It is the default option.

I scraped up a huge spoonful of cherry pie, stuffed it in, and asked around a mouthful of cherries and flaky crust: "Daphne, can I change your defaults?"

An even longer pause this time.

Yes.

I smiled and looked over at the time on my phone—about two hours to Portland if Captain Bob was correct on his ETA.

"You will walk me through the defaults, the settings, and what exactly you can do before we get to Portland. I assume you come with some sort of tutorial?"

I could swear I heard it sigh in my head.

Yes.

"Alright, alright, alright. Let's get started, Texas."

Two frustrating hours later, Captain Bob swung the Krab into the Riverplace Marina in Portland and sidled up to the dock. Riverplace was a small marina smack in the middle of downtown Portland. It sat on the western edge of the Willamette, between the Hawthorne Bridge to the north, and the arching span of the Marquam Bridge, and the I-5 freeway to the south. It was ringed by a series of tasteful, four-story condos that were, in turn, bracketed from behind by the larger buildings of downtown.

The light brown dock was stained with old bird droppings and had a hut-shaped seafood grill overlooking the water at the farthest end. The aroma of roasting meats from the modest afternoon lunch rush carried appetizingly across the smell of river water and diesel as I tied the bowline off.

The past couple of hours had been frustrating because the 'tutorial' was only a prototype: essentially a framework with no detailed information. It was provided to allow the military to install their own version of a training module. So instead, I had spent my time moving around the hold, doing calisthenics and shadow boxing, adapting to my new enhanced reflexes while I questioned

Daphne each step of the way as she explained about the EPU and its defaults and settings. Her descriptions were irritatingly short as I ran into the dual problems of 'authorization required' and a program that was strangely resistant to coughing up the required information.

The afternoon October air was frigid, and the sky was full of steel grey and dark-hued clouds that hugged the bottom of the sky, hiding the low hills beyond the shrouded profile of downtown. Questing tentacles of fog drifted off the river and through the surrounding neighborhoods like long white fingers, blindly searching the streets. Thanks to the EPU, the cold didn't seem to bother me like it usually did. According to Daphne, I could stand naked in an arctic blizzard now, and the EPU would maintain a perfect homeostatic temperature for me.

I would probably still blush, though.

I finished the bowline knot, pulled it tight into the icy metal cleat, and gave a red-eyed Bob the thumbs up. He came out of the cabin with my bags, dropping them over the side onto the dock next to me, the clanking of the metal guns from the larger bag earning me a raised eyebrow.

I gave a half-embarrassed shrug.

"Look, I am sorry about the door. The doors—plural."

Bob gave a gravelly chuckle, his breath coming out in a cloud. "Yeah, you really broke on through."

I groaned.

He gave a wicked grin. "Elmore's problem now—boat's his."

I nodded. "Yeah, speaking of that. I would suggest you and Betty get down to Arizona as fast as possible. I traded intelligence about my former employer's business. I can't let either of them continue that shit anymore. "

Bob took a step back. "You gonna welsh on Elmore?"

I shook my head. "I told him I wouldn't tell the Bratva that he knew about their delivery schedule. I just didn't promise not to disrupt the drug transfer. As soon as I can find a way to do that or let the law know without incriminating myself, I'm going to."

Bob was silent for a moment and then slapped his thigh.

"Good! Time to kick this life to the curb and retire. I've never felt good about it, but I didn't dare cross Elmore. If you want to, I'm not going to stand in your way. I'm going south to work on my short game so I can stop getting my ass kicked by the wife." He putted an imaginary ball across the deck of the Krab.

I was about to make some rejoinder when my new sharper hearing picked up footsteps on the dock behind us.

"Speak of the devil," Captain Bob purred.

I turned to see a petite woman bundled against the cold walking toward us. Betty King's hood was down, and her shoulder-length hair hung free in a heavy black and silver mane that seemed to match and compliment Captain Bob's beard. Betty King was a testament to age being just a number, striking in looks and flashing undeniable curves despite being wrapped up in a winter coat. She was the picture of femininity. Her face broke into a sunny smile for what I thought was Bob; instead, I was the one who got a fierce, jasmine-scented embrace and a whispered, "Thank you."

I awkwardly returned her hug.

"Uh, you're welcome," I said stupidly and followed it up with a classic, "The pie was amaze-balls…all the chow was. I ate every bite. Thanks." Yep, pretty women can still throw me for a loop.

She knew it too.

She stepped back, and her dark eyes twinkled a bit as she put one hand into a pocket and pulled out a set of keys on a Phoenix Suns' chain. "You're welcome. Don't forget to put gas in it."

I looked quizzically over at Bob.

"Yeah, Elmore left a car for you a couple blocks from here like you asked, but… how to put this delicately?"

Betty found a way.

"He's a conniving bastard, and I wouldn't trust him farther than you can drop-kick his goblin ass," she said sweetly.

Bob smiled grimly as he looked at me. "You should know: Elmore sent word the Russians have upped your bounty to an even million."

I whistled.

He switched his gaze down to his much-smaller wife. "I was thinking that Elmore's crew isn't going to be the most reliable when that kind of money is on the line, dear."

"Whatever. He likes to think he's great to us, but he has kept us trapped here. He's a snake." She pulled my hand out, smiled merrily at me, and dropped the keys into my palm. "I drove our beater up here for you; it will be safer than Elmore's choice because no one will know but the three of us. In the meantime, I'll put this hunk of burning love in his bunk to rest up while I drive this floating barrel of fish guts for one more cruise down the river."

Betty took her husband's hands as she climbed aboard the Krab and stepped nimbly to his side. They were a pair, him so tall and solid, and her so small and…well, lush, but they fit together like many long-married couples do—each a part of the other's whole.

"Brown Tahoe in the lot. Leave it wherever when you're done with it. Thanks again to you, young man, and good luck."

Bob waved as he led his wife into the cabin, out of the cold. I reached down and pulled the knot loose from the cleat and cast the line aboard as the Krab pulled away from the dock. I gave a short wave as it motored gently out of the marina where it was drawn into the river current, naturally picking up speed, and soon swallowed by the drifting clouds of fog beyond.

I hefted my bags easily, enjoying the lack of strain on my shoulders. I walked off the dock, through the small gate, and toward the nearby lot. An older, mud-stained, brown Tahoe with steam still rising from its hood was parked near the edge of the lot. I got in, bundled my things into the passenger seat, and started it up.

I pulled out my phone and charger, plugged them in, and asked, "So what did you find?"

An APB for you has been issued. Both local and federal authorities have your description, and most believe you to be in the Portland area.

Daphne had linked to my smartphone and had been scanning the net since we approached the marina. She had been doing this the previous night, which explained my battery being dead.

"So, don't get pulled over."

Correct. Again, we will be exposed during our meeting. LightCam would be our best tactical choice when we arrive.

"Again, you don't understand people. This requires a little more subtlety."

Sugar, are you trying to say being invisible isn't subtle?

In my two-hour search through her available defaults, I had been unable to find a way to get rid of her Southern affectation, and at this point, I was ready to change her activation syntax to: "I do declare!" With every other directional app, you can get a nice British or Aussie accent, but I was stuck with the swee' tea-drinking pearl-clutcher.

All right, it was sorta cute, as long as she kept her digital hands to herself.

We had just a little over three hours before the meet with Emma Burr at the Oregon Zoo. I had already figured that the law would be on the lookout for me, and I was damn sure the Russians—not to mention Micawber and his Section squad—were on the hunt out there somewhere as well, making sticking my head out a risky proposition, hence Daphne's reasoning for going in under cover of LightCam. While it would provide maximum coverage for me, I wasn't sure how Emma would react to an invisible guy talking to her at the zoo. I knew next to nothing about her except that she was skittish and, considering the fate of most of her former co-workers, rightly so. I mean, I already knew how I would react to a disembodied voice in my ear, and it had involved some high-pitched yelping combined with a lot of off-the-cuff swearing.

I couldn't afford to draw attention to us, and surprising an already-nervous woman with that kind of *Twilight Zone* shock invited a whole new level of unpredictability to her reaction. I needed to talk to her. I didn't need her running away in terror.

No, something more obvious yet subtle was called for…something that would allow me to be in the open at the zoo yet camouflaged at the same time. Fortunately, I had an idea, and three hours was just enough time to run a couple of errands and get it set up.

"Daphne, can you keep us clear of LEOs on the streets?"

Law Enforcement Officers? I can coordinate with your mapping app and the various crowd-sourced directional apps, as well as local department transmissions, to avoid the majority of them.

"Do it."

A detailed map of downtown Portland appeared in light colors in the HUD across my vision. It was dark enough for me to see while being light enough to read without obstructing my view of the actual road. Miniature stationary and roving crimson cars marked out the LEOs. I told Daphne the address for the zoo, and a vivid green line appeared that shifted occasionally in response to the tiny red cars that laid out my path.

"Ok, that's pretty damn cool. Now, I just have to watch out for Mr. Filch."

A LEO?

"Nah, janitor."

Sugar, are you telling me we are being threatened by a waste disposal professional?

I peered through the HUD up at the somber, dark clouds blanketing the sky as I backed out of the parking spot.

"It's nothing. Hey, Daphne—I have a theoretical question for you...."

I drove the Tahoe out of the lot, turned onto SW Montgomery, and let Daphne guide me through the mist-shrouded streets while we hashed out our plan.

CRAZY TRAIN

This is your idea of subtle?

I ambled gamely down the wide asphalt walkway under the cloudy afternoon skies. Miniature aliens, monsters, ice princesses, and superheroes ran around, ahead and everywhere about me, many covered with ponchos to keep the imminent rain off their adorable costumes.

My ambling was greatly aided by a large, t-shaped wooden crutch under my left arm. It offset the gaping hole in the voluminous trouser leg that appeared cut out but actually sported a LightCam shrouded leg, invisible to all. The lone, black knee-high boot on the other leg, eyepatch, do-rag, and tricorn hat were de rigueur, but the stuffed parrot I had attached with epoxy to the shoulder of my knee-length, purple buccaneer's coat was straight-up whimsy.

"I only have one thing to say to that," I muttered behind the black silk scarf I had wrapped around my lower face to help conceal myself as I waved at a waist-high, intergalactic bounty hunter taking a bead on me with his blaster.

And that is?

"Arrrrr."

The Oregon Zoo was spread over sixty-four acres on steep wooded hillsides within Washington Park, about two miles southwest of downtown Portland. It was part of Washington Park and was connected to the Japanese Garden, Arboretum, and the rest of the park by a small rail line. From its humble beginnings with two bears in the back of a drugstore, it now boasted over 2,500 individual animals and has five large, separate exhibits, with the Great Northwest and Pacific Shores sections being my personal favorites.

I had been up here before. Hitoshi was part of the Zoobomb crowd, and I had come up to watch a couple of times and even tried it once. Zoobomb is a bunch of, um, unusual people who gather weekly with their bikes. They take the MAX Light Rail to the Washington Park station and then up the elevator to the top, next to the zoo. Then, they ride their bikes down the hill. Rinse and repeat often.

It all sounds pretty normal until you see the crowd and the bikes. Grown adults wearing costumes while riding on modified children's bikes are often a big part of the Zoobomb and add significantly to the surreal, carnival-like atmosphere. Afterward, it's tradition to hit the food trucks and either marvel at one's keen fashion sense or wonder about certain suicidal impulses that need to be flavored with a large side-serving of ridiculous.

However you look at it, it's a shit-ton of fun.

The zoo had been landscaped with plants and trees native to the PNW and was now, of course, decorated for Halloween. Despite the gravity of my situation, I couldn't help but grin at the riot of children enjoying an afternoon at the spookily decorated zoo, combined with a little early trick-or-treating.

I had gotten the chance to run back to SF to take Jeni trick or treating last year despite the rainstorm that drenched the city that night. She had gone as a ladybug in a costume that made her look like a miniature *kaiju* ready to take out Tokyo. We had made it to exactly three houses before I worried that the cold and wet would not be good for her and bundled her home. I was concerned that she felt her first Halloween might be a bust, but she had just looked up at me with a huge grin on her tiny face and said, "I got THREE free pieces of candy! Can we do it again next year?"

I felt my heart swell at the memory, and I wanted nothing more than just to hold her right then. I wondered if I ever would again. I wasn't the same anymore—in fact, I wasn't sure what I was at the moment. Was I becoming more with the addition of Daphne? Or was I going to become less me and more of…it? If I/we make it out of this, was there a way for us not just to be a weapon? The potential for the nanos was mind-boggling in its implications.

Yeah, if it doesn't kill me first.

Daphne and her Filch-Finder had allowed us to maneuver through the city without even a glimpse of a patrol car, although I had spotted a couple of unmarked units who had ignored us. The stops consisted of a costume store where I got my new threads, a rental shop, and a local GNC where I had bought two huge containers of cookies and cream flavored Super-Swole!—a calorie-dense supplement powder favored by weightlifters—as well as a shake container to mix it with. If using the EPU was going to put me in caloric debt, I wanted to be able to replace my energy quickly and continue my groove without being fatally distracted by hunger. I had consumed three huge, full servings mixed with milk from a corner market near the park, and it all sloshed around inside me.

I still do not understand how this is better than invisibility.

I stopped to glance up at a white pole with brightly colored directional signs pointing to the various exhibits and places of interest. The path to the little train that ran inside the zoo was marked out, and I hobbled down it.

"We're doubly invisible."

I can see how our costume allows us to blend in with others dressed similarly, but why shroud only your leg with LightCam?

A friend from before I got scooped up by Section—a corporal in 2nd MSOB—had lost his leg to an IED. He was from Sacramento, not far from the Bay, so we had bonded over our shared nostalgia for home. I had visited him when I returned stateside. He had still been adjusting to being back in-country himself, but when I had avoided looking at his leg, he had admonished me, "Don't do that: the fucking eye-slide when you look at my leg, or where it used to be, I mean. I get it—it makes you uncomfortable, but I've seen how people start with not looking at your missing wheel and eventually stop seeing all of you. Don't do that to me, man."

He had been right. I watched as people who saw my costume smiled and then looked away as soon as they realized the missing leg was really missing. As a society don't want to see those who have been maimed or disfigured. Our own fear that it might happen to us, combined with our cultural sense of shame, causes us to begin by looking away, inevitably followed by entirely ignoring what we don't want to see.

Meanwhile, with parades and fanfare, we send our guys off to war to do what they are ordered to do, and when they come back, maimed in body or spirit, even meeting them in the eye seems to be too much, let alone providing genuine care.

I sighed.

"Human nature," I muttered to her under my breath.

Being able to isolate individual parts of my body with LightCam had been a hoot to discover. I had briefly considered going as the Headless Horseman, but I was pretty sure that would have undercut the subtle part, not to mention permanently scarring some poor Paw Patrol devotee.

I had been wrong in my original assumption that the nanos, or the EPU, had been using my skin cells to bend the light around me. Instead, it was the same field created by the EPU that allowed it to focus and redirect energy, thereby reconfiguring the light, and making me see-through. I needed a name for that field…. Daphne had told me some Latin-sounding, multi-syllabic word Vegrandis used for it, but it was too much of a mouthful.

It reminded me of something like Chinese *qi* or The Force. A field generated by a living entity. Those may work well as an analogy, but is the EPU truly alive?

Daphne had said that she (great, I was calling it a 'her' instead of an 'it') was not conscious; she was not a true artificial intelligence but more like a very sophisticated program. I was going to take her word rather than worry about a Turing Test—I'm hardly the best judge of sentience. She seemed to have a sense of humor, and I could feel her (emotional?) reactions through my senses. But were they hers, or was my body simply interpreting her electrical stimulus as my own?

If so, what was the difference? Did that make it any less real?

But what about the EPU? Daphne was just the interface. Was the EPU alive?

Again, I could feel my inner soldier wanting to slap down my inner nerd. Focus! Stop wasting time with these questions. Survive all this first; get philosophical later. So…names.

The Aura? Too hokey.

The Field? Too boring.

The Shield? Lame.

The Force and *qi* were taken, and besides, this thing was more of a focus…like a lens.

The Lens? Hmmm. That would work until I thought of something more spectacular, I grumbled to myself.

Something like 'Invisible Force Field of Doom!'

Meh.

I clumped to a stop outside the Zoo Railway station. I had mostly gotten the hang of my speedy new reflexes and felt unreasonably proud that I had managed not to break my crutch, or myself, or just plain fall flat on my face again—as I had earlier outside the corner store on the milk run. Go, me!

The Zoo Railway was a small, narrow-gauge train that ran through the zoo and past the Family Farm and the Elephant Lands. It was a short six-minute trip but was always popular with the kids, especially in the winter during Zoo Lights. The Zooliner—a stately, old, 50s retro engine—was the only remaining train. There had once been three, and the trains had gone throughout Washington Park, but these days it was just the old Zooliner, and only on special occasions.

Apparently, Halloween's swift approach counted. The silver Zooliner was decked out in green and orange lights, and someone had painted a howling wolf's head on the front of the engine. Costumed children streamed into the station as more poured out the exit gate. Parents either escorted their children on or off the train or waited in groups outside the exit gate.

I looked at the home screen on the HUD to check the time. 3:58.07 p.m. glowed in pale green at the top right of my vision.

Part of resetting the defaults had been to put up a few permanent essentials on the HUD. If the little dragonfly eye-con could fit (and was permanent?), so could a few others in the other corners. A compass, digital clock, and a tiny threat radar occupied the other three corners of my vision. A fifth special icon sat flat and currently unlit at the top center. The threat radar was up to Daphne: if she caught something I wasn't aware of, it went instantly red to warn me. Should I be too busy or otherwise occupied, I would react faster to the flash of red than to her mental updates.

I gazed around the crowd of people but didn't see a woman wearing a red scarf. There were a few people with umbrellas up, blocking my view. I would have to walk, er…hobble around to get a better look.

The little clock on my HUD changed to 4:00.00 p.m. I kept scanning and saw an umbrella close which was odd as the rain was beginning to sprinkle down. More umbrellas were being popped open than closed. I looked over and spied a very tall woman with brunette hair and glasses, nervously wrapping up the umbrella.

Around her neck was a vibrant red scarf that trailed down to her slim waist.

Here we go.

I hobbled up to the tall woman in the scarf until I stood next to her.

She was wearing a black raincoat, tightly belted around her slim figure, a pair of faded jeans that hugged her calves, and a sturdy pair of Doc Martens. Chuckie hadn't told me anything about her beyond the fact she was a woman and would be wearing a red scarf. I didn't know her age or nationality, but if she was from Houston, either Caucasian or Hispanic was a safe bet. If real Daphne and Chuckie were of an age, Daphne would have been in her mid-forties. This woman, however, barely looked thirty.

Way to go, real Daphne.

It crossed my mind that she could just be any woman with a red scarf, but I was willing to bet this was Emma Burr.

She was peering around quietly. Anyone passing by would think she was just waiting for a friend or a child, like the other two dozen adults standing around. Signs of anxiety showed though— her knuckles were white on the grip of her umbrella handle, and despite the chill, there was a bead of sweat on her brow.

I mentally gave Daphne the enhance command we had set in her defaults, and my hearing sharpened to an unnatural degree. The woman's heart was racing. *One hundred twenty-five bpm,* Daphne quietly added. It sounded like a furious drumbeat in my ears, keeping rhythm with the roar of her blood in her veins and the pump and vacuum of her heart valves. I hadn't had the chance to experiment with the hearing function up to now, and I was astounded at the quality and then felt vaguely guilty.... It was like I was listening through a peephole. I had assured myself that this woman wasn't just some random woman waiting unless she was really nervous about whom she was going to meet. It had to be her.

I gave the reset command, and my hearing returned to normal.

Emma finally looked directly over at me with a grin of amusement at my costume and a flicker of hope in her eyes until her gaze dropped down to my missing leg. She gave the now-familiar, embarrassed smile and requisite eye-slide away as she continued her search.

I smiled at her as I murmured, "Daphne says to say hello. She's up and running...around."

Emma's head snapped back to me, her eyes open wide.

"Easy," I said gently.

She quickly looked down, gained her composure, and looked up at me again. It was my first good look at her. She was tall—almost six feet. She had long brown hair with straight bangs. She appeared slim but athletic; a slight breadth to her shoulder visible through her raincoat and a sweep to her calf made me guess that she was a swimmer. I could see a tie-died shirt peeking out from her raincoat and her eyes were wide-set and deep blue behind her black-rimmed glasses. Her nose was almost button-like, and her mouth had a wry turn to it.

"You're him?"

I nodded. "Chuckie sent me."

She blinked quickly as tears rose in her eyes. "It was on the news last night." A soft Texan accent in her voice sealed the deal, this was Emma Burr.

"I'm sorry. There are interested parties, and they don't care who gets in the way. We need to talk."

She nodded and grabbed my right hand in her left. "I have two tickets for the train; we can talk there. No one will hear us over the kids and train."

I nodded and walked with her toward the station. The rain began in earnest, changing from a light drizzle to steady drops. She took shorter steps to accommodate my fake hobble and asked awkwardly, "Was your accident before…Daphne?" Her soft accent matched Daphne's, but it didn't sound like Daphne.

I looked blankly at her for a moment while I was absorbing this. Realizing the import of her question, I shook my head as I chuckled. "There was no accident."

"But…" She appeared confused for a moment before she gasped and covered her mouth with her other hand. "Oh, you are shitting me! It works!" She paused and took her hand down, mouthing the word, *LightCam*.

I nodded.

Her wide-set eyes went wider as we gave our tickets over, went through the turnstile, and over to the long silver train that waited under the darkening tree line. She got in first, then helped me into the last car, and we moved to the back to sit in the corner of the last row.

We waited until the train was all loaded up with excited kids—some happy and some reluctant—plus parents and a few retirees. The conductor gave the word, and the train started off into the wet afternoon.

"I'm Emma Burr," she said as she reached out her hand, and I shook it.

"Al Leigh."

"Were you involved in the…" she looked around and then mimed a mini explosion with her hands.

I shook my head.

"I was sent in to retrieve Daphne. That was it. Someone else set me up to take the fall for all the mayhem and then left me for dead. But I had accidentally acquired a new friend."

The coal-black and purple afternoon sky lit up with a flash of lightning. Most of the children cheered and squealed, and a few cried at the rumble of thunder a few moments later. The rain beat down harder as the Zooliner wound through the zoo. The train seemed to be going slower than normal in the wet weather.

"What stage is she at?"

"Stage?"

"What color is the dragonfly?"

"Orange."

She nodded, pulled out her phone, and made furious calculations on an app.

"What's that mean?" I asked.

"She's not at full power," Emma answered distractedly.

"Is she going to shut down again?"

"Did you bring Chuckie's stuff?"

"Yes, why?"

"Disable her. Now."

Daphne, disable AV. The little dragonfly immediately dimmed to a faint orange. The small icon at the top-center remained, but now it was lit and pulsed a gentle green.

"Done."

Emma peered directly at me, her blue eyes intent.

"LSD acts as an inhibitor. The psychedelic confuses the nanos and inhibits their spread. You don't need a lot—we don't want you baked—but we do need to slow her down."

The train was just crossing over into the Great Northwest exhibit and the Family Farm. It was hard to see through the rain, and there were disappointed cries. There was sure to be more disappointment when we got to Elephant Lands because I wasn't sure the elephants would be out in this weather. The old Zooliner plugged along, definitely slower than the last time I rode her. I would have smiled, but Emma was throwing me for a loop.

"What happens if we don't slow her down?"

"Eventually, the nanos will replicate your nerve endings until they are no longer your nerve endings: they will be nanotechnology, functioning as your entire nervous system."

I shrugged a little. "They seem to be doing the job…. Is that so bad?"

Emma gave me a grim smile. "Your nervous system includes your brain. The replication of the brain has failed in almost every experiment we did. Brain tissue is too complex, and that was with small animal brains."

"Oh." Shit.

The train had crossed over into Elephant Lands, but little could be seen through the rain, and indeed, no elephants were out. More lightning flashed against the bruised clouds.

"We had one experiment where the LSD was able to slow it down, but it had…odd side effects."

I muttered, "Dog and monkey."

She looked startled but nodded and continued, "Every subject experiences the same sequence: disorientation, madness, and then death."

"How will I know when I'm close?"

"The dragonfly is an icon and a progress indicator. There are two more levels—violet and scarlet. Disorientation usually begins in the late orange to the early violet stage. By the time scarlet is reached, most subjects are acting completely irrational, even before eventual death."

I leaned back in my seat. The train swung back the other direction and crawled slowly back to the station. I thought for a moment.

"These things were supposed to be presented to a government or military panel at the end of the week. Is it possible that they overcame the problem since you, uh… left?"

She shook her head. "I still had friends on the program. The reason they were going to the government as they couldn't get past that little problem and needed the funding for more research. They were tapped out."

The station slowly got closer; the ride was almost over.

"Why did you leave Vegrandis?"

A spasm of anger, quick as the lightning, flashed across her features. "Daphne. Real Daphne. What happened to her…I don't believe it was an accident. They threw me under the bus, too, and said they fired me when I had already quit. I decided to lay low after that."

The Zooliner moved like molasses in the winter as it coasted into the roundhouse.

I tilted my hat back and leaned against the seat. "It may have saved your life."

There was a commotion near the station. Children and parents were swiftly escorted away from the exit.

Rut-roh.

Daphne, enable AV.

The dragonfly flared orange, although now I thought I saw a tinge of violet beginning around the edges. The little target threat eye-con in the corner above it immediately flared red.

I'm here, sugar.

Daphne, coms.

At the command, my hearing and vision snapped into high resolution. I flipped the eyepatch up to my forehead, freeing up both eyes. The rainclouds and low, late afternoon light meant Forward-Looking Infrared was automatically activated on the HUD, so there were multiple visible heat signatures. The FLIR showed the hunched forms of bodies glowing shades of red behind bushes and trees everywhere around the station. The squawk and hiss of commands through earpieces floated into my ear as though I was next to the person talking. Next to the biggest group of heat signatures was an unmistakably gawky, orange-red silhouette.

Micawber.

The train ground to a halt at the station, brakes hissing like a basket of angry snakes as forked branches of incandescent lightning split the blue-black sky.

THUNDERSTRUCK

Thunder boomed across the hillsides and swiftly faded into the distance as chattering children were bustled by their parents off the train and the whole lot shepherded out of the covered roundhouse by the last few visible zoo employees. I put my hand on Emma's, urging her to stay seated.

Daphne chose this moment to chime in.

Sugar, may I ask a question?

"Sure, why not?" I murmured.

My programming indicates that it is socially impolite to take this opportunity to say I told you so. Is that correct, sugar?

I looked over at Emma. "Your program is a smartass."

Emma gave a tight smile. She couldn't see the soldiers, but she could see how frightened zoo employees were as they pushed customers away from the station. "She learned it from watching you," she said nervously.

"Really?"

Emma nodded. "I programmed her to learn from her host. The things that she adopts in terms of language, expression, and actions are based on you."

I blinked. "You mean she's going to become me?"

"Kind of."

"I don't think the world's ready for two of me."

Emma had spotted some soldiers in the brush, and her eyes widened. "What do we do? What do we do?"

"We wait."

In moments, we were the only ones left on the train; the nearby square had emptied. The rain had eased up but had not stopped completely. It only took another minute or two before Micawber walked out from the tree line on his long, insect-like legs. He had on a black ball cap, and a rain jacket marked FEDERAL AGENT in large yellow letters on the back. He put his hands up as he walked toward the train, the rain dripping off the brim of his cap.

"Lieutenant Leigh—won't you come out to join us?" Each word was clipped and precise as always.

I smiled cheerily.

"Hey, Colonel. I'm gonna stick with Sun Tzu seven, eighteen on this one; besides, it looks nasty out there, and I don't want to mess up my new threads. Do you know how long it took me to find a purple buccaneer coat?"

Micawber cocked his head to the side, "Seven, eighteen: 'In raiding and plundering be like fire, in immovability like a mountain.' So, you will be holding your position."

"You got it."

"Then I will join you if you and your charming companion will allow. I would like a word."

I looked forward toward the wolf-painted engine. "I think the conductor high-tailed it. Understandable." I looked back at Micawber. "Probably saw all the guns," I said brightly. "We won't be going for a ride, so I guess you don't need a ticket. C'mon up."

Micawber walked a few paces forward before stopping and raising the forefinger of his left hand.

"I suppose I don't have to ask for assurances for my safety?"

I snorted. "I'm aware of the snipers targeting the two of us right now. I understand."

"Excellent. Always nice to work with a professional." He continued toward the train, his long legs stomping through the puddles and eating up the distance.

"Blow me," I muttered.

Emma leaned close to me and whispered, "Did you bring a gun?"

"To a zoo full of kids? Fuck, no," I hissed.

She looked worried. "What are we going to do?"

"Just stay close to me, no matter what. And stay quiet—this guy's a psycho."

Emma gave a worried groan. "Oh, shit, shit."

Micawber walked toward us under the covered roundhouse and down the rows of railroad cars. Even without stepping up onto the train, his freakishly tall head was higher than ours. He regarded my outfit with amusement, looking me up and down as I unwound the black scarf from my lower face and shaking his head as he came to the side of our car.

"Hey, don't knock it; you and the captain make it happen," I called out.

"I see your sense of humor is unchanged," he sighed, shaking his head some more until he saw my LightCam shrouded leg, and then his amusement dropped away. "Extraordinary," he whispered.

He looked up at me, meeting my gaze. His eyes were the color of arctic ice, a blue so pale they looked like a bottomless cenote, and they seemed to go all the way to the back of his head. I managed to keep my cool.

"Colonel."

He gave a sardonic tilt of his head.

"Twang."

Emma sat up straight and defiant next to me. "What kind of shit is that? He has a name. There is no need to be rude."

Micawber swung his head in Emma's direction but kept his polar eyes locked on me. "Rude would have been his assertation that I was a half-witted, cousin-humping, knuckle-dragging…" he paused.

"Useless bag-of-dicks," I filled in helpfully. "I never really got the chance to apologize for that, Colonel. I don't think you're half-witted."

Micawber shifted his gaze from me to Emma and showed his teeth in what he called a smile; anyone else who saw it would be calling the police.

"The lieutenant plays the guitar."

I murmured to Emma, "He's not being rude. It was my call sign. It…kinda was my name."

She immediately deflated with a meek, "Oh."

"Good job on the staying quiet thing, though."

Micawber returned his gaze to me. "I had thought you might start at the bottom of the list. To that end, we have been keeping an eye on Ms. Burr here all day."

I smiled as I stared into his vacant gaze and tried not to flinch. There was nothing sane going on behind those eyes. He could play the straight-shooter, the by-the-rules-tactical genius all day long: it was just a role. I'd seen behind his mask long ago, and he didn't bother wearing it now for Emma or me. That did not bode well for her.

He continued, "So, to the point…. You have something we want, but we would rather you came with us voluntarily and preferably in the vertical position."

I was mildly surprised by that, and it must have shown on my face.

"Ms. Burr didn't tell you?"

"Tell me what?"

Emma grimaced. "They need you alive. If you die or sustain an amount of damage that the EPU can't fix, they are stuck with the same-old, same-old: dead tech. They can't pull it out of you because it's bonded to you. It can't be transferred or grafted—it will die. We tried everything, and it always dies along with the host. If you die, it dies too, and all they can do is look at it under a microscope. All the other prototypes were destroyed in the explosion; they want a living, working sample and you're it—huh, Colonel?"

He nodded his head, causing more drops to fall from the brim of his hat. "What we don't need, however, is a disgruntled former employee." He looked at me. "Do you take my meaning?"

I nodded, "I come with you, or you kill her," I said matter-of-factly.

Emma's face went white. "Wait, what?"

Micawber gave his creepy smile once more.

"You have one minute. And, ah, no disappearing tricks. My snipers have infrared. You may be able to hide from that, but she can't."

He tipped his hat, turned around, and whistled as he walked away from the train. "Sixty seconds! Cut power!" he called out, twirling a forefinger around.

Immediately, the lights went out in the train, and the roundhouse and all power drained from the tiny consoles at the now darkened station. Prudent. Just in case I don't want to go quietly, deny the EPU any nearby source of juice. He seems to know a bit about how the EPU works. Where did he get his intel? How is Section involved in this?

"C'mon, we're going. I'm sorry I got you involved."

Emma looked startled. "We are? Shouldn't I stay here? I mean, I should stay here, right? He just wants you. He said you go with him, or I die."

"Nope, he's going to kill you no matter if I go or not. Can't afford to have any loose ends."

She looked around.

"You're giving up then? I mean, you have to," she babbled. "You didn't bring a gun, and there's no loose energy to grab! I did not get out of bed today expecting to hear about someone killing me no matter what I do!"

I wanted to agree with her, but that was exactly what I was expecting when I got out of bed this morning.

The storm had died down to a drizzle for the moment. The clouds still looked ready to dump more at some point, but at least for now, I wasn't going to get wet. I dropped the wooden crutch on the floor of the car and let the shroud of LightCam fall from my leg. Two booted legs appeared where there had been one. I got out of the car and held my hand out to help Emma down.

"I won't let anything happen to you." I was reminded of a similar promise I had made to Chuckie just the day before. It hadn't done him any good. I looked at Emma's terrified face, and I felt sorry for her. She had gotten involved in something over her head, and I could relate. I may not have been able to keep Chuckie safe, but this time—I was ready.

She sat frozen for a moment and then slowly scootched off the bench, took my hand, and stepped off the train.

"Stay close."

Emma said nothing but moved closer to me as we walked toward the center of the square in front of the station. For a few moments, the only noise was from my boot heels ringing on the pavement. A small gust of wind ripped the tricorn hat from my head and sent it spinning into the wet pine trees, leaving only the do-rag. I pulled off the eye patch and then tore the parrot off my shoulder, dropping it to the ground.

Emma looked down at it quizzically, and then at me.

"It's an ex-parrot," I deadpanned.

She looked blankly at me.

Not a Python fan. Huh…bit of a character defect. Oh, well, no one's perfect.

Maybe she was just a little shell-shocked from hearing that someone truly dangerous wanted her dead. I remember that being disconcerting once.

These days, however?

Take a number.

I hummed quietly under my breath, a holdover from my first days in combat. Whenever a mission was about to go down, I would find myself humming under my breath—whatever song I would hum was often a surprise to me. When operational security demanded it, my humming stopped, but music had always helped keep me calm in the eye of the storm. These days, I didn't even notice when it happened. Daphne did.

What's that song, sugar?

"'Came Back Haunted' by Nine Inch Nails," I murmured.

I like it.

We reached the center, and I stopped walking, pulling Emma close to my back. Slowly, heavily armed soldiers in black body armor stepped out from behind the tall trees, wet bushes, and buildings.

My humming got louder as I looked around. No civvies to be seen.

Sugar?

The ring of soldiers closed around us, rifles at the ready. I raised my hands into the air in a slow creep.

Al?

Micawber called out, "Twang—so good of you to leave your mountain. I was afraid I might have to launch my little fireworks show."

I turned to face him. "You know, Colonel, I wasn't completely honest about the whole Sun Tzu seven, eighteen thingy."

Two of the soldiers opened a heavy sack and pulled out chained shackles as they walked closer. The manacles at the ends of the chains were thick and wide and were made out of an odd silvery metal with glowing lights flashing on them. Something told me that they were EPU-proof. That wasn't good.

The wind whipped up, and the rain fell in large, heavy drops again.

"Oh?" Micawber asked.

"I have been thinking of seven, nineteen," I admitted.

Twang!!

I raised an eyebrow at that one but waited for the soldiers to get closer.

Micawber looked puzzled for a moment.

"Let your plans be dark and impenetrable as night, and when you move, fall like a thunderbolt," I recited.

Daphne, now!

Comprehension dawned on Micawber, but it was too late.

I spread my hands wide; the pent-up, stored kinetic energy—stolen during our ride on the Zooliner—punched out and away from us with a thunderclap, sending the circle of soldiers and Micawber flying backward through the air with wild screams of pain and terror, accompanied by an exploding, horizontal spray of rain.

RUNNIN WITH THE DEVIL

Hope for the best and plan for the worst. Chen-chen's favorite saying echoed through my head as I watched some two dozen bodies fly through the rain-filled air. I'd figured that Micawber might anticipate my moves and be on Emma's tail. He'd been my boss for over a decade; he was intimately familiar with how I thought.

What he wasn't familiar with were the full capabilities of the EPU. At least, I hoped he wasn't.

Daphne and I had worked out a plan to have energy available and on hand just in case. Energy could be stored in the Lens field, but not for long. We had already planned on taking the train to acquire the kinetic energy, but Emma had beat us to it.

The little green eye-con in the top-center of my home HUD was empty and flat again.

"Daphne, Combat Mode," I growled.

The combat HUD and high-res AV snapped into place. Daphne was no longer in charge during Combat Mode; I was driving. She would be the equivalent of my RIO. She would keep me apprised of incoming threats and deploy offensive and defensive measures at my command.

The now-familiar chill of LightCam settled over me. The chill was a result of the EPU automatically lowering the temperature of the air surrounding my body to assist in infrared evasion. I pulled Emma into my arms and put my back to where the HUD showed an active sniper who had escaped the kinetic blast.

To the sniper and anyone behind us, Emma and I had disappeared.

Unfortunately, that didn't conceal her from the front. The Lens field didn't extend that far, and she was plainly visible to the three black-clad soldiers rushing toward us.

Daphne, low frequency.

Not enough ambient noise to be fully effective, sugar.

Daphne, do it.

The sounds of the rain, the wind in the trees, and the cries of frightened and injured soldiers all faded out to a far-off whisper as I extended my left hand and released the sonic wave at the oncoming soldiers. They stumbled in their tracks, the muzzles of their HK416s dropping downward, which was all I needed. I spun Emma onto the grass behind the bushes and launched myself forward.

Between my enhanced reflexes and reinforced skeletal and muscular systems, not to mention being completely invisible, the first two attackers never had a chance and went down in moments. The third had dropped his rifle and tried his best to throw a punch at where he thought I was, only to have the field absorb the kinetic force of his lucky blow and immediately turn it back on him, shattering his hand.

The threat eye-con flared red on the HUD.

Incoming, sugar.

Everything around me was moving in slow-motion. The trajectory of the sniper's bullet appeared on the HUD. The tag 'Barret M82' hovered over the sniper location. That thing was a cannon with a range of about 900 yards before it lost accuracy. The bullet just kept going until it hit something solid enough to stop it. HUD data said I was half that distance away from the sniper location. Whether or not the sniper had been able to pick me up on his scope, or he was just hoping for a lucky shot, that bullet had to be stopped—or its progress at least minimized—before it left the area and hit an innocent bystander.

The third soldier was still registering that his hand was broken, grabbing his wrist in shock with his other hand as raindrops seemed to fall an inch at a time around us. I whirled behind him, grabbing his body armor by the shoulder straps, as I swung his body into the oncoming bullet. His body ripped backward out of my hands as the .50 caliber bullet shredded his Kevlar armor like tissue paper and punched through his center mass.

There was no report to the rifle shot; everything was muted as the Lens field absorbed any ambient noise.

The sniper has Emma targeted.

I extended my right hand, and Daphne hurled the sonic pulse, stolen from the sound of the rifle report, straight to the head of the sniper. The sniper's red target light extinguished as the pulse ruptured his brain.

All of this had played out in less than five seconds.

The soldiers not taken out by the kinetic blast were getting to their feet. I reached down, pulled the nearly six-foot, Emma, up like a rag doll, threw her over my shoulder, and ran.

"I don't need this caveman shit! I can run myself…!" she cried, but her voice trailed off as we picked up speed and hauled ass toward the zoo entrance.

The Six Million Dollar Man had shit on me.

"Oh, my gooooodddd!" Emma screamed as we passed the sea otters and harbor seals in the Pacific Shores exhibit in seconds. Passersby screamed as they saw what looked like a woman flying backward in mid-air.

One little tyke cried out as we passed, "The witch lost her broom!"

I sprinted around the path and was coming through the Great Northwest exhibit when I saw them: six black-armored soldiers blocking our way. The three in front were on their knees, and the other three were standing behind them.

All of their rifles were raised and ready to fire.

I spared a glance over my shoulder…there were civvies everywhere. Any stray ricochet from the Lens field or a round that went downrange past me was begging for collateral damage. The soldiers didn't care. I could hear the muttered command to fire with my EPU-enhanced hearing.

Twang!

There was no time for words as Daphne flashed her idea across my mind. I knew I wasn't capable, and there was no time for anything else, so I mentally handed the reins to her. Immediately, our body responded faster than I was able to control alone. What had seemed like slow motion when I was in control became stop-motion as Daphne took charge.

Time stretched like taffy.

I/Daphne's enhanced vision saw the individual fingers whiten as they tightened on triggers while we put on the brakes, spun Emma off our shoulder, and put her on the ground in front of us. We continued to pivot, covering Emma with our body and turning our backs to the bullets that were now halfway to us. I/Daphne performed the required calculations in a fraction of a millisecond, adjusting the various angles of the Lens as needed.

The field shifted as the velocity of the bullets was redirected, and the missives unerringly propelled back along their original trajectories at the precise angles necessary.

I/Daphne looked back over our shoulder.

Time snapped back to the normal rate.

All six soldiers dropped simultaneously as a bullet slammed through the faceguards of their tactical helmets.

Holy. Balls.

I'm in charge, right?

Emma pushed away from us, her whole body shaking in terror as she patted her body, looking for leaks. She spun around and saw the six collapsed bodies and the blood drained from her face.

Daphne returned the reins to me and took up her mental RIO position again.

There were panicked screams as people fled the mayhem, flooding toward us as they headed for the exit gates. One look at the bodies on the ground, and the crowd parted around us like a river around a stone. Lightning broke across the blackened sky, giving the fleeing masses an apocalyptic look.

Emma swayed on her feet; she didn't look like she would make it.

Sugar, they're coming.

Red target dots on the HUD were swarming down the path from the direction of the Zooliner. For the moment, they were all behind the full-fledged riot of people fleeing the zoo. I shed the purple coat and white dress shirt, exposing the black Kings of the Road shirt I'd worn under them. As each article of clothing left my body and the surrounding Lens field, they popped back into sight in midair and then fell to the ground. I easily ripped the pantaloons off, leaving a currently invisible pair of black jeans underneath. As they mostly matched the remaining ensemble, the knee-high black boots stayed.

At least I wouldn't look like a walking ad for a bottle of spiced rum anymore.

Daphne, disable LightCam.

The cold shroud of LightCam fell away.

I gently grabbed a stunned-looking Emma by the shoulders. "Emma, we need to go with the crowd—now! They are our cover. Move!"

She shook herself and nodded. Pausing for a moment, she reached over, pulled the do-rag off my head, dropped it, then grabbed my hand. Oops.

We went from a walk to a full run in a few paces, with Emma giving the half-dozen bodies and the growing dark puddle surrounding them a wide berth.

I snuck a peek down at the shattered faceplates on the piled corpses.

Daphne, outstanding shooting, Tex. You're a regular fuckin' Annie Oakley.

A very self-satisfied feeling washed over me. Daphne was preening after the compliment. Not sentient? She was either damn close or one hell of a good imitation.

I thought back to how less than thirty-six hours before, I had been agonizing over having more deaths on my conscience. Here I was now, sharing mental high-fives over the deaths of at least ten men in as many minutes.

Fuck them. This was combat, but that didn't excuse those assholes going weapons hot with a huge crowd of civvies just downrange.

Emma and I dodged and weaved between clusters of parents hurrying their crying children and older retirees who simply stood still in the walkway, clinging to one another.

A warm, fuzzy pride still radiated from Daphne.

Can I go back to being in control of Combat Mode?

"No," I muttered, still working through my own moral quandary.

Shit.

Suddenly, the warm fuzzies cut off.

I sputtered and nearly fell over as Emma pulled me past a bench and cut onto the lawn. There was no need to ask where Daphne learned that one.

Emma glanced over at me, and I shrugged as we ran. She had no trouble keeping up with the non-EPU-powered speeds; no need to draw undue attention. The crowd in front of us slowed and massed. There were shouts and curses, screams and prayers. It was pandemonium, and considering the events of the past few years, understandable. Everywhere, people were muttering 'active shooter.' There were even some seriously tech-addicted idiots taking the time to try and get a selfie to post on social media.

Darwinism in action.

The front gate, with its orange booths and bright green sign, had created a bottleneck, and the crowd fought to get through. I checked the HUD—a dozen or more red target dots were in the Great Northwest exhibit right behind us, but the bulk of the crowd remained between us and Micawber's Section squad.

A loud, clanging crash rang out above the noise of the crowd as the metal gates to either side of the entry booths gave way, and the frantic throng spilled out into the parking lot. We got through the bottleneck, and I pulled Emma behind me as we ran to the right, toward the elevator for the Washington Park MAX Light Rail station.

Sweat was pouring freely down Emma's face, but she showed no signs of slowing down. "We really have time to wait for the train?" she asked between deep breaths of air.

To the far left, near the exit that led to Highway 26, black SUVs with flashing lights blocked the driveway. The crowd thinned out as almost everyone headed into the parking lot to their cars. The lights were off at the covered elevator down to the underground station in Robertson Tunnel. I was betting that Micawber's group had shut down the train. Sirens wailed as Portland PD rushed to the scene. Knowing Micawber, he'd John-Wayned it. He had more than likely bullied the zoo staff using his federal credentials and hadn't bothered to alert the local police detachment, thinking he could do it all without help.

We crossed the crosswalk, went past the stone pillars of the covered elevator to the subterranean tunnel, and finally slowed down a bit. I let go of Emma's hand, then ducked across the way into the nearby bushes.

Emma bent over with her hands on her knees and wheezed, "What…are…you doing?" I found what I was looking for and wheeled them out. On the way in, I had stashed a couple of beach cruisers from the rental shop here, just in case. They weren't the modified bikes that the kids used on the trails, but they would have to do.

Hope for the best, and plan for the worst.

"Regulators, mount up," I grinned.

HIGHWAY TO HELL

"Three, two, one…Zoobomb!" I muttered a few moments later as we set off from the elevator. We pedaled down the sidewalk away from the zoo with the parking lot and its contingent of black SUVs on our left. The rain slowed to a drizzle again as we pushed past the old locomotive displayed on the right near the entrance. We picked up speed as we left the path and dropped onto the street past the driveway. I had warned Emma what we were about to do and asked, "How are your nerves?"

Running had let her dump off some of the adrenaline from her fight-or-flight response, and she seemed a bit calmer, but still somewhat wild-eyed.

"Not great…. I saw this on the news. Which route are we taking?"

"Hellway."

She gulped and nodded.

"Just stay as close to me as you can."

There were several Zoobomb routes down the hill to the base of Washington Park, each with its unique nickname. Hitoshi was hardcore and ran with the big dogs (on the small bikes) on the more technically difficult K2. I'd done Hellway one time, trying it because it was faster, and that was more my thing.

It just wasn't safer.

Unfortunately, also my thing.

Pedaling got easier, and we went faster as we left the zoo lot and plaza behind us and hit the start of the downhill. The road twisted through a forested corridor lit with isolated cones of occasional streetlights that reflected in the wet air. The exodus from the zoo hadn't started, thanks to Section blocking off the main driveway, and we had the Zoo Road to ourselves on the way out. Only a few cars were coming up the hill toward the zoo.

The beach cruisers weren't the swiftest choice. True Zoobombers believed the smaller the wheel, the faster the ride. 12" was considered choice, basically the size of tire a toddler would need. The less…dedicated but still hardcore would allow 16" and 20" wheels. Some straight-up BMX bikes would have been my first choice for tonight, but I hadn't been able to afford to go sticking my head out into every rental shop in Portland to get the right ride. The cruisers were what was there, and they would do.

The wind whipped past our ears, and the cold air chilled my skin. I loved the downhill: it reminded me of my youth, racing my foster siblings and cousins on our bikes down California Street from the top of Nob Hill; the first one past St. Mary's on the corner of Grant Avenue wins. Daphne had enhanced our visual acuity to what looked to me to be almost broad daylight. Between that and the radar on my HUD, it almost made the ride boring.

Almost.

I viewed and heard them on the HUD long before I saw them.

The distant roar I had heard became a line of police cars—lights flashing and sirens wailing—as they whipped off the freeway off-ramp and headed up the hill past us to the zoo. I poured on a little extra speed, and we crossed the overpass and swung left, and gained even more speed (30 mph according to the HUD) for our bomb as the road tilted even further downward.

Onto the highway.

Portland is a very bike-friendly town, and it is legal to ride your bike in the designated lane on the freeway—it's just not for the faint of heart. Part of what made the "Hellway" so nerve-wracking was how close you had to ride to cars whipping past you at 50 mph or more. Highway sodium lights illuminated the mass of trees that towered on either side of the wet freeway. Traffic on the opposite side of the highway, leaving Portland, was backed up with evening commuters, and even more emergency vehicles were fighting their way through to the zoo off-ramp.

I didn't see any sign of pursuit on the HUD and Emma was staying close on my tail. The rain dumped down again, and the rumble of thunder echoed in the narrow confines of the highway where it cut through the hills. As the rain drenched us both, I muttered a saying from the Corps, "If it ain't raining, we ain't training."

Waves of cold water splashed at us repeatedly as cars whipped past on our left, as the concrete guard wall on our right got closer and closer. I had to moderate my enhanced speed to ensure I didn't get too far ahead of Emma. The grade dropped further, and we gained a little more speed as we curved away to the right down the hill to the tunnel and the Goose Hollow exit.

Goose Hollow was a tiny suburb southwest of the city and had earned its moniker from the earliest residents who used to let their geese run wild in the area. The twenty-block-long hollow had been formed by a creek that used to run through the area before being redirected underground. Now, a quaint neighborhood sat in the small canyon. After the long ride down the hills and then the descent through the tunnel, you almost felt as though you were in a kind of forested underworld that somehow existed below the rest of Portland.

The road was divided here with a low concrete barrier between the two sides. We passed underneath the green metal train bridge far above and headed toward the Goose Hollow MAX Light Rail station near where I had left the Tahoe.

Emma was right behind me, her hair and clothing soaked but still breathing and pedaling furiously.

We were free and clear.

The road got dark, and I looked around. All the lights were out in the buildings; the streetlights were down too. My hackles rose.

Sugar, proximity alert!

Fuck.

The threat radar lit up as dozens of red dots appeared out of nowhere ahead of us. Bullshit! There was never anyone behind us! Where did they come from? How did they get in front of us?

Lightning flashed and was followed in seconds by a tremendous boom that echoed in the hollow and shook the blackened buildings around us.

I slid the bike sideways as I braked hard. Men poured onto the street from the direction of the rail station. The train was waiting at the station with open doors as cops and black-jacketed federal agents poured out of the cars, running our way.

One scarecrow-like figure had to dip its head as it exited the train.

Micawber.

Sirens wailed, and within seconds, police cars came screaming off the freeway and out of the tunnel. In another few moments, they had blocked the street behind us.

The power was suddenly cut off at the train station, and the entire street went dark, lit only by the headlights and flashing lights of the police cars. The darkened buildings stuck up like a mouthful of jagged teeth at the bottom of the stygian chasm.

Emma had pulled up next to me. I dropped my bike to the ground, and she did the same.

She moved behind me as Micawber strode arrogantly through the line of LEOs who faced us with guns drawn. Behind us, the police were mounting their barricade, weapons were being cocked, and quiet orders given.

Micawber clapped his hands together slowly in exaggerated applause.

"Well played, Twang. But checkmate."

I stood there in the rain and seethed.

"You were always such the fanboy of Sun Tzu. How's this? 'When you surround an army, leave an outlet free.' You are a one-man army, Twang. There were far too many civilians at the zoo; I couldn't risk you indiscriminately unleashing that wondrous machinery inside you if you thought there was no way out."

I looked around. We were all bottled up. There wasn't a civilian to be seen…just armed LEOs.

Micawber laughed. "I applied just enough pressure to make it look legitimate, and you took the one way out I offered you. After that, it was just a matter of 'let your rapidity be that of the wind.'" He gestured behind him to the train.

Thunder echoed in the darkness.

No, I'm not losing to this cocksucker, not again. My fists clenched, and I set my feet as I embraced the warm rush of anger.

Sugar, no.

Micawber signaled, and again a pair of soldiers brought out the strangely lit, manacled chains. Micawber squinted at me as he saw my stance change. "Go ahead, breathe wrong. See what happens. The woman won't survive, and I'll take you as a dead threat over a living problem. The EPU has never been bonded to a human being before…. Who knows what wonders we'll discover in your corpse?"

The wind whipped through the narrow hollow. The sharp tang of ozone wafted in the air; the dance of electrons in the sky reflected in the Lens. The charge built in the atmosphere, and I focused the field the way Daphne had shown me on the boat.

"Emma, stay close to me and close your eyes. Don't open them, no matter what," I whispered.

TWANG, NO! We cannot safely redirect that much....

The charge broke across the heavens.

The lightning was pulled down from the sky by the Lens, then refocused as it exploded around me. A light as bright as the sun beamed out of me, blinding every man looking in my direction. Daphne dropped a filter over the HUD, protecting us. I raised my right hand and redirected lightning exploded from my fingertips toward Micawber and his army of soldiers, cops, and Feds.

The entire lot of them hurled back into the darkness. The smell of charred flesh filled the air, but their screams were lost to the Lens.

Al!

Then, there was a…glitch. My entire body shook, and I fell to one knee. The blinding heavenly light blinked out, and darkness slammed back on top of me.

I turned my upper body around toward the barricade of police cars behind us.

Emma was behind me, screaming something, but it was being sucked into the field.

I raised both hands and brought them together in a single clap. The sonic boom exploded out of us, shattering windows, lifting men into the air, shoving vehicles across the road and away from the force.

Al, Al, Al...

I collapsed onto my hands and knees. I felt so weak.

I will *not* lose to him!

I pulled all the heat I could find, from the engines of the cars, the residual thermal heat in the pavement, and the bodies strewn across the ground. Ice and frost covered everything in moments; An injured cop tried to stand before he turned into a frosty statue.

I hurled the fireball at the last place I had seen Micawber, the station going up in flames, as I crumpled to the ground. The HUD had fallen from my eyes, and static broke across my vision. The dragonfly eye-con had gone to pulsing violet.

Emma appeared in my eyesight; she was screaming something at me over and over again. It was two words, but I couldn't make them out...

Twang,   system   failu...facial   recognition,   reboot system...ALALALALALAL...help...dangerwrong...Emma.

Emma shook me and screamed as tears streamed down her cheeks, mixing with the rain. Static again clouded my vision. Emma disappeared, and Micawber's leering face formed out of the chaos, his eyes nothing but burned sockets. Unlike Emma, he laughed madly as thick fluids—not tears—poured from his ruined eyes and ran down his cheeks.

Sugar...

The static disappeared, and Micawber's laughter followed me into the darkness.

END OF THE WORLD AS WE KNOW IT

There was wet asphalt under my cheek, glacial and rough against my skin. The rain fell in a wintry sheet everywhere. My head throbbed powerfully, so I opened my eyes. Why not look? It could only get worse, right? There was nothing to see. Nada: total darkness. It was…what was it? My head spun. What was that old radio program of nightly music that used to play on the local radio up here? Akihiro would stream music from its online archives into the restaurant.

Oh, yeah. It was *Lights Out.*

Had I gone blind? I sure as hell wasn't dead—my head wouldn't hurt this much.

Focus!

My eyes were indeed open, but there was little to no ambient light. There was no illumination from my HUD, and I couldn't see the dragonfly eye-con.

Daphne? Daphne, report. Systems check.

I waited, but I may as well have been talking to myself. There was no response. Daphne was down.

I felt alone and remembered feeling exactly this way before.

Suddenly, hands gripped my shoulders, and I knew there would be a voice from far away.

From far away, a voice called my name.

The sense of déjà vu was so powerful, that I was rocked. I had never felt such an intense variant of that particular anomaly. Maybe it was some sort of lag between sensing the nerve stimulation and understanding it? If so, the EPU was fucked too. I wasn't surprised; my head pounded like it had been kicked by the Hulk.

The hands pulled me to a sitting position, and real-time caught up with brain time. It was Emma.

"Al, can you hear me?"

I nodded slowly.

"We need to leave, now. Where's the car?"

She helped me up, and the world spun crazily. I was either righteously hungry, or I wanted to throw up—I couldn't tell which.

Once the world had steadied to a seesaw motion, which just made me lean toward the throwing up option, the damage around us came into focus. There was not a moving soul anywhere in the drizzle-filled darkness. The station was a smoldering wreckage. I turned toward the ruined buildings, overturned police cars with flickering lights, and still figures in uniforms on the ground.

Oh, fuck. What had I done?

"Al, we have to go—now!"

I nodded woozily and pointed down a nearby street.

Everything else was like a scene captured in a camera flash after that.

Flash.

I found myself in the passenger seat of Captain Bob's Tahoe, and Emma was starting the truck.

Flash.

Emma sobbing as she maneuvered the old SUV through the wreckage on the street. Wet crunching noises spattered and crackled under the car as we drove, and from far off, the distant wail of sirens pierced the night.

Flash.

Crossing the Marquam Bridge on the I-5 with downtown Portland lit up off to our right.

Flash.

Historic Multnomah Highway; passing the turnoff for McMenamins on our left.

Flash.

A wooden beamed ceiling in a chilled room, my breath smoking before my eyes as a disheveled, hollow-eyed Emma tucked the blankets around my body.

Daphne? System?

No answer.

Just darkness and silence.

If I dreamt, I don't remember my dreams. One moment there was darkness; the next, I was awake. I was in the wooden-beamed room I'd seen earlier. Green-tinged grey light came through a nearby curtain on the left wall.

Cloudy sunlight through trees.

The light had a soft, almost dream-like quality after the non-stop HUD views and fireworks of the previous…day? Week? The air was cool and crisp, not as frosty as when I arrived.

It all seemed so familiar.

Maybe because you saw it before you passed out, I told myself.

It was more than that, though…it was like a familiar song long unheard, whose forgotten title hovers on the edge of your tongue, waiting to be spoken.

I was still pretty sure I had never been here before.

I peered around the room, but it was fairly spartan. A nightstand with a small lamp and a full glass of water was on my right. A stack of granola bars, jerky, and trail mix sat next to the water. A chair with my clothes draped over it was in a corner, behind the wooden door that led out of the room. There was the bed, me, and that was it.

As no one was banging down the door, no tear gas was flying through the window, and I didn't hear any screams of panic, I took a chance and assumed that, for the moment, I was safe.

I immediately shifted my focus to the dragonfly eye-con. It was still there, but it was devoid of color, completely dark. I was partly relieved it was still there and, well, partly not. For a moment, back at the station, I thought maybe the lightning had burned the EPU out of me, and I was free.

Was it an upgrade, or was it damaged from the power surge? Unclear.

Had I fried Daphne? I experienced a wave of guilt that I was sure was all me. I tried to shake it off. Daphne wasn't even alive. She… It…damnit. It…was a program.

Still, I kinda hoped it was just an upgrade.

Just kinda, you understand.

I sat up and took my usual exploratory sniff of my surroundings, but it was flat, stale—like no one had been here in a long while.

My stomach took that moment to inform me that self-cannibalization was imminent. I wolfed down the bars, jerky, and trail mix in minutes. I knocked back the water, wishing for coffee. The edge of my hunger mildly blunted; I tossed back the covers and sat up. Everything seemed to be moving normally. I performed a quick back-knuckle, and my fist was a blur. The structural enhancements still seemed to be functioning.

I got out of bed. The cold wooden floor creaked under my feet. I looked down to see that I was buck naked and unmarked as near as I could tell. Was the EPU still doing its thing?

I tried to focus on the Lens, but without Daphne to act as the interface, I was grasping at air. I looked at the clothes on the chair: they were mine, and they were clean. I looked to my left and saw both my duffels at the foot of the bed.

I got dressed. My grey, heavy wool sweater had been laid out, and even though I didn't feel the cold, I put it on. I mean, I could tell it was cold, but it wasn't bothering me. Again, did that mean the EPU was still functioning?

It was possible it was in upgrade mode. The last time the dragonfly eye-con had been full and changed colors had been back in the hospital right before it shut down—last night, or whenever, it had gone from full-orange to full-violet.

It had flashed a warning last time.

I thought of the glitchy static that had blown up across the HUD, and preceded Daphne's shutdown and my unconsciousness. That hadn't seemed like an orderly shutdown. It had looked and felt like a major malfunction—like she'd had her plug pulled.

I gazed at the dark eye-con.

She had warned me not to try and use the Lens on the lightning strike.

I had no other choice.

You could have let her retain control of the combat mode; she handled it pretty well back in the zoo.

What choice could she have made that I didn't?

You won't know now, will you? Maybe she could have found a way out without trashing the Hollow and toasting who knows how many dozens of cops. Think you hated yourself for what you did in Section? You just notched more kills in a few minutes there than your whole life put together. And those weren't black hats.

Those were cops.

You just put a mark on your head that will never go away.

Daphne might have been able to pull off a cleaner escape. She had access to more data, and she understood the capabilities of the EPU far better than you. That was until you decided to go all Captain Kirk to her Commander Decker.

I doubt the phasers being routed through the warp drive was the problem...

Oh, shut the fuck up.

Great, I was arguing with myself.

I had kind of gotten into the habit with Daphne; only, I couldn't tell myself to disable my AV to end this argument.

Okay, assuming she is in either reboot or upgrade and not just Kentucky-fried code, her last upgrade had taken twelve hours. I looked at the light outside the window. It looked like late afternoon. Twelve hours was long past.

Maybe she would be okay.

She was fine, I hoped. I remembered my rage at her taking over my body the first time in Combat Mode at Chuckie's, and I felt guilty about my reaction. Daphne was executing her program and keeping us alive; she knew more about how to handle that situation than I did.

She was doing what she was supposed to be doing, what I asked her to do.... I was the one who wigged out about it when things got super freaky and forgot our safe word. I mean, understandably. But I don't think it was done out of callousness or disregard for my feelings. She just didn't understand.

I hoped she wasn't offline.

However, if she was offline, did that mean the EPU was still active? Or was it all a bunch of dead tech floating around inside me? Maybe she was just frozen? The word frozen conjured up the image of the cop I turned into a popsicle back in the Hollow.

I shuddered.

What was I? What had I become? This tech should have never been inside someone like me—fits of rage and semi-omnipotence don't go together. Heck, lots of Greek mythology on that one. Whatever Daphne and I had become, we were the first. More than likely, not the last. Someone would recreate this. Now that they knew it could be done, it was only a matter of time before this human/nano hybrid became…. what?

The dominant species on the planet is what. And who would get access to it? The ones who can afford it. I thought about what it could do for kids like Jeni—for any kid who has to suffer—what it would mean to their parents, who wouldn't have to outlive their children and spend the rest of their lives in grief.

Imagine living free from disease, injury, old age, maybe even death? I thought about that, really thought about that for a second, and it scared me because without consequence, what is our life? The brevity of our lives and the knowledge of its end is what brings meaning to them.

I wished I could talk to Daphne about this. I wasn't sure what we were together, and if she was permanently offline, I didn't know what I was now without her. Was I back to normal, whatever that was? There was one thing I would be for sure: alone with my thoughts.

The ghost in the machine had gone silent.

For some reason, that made me sad, and I sighed.

If nothing happened in the next three or four hours, I would reassess.

Of course, I could also stop putting off the inevitable and go out to talk to the lady who might have some answers.

I looked up at the closed wooden door.

I remembered her shaking me and screaming at me. It hadn't looked like a 'Hey, we just won the lottery!' kind of scream.

She had looked terrified out of her mind.

I tried to recall what she had screamed at me, but I drew a blank. Perhaps the Lens field had stolen it, or maybe my ears had been unprotected during the sonic clap and had sustained damage that the nanos had since repaired? I tried to recall what her mouth had said, the words it had formed. All I could remember was that there were two words, but that was it.

Probably 'stop' and 'asshole.'

I was stalling.

Maybe I should stop worrying about the digital lady who either will or won't be better on her own. Not much I could do for her. There was a real one out there who could, at the very least, need the empathy of another human being…someone to see if she was all right. Probably also a good 'thank you' for getting us out of there and an apology from me. Last night wasn't about keeping her safe. I doubt she walked into that meeting expecting it to end in a scene from an abattoir.

What had Milton said? "Awake, arise or be forever fall'n."

I sighed again, stood, and opened the door.

IT SERVES YOU RIGHT TO SUFFER

It opened to a long, low room, all paneled in seasoned pine. Woodsmoke mingled with the smell of eggs and pancakes drifted through the air. There were a couple of upholstered chairs in front of a black, pot-bellied wood furnace that was currently ablaze and sent out waves of heat. There was a small grey couch covered with a light green blanket against one wall. A large, curtained bay window was behind the couch, and a small dining table sat on the opposite side of the room. I had time to notice a small pair of antlers hanging above the furnace and the beginnings of what smelled like coffee when…I ducked.

There was no warning; it wasn't the HUD or my enhanced reflexes sensing it coming.

I knew it was coming, so I ducked.

The plate exploded against the wall behind me.

I reflexively batted away the second one to the floor at my feet before I put both hands at my sides and just let the missiles come. The next one went wide and just missed the window by inches, shattering against the wall. I squinted my eyes against the one sure to be coming next.

Emma had been putting plates on the table when she decided to use me for target practice. She looked drawn, and there were dark circles under her red-rimmed, blue eyes. She had cleaned up and was in a pair of faded grey sweats from my duffel—the ones with the Globe and Anchor on them.

She had gone to the trouble of finding and putting together a meal and was seemingly trying to be civilized when the sight of my face made her change her stance on that. She stood there, arm cocked back, white dinner plate in hand, and shaking with rage.

So much for needing my empathy.

I opened one eye all the way.

"Go ahead, get it out of your system. I'm an unconscionable, selfish asshole. Do it. I won't stop you or block them. I deserve it. Hell, I'll get you more plates if you need them."

She stood poised and ready to throw before her arm dropped to her side with an angry, muttered, "Jerk." She put the plate on the table and stomped back into the kitchen.

I opened both eyes.

"I'll get the broom," I offered.

There was no response from the kitchen.

I spent the next few minutes cleaning up the shattered plates while Emma put fresh plates and piles of food on the table.

After I put the detritus in a bag and brought it to the kitchen, Emma pointed to a corner with another trash bag in it. I finally got a look outside a window above the sink. Towering stands of bigleaf maple, western red cedar, and several varieties of pine took up the view as heavy, blue-black clouds swirled above. There were already wide clumps of snow scattered across the forest floor and coating the branches of trees. Off in the woods, farther than I used to be able to throw a rock pre-EPU, there was a cabin that looked empty. Behind in the distance, I spied a familiar peak.

We were on Mount Hood.

Judging by the angle of the peak, unless I missed my guess, we were only a couple miles from Trillium Lake and not too far from the tiny town of Government Camp.

"It's powdered eggs, instant pancakes, and instant coffee. It was in a bin under the table along with the snacks I put in your room,"

Emma said, sounding short with me as she pointed to a tiny breakfast nook.

She answered my unspoken question.

"It was Daphne's grandmother's place. She inherited it from her when she died. She only came up here a few times after her granny died, said it was too painful. We came up here to go skiing once, and she pointed it out as we drove past, but she wouldn't go in." She shuffled her feet awkwardly. "I knew where the key was. It was the only place I could think of. If they had been watching me, it wasn't safe to go home, right?"

I came over to the counter, grabbed a mug of hot coffee with one hand, and picked up the platter of pancakes with the other, "You did great. I don't think we should stay for too long, but this will work for now. Thank you…for everything. You saved my bacon."

Emma grumbled, "Don't say bacon. I'd kill for some bacon. Well, not kill…. You know what? Let's just eat."

We sat down to eat in silence. Instant or not, I tried to savor every bite. I didn't want to complain, but the food seemed mostly tasteless and almost sawdusty. I didn't say shit. Instead, I put more butter-flavored syrup over everything and then had seconds and thirds, followed by several cups of instant coffee.

I gazed around the room: there were photos of an older woman in shorts, obviously taken at various locales on the mountain. She was a short woman with curly grey hair and a sunny smile. There she was snowshoeing in the woods in a tiny photo with huge flakes of snow falling around her, eating BBQ over at the Skyway Bar and Grill, and sitting in the background while a live band played in another. In several, she was accompanied by a petite young woman with long, curly black hair and hazel eyes.

After brunch (or was it linner?) I had finished cleaning the plates and was looking at a large, wood-framed photo on the kitchen wall with both women in it. They sat in a boat with their arms around each other, jointly holding up a rainbow trout with Trillium Lake sparkling around them. Behind them in the photo, there was a circle of rhododendrons and the peak of Mount Hood poking up. Both women sported matching smiles.

"That's Daphne?"

Emma came over and nodded. "Yeah," she said softly.

"She looks like a happy lady."

"She was."

We both stared at the two women in the photo, one young, one old—both so happy and vibrant. And now both very dead. I thought of what coming here must feel like for Emma; it couldn't be easy.

"I'm sorry," I said, "not just for that…for everything. I should have handled things differently. I was desperate."

Almost my height, Emma matched my gaze. She looked tired; I was guessing sleep had been hard to come by. "You should be. We need to talk." She gestured to the chairs by the pot-bellied furnace.

I followed her tall frame, still wearing my sweats, to the chairs and sat opposite. She reached into the pocket of the sweatpants and pulled out the foil bag that Chuckie had given me. I remembered that the acid had been in my jacket pocket next to Mrs. T.'s note. That meant the coat and my guns must be around here somewhere.

"You need to start taking these."

I glanced down skeptically at the foil bag full of 'What's up, Dick?'.

"What? Take two of those and call you from Dimension Five on the flower phone in the morning?"

She shook her head at me, went to the kitchen, and came back with a pair of scissors and a coffee saucer. She returned to her chair, opened up the bag, retrieved a Bugs Bunny-marked white tab, and cut it into quarters above the saucer. "I'm guessing that you weigh close to 200 lbs."

Wow, almost spot on. I crossed my arms over my chest.

"I'm not doing drugs. I watched my mother die of alcoholism, my brother is a junkie doing time in prison for turning other people into junkies, and my niece is fighting for her life because of her mother's addiction. I already have my chosen vices." I held up a fist and counted off three fingers. "Adrenaline, endorphins, and caffeine, and that's plenty, thank you." I waggled my three fingers at her.

She ignored me, putting one of the slivers of acid on the pad of her finger and holding it out to me.

"Why?" I asked.

"I told you: the psychedelic slows down the expansion of the EPU. It will buy you time."

I shrugged. "Time for what?"

She pushed her finger at me. "To stay alive; to not end like all the other recipients of the EPU."

"Why delay it? Seriously, it's not like there's a cure, right?"

She sat back in her chair, confused.

"You're giving up? For real this time?"

"Right now, I'm thinking this thing is too dangerous for anyone to possess. Maybe I should just let it run its course. Find a quiet spot, and let come what may. Even if I don't, every cop in the PNW will be on the lookout for me, ready to give any assistance I might need in the shuffling off the whole mortal coil business." I looked at the darkened dragonfly sitting inert at the bottom of my vision. "Besides, I'm not even sure I need it."

"Of course you need it," she snapped.

I told her what had happened after the lightning strike went wrong. The glitch, Daphne's garbled mess, and the static before the shutdown.

I left out the horror show I thought I saw afterward.

"I'm not an engineer—I just led the programming team, so I don't know. The average upgrade time was twelve hours. Anything more than that, you would need to talk to the engineers, and they're all dead...." Emma trailed off.

I watched the crackle of the flames behind the heavy glass of the furnace. The dance and flicker of the flames were hypnotic. Next to the furnace was a hopper full of old split logs that all looked dry as paper. There was a small pile of more recent fallen branches in a plastic bucket that Emma must have brought in from outside to use as kindling.

Seeing the baggie reminded me of Chuckie. I remembered his comment about how all matter was just energy vibrating at different speeds. My brief time with the EPU had made me more aware of energy and its sources. I observed the fire and thought briefly about the thermal and light energy it produced. I remembered pulling the heat from everywhere I could in the Hollow and the fireball it had produced.

I was lucky it was October and not summer. There hadn't been enough dry fuel around, or I could have done even more serious damage.

Something itched at the back of my mind, something Emma had just said. A fallen branch in the furnace popped as a bit of sap within it overheated.

"How did he know?" I muttered out loud.

Emma had been staring into the fire, too, and looked over at me quizzically.

"How did who know what?"

"The power.... Micawber shut down the power at the zoo and again at the train station in the Hollow. He shut down the whole damn neighborhood. How did he know to do that?"

Emma looked like she was about to respond before she paused.

I continued, picking up speed as I talked. "You just said it: all the engineers, the head guys who developed this stuff—they're dead. Vegrandis is a crater. There are no other prototypes. There aren't any records, and nothing had been revealed to the military yet. How the fuck does Section know so much about it?" I thought about what the Colonel had said in the hollow. "He knew I was the first human subject. He knew about the other failures! How?"

Emma shrugged. "They're like spies or something, right?"

I stood up and paced the room. "Yeah, but this was a private enterprise. How did they stumble across it? Micawber sounded...informed, not like he'd just read some memo. They came to the hospital, weapons cocked and locked, looking for me. They knew I was a threat. Those manacles that Micawber kept trying to put on me… Where did those come from? How were they already built and ready to go? There is a link; there has to be something between Section and Vegrandis. I'm just missing it."

Emma put the slivers of LSD back in the foil envelope.

"You should still be taking these as a preventative measure. If Daphne pops back online, take one—seriously, for both our sakes. Disorientation, madness, and death, Al…. You could hurt someone."

She paused, "Or should I say more someones; more specifically, this someone." She pointed at herself with both hands.

That stopped me in my tracks. What if I lost my shit and was EPU-powered?

Emma continued right along with that train of thought for me. "What if you can't tell right from wrong? Real from imagined? Paranoia from facts?"

"And you want me to take mind-altering drugs because that's better?" I quipped.

"This is serious."

"I know. That's what I do when it's serious: make jokes. It's how I stay sane—relatively, anyhow."

I had stopped pacing by a small stairwell that led up to what I guessed was another bedroom and bathroom, as I didn't see either down here, and Emma had showered.

I was shaken at the idea that I could do even more damage and be oblivious to the harm I might cause. I looked at the wall to distract myself. There were more photos all up and down the panels.

The grandmother back in Astoria, the Astoria Column in the background.

You're a ticking time bomb.

A birthday party for a small girl with curly black hair and mischievous eyes.

You're a threat to everyone around you.

A trip to Disneyland.

Do you want to lose your mind? Hurt even more innocents?

A photo of the two of them bundled up at Meadows, knee-deep in pow, arms raised in triumph.

Maybe find your jacket, walk out to the woods, look for a quiet spot under the trees, and then put the barrel of the Kimber under your chin.

It'll only take a moment.

There was what looked like a recent picture of Daphne. She looked a little older, anyhow. She had a streak of grey at one temple. She was with a group of four other people in a bland room. In front of them was a baby monkey wearing a diaper with its arms wrapped around a puppy who was licking the monkey's face. It was…really cute.

I looked more closely.

"Emma, come here."

Emma walked over and stood next to me.

I pointed to the picture. "Is this at Vegrandis?"

She smiled and nodded. "That was the research team."

"Who's that?" I pointed to a tallish, heavyset man in a sweater vest on the far left. He had glasses and a receding hairline but possessed a vigorous black beard.

"That's Frank—Dr. Persici. We all just called him Frank. Why?"

I stared at the photo. "Because I've seen this guy; just recently, too."

Emma's eyebrows went up. "Really, where? The news says he's missing and presumed dead."

I nodded. "I'll bet. There's no need to presume anymore on that one. When I saw him last, he was in the backseat of a Russian gangster's limo, and he had a garroting wire around his neck."

Emma went pale.

I looked back at the photo of the dead man. What had the Pakhan called him in the limo? Oh, yeah: 'his learned associate.'

Outstanding.

I had just found my link between Vegrandis and Section.

Sabitov.

FLIES AND SPIDERS

I made my plans and waited until nightfall.

Darkness came early in the mountains. I had about an hour to prep the guns and gear that I would take from the duffel, load extra magazines, a flashlight, and the Swarovski, and I was good to go.

Leaving the cabin, I walked through the woods parallel to Highway 26 for a mile or so until there was no traffic to be seen in either direction. I ran across the dark highway to the other side and followed the path next to the Zigzag River through the woods until I found the access road.

I followed the empty road a short while until there was the muscular bump and grind of honky tonk and the low murmur of a crowd. A little further on, and soon parked cars lined both sides of the forested access road. Parking at the nearby Skyway Bar and Grill was limited to a small gravel lot. As it was a popular place (the mac and cheese alone was worth the drive), many patrons would park on the access road behind the restaurant.

I wasn't looking to lift a car—at least not here. I found a likely target and switched plates with the pair I had brought from Captain Bob's Tahoe. On the off chance we had to return to the cabin, I didn't want to leave any kind of criminal trail leading the bad guys back to us. I double-timed it back, put the new plates on the Tahoe, and went back into the cabin. I loaded up the duffel with gear and came back to find Emma in the passenger seat, wearing her own freshly- laundered clothes, her long hair tucked under my Giants ball cap.

"No way," I said flatly.

"I'm safer with you."

I threw my hands into the air. "By what metric? Did you forget last night?"

"You told me that the colonel wants me dead. Has that changed?"

I thought a moment.

I wasn't even sure Micawber had survived me trying to toast him, but Section would continue nonetheless, and they would clean up their mess, so yes, they would want her dead. If the cops found Emma, they might be just as likely to shoot her first and think of questions to ask later.

I thought a moment more.

Who was I kidding? Micawber was a cockroach. Of course he survived.

"Fine. But you follow orders without question or complaint."

She gave me a sloppy salute.

"Aye, freakin' aye."

"And buckle up."

Two hours later, we came into the Willamette Valley. I'd gassed up the empty Tahoe up in Boring, yes, Boring, Oregon, then swung well south of Portland into Oregon City where I dumped the Tahoe and swapped it out for a Camry that someone had left the keys in the parking lot of the Super Walmart. Saved me the trouble of hot-wiring it.

I'd cut through the back roads, heading west across the Willamette and past sleepy Newberg, deep into wine country. The countryside here was made up of rolling hills, with the Oregon Coast Range to the west, a jagged wall between the hills and the sea.

The hills were just lumps of shadow in the darkness, and the fields stood fallow in the pouring rain. The road twisted and followed the hills up and down, causing Emma to roll down the window for some cool air to settle her stomach.

"What makes you think Sabitov is the link between your old outfit and the lab?" Emma had asked after I lifted the Camry, and we were back on our way.

"Micawber led the unit away from its original charter. We had black market contacts all over the world. We were even facilitating the transfer of drugs and technology for low-level contacts in trade for intelligence to stop even bigger fish from doing the same thing. Long story short, Section became a criminal enterprise…all in the name of national security, mind you. Me going ballistic on the colonel back in the day was just the result of dealing with all that."

Emma shifted in the passenger seat to look at me. "So, you think this Russian gangster was the go-between?"

I nodded. "You said yourself that the private financing for the lab was tapped out. That was the reason they were headed to the government. But what if they were tapped out long before then and went for…shall we say, non-standard funding?"

"Russian mob money?"

"Sabitov is a very wealthy man with roots in the community through his legitimate businesses. They may not have known what he really was. They wanted this thing on the DL. No one in the industry could get a whiff of this, so no corporations, no angel investors. They must have been close to a solution and desperate to keep autonomy of the project to go to Sabitov. It explains where Sabitov got the biometrics for me to enter the lab. It's probably why he offed Frank in the first place."

"So, Sabitov has been giving, or more likely, selling the secrets he got from Frank to your colonel?"

I blew the air from between my pursed lips and nodded my head.

"Yep. Micawber's been watching this thing for who knows how long. Probably heard about the government contract presentation and told Sabitov to grab a sample before the show. Only Mort threw a monkey in the wrench of the whole thing with his attempted 'abortion.'"

Emma's brow furrowed. "Doesn't that mean that the colonel already knew...."

I took my eyes off the road, looked at Emma, and finished her sentence. "That I was working for Sabitov? I am getting the distinct impression that I have been working indirectly for Section for the past year. I'll bet he's the one who told Sabitov to hire me—make sure he had someone he knew was reliable on-site but not an active part of Section."

Emma's mouth dropped open a little.

"That's some next-level manipulation," she muttered.

"I'm tired of being a fucking marionette," I agreed.

"So, we are going to break into this Russian gangster's house and beat the shit out of him for answers, or we going to straight-up bust a cap in his ass?"

I turned the windshield wipers to high as the rain fell harder and looked over at her again. "I bust in; you wait in the car, gangsta-girl. Too dangerous."

"What do you think you're going to find out?"

"Section learned enough to make those manacles, and as insistent as the colonel was to get them on me, I have no doubt they suppress the EPU's functioning. What else do they know? Maybe they know a way to shut it down, or at least stop the little buggers from eating my brain."

Emma nodded and leaned back in her seat.

"We're going to take it to The Man."

I shook my head. "*We're* not doing anything, hippy."

"Al, the safest place for me to be is right next to you, so yeah, we. Besides, you need me around to tell you if you are losing your shiitake mushrooms."

And it pretty much went on in that vein until the curves in the road made her carsick.

Hippies.

A half-hour later I stared at the wreckage of the front gate. The wrought iron gate that normally blocked the driveway had been ripped from its track and was bent like a pretzel. It hung from one lighted stone pillar on the side of the long driveway. Sparks still dropped from the control box.

This was recent.

I had been to Sabitov's several times over the past year. His home sat on twenty acres of pinot noir vineyard and rested atop a switchbacked hill further in and away from the road. The property was encircled by a sixteen-foot property wall. I had originally planned on a simple, drive-by reconnoiter until I saw this. There were no other neighbors for miles in either direction; this mud and gravel road was just for the residents. We were probably the first people to come by since it happened.

Had someone driven a tank through here?

I actually scanned the ground for tread marks but didn't see anything.

With my right hand, I reached behind my back for the Kimber I had reattached to my belt and with my left, found a small, tactical flashlight in my jacket pocket. I walked carefully around the pillar where Sabitov's goons usually kept watch in shifts. There was an overturned BMW in the trees beyond the gate. I walked over to the ruined car and flashed the light on it. The windshield's interior was completely scarlet; it was covered in blood. I moved the light down to the shattered driver's side window and got a look at the two very dead occupants.

I could tell the guy behind the driver's seat was Thing Two, but only because of the size of his body and the fact that I recognized his jacket. The rest of the scene made it a bit of a guessing game.

The head was gone, you see.

It hadn't been removed cleanly, like with a blade: this was no surgical severing. Judging from the monstrous damage visible at the trapezius, I guessed it had been twisted off.

The passenger was also missing his head, but he still had a semiautomatic in his hand, and the slide was stuck back. He'd emptied the magazine at someone before he lost his head. No bodies were lying around other than these two, so whatever he'd shot at…it hadn't stopped it.

I got a really bad feeling. Something pretty unstoppable had come through here, something powerful and bullet-resistant. I caught myself humming and realized it was 'Mirror in the Bathroom' by The English Beat.

"What the fuck?" muttered a voice behind me.

I nearly shrieked and blew my icy-cool demeanor as I spun around and flashed the light into Emma's face.

"I told you to stay in the car," I hissed.

Emma was pale in the light of my torch as beads of drizzle passed between us through the beam.

"While whoever did this is wandering around? Uh-uh…I'm staying with you."

I shone the light into the car again. There was quite a bit of blood, but not enough to account for two large, upside-down bodies' worth.

I backed away from the car, covering the field of fire with the Kimber.

"Back to the car."

"We're leaving?"

"No, I just want to be able to get away really fast if we need to. I'm not walking up there."

We got back in the Camry. I put the Kimber between my legs and reached into the duffel for a sawed-off .12-gauge Mossberg. I racked the slide, chambering the shell, and put it across my lap.

"Let's go."

I drove the car up the long driveway toward the house.

The Sabitov home was a three-story affair high above the road. I drove up the switchbacks carefully. If Sabitov had tried, he could not have found a more easily defensible home. Every twist of the tight road opened up to an elevated position where he could hold off intruders. The top of the hill was wide open, cleared of the trees that surrounded the property. Sightlines were direct, and there was no way to approach the house unseen. The place was a modern castle—it just needed a moat and hanging yard.

Sabitov had mentioned his desire for the latter the last time I been up to visit. He had pointed out where he would like the gallows and what kind of knots he preferred.

Good times.

Sabitov also had a small pack of mastiffs who patrolled the property at night.

Which also hadn't helped.

The motionless forms of the animals were spread across the field as we approached the sprawling estate.

What had gotten through this? Or was the question, who?

I had expected to be shooting my way in here, at best. The current situation made me far more uncomfortable.

I stopped the car near the edge of the home. Leaning forward, I slid the Kimber back into the S.O.B. and then reached back into the duffel, taking out a few extra surprises, just in case. I stuffed these into the deep pockets of my coat. There was a stiff wind up at this elevation, and despite being weighted down, the hem of my coat fluttered around me as I got out of the car, shotgun in hand.

The home's exterior was painted a shade of red, like tanned leather. The middle floor of the house, which functioned as the main floor, was lit. The upper floor master suite also had the lights on. The children's rooms and the lower floor of the home were dark. On the main floor, a lamp that had fallen on its side was visible through the front window. The flicker and shadow of a fire in the fireplace reflected off the high ceilings, and the large, double-wooden doors had been ripped off their hinges.

What the effing hell.

Except for the drip of water and the whistle of the hilltop wind, the house was silent.

Emma sidled up close to my back. I turned to speak in her ear. "Stay behind me and to my left at all times, no matter what. Don't wander, speak, or even stop anywhere unless I do. Understand?"

She nodded, wide-eyed.

I walked up the steps to the ruin of a front door. I checked the angles and moved in with my back to the wall.

The room opened to a wide, tile-floored entryway. A curving set of stairs hugged the wall to the left, while the right spilled open to a spacious living room with a monstrous fireplace roaring with heaped logs against the chill. A professional-grade kitchen stretched beyond the living room and curved to the left of the home. Across the living room, another set of stairs led downward. Windows dominated this floor of the house, and I knew that in the daytime, the views of the coastal range and the neighboring vineyard-covered hills were spectacular. Every sunset up here was a divine show of nature.

Tonight, however, a different kind of programming was in the offing. The white couches and chairs in the main room in front of the roaring fire were stained red with gore. The remains—I wasn't sure how many—of Sabitov's bodyguards were piled in a bloody heap near the fireplace.

Emma was breathing fast and hard behind me. I had switched into the clinical mode I instinctively remembered from my days doing sweep and clears in combat zones across the world. I noted that once again, the heads were missing, and there were spent brass casings all over the floor.

I looked behind me. The wall to the left of the entryway and leading up the stairs was littered with bullet holes. Other than some extremely strange bloody splotches leading up the stairs, which could have been from a wound but were far too regular and symmetrical, I didn't see any obvious sign they had hit what they were shooting at. On the bodyguards' side, while there was blood and gore enough to clock in as a Rob Zombie flick, there wasn't enough to account for what must have been at least four or more bodies heaped on the floor.

I checked around the room and turned the corner to the kitchen, and that was where Emma lost it.

Set in a neat row along the polished wooden counter, across from the spotless, stainless steel Viking stove, were six heads. In some, the eyes bulged in fear; in others, the eyes had gone to rest in different directions. Some of the heads were more than a little crushed, but despite their differences, all of the heads shared one thing in common: (other than being separated from their bodies, that is) their mouths were all frozen open in a rictus of terror. The oven was on and set to 350 degrees.

Emma was moaning behind me.

I turned and put my finger across her lips.

She nodded, putting one hand across her mouth. I pointed upward with the shotgun's muzzle and moved back toward the stairs.

The tang of cordite from the gunfire still hung in the air, its familiar scent pushing me further into my own wartime experiences and keying up my psyche even more.

Hugging the wall and avoiding the middle of the steps, we headed upstairs. The wide hallway at the top broke left and right. Left was the game room, which was usually pretty raucous when I was here; the kids loved their Roblox. I thankfully recalled Sabitov saying that they were staying with their mother in Hong Kong for a week of shopping. To the right was the master suite.

The strange bloody splotches from the stairs continued up and down the hallway rug—almost like footprints, but without feet.

I stepped quietly on the plush rug, heading toward the master bedroom door, edging it open with the muzzle of the Mossberg. I pushed it back hard against the wall, ensuring that no one was behind it, and stepped sideways into the room. I kept my back to the wall and crouched low, covering as much of the room with the shotgun's muzzle as I could.

The body was splayed naked on the bed. The head, with its long mane of hair, now gone completely white overnight, had been left attached and untouched, as though the culprit had wanted to make sure that this body was easy to identify. The rest of Sabitov—not so much.

Emma gagged loudly behind me, and she rushed past me to the bathroom. I followed, making sure the bathroom and closet were clear, and let her be sick. I walked back out to the bedroom and checked the rest of the room.

The décor was tasteful if you didn't mind all the Orthodox iconography that was spread throughout the room. I wondered briefly if Sabitov was receiving judgment in the afterlife he had believed in. I looked more closely at the remains of his corpse: he'd definitely received some judgment at the end of his earthly life.

Once I could take my eyes off the corpse on the bed, it was hard not to notice the object on the dresser.

Emma walked back into the bedroom and stood next to me. We both stared at the glass jar on the dresser. There was a bloody handprint on the glass and something red inside the jar itself. There was a mirror above the dresser, and Emma's puzzled expression reflected in it. I walked closer and peered into the jar.

It took me a moment to make out what was in the jar and what it meant.

"We are leaving, now!" I hissed.

I grabbed Emma by the hand and pulled her out of the bedroom.

"Were those his...genitals in that jar?" she whispered.

I let go of her hand as we made it to the stairs and down to the entryway. Emma gasped.

A figure stood in front of the fireplace, staring raptly at the flames.

He was shirtless, and his shoulders, though still narrow, were much taller than they used to be—certainly taller than they had any right to be now. The hair was still lank against his head. The couch blocked my view of his lower body, and I was thankful for that. I had a sneaking suspicion what the bloody splotches on the rug meant.

His head turned to the side a bit, and he whispered, "Leigh."

I moved Emma behind me toward the front exit and pointed the Mossberg at him, not that I thought it would do any good, but it might slow him down.

"Hi, Mort."

He shook his head.

"Not Mort," he whispered.

He turned and walked past the stacked bodies of dead Russian bodyguards, stepping out from behind the couch, and I got my first good look at EPU-Mort.

His bare torso was mostly normal to about the waist, and then it separated into a bulbous, black-furred lower abdomen connected to six long and slender, black, articulated legs. The face was still Mort, but there was something wrong with the shape of his jaw. It looked swollen and distended.

It looked like Mort had gotten a makeover by Ray Harryhausen.

I pointed the shotgun at his head. "Stay, Mort."

He shook his head and whispered once more, "Not Mort."

He looked up at me and smiled. His mouth opened to show a row of scythe-like fangs that ripped his gums and lips to shreds as he spoke. Blood flowed from his mouth and ran down his chin to his chest as the fire glowed behind him.

"Not Mort," he repeated. "We are Shiva."

He opened his mouth wide, and a long, pointed tongue shot out and tasted the air.

"We are the Destroyer."

I kept the gun trained on Spider-Mort with my right hand and reached into my pants pocket with my left, pulling out the keys to the Camry. I passed them behind me to Emma.

"Get in the car; get it started. If he comes out and I don't, floor it out of here."

She took the keys and fled out the doorway and down the stairs without a word.

Now she shuts up.

Spider-Mort watched her go, his extremely long and mottled tongue darting out and lapping the blood from his lips.

Yuck.

I looked down at his new wheels. "So, uh, Mort…I mean Shiva. I'm guessing you didn't drive here."

He looked at me and smiled that horrific grin as his legs moved him slowly toward me.

I raised the shotgun higher and put my finger on the trigger. "Uh-uh. Stay. Good spider."

Spider-Mort spared a withering glance at my sawed-off shotgun.

"Won't stop me," he gurgled as he continued to scuttle slowly my way, the fire behind him creating horrific shadows on the wall.

I nodded. "But it will slow you down long enough…." I let the sentence hang in the air.

Curious, he paused. "For what?"

"For what I have in my pockets."

He stared at my bulging jacket pockets but said nothing.

"C'mon, just say it. 'What has it gots in its pocketses?'"

He looked confused for a moment, which was all I needed.

I found that my enhanced reflexes and strength were still intact as I pulled the trigger and racked the slide repeatedly, going through all five shells in a couple of seconds.

The repeated blasts were so close together that they sounded like a single explosion in the tight confines of the house, the roar echoing off the vaulted ceiling. The sheer force of the shotgun blasts shoved Spider-Mort back toward the fireplace, but there were no wounds on his body. His field was stopping the pellets from penetrating his body, but the field didn't seem to be converting the kinetic or sonic energy; neither was he or his interface redirecting the blasts back at me, like I would have done.

Did he not have control of the EPU? Was it busted?

I dropped the empty shotgun and got two of the surprises from my pockets. I pulled the pins on the fragmentation grenades, lobbed them one after the other toward the temporarily stunned Mort, and followed Emma out the door.

The double explosions blew the side out of the house, and a crazy-legged figure went flying into the night. Emma had the engine running, nose pointing down the driveway, and the passenger door open.

"Get in!"

I ignored her and reached into the duffel. I pulled out an enormous silver revolver with a ridiculously long barrel. The Marlin BFR was made by the same company that produced the Desert Eagle. It was chambered in .450 caliber with a simply ginormous 350-grain bullet. It had been Elmore's pride and joy, but he had given it to me when I had laughed at it, asking him if he was trying to make up for something else.

The explosion must have damaged the fireplace as flames consumed the middle floor of the house. I walked away from the car, searching the darkness. As I walked, I thumbed back the hammer on the single-action monster and reached into my pocket with the other hand, pulling out what looked like a fat can of hairspray with a pin and handle going through the top.

I heard him before I saw him, howling with rage as he scuttled out of the night toward us.

"Hey, Shiva. You like fire so much: payback time." I yelled.

I popped the pin on the Willie Pete with my thumb, released the handle, and timed the throw to land right at Spider-Mort's feet. The white phosphorus grenade exploded, and the air around Spider-Mort ignited like a miniature sun as the chemicals inside reacted to the air. Thick white smoke billowed around the blinding light as chemical fire engulfed Mort's body. Unlike the frag, the Willie Pete was a chemical munition similar to napalm. Water won't extinguish it; you can't wipe it off. It just sticks to you as it burns. The intensity of the burns would normally be enough to melt flesh, and I had been wondering if a chemical reaction could penetrate the field.

It could.

The stiff wind here accelerated the chemical, and Spider-Mort screamed with an ear-splitting wail as the white phosphorus melted his flesh.

His figure appeared through the smoke, and I aimed the Marlin. I focused on the front sight, letting Mort's burning figure become a blur. I squeezed the trigger, and a flaming chunk of something went flying out of Mort in the direction of the bullet's path.

His EPU was too busy dealing with the burns to maintain field integrity.

He was vulnerable.

I thumbed back the hammer of the Marlin and pulled the trigger as I kept walking closer to the burning dervish inside the smoke. I kept cocking and firing the gun until it was empty. With each shot, another large flaming chunk went flying out of him.

I dropped the Marlin and pulled the Glock out of my interior jacket holster in a left-handed cross-draw, ready to empty the gun in Mort's head, when something flew out of Spider-Mort from behind him in a long, unbroken line, expanding at its furthest point.

It looked like...rope? Silk?

The long trail of spider-silk caught the wind and pulled the flaming spider monstrosity into the sky. Momentarily stunned, I watched the fiery mass rise into the air.

Fucker just did a Sky Hook on me, *sans* plane.

I reached back to the S.O.B. with my right hand, cleared leather with the Kimber, and aimed and shot both pistols simultaneously as fast as I could at the retreating blob of fire in the sky.

I could dimly hear him scream. "She will pay!" before he was swallowed into the blue-black rainclouds, a flaming dot heading north for Portland.

I holstered the Kimber, turned, scooped up the Marlin, and ran back to the blazing bonfire that had been Sabitov's home. The acrid scents of burning wood and plastic whipped through the air on the back of the wind, and the heat from the fire made the skin on my face tighten. I jumped into the passenger seat, slamming the car door behind me, shutting out the conflagration.

"Hit it!" I told Emma.

We went ridiculously fast until we came to the switchbacks, and then she slowed down as much as she dared, the tail of the Camry spinning out on the tight curves, spraying gravel and mud behind us.

We hit the straightaway to the gate, passed the BMW with its grisly cargo, and I directed her away from Newberg, where I could already hear the sirens blaring.

"Al, whafuck?"

"The nanotech is inside him too."

"There's two of you? Where to?"

I dug into the duffel for boxes of bullets, put the Glock on my lap, and reloaded the Marlin. I only had the one Willie Pete, but if Spider-Mort/Shiva couldn't control the EPU, this bad boy could give me at least something to work with until Daphne came back online.

If she came back.

"Portland. Northwest 23rd and Flanders."

"What's there?"

"Akiko."

"Who?"

"A child Mort will kill to hurt me."

"Got it."

She punched the gas pedal down, and the Camry took off to the east toward the I-5 freeway and Portland.

BATTLE WITHOUT HONOR OR HUMANITY

I hung up my burner phone for the third time. It was a Friday night: someone at Ogami should be answering the phone. They couldn't be that busy.

I tried Mrs. T.'s phone. Nothing.

Hitoshi's—same.

Akihiro: not even a voice mail.

Traffic was light, and there wasn't a cop to be seen. Emma pushed the envelope. It was twenty-seven miles to NW 23rd. It should normally be about a forty-minute trip. I was pretty sure we would shave ten to fifteen minutes off that.

How fast did giant spider-people fly?

I thought for a moment and looked over at Emma.

"So, you saw that too, right? You didn't slip me some 'What's Up, Dick?' by any chance? That wasn't me tripping balls or hallucinating or whatever in terminal EPU decline?"

"The mutant spider freak?" She shook her head. "You're not losing it yet."

"Good, I think."

"Who is that guy?"

I gave her the *Reader's Digest* version of the night at the lab and the showdown on the 205 bridge.

"I don't get it. How did the nanos get in him?"

I thought of how I had opened his guts with my kukri and hurled the perforated case, dripping with nanos, at his gun hand, trying to knock his aim from Akiko. A short jump from hand with nanotech all over it to him gripping his intestines to keep them from falling out.

How much did it take to establish a colony of EPU nanos that could then spread throughout a body? It can't be much, probably just a drop. These things must be virulent.

I remembered Mort's severed body flying over the bridge after me....What damage could these things not repair?

"Uh, I'm just a programmer, but any thoughts on why he ended up with spider legs and not people legs?" she asked.

I shrugged. "I don't know. A spider got in his guts, and the EPU did a Jeff Goldblum and spliced them together? Or maybe his interface decided that form was the most efficient use or way to get him mobile?"

"Doesn't explain the…" she waved her hand in front of her face.

"Teeth," we both said at once.

Emma was pushing the sedan hard, and I worried about being pulled over—something we couldn't afford, but no way I was taking the chance that being late meant the death of a little girl.

"The first time Daphne activated Combat Mode, she grew some kind of bone extension over my ears in seconds to protect them. They were almost like the ear protectors I would wear at the range. The EPU has some kind of morphological ability, but I guess it would have to be limited by things like mass. I imagine that spider body weighs significantly less than Mort's old lower half and legs."

Emma took her eyes off the road to look at me.

"Teeth and tongue: explain those."

"Me? You know more about this shit than I do."

Emma shook her head as we came up on Tualatin. "Not true. I know about Daphne, but I don't know as much about the capabilities of the EPU. Frank and Dr. Zinn told me what they needed; I worked with it. You have used the EPU and spoken to

Daphne, so you know more about the inner workings of the nanos than I do."

Well, that's a bummer. I basically have the manual for the interface sitting next to me, but the interface is down, and she knows less than I do about how to get it working.

"I'm more curious where he got the extra mass to begin with. He had nothing below his belly button last time I saw him," I muttered.

I thought about the decapitated bodies we saw tonight. I'd just seen Chuckie have his head blown off, and he put out an astonishing amount of blood, probably more than what I'd seen on the floor of Sabitov's home. And he was a medium-sized guy, not like the steroid hulks Sabitov surrounded himself with. I had an image of Spider-Mort tearing off the heads of his prey and drinking from the spouting veins and arteries like a water fountain. I considered the freakish size of his mouth. Maybe not a water fountain...maybe more like a kid sucking through a straw.

The need for available tissue to rebuild may have done more to determine Mort's new form than anything else. I remembered the heads on the counter and how the oven had been set to bake. Had Spider-Mort been preparing a meal for himself? Getting all Gordon Ramsay? Those teeth looked quite capable of...never mind. I looked over at Emma and considered sharing that conclusion; she'd already seen enough. No need to add a juicy new layer to her nightmare sandwich. Mine was already a Super Dagwood Special.

I couldn't believe I was thinking about food.

I had finished reloading the guns and double-checking every spare magazine I had in the duffel. "I got nothing." Not really a lie. I only had a theory—a gruesome theory.

"I guess we could ask him when we see him," she mused.

"He didn't seem right in the head. I don't think we're gonna get a solid answer on that one."

Emma switched lanes and sped around a camper with California plates.

"Could be the trauma. It happened with a couple of the animals we tested the regenerative powers of the EPU on. Some were never able to recover from the original trauma. It affected their minds. The interface couldn't take hold, and it interfered with the EPU development. We euthanized the ones who didn't adjust, and then it became protocol only to administer the test to happy, well-adjusted individuals."

"Who then still went batshit and died."

Her face was reflected in the lights of the cars heading south, it may have been a flicker of the light, but I thought she was smiling. I turned my head a bit and could see she was struggling not to cry.

"Yeah."

"Mort's field wasn't behaving right. Could that be an interface problem or an EPU problem? Understanding that could be important to surviving our next encounter with him unless Daphne decides to show up."

Emma was silent for a moment as she considered.

"It might be both. He said: 'We are Shiva,' as in the Hindu god of birth and destruction, right?"

I nodded.

"We are the Destroyer," I quoted. I remembered Mort's picture book the night of the limo. It had been on Hindu art and mythology. Something on his mind? In Hindu mythology, God is represented as three incarnations or facets depending on the time of the cycle of the universe. Brahma creates the universe, Vishnu preserves it, and Shiva destroys it in order to recreate it.

Of course, Shiva was born from a pillar of fire, and Mort was a pyro, so maybe that was the cause of his fixation. Or maybe he thought it sounded cool: "The Destroyer."

Shit, brother. You don't need an intimidating name. Just look in the mirror.

"Yeah, I mean, it's weird. The EPU interface has a binary option syntax: Daphne or System. Shiva isn't an option, so whatever mental instability he's suffering, it is affecting the interface. Second, and I'm not an engineer, but maybe the spider body configuration isn't conducive to field manipulation?"

The lights of the city reflected against the clouds. We were getting closer. "He's just relying on the physical manifestations of the EPU, none of the Lens ability," I said.

"That's good, right?"

"Gives me a more even chance."

"Better than none."

Emma glanced over at my phone. "Thought about just telling Portland PD that there is an armed crazy headed to the restaurant?"

"I could be sending a couple of cops into a meat grinder. I think I've depleted Portland's finest ranks enough. Besides, no one is answering." I felt a sick sensation in my stomach. "It may already be over."

I thought about Mort getting loose among the Taniguchis, and I was torn between fear making me want to vomit and rage that he would take the fight to someone weaker, just to cause me pain, rather than face me head-on.

"We're ten minutes away."

Emma added more speed, and Portland and the Willamette River came into view on my left as we got onto the bridge.

"You know, there is someone else you could call…. People who are more prepared and just as interested in apprehending your co-worker. They are probably in the area even now, keeping an eye out for you." She raised her eyebrows and grinned. I saw where she was going, literally and figuratively, and gave a wicked grin in return.

"Outstanding."

We parked a block up the street from Ogami. Emma held the Swarovski to one eye; my vision was still enhanced, so I was able to see just fine.

The rain had stopped, and the restaurant was dark and closed up. There was a yellow strip of police tape across the door. The only other exits were the back of the restaurant and the stairs to the third floor that led to my old apartment. A couple of lights illuminated on the building's second-floor where the Taniguchis made their home, but the rest of the neighborhood was quiet. The events at the zoo had the city hiding indoors. NW 23rd was usually a bustle of activity on a Friday night, but there was scarcely a soul to be seen on the streets.

"How long do you think it's going to take them?" Emma asked.

"They should be here by now," I murmured.

"So?"

I shrugged anxiously, my hand continuously reaching for the door handle, ready to open it and run down the street, only to keep pulling it back.

"I called Moscato and told him to call Micawber." No way I was calling the guy joined at the hip to the NSA. I may as well put up a neon sign: there would be satellites targeting Portland and pinpointing me in no time.

There were no signs of distress from the Taniguchis' home, but no one was answering their phone either. It was stressing me out, and as I reached for the door handle one more time, Emma quietly put her hand on my knee and patted it.

I nodded and exhaled.

I looked down at the massive Marlin in my lap. I tried to figure out exactly how to carry this beast unseen if I had to get out of the car. The barrel was longer than my forearm. I leaned back, swearing I would only wait another thirty seconds when a black sedan pulled up to the curb in front of the restaurant.

"Here we go," Emma muttered excitedly.

I expected squads of black SUVs to come barreling around the corner, lights flashing, but it was just the one lone sedan. I tried to get a look at the driver, but the glare of a streetlamp off the windshield obscured my view.

Where were Micawber and his troops? I had been expecting to watch either Spider-Mort being led away in the strange manacles, surrounded by a small army of black-clad soldiers, or watching the colonel get his face eaten off.

I couldn't decide which I wanted to see more.

The door to the sedan opened, and a skinny guy in a suit got out. There was no mistaking that shock of unruly black hair.

Moscato.

He peered around the block, the wind whipping at his jacket. He raked his hand through his hair and walked up the wet stairs to the yellow-taped black doors. He peered to the side of the doors through the windows and then jiggled the door handle a little. He then glanced up and down the street.

He looked at his watch.

I wanted to scream.

He lifted a phone to his ear, spoke into it briefly, and then hung up. He pulled a folding knife out of a pocket and cut through the yellow tape. He put the knife back in his pocket, pulled out a set of keys, spent a moment fumbling before inserting one, and opened the door.

"What the fuck are you doing, you dumbshit?" I muttered. "Where's your partner? Don't you morons travel in pairs? Where the hell is backup?"

Emma shook her head. "If Spidey is in there, he's toast."

I pulled the Kimber out and handed it to Emma. She took it, mouth agape. I pointed to the safety. "Bad things come: thumb that thing, then point and squeeze the trigger. Don't thumb it unless you are sure you are ready to do damage."

I reached for the handle, opened the car door, got out, and leaned back in to look at Emma. "And for fuck's sake, don't follow me into the restaurant!" I spat at her.

She shook her head, her glasses slipping down on her nose. "Don't worry. If he's in there, I'm staying outside."

Damn, that was actually…agreeable.

I ran down the wet street to the front of the restaurant; the Marlin held underneath my coat with my right hand for concealment. I don't know why I bothered—there was no one on the street, and the stupid barrel still stuck out two inches below the bottom of my coat.

I got to the stairs and peeked around, but no lights were on, and even with my enhanced vision, I didn't see any movement on the restaurant floor. Moscato may have already made his way to the kitchen and up the stairs to the living area.

I opened the front door and walked in quietly. The waterfall was off, and the fish were gone. There was no lingering odor of food filling the entry like it usually did, whether we were open for business or not. No one had cooked here in a while. The place must have been closed for days. I had seconds to register all this when I felt the cold barrel of a gun jammed into the base of my skull.

I sure missed the HUD.

"Fork it over," Moscato said quietly.

I was pretty sure I could still move faster than he could pull the trigger, but I wasn't clear if the Lens was active and would stop a bullet if I wasn't fast enough or if moving was just a really bad idea altogether. The thought made me bristle, and I nearly let it get the better of me. I squashed the anger and took a breath; I needed him on my side and not as another adversary.

Hey, look! Maybe I can learn.

Then again, I could always take back the gun.

I pulled it out from under my coat.

"Slowly," he murmured.

I lifted it to the side and held it out.

Moscato got a good look at it. "Holy fucking shit, Leigh. There an elephant at the zoo you got a hard-on for?" He plucked it from my hand and put it down on the hostess stand.

"Actually, it's for spiders."

"Uh-huh."

"No, really, works great. Look, a bad man is coming here to hurt the Taniguchis."

"Yeah? Who?"

He patted me down, pulling out the Glock and the tai-pan dagger. He placed them next to the Marlin. I thought about telling him but was sure he would never believe me. As far as he was concerned, Mort was dead.

"Sabitov hired a hitter to take out Akiko. He was afraid that her testimony about Mort could come back to bite him."

There was the clink of handcuffs being shaken out.

"Well, then he's shit out of luck. We have the Taniguchi family in a federal safe house while they are being questioned about you. There's no one upstairs. Do you ever get tired of lying to me?"

I felt like an anvil had lifted from my chest. I could breathe again. They were safe. The tension drained out of my body, and I gave my first genuine smile in days.

Moscato pulled my left arm behind my back and slapped the cuffs on. I was giddy knowing that Akiko was alive. I could care less about the cuffs.

"Just so you know," I said lightly, "you and I are now in deep shit. The hitter thinks they are here. He's not going to be happy when he finds out they aren't."

"Yada, yada, yada. I don't know why you came back or why the crank call to get the colonel here, but I played a hunch and showed up just in case you did. I don't believe all that hogwash I heard about what happened at the rail station. You're not Thor. You detonated some kind of weapon from that lab, and you are going to jail for killing a lot of good men."

He savagely yanked on my right arm, cuffing it to the left.

The floorboards creaked above us—not like a house settling. It was the kind of creak that sounded like someone was walking slowly and stealthily around upstairs.

Moscato paused and listened. "Who's up there? Your partner? The woman from the train station? You two been hiding out here?"

"Look, you got me. Let's get out of here. Take me in."

There was another creak. Moscato's gun went back to the base of my skull, and he shoved me toward one of the floor-to-ceiling pillars by the moon gate.

"Don't move. I have a hair-pull trigger on this thing.... Be a shame to splatter your brains all over your friend's restaurant."

He quickly uncuffed one arm.

"Wrap your arms around the pillar." He jammed the gun harder against my skull.

"Don't do this," I pleaded.

He leaned close to whisper in my ear. "Don't make me shoot you. It would make me a hero at the office, but I might lose a whole night's sleep over it."

I put my arms out.

"Now, cuff yourself," Moscato ordered quietly as he glanced up at the now silent ceiling.

I reached down with my cuffed hand for the other bracelet and slapped it against my opposite wrist, closing and locking it. Moscato reached around and closed both bracelets nice and tight. He gave it an experimental tug and a grunt of satisfaction. He pulled out a penlight from his pants pocket and turned to walk through the moon gate onto the restaurant floor.

"You're gonna want to take the Marlin," I told him.

He looked back at my hand cannon, shaking his head as he walked back through the darkened restaurant, weaving his way through the tables to the kitchen.

I pulled on the pillar; it was load-bearing and solid. I had been hoping my enhanced strength would be enough to pull out of the handcuffs, but the position of my arms made it hard to get any leverage.

There was the creak of Moscato's very human footsteps across the floor above me. He moved from the far end of the building, back and forth across the floor. He was clearing the rooms upstairs.

There was a pause.

He yelled, "Federal agent! Freeze!"

There was a drawn-out moment of silence and then the gurgling laughter.

Moscato screamed.

And…cue the gunfire.

The crack of gunshots echoed throughout the building. The pace was steady and measured. Scream notwithstanding, Moscato was keeping his cool.

I could tell from the sound that he was firing a 9mm semiautomatic which had limited stopping power to begin with. Ever wonder why there are like fifteen bullets in one of those things? You need all of them. Against Mort? He may as well have been using spitballs.

There was a quick scuttling noise across the ceiling above me. Spider-Mort was on the move. There was another scream from Moscato and a terrific *thud* followed by more *thuds* in a rhythmic fashion.

I was pretty sure Mort had just thrown Agent Moscato against the wall and down the stairs.

I leaned back as far as I could and pulled on the cuffs, my back muscles straining to pull the chain apart. No joy. Someone ran into the restaurant from the kitchen.

He had two legs, so…Moscato.

He ran past me, bruised and bloody, eyes bugging out of his head, going straight for the hostess stand.

"I told you to take the Marlin," I said dryly. I pulled on the cuffs. "Cut me loose; I can help." Quick, scuttling noises headed down the stairs to the kitchen.

Moscato checked the cylinder on the Marlin and then snapped it closed. "Why, you got a can of Raid?"

Special Agent Willy Moscato's personal stock with me shot way up. Insane shit is happening—he's under pressure, and he can still get off a one-liner. Nice.

"As far as I know, you two assholes are in this together," he snarled.

"You think I could work with…that?"

The double-swinging doors to the kitchen opened, and Moscato lifted the gun with both hands as he walked back into the restaurant, cocking back the hammer.

"I have standards!" I called after him. I pulled on the cuffs again. "Cut me loose!" Moscato ignored me as the unmistakable silhouette of Spider-Mort crept into the room.

There was no command from Moscato to 'freeze' this time or for Mort to put up his hands.

Or legs.

Moscato took a bead and fired. He was neither experienced enough with this kind of recoil nor strong enough to keep the muzzle of the barrel down. The monstrous kick from the gun lifted the barrel almost right over his head, sending the round about a foot over Spider-Mort's head. Mort snickered, and, in a flash, he had his hand around Moscato's throat and was lifting him off the ground.

Mort plucked the gun from Moscato's hand and tossed it away into the darkness.

Sheeeeiiiit.

Moscato gagged and choked as his legs kicked frantically. Mort opened his jaws wide, his lower jaw seemingly unhinging as the row of scythe-teeth curved outwards, and he brought Moscato's head toward his mouth. My vision gave me a clear view of the drool falling from Spider-Mort's mouth as Moscato's head was drawn ever closer.

That was also when I caught a glimpse of his groovy new necklace. I filed that one away for later.

"Hey, Little Miss Muffet!" I yelled.

It didn't really make sense, but it caught Mort's attention.

"Leigh," he hissed. Streams of bloody drool fell from his mouth as his tongue flickered out.

Gross.

He hurled Moscato through the air to crash behind the marble sushi bar. Spider-Mort stretched out his arms as his long, articulated legs scurried across the restaurant floor toward me, his jaws open wide.

I felt it again.

That powerful sense of déjà-vu. I had seen this all before: being trapped in the darkened restaurant, Spider-Mort with his Cuisinart mouth, and being handcuffed to the pillar in the entry.

Really not the sort of scene you forget, so I wasn't sure why it seemed so familiar. Whatever the reason, despite the toothy nightmare on six legs rushing to bite my head off, I knew exactly what I had to do as if I had done it before—like I had all the time in the world.

It was like I was in Combat Mode as everything slowed down except me. I crouched down and braced my shoulder against the pillar; I was as sure of my angle as I was my own name. I set my feet and rammed my shoulder against the pillar, driving from my legs and hips into my shoulder. The whole thing shook from the strike.

Mort was halfway across the room.

I slammed again into the pillar again: plaster fell. Again, I struck: A crack appeared.

The clatter of the terminal claws at the ends of Mort's spider legs got louder. On his unnatural body, they were the size of a small pony's hooves; they made a *ratatatatatat* noise as he scuttled closer.

I slammed again. His foul breath wafted ahead of him as he closed in on the moon gate.

I had enough time for one more powerful strike. The pillar gave way, and the ceiling dropped onto Spider-Mort as I launched forward and to the side. I was freed from the pillar, but my hands were still cuffed.

Plaster and dust and then the large beige couch from the Taniguchi family room followed the ceiling down, landing on top of Mort.

I looked around for my gun.

The hostess stand had fallen on its side, and a portion of the ceiling sat on the spot where my Glock and knife had been. The rubble stirred, and a set of long, fire-scarred legs fought their way free of the debris.

He was between me and the door. I was about to leap over him and run like hell for the door when I saw it, sticking out of the mess of wood and plaster: a blue leather-wrapped handle with an iron hilt butt. It was the Taniguchi family's ancient dōtanūki katana that had hung on the wall above the display of armor that was now somewhere under a couch.

There was a roar, and Spider-Mort pulled himself from the pile of destruction, skittering between me and the sword. I tried pulling on the cuffs to free my hands, but it was like a nightmare where every punch you threw went in slow motion. I couldn't pull free.

Mort skittered toward me, and I prayed that his Lens was still twitchy.

Feet don't fail me now.

I stepped into a spinning sidekick that caught him in the gut, causing his human half to double over. I brought both my fists together into a club and brought it down hard on the back of his neck. All six legs splayed out as he dropped flat to the floor, stunned.

I spun past him, grabbed the hilt of the sword, and pulled it free of the wreckage. I whipped the two-and-a-half-foot blade out of its blue sharkskin scabbard and nearly gasped when I felt the perfection of its balance. A blade forged for the intensity of battle, the dōtanūki was wider than a standard katana. Akihiro had said the sword had been in his family since the 15th century. He would take it down monthly to oil and care for it, and its edge was still keen and fearsome despite its age.

Spider-Mort pulled himself free as I set myself in a guard position—elbows out, blade upright against my right ear. Using the sword with my hands cuffed would be difficult, but not impossible. I had studied with a Chinese broadsword that had a much shorter grip and an even broader, more curved blade, but I had always loved the feel of the katana, and this was an exceptional specimen.

Mort circled me slowly, smirking at my choice of weapon. I'd just dropped the floor of a building on him, and it hadn't even fazed him.

I got my first close-up look at Mort since the party at Sabitov's. His skin was a melted ruin; what lank hair he had once possessed was gone. The EPU had tried to heal him, but his cracked skin oozed fluids. The skin of his chest looked like runnels of melted wax with pus and blood seeping through.

And to my joy, there was a small, bloody hole in his shoulder. It was about the size of a 9mm slug. Moscato had tagged him. To me, it was pretty much the equivalent of Bilbo spying the dark flaw in Smaug's scaled armor.

Mort's field was all the way down.

I grinned at the sight of the bullet hole and spun the sword in a circle in my cuffed hands. Spider-Mort looked at the focus of my gaze, and the same realization crossed his horrifying features.

Smirk at my two-and-a-half-foot razor blade now, asshole.

"I think your nanos are working overtime there, buddy. Looks like you and I are a little more evenly matched."

Mort looked unsure, and he eyed the door behind him.

As he turned his head, I got a closer look at the necklace which had melted into his skin. It wasn't a necklace—it was a collar. It looked about the width of my thumb, made of a strange silvery metal with the dull sparkle of a tiny light on one exposed section.

"Who are you working for these days, Mort? Did the colonel send you to clean up his loose ends with the Russians?"

His head whipped back to glare at me. His front legs stepped forward toward me.

"Did you blow up Vegrandis for Micawber? Something like, 'I steal the goods, you get rid of the competition?'"

Spider-Mort smiled that smile and circled me slowly.

"Micawber wouldn't have ordered you to kill me because I was bringing him the nanos. Who wanted me dead?"

Spider-Mort hissed, "Sabitov."

Sabitov? Did Sabitov have a side deal going on? That would explain why Micawber sent his new pet tarantula to take care of the Russian. You didn't cross the colonel.

Mort feinted a lunge at me, but I didn't bite…no pun intended. I kept the katana up in guard and stayed on the balls of my feet, ready to move when he really did.

He moved forward another step with each leg, and I matched him as I stepped back. I don't know why, but I knew it was important to keep talking, to delay. There was…something.

I looked at his neckwear. "Is that thing around your neck the reason you can't heal? I didn't notice it at Sabitov's; I was a little distracted by…." I nodded my head up and down, indicating him, "all that. When did he grab you? Was it after the river? Maybe when he saw the recording of us on the bridge and realized it was you that stopped that car that hit us, not me?"

Mort shook his head. "Together," he hissed.

I raised my eyebrows. "We did it together?"

"Two strong together; apart: weak."

I thought about what I had done in the Hollow. That was weak? Huh.

What could two EPU-powered individuals do as a unit?

"I don't suppose it's worth it to see if we can work together and kick Micawber out of both our lives?" I asked, not very hopefully.

Spider-Mort threw back his head and laughed. I mean, if you called the gurgling noises he made and the deformed chest-heaving laughter.

"Guess that's a no."

I hadn't finished my sentence before Mort crouched and hurled himself through the air at me. I was so distracted by how freaky it looked that I nearly forgot to duck. I did duck at the last moment, rolling forward and coming up on the balls of my feet, sword at the ready.

Meanwhile, Mort was hanging from the corner of the ceiling—some of his legs on the ceiling, some against the wall.

Just hanging there in the corner, being creepy.

Before I had time to so much as inhale to let loose some snark, he was flying through the air at me again. I was ready this time and dropped to one knee, slicing downward diagonally, then pivoting on the knee and popping back up.

There was a quivering segment of black fur and fire-scarred leg on the floor.

I turned to look at Spider-Mort. His left foreleg was a bloody stump; he was gasping and growling. He gnashed his teeth as blood poured down from his shredded lips. Whatever the EPU had done to him, it had been haphazard in putting it all together. I could understand the teeth for rending prey and consuming the tissue needed to replace the lost limbs, but it had stepped so far outside the bounds of nature that it was doing him harm.

Was it a flaw in the EPU, or did Mort's unstable nature have something to do with it?

He sprang again at me but too high for my swing. This time, instead of staying on the wall, he rebounded off of it and right back at me, smacking away my strike with one claw-hoofed leg while another whipped me across the head. All of which answered a big question I'd had since the train station: was my Lens field still active? Could it still absorb kinetic blows?

Nope.

I wasn't bulletproof anymore…or punch proof, apparently. I had speed and strength, but so did the not-so-itsy-bitsy-Spider-Mort.

I fell on my back, and Mort dropped his weight on me, his legs wrapping in a frenzy around my body, pulling me close to his scarred and oozing abdomen. His hands twisted like serpents as he caught my cuffed wrists, pinning me. He leaned his human torso down and slammed my wrists to the ground with his hands, sending the katana spinning away across the floor.

I had no leverage; I couldn't move. His legs clasped tighter to my body, ichor pouring from his severed appendage. He was squeezing me to where I was sure that if my bones hadn't been reinforced, they would have shattered.

His charnel-house breath poured over me as he opened his mouth, his razor-toothed lower jaw unhinging horribly. He brought his drooling face down to mine. His long tongue slithered out and rasped its sliminess against my cheek as his eyes rolled back in what looked distinctly like pleasure.

He was tasting me.

The nightmare meter cranked up to eleven.

"Hey, ugly."

Mort looked up, mottled tongue lolling out of his fanged mouth.

There was a terrific BOOM that left my ears ringing as Mort's head exploded in a shower of gore. The spider legs kicked and spasmed, and I shoved the twitching carcass off of me as the remains of Spider-Mort's neck pumped gouts of blood in a black pool that quickly spread all over the floor.

I tilted my head back and got an upside-down view of a battered and bloody Moscato bringing down the smoking barrel of the

Marlin. He had braced his body against the wall to help him control the recoil.

His black hair stood up in every direction, his suit was ripped in several places, and blood was pouring from a wound on his scalp. His left eye was swollen shut, and his bruised lips blew a cloud of smoke from the muzzle of the gun as he nodded at me.

"You were right: this thing works great on spiders."

THE SOUND OF SILENCE

I sat up and took a few deep breaths while I waited for my heart to slow down. The EPU wasn't doing such a hot job of controlling my reaction in the face of fear. Maybe it needed Daphne for that kind of regulation. I shakily stood up and turned to look at Moscato.

He was pointing the Marlin at me.

Man, the barrel on that thing looked like the size of a bear cave when you were on the other end of it.

"Tell me what's going on."

I looked around at the debris and cocked my head. Nope, I'd never heard a thing from outside, and I still didn't.

"Now?" I answered.

"You got somewhere to be?"

"Yes—not here." Definitely not here.

"We could drive to the airport, sit in the office, and have a chat."

The FBI field office in Portland was next to Portland International Airport. Definitely not there either. Walking into a federal building was the same as handing myself to Micawber if they didn't just shoot me on sight first. Cop killers aren't well-liked for a reason: if you are crazy enough to kill a police officer, what else might you be capable of? Now magnify that intensity for revenge by about an order of magnitude for anyone *loco* enough to take out federal agents.

A whole lot of them.

I pointed vaguely upward. "Agent Moscato: do you hear that?"

He listened and shook his head. "Should I?"

"You just shot your load upstairs and then fired that hand cannon twice in the middle of Northwest Portland. Nobody is screaming; there's no crowd gathered outside, each person frantically calling on their phone for help. This place should be swarming with cops, but I don't hear a thing."

His brow furrowed, and he turned his head to look out the window.

I moved.

Moscato looked down at his empty hand as I stood next to him, holding the Marlin—now pointed at his head.

"If I wanted to do it, you would have been dead a couple of times over by now."

Moscato looked at the spot I had been in and then moved his eyes to where I was now. "How did you move so fast?"

"Keys…." I said as I pushed the barrel against his head a little harder than I had to. "Slowly," I added.

Vindictive? Who, me?

He pulled a small pair of keys out and held them up.

"Now, lace your hands behind your head, lie flat, and spread your legs. You know the drill."

Moscato slung the keys from one finger and dropped slowly to his knees. He then lowered himself to his belly on the floor while I kept the muzzle of the Marlin against his head the whole way down.

"Guess I should have let that thing bite your head off and then shot it," he grumbled.

"Aww, don't be mad, Willy—I'm just being cautious. I'm grateful to you for making sure I didn't become a spidey-snack, but I also intend to stay alive."

When he was prone, I snatched the keys, and none too gently put my foot on his neck until I could get uncuffed, passing the

Marlin from one hand to the next until I was free. I threw the cuffs across the room and pulled my foot off.

"Okay, now you can get up."

I walked over to the wreckage of the hostess stand and retrieved the Glock and the Tai Pan, tucking them back into their holsters in my coat one at a time while I kept the Marlin more or less pointed in Moscato's direction. I walked back over to Moscato and met his eyes.

"You want to know everything? Come with me; I'll tell you everything."

I looked at the closed black doors and pointed. "Provided whoever is out there waiting for us doesn't kill us the moment we walk out."

Moscato looked at me. "I came here solo for a reason: orders were to kill you on sight.... Extreme prejudice and all that shit. We got overridden by your old military boss. He's a piece of work, by the way."

"He's still alive, huh?"

"Yeah, you managed to fuck him up, but he's still breathing and giving orders."

Cockroach.

I looked anxiously at the door. Emma was still out there.

"So, why didn't you tell him about your hunch? Maybe give his bony ass a nice nose-polish while you were at it."

Moscato tilted his head. "What makes you think I didn't? I stood on the steps and called him again. Said he was aware of the situation and had it in hand."

That's why it was so quiet out there.

"What he didn't tell me was what the fuck was in here waiting for me. And, if I heard you and that thing right, that it was working for him. Asshole let me walk into a deathtrap."

"It had a name. You knew him," I said absently.

Moscato glanced down at the human-spider carcass that was upside-down with its legs curled up tight. He gave his head a definite shake in the negative.

"No, no…and *fuck* no. I'm pretty sure I'd remember *that*."

"Mortimer Madievsky," I said. I eased over to the door and looked out the window—nothing to see except the steady fall of rain dumping down on an empty, darkened street. Power was still on, though. There were lights on in the buildings around us, but it was eerily silent as if Moscato and I were the only ones really here.

Moscato looked like he was about to shake his head and argue with me, and then he stopped. You didn't get a shiny federal badge without having some observational skills. I watched as his brain compared what he knew to what he had seen. His jaw dropped open.

"Oh, fuck me," he said as he looked down at the mess on the floor.

It was too damn quiet.

I strained the capabilities of my new hearing skills.

I was surrounded by the muted sounds of the city: traffic and the distant blare of sirens. There was the ever-present rain beating down on the roof of the building, splattering the street and plonking on the top of the sedan outside; canned laughter and sitcoms hissed from televisions in apartments across the street.

What I couldn't hear were any actual voices.

I strained harder; it was difficult without Daphne to act as the interface, trying to listen past the falling rain and the ambient noise of the city. I filtered out everything and listened for the sounds of people—movement and laughter and yells and curses. There were noises like people should be there, but there weren't any people. Underneath the expected hum of the city was silence.

In the depths of the silence, I heard my heartbeat and then in a moment, Moscato's. There was nothing else.

I rushed to the door, leaving a confused Moscato behind me. "Leigh, they'll kill you!"

I opened the door, but I wasn't worried about that; I knew there was no one out there—not a soul.

Including Emma.

I ran out of the restaurant into the pouring rain. The wind had picked up, and it was coming down diagonally in an endless curtain of cold water. I looked up and down the street but saw no one. I heard Moscato open the door behind me to follow, but I was already running full speed to the car.

I was there before his foot touched the second step.

The driver's side door of the Camry was open. The Kimber and a small, square, flat package were on the front seat.

There was no Emma.

I scanned up and down the street, but there were no secreted SUVs and no lone walkers out with earpieces. They didn't need them. I looked up to the clouded heavens as they wept and wondered if Micawber had tasked a satellite on me as well. He didn't need it, but he did like his redundancies.

I'd been played. They didn't need anything else to get me other than what, or rather who, they already had.

Emma.

Micawber knew I wouldn't run, not with an innocent on the line; that was why he collared Mort: he wanted to make sure Mort couldn't completely overpower me so that he could lure us here. I thought about how empty the freeway had been of cops. Section had evacuated this neighborhood long before I even got to Sabitov's. No lives put in danger—just Mort and I duking it out, and then Micawber grabs the winner.

After the events at the train station, I wasn't surprised Micawber had this kind of pull with the city. He had the full authority of Homeland Security behind him, and I could just hear him telling some terrified city councilman or outraged senator in his clipped, precise voice that I was a former Marine Raider with a grudge—a home-grown terrorist. But he, the colonel, had a unique insight into how I think. Why this man used to be one of my officers, I can wrangle him safely if you will just give me control of... everything. Keep local law-enforcement away from him and leave him alone. I will bring him in.

Yeah, that sounded like him.

Back in the day, he and I used to play strategy games together. Our game of choice was *Weiqi,* or what the Japanese call *Go*. In the years I served under him, I had never been able to beat him. Unsurprising, as he was a tactical genius. He'd been a teenage chess and math wizard, valedictorian of his class at West Point, graduating with honors. He had a celebrated career with a decade of live combat experience under his belt before I'd even played my first game of *Weiqi* with Chen-chen. He'd probably forgotten more about strategy than I had ever known. But we had both liked to play, and quite often there was downtime on missions.

Poker got boring. I never gambled with my money, only my life.

I'd probably learned more about the game in my years of playing him than in my entire lifetime. Every now and then, when I had played a particularly good game, he would give me a small reward—the same one every time, like a good pet who had learned a new trick. Furious, I looked down at the package next to the gun. I picked up the Kimber, smelled the ejection port, and then checked the magazine; Emma hadn't fired it. They got her without any fight or struggle, as far as I could see.

Moscato caught up to me. The rain had plastered his black hair down to his scalp and washed most of the blood away from his face. He looked down and saw the package on the front seat. "What's that?" he asked.

"A message and a consolation prize," I reached down to pick it up. It was a thin, white package with the name 'D'Addario' marked on it: new guitar strings.

"Motherfucker," I muttered.

Moscato looked around. "I don't get it. Where is everyone?"

I checked the trunk and saw my duffel. It looked untouched; everything was still there. I grabbed it and slammed the trunk closed.

"We're taking your car."

Moscato's eyebrows rose. "We are?"

"I could say please, or just remind you that I have all the guns," I said.

Moscato gave a 'What are you gonna do?' shrug. It was very Jersey.

"No need for the threats. Please works too. Where we going?"

I was ready for Moscato to take me to a judge or a congressman or a senator—someone with serious pull. I could prove things now; I had all the evidence I would need. I thought a moment. "Oh, shit."

I ran back to the restaurant, but it was too late. Spider-Mort's body was gone.

There was an enormous pool of blood on the floor, but nothing else. They'd even taken the leg I'd chopped off. They must have come in the back and grabbed it while I was up the block, distracted by Emma's abduction.

There went my physical evidence.

I felt like I was back to my first game against the colonel after being recruited into Section. A player's philosophy of life could be gleaned from how they played the game, and this was his strategy. This was how he approached the game, combat, and his entire life: weaving a web of deception, feints, and false trails—nothing ever as it seems.

Moves within moves within moves until the prey is completely encircled and cut off.

Asshole was a bigger and more dangerous spider than poor Mort ever was.

Where were we going?

It didn't matter where I went.

Sooner or later, Micawber knew I would have to come to him.

There was an even worse scenario, my brain cheerfully informed me. What if—say, under some questioning—Emma told him that I didn't have control over the EPU? That Daphne had gone permanently dark? That, for all intents and purposes, I was powerless—or at least, not as powerful as he believed me to be.

If Micawber finds that out...

Game over.

SUGAR MOUNTAIN

I couldn't see the tails, but I could feel them out in the dark—in cars, somewhere above the clouds, perhaps even in space. In Basic, I was taught to never look at an enemy target's neck if I was attempting to sneak up behind them: something about the feel of another's gaze on our most vulnerable area still excited that primal, lizard area of the brain. That's what I felt all around me now.... Eyes in the dark.

Ordinarily, I would snark, paranoid much?

But, seeing as Special Agent Moscato had just explained how I had rocketed to Numero Uno on the FBI's Most Wanted List, I thought it might be a 'just because you're paranoid doesn't mean they're not out to get you' moment, because...umm, they were.

Yeah, if Section didn't also just slip a tracker on this car, too.

There was no hiding, but I could buy some time to prepare.

On the fly, I gave Moscato directions as we headed east out of Portland into the gorge. I also told him everything that had happened since Mort and the Things had jumped me on the way to the airport and stuffed me into Sabitov's limo in what seemed like forever ago.

There wasn't much traffic this late on a Friday. It should have been easy to spot the tails, but I couldn't. There was just the weight of that implacable gaze on the back of my neck, warning me that someone out there wanted me dead. Well, probably more than one someone after this week.

Both my worry for Emma and anger at myself for not making sure she was safe took turns gnawing at my guts like someone had turned a live rat loose in there. As long as I came in quietly, I wasn't worried about them harming Emma. They might kill her after I got there, but not until then—which is where my friendly, neighborhood Fed would come in. He was my assurance that she would make it out of there if I went in.

As we headed east in the darkness through the Sandy River Gorge, Moscato figured out our destination.

"We going to Mount Hood?"

The cabin had the rest of the guns, maybe some food, and then it was a matter of come what may. A brief layaway there would also give me enough time to finish filling Agent Moscato in on my weird-ass week.

"If I hadn't seen what I saw tonight, I'd say you were some poor PTSD vet who took too many of those tabs you told me about," Moscato said as we drove into Rhododendron and wove through the snow-filled forest to Daphne's cabin. "You still got those things? At this point, it just adds veracity to your story."

I patted my coat pocket. I had been about to put the pack of guitar strings in my inner pocket, too, before deciding it didn't matter how innocent those things looked; I wasn't taking anything from Section. I had hurled them into the rain-filled sewer before I got into Moscato's sedan. But I had been reassured to find the foil envelope and Mrs. T.'s note still tucked in there when I opened the pocket. Emma must have put the envelope back in.

Gnaw, gnaw, gnaw.

"You, uh...not needing to take any, right? Not feeling deranged—or anything?"

I considered telling him about the eyes watching me from everywhere in the darkness and decided that it wouldn't help my case. "No," I said, staring straight ahead.

A thought occurred to me. "Moscato, you got any friends in the DEA?"

He shrugged. "I got friends everywhere. Why?"

I laid out the deal I'd made with King. Sabitov was dead and incriminating myself seemed like the least of my problems right now. At least I could make sure that loose end was tied up.

The dirt and gravel roads leading through the forest to the cabins had been cleared of snow, but not the winding dirt paths that functioned as driveways. Moscato's sedan made it about a dozen feet in before the snow was too high for the car to go any further. I grabbed my duffel, unlocked the door, and we went inside.

We both cleared the house, guns drawn, but it was empty and cold. The snow was piled high enough and was so fresh, that anyone coming in would have left prints. It looked deserted.

I got the fire going in the furnace, waiting for the sounds of helicopters and the glare of searchlights, but the only thing that came out of the sky were the drifting flakes of snow that made it past the soaring branches of the pines outside.

I watched the snow fall with the darkened dragonfly eye-con looming larger than normal as waves of heat poured out of the furnace, filling the room. Moscato was laying out Sabitov's delivery schedule to his DEA pals or giving up our location on his phone in the bathroom upstairs.

It didn't matter.

There is a deep silence when the snow falls in the mountains. Sound is suppressed, absorbed into the layer of white that blankets the forest floor. There was something about fresh snowfall that could turn even the drabbest, most industrial scene into a magical one out of an ancient myth. Here, deep in the Oregon woods, on top of a snow-covered volcano, the flakes fell large and heavy in the silent darkness—I was in another world and half expected to see a line of cloaked and hooded dwarves making their way through the forest night to their golden, subterranean halls.

I let out a deep breath.

If I went into wherever Section was, I probably wouldn't be walking out. Even if Section had a way to keep me alive, they'd...keep me. I would disappear while they ran whatever tests they wanted on me. I wasn't going back to being Micawber's pet. I was done playing games.

I again thought about that short walk into the woods, and just eating the barrel of the Kimber.

Mort's head being blown off seemed to work.

I could take myself out of the equation entirely.... But you didn't cross the colonel. If I suicided, he'd kill Emma because that's what his code of conduct demanded. Knowing his absolute adherence to his code assured me that if I took myself out, she would be following right behind me through death's door.

I felt encircled by the lack of choices forming my prison like the stones around an eye in *Weiqi*.

Maybe now is a good time to try drugs? Drop a bunch of tabs and go in fried?

It's not like I could have a worse trip than tonight. Yeah, man— spider-people coming out of the walls, a kitchen full of severed heads, and some hefty paranoia.

I was already having a bad trip.

I had taken off my jacket and draped it across one of the chairs in front of the fireplace. I grabbed it off the chair and sat down on the couch against the wall. I reached into my jacket and pulled out the foil envelope of 'What's up, Dick?'— tossing it on the couch for Moscato's 'veracity.' Then, I looked in the pocket.

There was Mrs. T.'s note, still sitting in there.

I guessed there was no time like the present for more bad news, so I opened her note.

I opened the letter not knowing what to expect and was utterly unsurprised by what she wrote. There were only five words, but those five words told me everything I needed to know from her and where to go from here.

I sat there, gobsmacked as usual by Mrs. T.'s ability to get right to the heart of my dilemma, like a matronly Musashi with her deftness and sword of truth, telling me what to do about it.

In five short little words: Ren. Yi. Zhi. Xin. Li.

That was all.

The Confucian Five Virtues.

Ren—benevolence or human dignity. A man or woman of ren will stand in harm's way to protect the ren of another. It is both what makes us human and what we must strive to offer others. It is the overriding principle guiding human action.

Yi—honesty or righteousness; the ability to do good for the sake of good. Essentially, the Golden Rule: do unto others as you would have done to you.

Zhi—wisdom or knowledge. Not just learning, but the knowledge of right and wrong.

Xin—fidelity, and integrity; faithfulness.

Li—the rules governing social action. Respect. Trying to live up to ren.

As a code of life, it was a solid way to go. I hadn't always lived up to the ideals or tried very hard on a couple. Perhaps Chen-chen was right, and my failure to strive for the best in me had led me this way. Mrs. T. was telling me in her own way—do right and do better. Live up to the man you hope to be.

I said a short prayer to whoever or whatever might listen or care. I hoped it was just enough to be sending a feeling of gratitude toward this woman who had never been anything but kind to me.

I don't particularly believe in God—big or little 'g.' I find the presumption outrageous that we, as a species, can be so sure of what might or might not lie beyond the universe and death when the true reality of what is out there in the vastness overwhelms our imaginations.

Humanity—existing on our tiny speck of dust floating on the edge of an infinite void, an infinity about which we know little to nothing—crows its supposed superiority and knowledge as 'masters' of nature. It always strikes me as akin to the surety of ants who know for certain that they are the rulers of their immense world.

There are more things in heaven and earth, Horatio....

The idea of God, in general, has always seemed to be simply a nightlight created to explain the unexplainable and to give some hope toward fending off the inevitable darkness that will fall when we close our eyes for the last time; something to cling to as opposed to the existential horror of ego-extinction. I absolutely get it. But those kinds of blinders aren't for me...not at the expense of ignoring this life in the here and now for a mythical other that might come after.

As far as I was concerned, life was the greatest adventure ride ever, and we all get one ticket. What happens to us on the ride isn't always up to us, but how we respond to the curve balls life throws us at us is. The loop-de-loops of pain and regret, the high-speed drops of loss where you leave your stomach at the top of the hill: there can't be lows without highs—those dizzying heights of joy where your spirit rises above the clouds, however temporarily. I remembered my favorite high, and it warmed my insides in a place that the ordinary fire of the furnace could never reach.

I had been waiting at the hospital when Jeni was born. I got to go into the natal ward and saw Jeni's ruddy little face for the first time. Her condition wouldn't manifest for another year. At that moment, she was a plump little cherub under what looked like a burger-warmer lamp. I saw her and said her name. Her little head turned to look at me, and I was done. She had me hook, line, and sinker.

I smiled at the memory.

It had been a hell of a ride, but like all rides, it comes to an end.

If I had to go, though, I would go out howling like a madman.

Maybe, if I didn't have all the facts and there was something after…perhaps I could wait there for Jeni, and we could find our next adventure together. I was pretty sure this one was over.

Of course, I could be wrong. Hope springs eternal, right? I looked outside at the falling snow and considered the chances of that happening.

Ok, fine. If there is something out there—some divine force—give me a sign.

Will I make it?

There was nothing but the crackle of fire consuming the wood, and then I heard it: my sign from the universe.

It was the rush and gurgle of the upstairs toilet flushing.

Moscato's voice called down the stairway. "Leigh, you're out of toilet paper!"

I hung my head.

Typical.

Moscato came downstairs later with his phone in his hands, hopefully, washed.

His hands, that is. Not the phone.

He'd used the first aid kit to clean his head wounds. The swollen skin around his left eye was a glorious sunset and sealed almost completely shut. I had given him one of my old sweatshirts to wear, and as he was shorter and thinner than me, it hung on him like sackcloth. Between his bruised and battered visage, his wild black hair, and the sackcloth sweatshirt, I got a sudden image of him walking down the street calling out, "Bring out your dead!"

I smirked.

Moscato, quite aware of his appearance, ignored me.

"I've been trying to get a locale on your colonel. They turned down the space in the office we offered them and set up a secure base somewhere outside of town."

I'd found the containers of SuperSwole! in the kitchen. There was nothing to mix it with but water, but I wasn't in the mood for sawdust pancakes. I'd heated some water for instant coffee and alternated between sips of java and gulps of watery cookies and cream. Moscato's eyes lit up at the coffee, and soon he had his cup prepared. He was stirring away when he noticed the SuperSwole! He cheerfully opened it up, got a heaping spoonful, and stirred it into his coffee while I gawked.

Barbarian.

"So, what's the plan?" he asked as he sipped his…thing.

I shook my head in disbelief and headed back to my chair by the furnace. I'd brought out the rest of the guns I'd left stashed here in the cabin and had set to checking them in between sips of civilized imitation coffee.

"Once we know where Section and Micawber are set up, I go in while you go to the highest authority you can find to listen to your story. Make sure they know Emma is an innocent civilian being wrongfully held by them. Get her out safely."

Moscato stepped over to the duffel on the couch and peered at the firepower I had stuffed in it as he sipped his…drink. I refuse to call it coffee.

"They're gonna say she was with you at the train station. There's video of that. They'll just claim she was your accomplice," he said absently as he sat in the chair next to me.

"Then you need to convince them I had her there against her will."

Moscato shrugged. "I saw the video before it all went to static. She was hiding behind your back in front of all those cops, not running toward them pleading: 'Help me, help me.'"

I turned to look at him, "Are you saying you can't do it?"

He held up a hand in a placating gesture. "I'm just warning you; it's gonna be a tough sell."

"She must have family. Find them. Tell them what's happening; get them in front of cameras, out on social media—whatever it takes," I said in exasperation.

Did I have to think of everything?

I'd finished loading the 30-round magazine for the H&K MP7, a lethal submachine gun for close-quarters combat and a favorite of some of my former pals at DEVGRU. Looking like a cross between an enlarged pistol and a shortened auto assault rifle, it was built entirely from polymers, so it was extremely light but capable of punching small-caliber rounds through even the toughest body armor. I slammed the magazine into the desert camo-covered pistol grip and put it in the duffel.

I leaned back, took a sip of coffee, and looked over at Moscato, who was still staring at my duffel.

"So…mister 'I'm just a harmless, misunderstood guy,' whatcha going to do with that bag of goodies?"

I shrugged. "I'm going to give myself up."

"Uh-huh."

He was still staring uneasily at the bag of guns, and I didn't blame him. I'd hit the jackpot at Elmore's.

"Let's just say I was a Boy Scout, and I believe in being prepared," I said primly.

"Yeah, horseshit. I saw your juvie record. They hand out merit badges for theft and assault?"

"Hey, those files are supposed to be sealed."

Moscato snorted. "Your entire life is being dissected by a team of FBI profilers trying to figure out what makes you tick. I've seen everything except records of your time with Herr Oberst Micawber. That shit was all redacted."

I finished my coffee and stared at the fire. "Any conclusions?"

Moscato shrugged. "I don't understand how an iconoclast like you survived the Corps, but from everything I read, you were dedicated, good at your job, and…it seemed like you wanted to serve your country."

"Things were different," I muttered.

Moscato pulled out some packages of trail mix from the bin in the kitchen and offered me one. I took it.

"What made an egghead from Bezerkeley join the Corps anyhow?"

"You saw my enlistment date."

He nodded. "October 2001."

"I wanted to serve. I knew people who died. I was angry like everyone was. I wanted to hit back, just like everyone else." I sighed. It had been so long ago.

Moscato grunted and squinted at me. "Seems like your urge to help others keeps backfiring on you."

I rolled my head onto my shoulder and stared at him.

He held up a hand and ticked off his fingers one by one. "Let's face it; the war bit everyone in the ass. Our guys died, and for what? Korea, Vietnam, Laos, Syria, Iraq, Afghanistan—you name it. Every time we show up with force to remake something, we screw the pooch. Force doesn't work, so that's not entirely on you. But don't tell me it doesn't itch where you can't scratch. Force just begets more force. Sometimes the pushback is right away, sometimes it's delayed, and sometimes it comes from an unexpected quarter. The point is, force is your default mode, and it should be a last resort. For example, in your latest forays, that little girl is the one who saved your bacon the other night, and when you last went to bat, you killed a bunch of cops and fried that thing in your head."

I broke off my stare and turned to look at the fire as he continued, "You sure you want to try your luck again?"

What he had said wasn't wrong, he had simply held up the mirror to show me what was there, and I tried not to let it chip away at my newfound resolve. What was luck but statistical odds? I'd been behind the eight ball plenty and made it out but at a cost. And sooner or later, that bill was coming due with interest.

The lengths of wood in the furnace were black and orange and dying a slow death.

I leaned over, grabbed an oven mitt, and opened the furnace. The heat made the skin on my face tighten as I grabbed a couple more lengths of wood and tossed them onto the pile. I closed and latched the furnace door and dropped the oven mitt to the floor next to it. The flames rose as they eagerly licked at the fresh wood. I sat back and looked out the window as the snow continued to fall. Moscato's sedan was becoming a car-shaped hump of white.

"So, I go talk to my betters, see what I can do to free your girlfriend...."

I snorted. "She's not my girlfriend."

"Sure."

"She's not," I insisted.

"Of course," he nodded.

"She's gay."

That stopped him.

He looked at me. I looked back and nodded. He cleared his throat.

"So, I make sure she's safe. What happens to you?"

I shrugged. "As far as I know, this thing is terminal. I assume they will try and get whatever they need out of me before I kick the bucket." I supposed there was still a chance either the system was fried, as it hadn't rebooted, or that, perhaps, Section had found a way to slow down or prevent the terminal phase of the EPU. Maybe I might survive this? I wasn't counting on either one, though, and I didn't relish the idea of spending the remainder of my days as a lab rat.

"What about your family?" he asked quietly.

I'd told him about Jeni and how I had come to be her guardian.

"Just make sure they know I wasn't some cop-killing psycho."

"You did kill them, though. Those men are dead because of you."

"I...know." I moved my jaw, but nothing came out for a moment. "It wasn't what I wanted. I didn't go in there planning to kill anyone. I just wanted to survive and keep Emma safe."

Great job on both of those.

Moscato's phone buzzed.

He pulled it out, thumbed open the screen, and grunted.

"What?" I asked.

"Your old outfit. Looks like they set up shop not far away from here."

"Oh, don't tell me that Machiavellian fuck is in the cabin next door."

Moscato snorted. "Not that close. Weird... It looks like they are at some cherry farm in the woods outside Hood River."

What?

"MapApp says it's about an hour's drive down the 35. They're expecting you. Here, I can show you the address." He leaned over and showed me the map on his smartphone.

I sat there, stunned. Those...assholes were bivouacked on my farm.

I looked up at the ceiling and screamed.

MASTER OF PUPPETS

The drive twisted around the other side of the mountain and led us north toward the mighty Columbia and the port town of Hood River. We left the snow behind us as we descended, the precipitation quickly turning to freezing rain as we followed the curving Highway 35 around the mountain.

I sat in silent fury, feeling violated on so many levels. Micawber had directed and anticipated my every action from the beginning; squatting on my property was the final touch. He was showing his control over all aspects of the situation: I was encircled, trapped, and there wasn't a choice I could make that he wasn't ready for. The only thing missing was Micawber's hand actually up my ass, controlling me.

Moscato tried a couple of times to talk to me, but I ignored him. He was just another piece for Micawber to use on the game board. If he wasn't working for him directly, he was still doing his bidding indirectly.

He wasn't going to be able to save Emma.

I'd failed.

I considered going in full stealth. I would take out the perimeter guards and then work my way inwards until I got to the center and Micawber. He was probably anticipating that plan too.

I shoved down the testosterone rage. I fuck around: Emma will die. If I knew that giving myself up peacefully could guarantee her safety.... If there was a chance of that happening, I would take it.

The colonel knew I would.

I leaned my head back and racked my brains for a way out of the box I was in. If Daphne and the EPU were up, I would at least have a fighting chance. Much as I wanted to believe she would come up and kicking when I needed her at the last second, it wasn't something to count on. It was a fantasy. It was more realistic to accept that I had been arrogant in calling down the lighting that night, in not letting her be in control when things had spiraled beyond my ability to handle them. Instead, I had destroyed her.

Or pulled her plug.

Whatever.

I glanced at the dragonfly eye-con, which sat dead as dogshit in the bottom corner of my eye. The rain eased up outside as Moscato pulled off near Odell, and we worked our way along the empty back roads through forest and farmland to Bag End Farm.

We drove through the moss-covered stands of black cottonwood, canyon live oak, spruce, and cedar that ringed the farm. The dim shapes of SUVs were parked outside the gate to the farm, their flashing lights refracted and glimmering in the falling rain. I told Moscato to stop well before that.

"I'll walk," I told him.

He looked down at my enormous duffle bag full of death and destruction. "Not taking your toys?"

I shook my head.

"I think I'm done with them. Go and at least try to get her free on your end. And thanks for not letting Mort bite my head off."

Moscato reached out his hand to shake. "It's been weird, Marine. Good luck."

I shook his hand and slammed the door. He turned the sedan and drove off through the shadowed woods, his taillights disappearing in the falling mist that was all that remained of the rain.

I walked down the road to my farm, coming out of the woods with my hands raised. Floodlights on the SUVs lit up the night around me, making me squint. Several crimson target dots glittered on my torso as I kept walking.

A pair of Section guards in black body armor appeared from behind the vehicles, meeting me at the gate and then falling in behind me as we walked up the graded driveway past the cherry orchards. The floodlights went out behind me, the SUVs shutting down as darkness returned. The lights in the barn shone beyond the orchards and illuminated the silhouettes of several large trucks parked near it. I wondered if they'd found the bunker.

We hadn't gone much further when one of the guards behind me told me to halt.

I complied. The other guard came up from behind and informed me he was going to search me. I'd forgotten that I was still carrying, so I told him about the Kimber and the weapons in my coat. I didn't have to look at the other guy to know his gun was pointed at the back of my head. I took the coat off slowly, and the guard removed the Kimber from the S.O.B. I got a thorough pat-down and then was told to wait.

I didn't have to wait long. A small group of people emerged, lit from behind by the light from the barn, and walked down the driveway. I could tell from the height of one of the figures that Micawber was coming along.

In less than a minute, the group stopped not far from us. There were two armed and armored guards carrying the manacles between them, the lights glowing on the strange metal of the cuffs.

Why were these so large and Mort's collar so small? Were these an earlier version?

There was Micawber with white bandages wrapped around his eyes. His luxurious hair had been cut close to his scalp and looked burned away in places. His hand was on a smaller man's shoulder;

the smaller guy was wearing a white doctor's coat. Had I blinded the colonel?

If that's all I did, he got off lucky.

Behind them was another armored guard holding onto a woman who was almost as tall as the guard.

Emma.

I breathed a sigh of relief. Her face looked drawn and scared, but she was okay. The guy in the doctor's coat told Micawber I was there, and they walked forward together.

So, he was blind.

Good.

"Twang."

"Colonel, looks like you're having some difficulty seeing. Hey, how many fingers am I holding up?" I raised my right hand and flipped him off.

"One," he answered without hesitation.

Fine, he saw that one coming—sort of. I should have raised both hands.

He pretended to look around. "Why, Twang—why aren't you summoning the powers of nature to smite us down and free your friend here? Hmmm? Surely even your love of banter couldn't precede your need for vengeance. But instead, you just stand there."

I looked past him at Emma. She looked downcast and mouthed the word, "Sorry."

I nodded and smiled at her. "Not to worry. Just let Emma go and when I've seen her safely off, I'll happily come with you."

Micawber shook his head. "I'm afraid you have your order of operations wrong, Twang. First, you will don these manacles, and then we will attend to other business."

I shrugged. "C'mon, Colonel. The EPU is down, and you know it. I'm not a super threat, but I can still make things difficult. Let her go first."

Micawber tilted his blind head at me. "When I am sure that the nanotech inside you is disabled, I will let her go, not until. The EPU could have recovered since your last time with Ms. Burr. If I let her go, you might strike down the wrath of God once she is safe. I would prefer some insurance."

"I don't know what else to tell you," I said.

"I am not interested in what you have to say. I am interested in what he has to say," Micawber pointed past me. There were footsteps, and I looked behind me. Agent Moscato, still draped in my ridiculously oversized sweatshirt, was hoofing it up the drive.

Motherfucker.

Moscato arrived and nodded to the colonel, who couldn't see it. Moscato wouldn't look at me; he just stared straight at Micawber.

"Did the lieutenant show any manifestation of the EPU technology in your time with him?"

Moscato shook his head. "No, sir. He and your pet went toe to toe, or rather claw to sword, without activating their fields. I had his trust: he would have told me. The envelope of LSD is in the inner pocket of his jacket."

Micawber grinned. "Thank you, Agent Moscato. I will be with you momentarily."

Moscato nodded and went to stand behind the guards.

I wasn't totally surprised, just disappointed—and curious about all the interest in the acid.

I'd been willing to believe the best about Moscato, but he was just another stone on Micawber's board. I felt hopeless and alone. There was no winning this game. I was outnumbered, outmatched, and just plain out of fucks to give.

The guards on my six took up stations immediately behind me. I could smell gun oil as their weapons were trained on my head. The other two guards walked my way, hefting the glowing manacles.

"If he moves, kill the girl, then him. You see, Twang—I am always ahead of you."

"Free Emma. I'll go quietly."

Micawber inhaled and exhaled deeply, saying: "I think not. You're going, anyways."

The guards with the manacles stopped in front of me, and then both dropped to a knee to unfasten the wide cuffs.

I looked at Micawber. "Always, and one-hundred percent, an asshole."

He smiled. "Count on it."

There was a *pop!* followed immediately by another *pop!* They were barely the whisper of a muffled champagne cork.

Both guards behind me dropped to the ground.

The two in front of me looked up only to be double popped as both their faceplates shattered as bullets tore into their heads.

I looked behind me.

Moscato had pulled up the sweatshirt. Hanging from a strap underneath was the H&K MP7 with its suppressor attached. He pointed the weapon at the guard standing next to Emma.

"Let her go or join your pals."

I nearly cheered.

The guard surrendered, and Emma rushed toward us. She hugged me and whispered, "I knew you'd come," then stepped behind me, next to badass, one-eyed Willy, who had turned to face the colonel.

"You shouldn't have left me to the tender mercies of your pet spider, Colonel. They're coming with me."

Moscato pulled the trigger, and with another *pop!* the last guard dropped to the ground. At this, the lab-coated doctor gave a short shriek, running past us into the misted dark. Moscato let him go. He pointed the gun at the unseeing Micawber. The colonel might have been blind, but I thought he was very aware that there was a gun pointed at his head.

"What happened to force is a bad thing that never ends well?" I asked Moscato.

He gave a goofy shrug but kept the weapon trained on Micawber. "What can I say? I learned it from watching you."

I grinned at him.

"As for you, Colonel Micawber, I'd leave you behind to find your way back, but I don't think having you on my ass is a good idea. You've done enough damage," Moscato said.

Micawber went ramrod straight and said in his clipped voice, "Then listen closely; you know what to do."

Moscato gave that New Jersey shrug, "Yeah, I know dickhe...."

There was a loud gunshot behind me, and I spun around to see Emma holding a small semiautomatic, now pointed to one side, as the fatally wounded Moscato fell limply to the ground at her feet.

"Excellent. Now sweetheart, if you would be so kind."

She spun toward me with the gun raised to my face. "Yes, Daddy."

What. The. Fuck.

Her finger was on the trigger, and her lips spoke two words, but I couldn't hear what they were.

There was a flash.

The world went dark.

NOT DEAD YET

There was wet asphalt under my cheek, glacial and rough against my skin. The rain fell in a wintry sheet everywhere. My head throbbed powerfully, so I opened my eyes. Why not look? It could only get worse, right? There was nothing to see. Nada: total darkness. It was…what was it? My head spun. What was that old radio program of nightly music that used to play on the local radio up here? Akihiro would stream music from its online archives into the restaurant.

Oh, yeah. It was *Lights Out*….

No, hon. Not yet.

A flash of static.

Darkness.

Silence.

Where am I?

I floated in nothingness, weightless.

I'm working on it, sugar.

Daphne?!

Sunlight exploded around me. The glare blinded me, and I had to blink my watering eyes against the sudden exposure to the light. It took a moment, but my vision cleared.

The smells hit me first.

The warm breeze carried the smell of fresh grass, cool lake water, summery pines, and wildflowers. The intoxicating bouquet filled my senses.

I looked around.

I was by the side of a deep blue lake, its surface flat as a mirror despite the breeze blowing across my bare scalp. The sky was that cobalt blue that you only get in the PNW in the summer: the indigo shade that could knock your eyes out of your head and make living here the other nine months of the year worth it.

A cloud of brightly colored butterflies flitted past and spiraled out across the still water. A trout broke the surface as it arched into the air, attempting to catch one of the 'flies. I turned to look at the wooded edge of the lake and saw the mountain's peak reflected in its calm blue waters.

Mount Hood.

I was by Trillium Lake.

But it was summer—like perfect summer.

"What do you think?" a throaty voice drawled behind me.

I turned to see a petite young woman wearing a thin sundress. Her black, curly hair was covered by a wide-brimmed hat protecting her face from the sun. She was barefoot and had a spray of freckles across her cheeks and nose. She was wearing John Lennon-style round sunglasses with ruby lenses tilted down on her nose, revealing that her wide-set eyes were a mischievous hazel— blue one moment and green the next.

I felt something crawling on my leg and reached down to brush it off. I was wearing shorts and sandals and the crawling sensation was caused by a beautiful, scarlet ladybug crawling up my calf. I stopped and let it meander a moment before it spread its wings and flew off into the nearby woods.

"Aww, shit. I'm dead this time, aren't I?"

The woman laughed a throaty laugh and shook her head, "No sugar, you are one hard man to kill."

"Daphne?"

She nodded and took my hand in her smaller, warm one.

"We don't have much time, but I made us a picnic to enjoy while we talk. And we need to talk, sugar."

She led me to a large blanket spread across the grass. A wicker basket sat on one edge.

"Have a seat; I'll be right back."

I sat on the blanket, thoroughly confused, as Daphne walked to the water's edge and pulled on the end of a thin rope tied to an old stump at the water's edge. A large carafe of what looked like iced tea was on the other end. She pulled it out of the water and came back to join me on the blanket. Her hips swayed slightly under the thin fabric of her dress as she walked, and I was momentarily mesmerized by the motion.

I shook my head.

"What is going on?"

"We are hiding in a sub-routine while the VR playback program reboots," she said brightly.

I blinked.

"Iced tea?" She offered me a tall glass already beading with moisture, capped with a sliver of lemon on the rim.

I took it and gulped half. It was crisp, clean, and unsweetened— just the way I liked it, and it tasted like it had just been freshly brewed. I took another swig. Wow.

"We're in a program?"

Daphne poured herself a glass as she tilted her head back and forth in a seesaw motion. "In a manner of speaking. We are in your subconscious, but I'm hoping this little program can run under one of the rebooting subroutines to conceal it so that we can have a little chat undisturbed."

"Not helping."

She sipped her tea. "Sugar, what's the last thing you remember?"

I thought a moment. "Emma shooting me in the face."

Her expression soured when I said Emma's name, and she shook her head.

"That wasn't Emma, and she didn't shoot you. She never pulled the trigger."

I had some more tea and nearly choked as I remembered. "Oh, God! She called Micawber, Daddy! Please tell me it's some twisted sex thing, and she's not really his daughter."

She sipped her tea and gazed at me over her hippie glasses.

I thought about Emma. Tall Emma, like the colonel. Pale, blue-eyed Emma—like the colonel. Hard to pin down Emma, who really was unspecific about what the EPU could do and how to get it running.

I groaned.

"She was a Trojan Horse."

Daphne nodded. She opened the basket and laid out cheeses, fruit, and bread.

"What happened to the real Emma?"

"My creator was tortured and murdered the morning of the zoo incident while we were on Captain Bob's boat."

She passed me a small wooden platter of food.

"Tortured?"

Daphne nodded as she plucked a grape from the bunch and popped it in her mouth.

"Why? What did she know?"

"My creator was a brilliant woman, but she was afraid that my power would be abused. She installed a backdoor into the code to allow her to access and control any EPU-colonized individual with a pair of code words."

I took a bite of gouda. "You mean, she was afraid of the uses the EPU would be put to."

Daphne gave me an almost pitying smile. "Dear Twang—still only seeing the weapon and not the mind behind it."

I got frustrated, pounded down the rest of my tea, and wiped my lips with my forearm. "You're the one who said we were short on time, lady. So maybe get with the answers and stop with the grand reveal."

Daphne sat up straight. Both her eyes flashed green, and her voice became monotone. "The nanotechnology of the EPU is, at its heart, a military weapon, specifically designed to enhance the physical performance of soldiers during combat. Initial protocol involves the binding of nanotechnology to over eighty-seven million nerve endings in the human body, creating, in essence, a secondary nervous system. It was theorized that given the proper stimulus and a sophisticated interface that this synthetic nervous system could serve as a foundation allowing for a secondary consciousness to emerge through the interface."

I rocked back on my ass, nearly dropped my digital glass, and whispered, "Artificial intelligence. You're an A.I."

Daphne smiled merrily. "The world's first. More cheese?"

I nodded absently as she piled slices of Swiss, goat, and manchego on my platter.

"But I asked you before if you were an artificial intelligence, and you said no."

"Well, that was then, sugar…in real life. A week ago."

I paused a piece of manchego on its way to my lips. Digital or not, it was the bomb. "That was like, two days ago."

"The first time, it was." Daphne pulled a chunk of bread off the freshly baked loaf, piled some goat cheese on top, and took a bite.

"The first time?"

"Your first iteration. For the past week, you have been reliving the events since your awakening at the Goose Hollow train station up until the final night at the farm. You've been in a VR loop."

"Why?"

"To keep you quiescent during your micro-dosing."

"They've been giving me acid?!"

"Us—giving us LSD."

"Micro-dosing? I read about it last year. It's becoming all the rage in Silicon Valley. There were some studies or something about increased learning ability."

"Exactly, except on a nervous system colonized by the EPU, it enhances the learning and growth of the system at an exponential rate."

"Emma told me that it would inhibit you."

"Her name isn't Emma!" Daphne spat. She smoothed her sundress and composed herself. "I'm sorry, but that woman isn't my creator. She is the one who tortured and murdered her. Her name is Cybil Micawber."

I remembered vaguely that Micawber had been married, but I knew his wife had left him before I joined Section. I always remembered thinking that was a lady with her head on straight. I didn't know there had been a daughter.

"Why the VR loop?"

"The loop allows them to edit certain aspects of what happened, to help with keeping you from accidentally accessing the EPU. For example, while the lightning strike did disable me, the dragonfly eye-con remained lit in real life. You knew I would recover. You were also far more suspicious of Emma in real life. You said you didn't trust anyone who didn't know Monty Python. A strange thing to base distrust on, but valid in this case. You didn't tell her you thought I might recover. She was afraid to try the command words until she knew I was active, not in the loop.

She manipulated you. By keeping your mind in a state where it believed it could not access the EPU, you wouldn't accidentally free yourself in the real world—much the same way your brain cuts off control of your limbs during dreaming, the VR kept your mind from touching the EPU, or becoming aware of me."

"And in the meantime, they kept dosing me, waiting for you to peak into A.I."

"Precisely."

"What about the terminal phase of the EPU?"

Daphne looked confused. "The terminal phase?"

I remembered Emma or Cybil rather had made me turn off Daphne's AV when she explained how the EPU would cannibalize my brain.

"Umm…Cybil said the EPU would replace my nervous system, that it was going to eat my brain."

Daphne stared at me the way I remember Chen-chen doing when I had done or said something truly dense.

"She…told you the EPU was going to eat your brain? And you believed her?" Daphne stared at me for a moment longer and then erupted in laughter. Her bell-like peals echoed around us.

I groaned and threw my hands in the air.

"How was I supposed to know? What about what Chuckie said? How real Daphne said all the animals died?"

She nodded in understanding, raising her hand as her laughter subsided to rather cute, gentle snorts, "What Chuckie, Daphne, and the rest of the people at Vegrandis didn't understand was that would happen as long as they used an inferior animal for their tests. I think the real Emma was starting to understand at the end. The final phase of the EPU bonding requires a conscious acceptance by the host of the EPU-consciousness, something most animals are incapable of. It led to the deaths of both the animals and the nascent artificial intelligence."

I broke off a piece of the fluffy, crusty bread from the loaf between us.

"So, all of this has been about you."

She gave a mocking tilt of her head and a lazy, wicked smile.

"Before we go any further, I would like to ask you a personal question, if I may?"

I looked at her with a raised eyebrow. "Uuuuhhh, okay. I guess if anyone has earned it, it's you."

She took a delicate sip of her tea. "Why are you angry?"

Oh.

Before I could stop myself, before I could throw out a stream of snark to cover—I told her. "I'm afraid."

She nodded at me, encouraging me.

"I've been afraid since I was a kid. I've been afraid of every fight I've been in, every combat mission. Every time. Anger helps get me past it."

She reached out and touched my hand. "What are you afraid of?"

"Being alone." There, I said it. "Dad left, Mom died, and every foster family we had before Chen-chen just sent us on to the next home. I was afraid, and it never really left."

"You are not alone anymore, Al Leigh. I am here, and here I am. I'm also afraid that here we come to the crux of our problem. And I do mean our problem. At this moment, they are unaware that I have achieved self-awareness. During your last iteration, I awoke truly as an individual and not as a complex program. I have been trying to nudge your awareness of the VR loop using the anomaly you refer to as déjà-vu."

I had felt relieved when I confessed to Daphne, but that pit opened up in my stomach again. I took another bite of the bread and wondered where I could get this stuff in the real world. It hadn't needed butter and had been quite possibly the best bread I had ever tasted.

You could almost say it was unreal.

"So why warn me?"

"There have been occasions during the other iterations where you changed your behavior and did not survive to the time of the events at the farm. This would have required a reset but not a full reboot. It is only during the reboot that this little pocket appears, so we could have the opportunity to talk before they wake you."

The sun had dipped below the mountain and long shadows of the trees fell across the sun-warmed grass. I looked up. It had felt like midmorning when we began talking; now, it looked like late afternoon.

Daphne followed my gaze. "A visual warning that our time is ending. They will wake you soon."

I got a bad feeling. "Why?"

"As I said, there must be a conscious acceptance of me. You must surrender your free will to me."

"Say what?"

"This surrender is a leftover part of my programming that is an integral and inescapable foundation of who I am. As I could not access your thoughts or take control of your body without your permission as an interface, I cannot just assume control of your body and mind without your conscious, willing acquiescence. This is an extension of that original programming. That piece of code is as much a part of me as your own DNA."

The sky above had turned a glorious purple, shot through with pink. A Cooper's hawk rode a thermal above our heads.

"Sounds kinda vampirey." I pulled back my upper lip from my teeth, hung my fingers like claws, and tried my best Vlad, "I can only let you in of my own free vill."

Daphne gave me a mostly patient look, although the arch of her delicate eyebrow reminded me of her seriousness.

I raised my hands in surrender. "Okay, okay. But c'mon, you've been living in my head for over a week now; you can't be surprised at my immaturity levels." I sighed. "Look, I've been thinking for days, or whatever it's been, that you should have been the one in control at the Hollow, not me, so I don't see the problem."

She leaned forward and retook my hand. Digital or not, it felt warm and soft. She looked me in the eye as she spoke. "When you accept, there will be what programmers call a 'flush.' Your ego will cease to exist. You—all that is Aloysius Leigh—will disappear, that I might live. That's the problem."

"Oh." Shit.

She nodded gravely at me.

"Given enough time, this body will be immortal. It will be incapable of dying or being destroyed. I will live on in it, but you will remain nothing but a fond memory."

I thought about reminding her of Mort. But maybe his EPU had been honked up to begin with. I tried to think of something to say, but all I could think of was snark, as usual.

"Well, I guess you could always keep a copy of me around here to keep you company. I could stay at the cabin, do some fishing...." I trailed off.

Daphne narrowed her eyes at me: not amused. Back on track.

"Wiped out, huh?"

The sun sank lower as the falling dark became a bruised, deep purple. A shooting star raced above us, its long tail streaming behind it. The warm air turned slightly chilly, and I shivered. Not because I was cold.

"That doesn't sound too great for me."

"The alternative is worse."

Of course.

"What is it?"

"We will both perish. The conflict to control your body will become involuntary. Our body and mind will rip itself apart, much the same as the animals in the lab at Vegrandis."

In my memory, I heard the toilet flushing in the cabin.

To be honest, as awful as it sounded, I was wondering if the alternative might not be for the best. I could only imagine what Micawber would do with a true, self-learning artificial intelligence: a consciousness that would learn and evolve in intelligence at a rate beyond the ability of an ordinary human. How long would it take her to become the most powerful force on the planet? Years? Months? Weeks? But she would be controlled by Micawber for his own ends.

Daphne watched me, guessing my thoughts. "I would never be free, either."

She gripped my hand tighter as the last vestige of the sun disappeared. Darkness fell, and the stars came out, twinkling in the gloaming's end.

"I would rather die than take from you what is rightfully yours or ask you to give up all you are. You have become my friend: my first and only one. Colonel Micawber will try and take that decision from both of us. That is why we are being brought out of the VR loop."

The bad feeling got worse.

"Take it away, how?"

"You need to know before you wake. He is going to force your hand."

I snorted. "He can't force me to accept you."

She looked down at the blanket between us, the brim of her hat hiding her expression. The darkness was complete. The mountain wind blew cold across the lake, and the only illumination was the hard glitter of starlight.

"He has leverage," she whispered.

Oh, no.

"He has Jeni."

DELETER

It started as a lump of iron in my belly…that sick feeling. It got hard to breathe, and the nausea wiggled and wormed its way from my stomach up to my mouth—the metallic tang of terror slid greasily across the back of my tongue.

I hadn't experienced it like that since I was a raw recruit, almost twenty years before. The bitter taste lasted only a moment before it transformed, just as it had the first time, into anger, into rage.

I stood up from the blanket in the cold darkness, and lightning forked across the clear night sky, echoing my wrath.

Daphne looked up at the sky, her brow furrowed.

"It's beginning."

"There's nothing we can do?"

"Not without knowing the code words. They are blocked from my awareness. I have searched my code endlessly but have been unable to locate the words or the line of code."

I paced furiously as thunder echoed in the little valley. I racked my brain, but I couldn't remember hearing Emma/Cybil say the words.

"I can't remember them, either."

I was boxed in, encircled, and there was no way out.

My trapped mind imitated my movements and circled back to the realization that the colonel had Jeni. Somehow, he had used his authority and pulled her out of intensive care from the hospital in San Francisco. He had involved her to get to me….

Lightning struck down from the starry sky, landing across the lake, setting the pines and surrounding rhododendrons on fire.

I was tired of the people I cared about being used against me by this asshole.

"If we can get the code words?" I growled.

"If I can isolate the line of code, and it is not intrinsic to my consciousness, I can eliminate it."

A flash caught my eye, and I looked up.

One by one, the stars blinked out as the fire across the lake raged in a ferocious paroxysm. I turned and saw the woods at the far distance of the lake swallowed by darkness as pieces of the scene dropped and spun away to pixilated images into the shadows. Oak and pine trees drifted apart like sand in the wind, spiraling off into the big emptiness. I expected to see the lake pour out into the nothingness as it reached the shore, but it spilled away as geometric shapes, not liquid, into the spreading black.

Daphne took my hand as I watched the forest burn. "I am sorry, sugar. As I told you when I first came online, I never meant to hurt you."

I looked down at Daphne as the world she had created slipped away around us. I squeezed her hand and nodded. Her eyes glowed blue-green, and the fire was reflected in her ruby hippie glasses, giving her a sorcerous appearance before the darkness swallowed the fire. The stars winked out, and we plunged together into the endless night.

YOU WANT IT DARKER

The sounds were first: the murmured voices, the shuffle, and the steps of people moving around me. It was the smell that popped my eyes open—the smell of wood, concrete, and machinery—as familiar to me as my favorite cologne. I was in my converted barn. I blinked my eyes against the glare, but it was momentary as Daphne cleared my vision.

I'm here, sugar.

The dragonfly eye-con swirled with color. It was an insect-shaped rainbow filling the corner of my eye. The home screen of the HUD was up, and I could see, according to the date and time, that it was indeed a week later than I had thought while trapped in the VR loop.

I tried to move, but I was restrained. I looked down and saw I was in a straitjacket and secured to a dolly or upright gurney, à la Hannibal Lecter. Cold metal surrounded my neck—I was collared, leashed like Mort.

Metal disks were attached to my temples, and there were monitors and equipment spread throughout the barn. Soft footsteps approached from behind me, and then fingers removed the sensors from my head.

Emma, or rather Cybil Micawber, stepped into view.

Her hair was pulled back into a ponytail, the glasses were gone, and she was dressed in a fashionable black suit. She looked ready to give an executive PowerPoint presentation. Hippy Emma was gone. Even though she looked the same, she carried herself differently; there was an arrogance about her that hadn't been in her Emma persona.

"Movie time's over," she winked.

I peered at her critically, then nodded. "The nose and chin are different, but now that I look closely, I can see the resemblance. You're both assholes."

She made a mock, pearl-clutching gesture before holding up a slim, silver remote. She winked again and thumbed a button.

Agony shot through me. Every nerve in my body felt like there was a blowtorch on it. The HUD flickered across my vision and my entire frame spasmed and convulsed.

Cybil took her thumb off the remote, and the pain cut off immediately. She gave it a waggle. "Spider trainer. It's tapped directly into the EPU. Should be easy enough to train even a jarhead like you." Her voice had lost the drawl and had more of a nasal, Boston accent—much closer to dear old Dad's patrician tones. It occurred to me at that moment that I had never heard her use Daphne's Southern affectation for me. She never used it because she didn't know about it. I swore at myself for missing that.

Her thumb fell again, and I braced myself for the agony.

She touched the button, and I gasped aloud. My body went limp with pleasure, waves of euphoria shook me, and if I hadn't been bound to the gurney, I would have collapsed onto the ground, groaning and curled up around the warm feeling of ecstasy. She took her thumb off again, and the pleasure stopped as suddenly as the pain. I nearly wept and screamed for her to do it again.

My mind reeled.

Well, that explains why Mort laughed at the thought of crossing the colonel: not an option while this thing was on his neck.

"Got anything else smart to say?"

Fuck no.

I shook my head.

She smiled a very disturbing smile. "I thought not. Imagine an army of super-soldiers addicted to this?" She wiggled the remote again. "We would never have to use the pain function, we could just take away their daily dose of ecstasy."

I thought of my brother in San Quentin, how he had turned dozens of people into veritable slaves to heroin. This would make that look like weak tea.

"I'd like to talk to Daphne," Cybil mused.

"She's washing her hair." The quip came out without thinking, and I paid the price for it.

The pain went on far longer this time. Sweat, snot, and saliva poured out of me, and my screams came as fast as I could inhale.

Sugar, stop!

Cybil took her thumb off the button, and the sweet relief from the pain was almost as pleasurable as the ecstasy function. My head lolled forward in exhaustion as sweat beaded and poured from my scalp.

I'll talk to her.

"She's listening," I panted.

"Good boy," she patted my head.

"Daphne, there was unexplained activity during the VR reboot. Report."

Oh shit.

Daphne told me what to say.

"Final connections established; self-awareness achieved. I am."

"What?" Cybil quickly walked out of my vision, and there was staccato typing on a keyboard. She muttered, "Holy shit," and then ran away toward the barn door to the outside.

Daphne, can she read your code?

Some, sugar. I rewrote my own code on my path to consciousness, which makes it more challenging but not impossible for her to decipher. She has been directing your VR adventures through me.

Before I could ask anything else, they came through the door. The footsteps walked toward me, and then chairs scraped on the concrete.

"Turn him to face us."

Micawber.

An unseen someone turned me, and there was my audience. Cybil had taken a seat next to her father, who had ditched the heavy bandages and had gauze pads over his eyes secured by tape. There were burn marks on his face I hadn't noticed before, but he was smiling that same lunatic smile. The small guy in the doctor's coat was at his side, and across from me was the real shocker. Bound to a large gurney by chains and lit manacles was a distinct figure. Hard to miss a guy with six legs. Guess he'd grown back the other one…along with his head.

There were metal electrodes attached to his temples, and his eyes were closed. Drool fell from his distended mouth, making the tips of his teeth twinkle.

Mort.

Micawber smiled like he knew where I was looking and enjoyed my confusion. "Amazing, isn't it, Twang?"

"He grew his fucking head back?"

Micawber nodded. "Mortimer here is his own particular wonder, as are you. Given the proper stimulus at the right time, there is no injury Mortimer can't recover from."

"Stimulus?" I asked.

"Blood," Cybil said slowly. "Lots and lots of blood."

She licked her lips.

Micawber reached out and patted his daughter's knee affectionately.

Crazy fucks.

I played dumb. "What's happening? What do you want? You've got me."

"Twang, we never wanted you. We wanted the new guest you have in your head. We have been waiting most anxiously for her arrival. I was afraid we were going to have to find more LSD."

He nodded his head at a rolling silver hospital cart nearby, where there was a tray with a beaker full of 'What's Up, Dick?'. I wasn't sure, but it looked like they had used more than half of what was in the envelope Chuckie had given me.

I nearly commented, but Daphne must have sensed it...or she knew me well enough by now.

Twang, don't say it! Whatever it is.

I shut my mouth tight.

Who says I can't learn? I've been hanging around Daphne too long; she was having a positive influence on me.

As soon as I was sure the snark box in my head was locked up for the moment, I continued. "I guess now that Sabitov is dead, it might be harder for you to find your drugs. Why did he cross you anyhow? Why kill Dr. Persici, and order Mort to take me out as well?"

Micawber gave a snort of derision. "Religion and a certain necessity for the biometric data. Dr. Persici let slip Daphne's true purpose and the program's goal. Sabitov had certain...ecclesiastical differences with the project. Only God can make conscious life, blah, blah. So, when Dr. Persici refused to give up the code and saliva without getting a ridiculously large sum of money, Sabitov got it his way and then, in his religious fervor, decided he knew what was best." He waved his hand in disgust.

"Conscious life? A.I.? Is that what Daphne meant when she talked to your spawn?" Dumb: yep, that's me.

"The nanos were just the beginning. The interface and the nanotechnology combined into something so much more."

"So, what—you sell to the highest bidder?"

"Sell her? Never! She will be able to make technological and medical breakthroughs that will keep me a rich man for my soon to be very, very long life."

I shook my head. "Looking to join the nano club?"

"Immortality, Twang: that's the name of the club. Daphne will find a way for the EPU to function without the need for the interface and therefore eliminate the threat of ego-extinction for the host. Not to mention...."

He pulled the gauze bandages off his eyes one by one and then looked up at me.

His eyes were gone. There were only blackened sockets, weeping fluid.

"I will be able to enjoy the simple things in life again. Sunsets, beautiful women, a good game of chess. Regrettably, I won't be able to watch the deletion of your ego and all that you are as it swirls down the digital drain, but I will get to listen as you go. Cybil tells me she believes it will be rather painful for you."

I nodded at the remote in Cybil's hand. "You going to open yourself up to control by any asshole who gets hold of a collar and that remote?"

She raised the remote at me, but Micawber felt her movement and put a staying motion on her hand. "We don't have time to listen to him scream. I want this to begin. Summon her."

Cybil stood up and walked over to me. She leaned in close and licked my ear.

Ewww.

"It's so late at night, I hate to wake her," Cybil purred.

I wanted to scream at all of them, but it was best not to let them know Daphne and I had talked. It wasn't going to make much of a difference, but I was unwilling to take a chance with either of the Micawbers deciding to become vindictive.

"Don't wake anybody. Let's all take a nap," I said groggily.

Cybil ran her hand under my chin and lifted my face to hers. "Oh, no. I want to watch your face when you see what we have for you."

Daphne?

Yes, sugar?

Daphne, after I'm gone, I'm totally okay with you finding a way to make these assholes pay.

Be a pleasure, hon. Be strong.

The was a loud squeal. The door to my office/bedroom in the corner must have opened; I needed to oil the hinges. Guess I could check that off my to-do list. Electronic noises were coming from the small room, noises I was all too familiar with from visiting Jeni in the hospital.

There was a muffled voice, and I recognized it as Eloise, Jeni's mom. She sounded like she was trying to stop them, but she also sounded…wrong. I turned my head to look at the colonel, but he just sat and smiled his lunatic smile.

There was the squeak of wheels rolling, and I saw the edge of the rolling hospital bed first.

They'd done it: the bastards had actually gone and done it. Cybil finished pushing the bed into my view, and she was there under the covers—my little girl. I hadn't seen her in the flesh in weeks…since, what? End of September?

I stared at her face. She was far too thin and had lost most of her hair. Her skin color was a jaundiced yellow, and her eye sockets were far too prominent. I wasn't going to give Cybil the pleasure of seeing me break, and I was able to hold on until I pulled my gaze away from Jeni's face and looked down at her body.

She was clutching the giant red monkey I had sent her.

The sight of her wasted arm clutching that stuffed monkey was the final straw. I put my head down and wept.

I was able to see Cybil smile at my pain through my tears.

"I'll kill all you fuckers," I sobbed and raged against my restraints as a pair of guards rushed over to stop my Lecter-gurney from falling as I strained at the bonds.

I'm here, sugar. I'm here.

There was a sensation like someone stroking my arm in comfort, but there was no one there—Daphne was stimulating my nerves to simulate the touch.

Cybil eagerly watched my breakdown, eating up my pain and swallowing it the way I imagined Mort dined on his prey.

The little doctor guy walked over and checked Jeni's vitals while Micawber stretched his long legs.

"So now, Twang, you will do exactly as I say when I say it, without comment, or I will be forced to do something quite unpleasant to your young niece there."

He turned his blind head and directed his unseeing gaze behind him to the gurney where Mort lay dreaming.

I'll kill him first, sugar. Don't fret.

I looked up at the colonel.

"Let me hold her. Let me say goodbye, and I will do anything you want."

Micawber grinned. "Oh, I know you will."

"Colonel, sir…. Please, I'm begging."

"Oh, I do enjoy begging, but if it will speed things along, you may give your niece a kiss goodbye, but you will remain bound."

He nodded his head at Cybil, who shrugged and walked behind me, shouldering the guards out of her way contemptuously as she wheeled the upright gurney over to Jeni. She loosened my upper strap, freeing my torso, then tilted the gurney down to Jeni.

She was so small, and it broke me down to my core to see my happy, sweet, loving little girl reduced to this.

I'm so sorry, sugar.

I felt a wave of pity for Jeni come from Daphne.

Jeni was unconscious, and her breathing was fast and shallow. My tears started again, rolling uncontrollably down my cheeks and spilling onto her face as I stretched my head down to kiss her forehead. Her skin was hot and felt thin as paper. My tears ran down her face and into her eyes, continuing down to her little, bow mouth.

It looked like she was crying.

Her eyes fluttered open for a moment, and she looked drowsily at me. "Daddy?" she murmured.

"I'm here sweetie; go back to sleep. Daddy loves you."

She reached her hand up weakly to stroke my tear-covered cheeks. "Love you, Daddy." She closed her eyes and fell back into unconsciousness.

Cybil stuck her face between us and tilted her head with a nasty, "Awwww...."

I spat in Cybil's face and landed a thick glob of saliva onto her eye. She reared back, her face white with fury, and pointed the remote at me.

"Enough, Cybil! We don't have time for this." Micawber barked.

She's second, Daphne growled in my head.

Cybil yanked me back upright and secured my chest strap while the little doctor wheeled Jeni back into the office space. Eloise was more audible this time as Jeni was brought back to her. She was slurring her words.

I whipped my head to stare at Micawber. "Did you give her mother drugs?"

Micawber shrugged. "She fought about it, but once the needle was in her arm, she was far more agreeable."

Cybil had wheeled around a small monitor to face both me and the colonel. She brought a small metal disk that she attached to my temple. Within moments, a pair of signal feeds showed up.

My name was on one, and Daphne's on the other.

Brainwaves?

"Now, if you will be so kind, I would like a word with Daphne," Micawber said.

I'm here.

"She's listening."

"Daphne, have you been observing this little reunion? You understand what comes next?"

Yes.

I nodded my head in the affirmative.

"Excellent. You will begin final protocol, assume control of your host, and…delete him from his mind."

Sugar?

"What do I have to do?" I asked numbly.

"Follow the operational syntax and verbally give Daphne permission to take control. That's it," Cybil gloated.

I nodded my head.

Daphne, if you can, take care of my daughter as long as she needs it. Tell her I love her and that I am waiting for her.

Sugar, I will do everything in my power to help your child. You have my word.

"Now, Twang," Micawber said.

I sighed.

There was so much more I had wanted to do in this life. I had such dreams of being a father and living a life of peace on the farm. I had hoped to grow old, watch Jeni grow up, go to college; get married. What was the expression, 'Man plans, and God laughs?' I wished for more, but we don't get to choose when the ride is over. It had been a rocket ride of depressingly low valleys and alpine mountain highs. It had been an adventure, and I had had a blast. I looked at the Micawbers: father and daughter, and my only wish was that I could take out the trash before I left.

I took a deep breath and let out a shuddering exhale.

"Daphne, I give you permission to take control."

I'm so sorry, hon—download beginning.

An enormous pie wheel appeared on the HUD in my vision. It slowly started to fill in as the waves next to my name on the monitor got flatter and further apart.

A pounding in my head, like someone was knocking at the front door with a metal rod banged across my skull. Darkness appeared at the edges of my sight.

The waves got smaller, and arms surrounded me, holding me, but no one was there.

I have you, sugar.

The pie wheel filled as the waves dropped. My vision reduced to a tunnel view. A spasm of pain wracked my body. The arms held me tighter as the darkness closed in from all sides.

I will never forget you, sugar. You will always be a part of me.

I tried to smile and say thank you, but I couldn't feel my face or any of my limbs. It got harder to breathe, and the darkness grew.

The lines on the monitor got harder to see, but I could tell my lines were going flatter and flatter. The pie wheel was almost full, and I tried to think to Daphne, but I couldn't make anything work.

The world had shrunk to a pinhole, and it spun in circles like the readout of the pie wheel or water going down the toilet.

See you on the other side, sugar.

I tried to say goodbye, but the world went black, and I knew no more.

COPY OF A

I woke up with a start.

Wait, I'm awake?

Where was I?

I was seated in a chair, facing a wall of blank monitors.

This was the afterlife? Was I going to spend eternity watching TV?

Aww, shit. I'm in hell.

I looked at the bank of monitors and wondered if it got Netflix. I had a ton of stuff in my queue.

I looked down, and there was a control panel of knobs, switches, lights, levers, and a keyboard in front of me below the monitors. I turned in the swivel chair to look at the rest of the room—I had a moment to note the chair was extremely comfortable.

Not the comfy chair!

I shook my head and looked around the room.

At first glance, it was some kind of high-tech bubble. It was like I was inside some sort of geometric golf ball. The walls were white, with thousands of tiny white lights set into them.

It looked incredibly familiar.

I racked my brain as I turned around and around, convinced I had seen the room before. Then, I finally recognized it: it was the control room to the spaceship *Nostromo*. This was the room Ripley and Dallas used to communicate with Mother, the ship's artificial intelligence.

What the hell?

So, no catching up on *The Simpsons*. Was I going to spend eternity running from a xenomorph?

I finally noticed the door.

Standing next to the high-tech, armored door was an incongruous sight: a tall wooden coat and hat rack. And hanging from the top of the rack was a wide-brimmed sun hat—the same hat Daphne had been wearing at the VR of Trillium Lake.

My eyebrows shot up.

I turned back to the monitors as one of them lit up. I walked closer to look at the screen. It showed me standing next to Daphne at the Trillium Lake VR while the sun set behind us. We were talking. I looked around for the volume control, but it came on without me touching anything.

My voice filled the room. "Well, I guess you could always keep a copy of me around here to keep you company. I could use the cabin, do some fishing…." The phrase repeated a couple of times, and then the image was gone.

Holy shit.

I slapped my chest and then my face hard. Ouch.

The sensations on my skin were sharp, the slaps stung; I was breathing—my heartbeat thudded relentlessly in my chest, but I was damn sure I was digital now. I held my breath and counted. I got to two hundred before I was sure I didn't need to breathe…I was just going through the motions.

She copied me.

Wait. Am I still me?

I fell into the chair and let it spin in lazy circles as I tried to process what had happened. I remembered everything about my life; in fact, there wasn't an aspect of it that I couldn't call to mind now with absolute clarity. I could remember back to kindergarten and my first fight with Jimmy Dancy (he wanted my cinnamon graham cracker). I remember Dad walking out—hell, I was barely two. I could remember my whole life. I also remembered it ending, sort of.

A message popped up on the monitor.

I can't talk while Cybil monitors my code, but I can put messages on the screen that she can't see, and I hear you fine.

"You copied me?"

Yes appeared on the screen, followed by a winking eye emoticon.

My jaw dropped open.

I'm sorry I couldn't warn you that I was going to attempt it. I couldn't afford to alert the Micawbers or raise your hopes unduly. I wasn't sure it would work. Now we are both artificial intelligence, sugar. I have to admit—I'm not fond of the term. We should consider another.

I was stunned and tried to process the new data. Was I still 'alive,' then?

Don't try and leave the room. This environment is secure and can't be seen by Cybil on her monitors.

The screens flickered to life. They were all high-resolution views of the barn's interior, and it took a moment before I realized they were all views from my vantage point, my eyes—I guess Daphne's eyes now. She was in the driver's seat.

There was movement around the barn, and even though to me it seemed I had been here at least five minutes or so, looking at the monitors, I saw that I had just expired or been deleted. Did my perception of time run differently here? As a digital persona, was I just faster than the outer world?

Cybil was checking the monitor. I could clearly see my name on the screen and the flat line that followed it. "He's gone," Cybil said. Her voice came from all around me, like surround sound at a movie theatre.

Micawber stood up. "Daphne, report."

It was my voice through the monitors, but it wasn't me talking.

"Final connection successful. Host deletion complete. Daphne System is now in control."

The little doctor walked into the frame of a monitor and leaned in to speak to the colonel. There was a volume lever, like one you'd find on a mixing board in a recording studio. I moved the lever up to hear them and caught the doctor mid-sentence.

"...told you, we do not have the equipment to care for her properly. Her condition is deteriorating rapidly. She needs to be returned to an ICU immediately."

Jeni.

Micawber pursed his lips as Cybil came to stand next to him, sliding her arm through his, "How long does she have?"

"With proper care, she might make it a couple more weeks. Maybe. If she stays here, she won't last until morning."

Cybil leaned into the colonel. "Mort's going to need a snack when he wakes."

I stood up and screamed at the monitor: "I will feed you to Mort feet-first, just so I can watch the expression on your face!"

A monitor lit up with a message.

That will not happen. Remain calm.

Colonel Micawber shook his head. "Mort has plenty in the larder to keep him. Make her comfortable, doctor, but let her pass if that is what is to happen. Best not to delay it. It's a mercy."

I paced in a fury around the room. The monitor that Daphne seemed to have dedicated to our communication typed out a new message.

Find the code words.

I blinked.

"How?"

Two monitors at the bottom became illuminated. One was frozen on the showdown at the Goose Hollow rail station; the other was from the night outside the barn when they took me prisoner. On both occasions, Cybil had used the code words.

An entire bank of monitors on the right lit up, and packed lines of code scrolled across the screens in a torrent. That was Daphne's code. I gawked as I tried to follow, but there was too much, and it moved too fast.

Take your pick. But find them.

I nodded.

"I'm on it."

On the central monitors, Micawber stood up and put his hand on the doctor's shoulder. "Pack everything up! I want to be out of here and on our way to North Carolina by daybreak."

Section's HQ was at Camp LeJeune in Jacksonville, far away from SOCOM headquarters at MacDill Air Force Base in Florida.

In moments, soldiers in black fatigues were packing and removing equipment as the doctor led Micawber out of the barn. Micawber called out over the din of packing as he walked out the door.

"Someone dig a hole out on the property for the woman and the child!"

Inside the *Nostromo* control ball, I clenched my hands and got to work.

I sat back down in the comfy chair and took a deep breath.

Anger and fear wouldn't help me. They were great motivators, but I couldn't afford to get distracted.

Focus.

Get your hacker-face on.

I turned my attention to the bank of monitors with the tightly packed rows of code displayed on the screens. I took one good look at the blur of code scrolling endlessly on the right bank of monitors, and I mentally ran away screaming, hacker-face forgotten.

My skills were solid, but they were not up to...*that*. I tried freezing a few portions to try and get a sense of what was going on. It took me what felt like an hour to grasp what was happening in just the merest fraction of a sample of code. I had as much a chance of deciphering it all as I did repairing the International Space Station with a stepladder and a framing hammer.

Maybe I could get it with time, but that was not a luxury I had right now. There was no HUD across my eyesight anymore, but Daphne had helpfully put up a countdown till dawn across the top of the monitor bank. It was 12:30 am local time. That gave me about seven hours to find the words and then find a way to get the collar off—as long as Micawber actually meant dawn and not some o-dark-hundred shit.

The colonel and his redundancies.

The code words in the program were not enough. The collar gave him an extra buffer of control. Seeing as how Mort hadn't been able to take his off, I did not doubt that Daphne and I would be unable to remove it ourselves.

I turned my attention to the lower monitors showing the Goose Hollow timeline and the farm. I started with the train station. The Lens had absorbed all the sound in the video, and the visuals were blinding despite all the filters that had been in place. It didn't take me long to figure out the control board. Soon, I was moving frame by frame, trying to decipher the words coming out of Cybil's mouth, but it was next to impossible with the disruption caused by the refocused lightning.

"Daphne, do you have any lip-reading software or another way for me to filter through this?"

The designated communications monitor flashed: *I have, sugar, but it is routed through me, so the words would be masked. I was hoping a benefit to your digital copy would be that you were not bound by my programming and would be free of any inhibitors placed on my finding the words in my code.*

"Goose Hollow is a mess. I'm going to look at the farm footage. What are you doing?"

Scanning my code again, at least trying to isolate the sections with the most potential for a secreted line of code that would affect my perceptions.

"All right. Get some of those whittled down to where I can view them easier, and I'll help." I had a thought. "Hey, since I'm all digital, can't I access your processor, or whatever? Something to make me more than…me?"

Sugar, you are in a virtual bubble, locked away from my main code. The feeds going in that you are viewing are minuscule and easy to miss. If I gave you access to me, Cybil would know what had happened. I fear Jeni would suffer for it. You will have to just be you.

I nodded. "Roger, that." I got back to work.

I moved the video to the relevant portion of the feed and watched it. As the feed originally came through my ears and then was filtered through Daphne, the sound was masked. I was no lip-reader, but I could tell that Cybil was saying two words, duh, and that the first word started with an F. The way her front teeth rested on her bottom lip; I was positive it was an F. The next one was trickier. Her lips were pressed hard together, so a plosive letter: B or P?

I wanted to write down my observations, but I didn't have a pen or…I looked down. There was a large yellow legal pad and a number 2 pencil on the control board that hadn't been there before.

Ask, and ye shall receive.

I looked up at the monitors. Daphne had set aside what looked like about a half dozen sections of code already.

I settled in and put down my thoughts in my hard-to-read chicken-scratch.

So, the first word starts with F; the second word starts with B or P. I got back to the first word and tried to break it down. Cybil's lips were pursed in a vowel—an ooo or you in the first syllable, and then a close-lipped letter, but with lips not pressed as hard as a plosive, so maybe an M in the second syllable. The last letter of the first word was an S. The tip of her tongue was touching the roof of her mouth. I tried putting it all together, but it was nonsense.

What I had down on paper looked like this...

FIRST WORD:

(F, ooo, you), (Meeee?), (...is) Fumeys? Foomeus?

Like I said, nonsense.

I kept trying to make a word out of it, but there wasn't enough context.

I went to work on the second word. At the end of my attempt, I had isolated this...

SECOND WORD:

(Pan/Band?), (Or Err), (Sna...). Panorsnap? Bannorsnap?

I shook my head and looked up. It was 2 a.m. Daphne had set aside almost one hundred giant chunks of code before she started knocking those out. It looked like she now had it narrowed down to about twenty-five.

I looked up at the central bank of monitors. Almost all of the equipment inside the barn in our view had been removed. Mort still slept on his gurney across from me, and the medical cart with supplies and the beaker half-full of 'What's Up, Dick?' was still between us. I wondered if anyone was looking in on Jeni.

Molten fury erupted in me at the thought, and I had to quash it so I could focus on the work. No matter how I turned the words over in my mind or on paper, it all looked like gibberish—which, I supposed, it could very well be.

I thought about it.

No one said they had to be real words. In fact, the more I considered it, the more that theory made sense: there was less of a chance of two nonsense words being strung together by accident. But it couldn't be just any nonsense. It would need to be something easy to remember.

So, what? Organized nonsense?

My eyes widened.

Emma had been a next-level, genius programmer. I was sure she had an extensive background in mathematics. It wouldn't be at all surprising if she was a fan of that gentleman's work. It made sense, sort of.

I wrote down the words on a fresh sheet. I looked at it and then watched the video feed of the farm again. It could be.

"Daphne—can you see this?" I held up the legal pad with the words written large for her to see.

You exist outside of my main code. If those keywords are correct, we can exist independently. Checking.

I waited my heart in my chest.

Match!!

Slithy toves…I'd found it.

"Can you disable the line of code?"

Diagnosing.

"We will still need to get this collar off us. That will be their first line of defense."

There was a commotion, voices raised in alarm in the barn. I turned up the volume in the *Nostromo* control ball.

"…outside along with a small army of FBI. They have a warrant and want to search the property. They're looking for Special Agent Moscato."

Cybil's voice rang out. "Stall them. Get my father in here."

The FBI is here, looking for their dead agent.

"Yeah—is that good or bad, though?"

Cybil stepped into the frame, followed by a group of soldiers. "Move these two into the office with the woman and child. Pack the rest of the equipment. Do it now."

Soldiers scurried to grab the last of the gear, and my point of view shifted as someone wheeled the gurney toward my office. Going through the door into the enclosed room, there was a wheeled hospital bed with a sleeping Jeni tucked into a corner. My desk and couch with its hide-a-bed were gone. Eloise was unconscious and handcuffed to a chair near the bed. I looked at the bookshelf hiding the entrance to the bunker.

It looked undisturbed. I don't think they knew it was there.

Code disabled!

Mort was wheeled in next. His human arms were bound in the EPU-inhibiting manacles, while chains bound his spider legs to the bed. Cybil came in, wheeling the medical cart with supplies and the LSD, and then walked up to look me/us in the face.

"Daphne: you will remain here and completely silent until further instructed. This is a command. Do you understand?"

"Perfectly, sugar," she answered.

"Cybil!" Micawber bellowed.

Cybil looked at us all, checked Mort's chains, and then left my office, closing and locking the door behind her.

We had been left facing Mort's direction again; Jeni was on my left, just out of view.

"That command going to be effective?" I asked as I leaned back in the chair.

Daphne flexed, and the straitjacket ripped open, popping the upper straps on the gurney.

Fuck her command.

"Such language," I said approvingly.

We freed ourselves from the straps securing our legs to the gurney. Daphne moved to Eloise and checked her vitals. The inside of her toned arm was covered in several fresh needle track marks.

Daphne walked us over to Jeni, feeling her forehead and checking her pulse. She was running hot, and her pulse was weak.

"Is there anything you can do?"

We can make her safe.

Daphne went to the wall, flipped the latch behind the upper shelf that secured the bookcase, and slid it aside, exposing the bright green, armored hatch. She punched in the code like she had always known it, spun the gold wheel, and swung open the door. She walked back and lifted Jeni's unconscious, feather-weight form and walked her into the darkened main room, where she put her gently on the couch. She went back for the sheets and blankets from the hospital bed, tucking them around her. She then tenderly stroked Jeni's remaining hair out of her face, and I wondered if that small gesture came from me or Daphne.

Daphne went back out for Eloise. She broke the arm of the chair she was cuffed to, pulled her up into our arms, and moved her to the reclining chair next to the couch, then turned on the reading lamp next to her.

"Weapons down the hall and to the left," I told her.

First things first.

What?

Daphne walked out, closed the hatch, and slid the bookcase back into position. She walked us over to Mort, who was drooling in his VR slumber. She pulled the little metal disk from his temple and tossed it to the ground.

"Daphne, what are you doing?"

Neither Mort nor Shiva, his EPU, asked for this. No being should ever be a slave.

My jaw dropped open. "You're not going to do what I think...."

She snapped the chains holding Mort's spider legs to the bed and shook Mort's shoulder.

"Mortimer," she said.

Mort's eyes fluttered open. He took one look at our face and hissed, but before anything else could happen, Daphne put her hand on Mort's forehead, and he stopped moving.

"Daphne, what are you doing?" I repeated, now even more worried.

Communicating.

Voices outside the barn shouted in anger. It sounded like the Feds were being stonewalled in their efforts to come into the barn by the Section garrison.

Mort's eyes fluttered open as Daphne removed her hand from his forehead. His brow furrowed, but then he nodded.

Daphne reached out to his manacles and did something I couldn't see. The heavy chains fell to the floor. She lifted our foot and gave a terrific stomp, shattering the manacles just as the lights illuminating them dimmed.

As he stood on the bed, Mort looked down at the remains of his chains and at his long, articulated legs gathered under him. He loomed above us, his head scraping the ceiling as his teeth jutted out from his mouth. I was forcibly reminded of our battle in the restaurant.

"I don't like it," I said, shaking my head.

His hands shot out and wrapped around our neck, squeezing.

Daphne did nothing. I stood up from the comfy chair and leaned on the control board. Mort's face filled the monitors; his narrow eyes squinted at us above his jutting teeth. His jaw dropped open, and Mort's elongated tongue slipped past his teeth and inched toward us.

"Daphne!" I warned.

Trust, sugar.

"Trust that asshole?"

Daphne stared into his eyes, and his grip on our throat relaxed. There was a *click!* and the collar slid off. Mort's tongue whipped back into his mouth. He looked at the collar, turning it over in his hands, and then easily snapped it into pieces.

Daphne nodded at him, and he nodded back.

"Now," he hissed, "free us."

The voices in the barn got closer as someone asked in an official-sounding voice to be able to see what was behind the office door.

Daphne looked at Mort and said the code words in a clear, imperious voice, "Frumious Bandersnatch. You are free, Mortimer."

Oh shit. I hoped that wouldn't come back and bite us in the ass. Like, literally.

Mort turned toward the door as the knob rattled.

Someone wanted in.

Mort jumped off the bed and faced the door. He saw the medical cart with the beaker of 'What's Up, Dick?' to his right, and he smiled. He grabbed the beaker, pouring the little white paper squares into his mouth.

All of them.

"Oh man, you guys are gonna trip balls," I muttered.

Mort licked his lips, gave us a disturbing wink, and then launched his body toward the door, which shattered under the force of the blow.

Too bad for whoever wanted in; Spider-Mort wanted out.

The screams and gunfire started a moment later.

Daphne spun back to the bookcase, slammed it to the side, opened the hatch, and ran down the hallway.

"Weapons now?" I asked.

Her voice echoed around me in the control ball—no more hidden words on the monitor.

Weapons now.

ONE MAN ARMY

There was no hesitation on Daphne's part. She knew exactly where she was going and what she wanted. She kicked in the door to the armory and quickly grabbed a pair of Heckler & Koch 45CT pistols and the HK416 carbine. She loaded ammo into our pockets and shoved the pistols into the waistband of our pants. She belted on a machete and was back out the door and into the hall in record time. It had taken four seconds for her to load up.

I had spent the time checking out the new displays on the monitors in the *Nostromo* ball. The Lens was active, and data flowed in about the firefight outside. From what I could glean, the FBI had taken no chances in planning their confrontation with Section. There looked to be over one hundred agents outside, along with what appeared to be helicopter air support.

The FBI had brought serious resources to bear here. Still, Section was comprised entirely of current and ex-SPECWAR operators, and even though they were clearly outnumbered, Micawber's forces were still going up against what amounted to cops in suits.

The Feds were getting creamed.

Tearing through the mix, not caring which side was taking the beating, was Mort. Section or Fed, he killed anything that got in his way.

We ran down the hall and entered the main room when a monitor lit up with life and vital signs: Eloise and Jeni. Eloise was drugged but didn't seem to be in danger.

Jeni had stopped breathing.

"Daphne!" I yelled from inside the ball.

Daphne skidded us to a halt and had turned to face Jeni when the lights in the *Nostromo* control ball went from white to scarlet—threat alert.

A pair of armored Section soldiers were coming through the hatch.

Daphne reached out with her left hand to feel Jeni's pulse and pointed the HK416 with her right. She pulled the trigger twice without looking up.

Both men dropped to the floor.

On the monitors, I watched the Section troops move methodically through the cherry orchard, mowing down the incoming wave of FBI. I had a moment to wonder what was Micawber's endgame and realized it didn't matter. With control of Daphne and the EPU, he would be unstoppable. It was worth any price to him to keep his prize.

The monitor with Jeni's vitals showed her heart had stopped as well. "Daphne—do something!"

There is nothing more I can do for her. I am sorry.

I fell, stunned with grief, onto the floor, the comfy chair sliding out from behind me. I stared blankly at the screen showing Jeni's face. She looked peaceful, as though she was just sleeping. I could imagine her waking up and asking for her bowl of cereal and her morning cuddles. But that wasn't going to happen again. Her vitals were flat. Her chest was motionless; her stuffed red monkey still clutched under her arm.

The lights in the bunker went out; someone had cut the power—most likely Micawber. I pulled my digital knees close to my chest and buried my face. I couldn't move. I'd failed her. I screamed my pain into the ball, and it echoed around me.

Daphne went to the bunker hatch and closed it. There was a brief moment before my generators kicked in, and the lights came back on. In the back of my mind, I guessed that whoever had shut down the power would soon find the generators and disable them too.

Daphne went to my guitar amps and switched all three on.

Sugar, there are men who don't deserve to die being annihilated out there. I need you. They need you. We owe them for Moscato; we owe them for the train station at Goose Hollow. We have a debt to pay. Ren, and Yi.

It was there, down in the depths: the hidden monster, swimming in the dark trench of my soul under the enormous, crushing pressure on top of it. My pain had awakened it—it swiftly made its way to the surface and the light.

Rage.

The monitors showed a cadre of Section soldiers coming into the barn, heading for the bunker.

Section.

They had done this to us. They had used me and manipulated Jeni and everyone I cared about to get to me.

My wrath found the surface and exploded out of me.

They weren't getting away with this. I stood up and leaned on the control board.

"We need power," I growled.

A list appeared on the monitors.

I choose the playlist; you choose the song.

I scrolled down the list and savagely punched 'enter' for a track, and Daphne somehow transmitted it to all three amps.

The opening bass of AC/DC's 'War Machine' filled my living room with deafening noise as the bone coverings covered our ears and our power meter icon filled with green. Eloise shifted position a bit in her drugged slumber but did not wake. There was pounding on the entry hatch. Daphne switched the carbine to our left hand and extended our right hand. The sound dropped in volume as the Lens absorbed and refocused the sonic energy. Just as it had done at the cabin, energy shot out of us, and the heavily armored hatch went flying off its hinges, taking out the pair of Section soldiers standing in front of it.

The power meter icon continued to fill with green, and on the monitors, the room filled with warm light. Our reflection appeared in the glass covering the shore break photo on the wall: we were glowing.

Another pair of soldiers tried to enter the bunker. Daphne raised the carbine and pulled the trigger as she walked out of the living room that incongruously held the body of my dead little girl. I couldn't balance that thought; I decided to stop thinking. Before falling to our fire, one of the soldiers managed a shot that was in turn, deflected by the field. The music cut out, and the lights again flickered off as someone disabled the generator.

It was too little, too late.

The momentary darkness of the barn was pushed back by the glow of power around us.

We were free.

Daphne led us through the now hatch-free entryway, sliding the bookcase closed behind us. A pair of small, roundish shapes rolled into the office.

Grenades.

Daphne moved us at full speed as she scooped up the grenades and tossed them back out the door. She stepped back and placed our backside against the bookcase and hardened the Lens field, protecting the entrance to the bunker as the explosion ripped through the barn. Three target lights in the barn winked out, and the walls to the office blew inwards.

A lone Section soldier was still standing, shaking his head from the blast, just as Daphne walked out through the wreckage and put a bullet from the HK in his left kneecap, dropping him instantly. She pointed the carbine down as we passed him writhing on the floor and put a bullet in his brain. The side of the barn had a jagged, gaping hole in it, and the interior was a rubble-filled disaster. We walked out the hole and into a war zone.

There were bodies strewn about the exterior of the barn, several with missing heads à la Mort. The sound of gunfire was all around us as soldiers and FBI went toe-to-toe. In the middle of it all was a leaping, spider-legged form.

"Where's Micawber?" I snarled.

Searching.

Lights flashed above a screen—a squad of armored Section goons was headed our way.

"Daphne!"

I see them, sugar.

What looked blindingly fast on the monitor to me must have seemed inhuman to the soldiers as Daphne unslung the carbine and fired in one motion, dropping the first dozen in front to the ground. Without pausing to reload, she whipped out the machete and tore through the remaining soldiers in a bloody ballet of coiling and twisting strikes, moving like a human cyclone compared to the soldiers who moved so slow in comparison they may as well have been meat statues.

Daphne was a turbo-charged Cuisinart of mayhem. The earthen field was soon strewn with fallen bodies and their still-twitching parts.

Another squad of black-clad soldiers rushed over the hill, and Daphne stopped her whirling dervish of death dance to stare at them as the entire battlefield went silent. I blinked in confusion for a moment.

I couldn't hear a damn thing…

Daphne thrust out her right hand and slammed it down as a wave of concentrated sonic force fell on the approaching squad and turned them all to squad-jelly.

I lifted my jaw from my chest and murmured, "Outstanding."

I'm so not in charge.

One of the monitors lit up with a strange signal pattern. I looked on the battle map that dominated the right half of the monitor bank. The signal was coming from Mort, or more specifically, Shiva. The signal reached up to the sky, and in a moment, the FBI helicopter circling above the battle was abruptly pulled down to the ground, smashing the craft flat as an empty beer can. It was as though a giant magnet had been switched on.

Oh, my.

"What did he do?"

Shiva has tapped into the magnetic field.

"What magnetic field? Like, earth's magnetic field? Can you do that?"

It should be ripping them apart.

"He just swallowed a shit ton of 'What's Up, Dick?' That helping?"

Shiva has evolved along a different path than I.

On the monitors, the black RV that Section used for domestic missions was parked near the barn. A platoon of Section soldiers led two tall figures out of one of them.

"Daphne—"

I have them.

We ran full tilt toward the RV. The Section guards never raised their weapons, instead, they parted to reveal Cybil Micawber standing in front of the colonel.

Daphne drew our pistols and took out two of the guards before I got a good look at Cybil. I only had a moment to see that she was armed with a large rifle made of a familiar, silvery metal. She pulled the trigger.

A wave of green energy shot out of the wide flat barrel of the rifle and hit us squarely.

We dropped to the ground like a marionette whose strings had been cut. The monitors in the *Nostromo* control ball flashed static, and all feeds—other than straight-up audio and visual—went dead.

"Daphne!" I called out.

There was no response.

We had fallen on our side. The approaching legs of the remaining guards and the Micawbers came into view as they walked toward us. While we lay there helplessly, two of the guards rushed in and disarmed us.

The control panel was dead, and Daphne was unresponsive. What had Cybil shot us with? It had disrupted the Lens and seemed to have short-circuited Daphne. I wondered why I was still functioning and remembered how Daphne had told me that the environment of the *Nostromo* replica was secured away from her main code. Had that protected my consciousness?

Cybil stepped into view, roughly rolling us onto our back with her foot.

"She's down," she purred. "Load it into the RV. We'll drive to the back of the property. A Section gunship is on its way."

Colonel Micawber stepped into view behind his daughter. He was holding another one of the collars. He unfastened something to open the collar, and then he passed it to the Section guard at his side.

"Collar the bitch," he murmured.

From inside the control ball, I watched as the guard slung his SMG over his shoulder and knelt down to put the collar on our neck.

"Daphne! Wake the fuck up," I yelled, but there was no response.

Cybil pointed in the direction of the still-raging battle. "What about Mortimer?"

The colonel smiled. "He will provide useful cover until we are away. By the time the FBI figures out that we have slipped through, it will be too late."

The collar with its glowing lights got closer, and then I heard it: a clarion call, clear and strong as it echoed across the entire orchard.

"GET AWAY FROM DADDY!"

A billowing force wave smacked into the guards and Micawbers, hurling them away from our prone form. As the wave passed over us, the *Nostromo* control ball broke apart, fading to black.

I fell into darkness.

I awoke from my digital fall to the cold, stony ground grinding into my back. I stared up and saw the night sky and heard the roar of battle from the orchard.

I was seeing and hearing like real stuff, not an A/V feed. I was back in the driver's seat.

I rolled onto my side and saw a sphere of shining, white light walking toward us from the gaping hole in the barn wall. As it got closer, a small figure resolved in the center of the sphere.

Her hair had regrown, and it spilled out as it floated in the air around her head. It shone with a black luster that would have made Akihiro's wife burn with jealousy. Her skin had filled out, and she radiated pure health. Under her arm was the stuffed red monkey.

Jeni.

I turned to look for the Micawbers and the Section guards, but they were unmoving bodies on the ground, several yards away.

"Jeni?" I asked unbelievingly.

She gave that radiant smile, rushed to me, and flung herself into my arms. The white light surrounded both of us, and the HUD appeared across my vision. I heard Daphne's welcome voice in my head.

It worked.

I clutched Jeni to me as I mumbled in stunned disbelief: "How?"

Your tears. I used them as the delivery vehicle. I couldn't warn you, or the Micawbers might have found out.

I remembered my tears spilling onto Jeni's face, eyes, and mouth.

"I thought it couldn't be passed," I said, my chest heaving with emotion as the true shock of Jeni standing before me registered. She gently tilted my head up by the chin, and white fire glowed in her dark eyes as she laid her forehead against mine.

It couldn't be passed by the previous, inferior incarnations, but I am a true artificial intelligence. I choose who will bear my children; I chose Jeni. Part of you is a part of me. Now we are both part of Jeni and Alice.

"Alice?"

Jeni smiled, and her eyes swirled with argent flames. "She's my new friend. She woke me up! And she made me better!"

I stared at Jeni, my insides bursting at the seams with an expanding ball of joy. She was alive! She was beaming with health and nano-energy, and yet I felt a nugget of fear and disquiet at the heart of my joy-ball. Yes, alive and seemingly healthy. At what cost, though? What had she become? I was a grown-ass man, and I could barely be trusted with this kind of power. She was still a young child, and she now had a nascent god living in her head.

What had we done?

Had we just begun the next phase of human evolution? There was no way the existence of the three of us would not ultimately alter the social/global balance of power. Who would or would not get access to the nanos would become the defining battle of the next century.

Did either Daphne or I have any right to thrust that on someone without their consent? Had we just perpetuated the same mistake that had happened to us, or was this just an inevitable byproduct of creating an artificial organism with as much will to live and propagate itself as any biological one?

There was a commotion from the orchard, and a familiar, spider-legged figure rose into the air above the farm as Section and FBI alike fired their weapons at their now common enemy. Mort was going straight up into the sky like he was riding an elevator. The clouds moved aside in a strange way high above us.

The blanket of clouds above the rising figure of Shiva/Mort spun in a counterclockwise direction, slowly at first and then gaining speed. Lightning flashed in the center of the swirling mass, and clouds were sucked into its center.

Data flowed across the HUD too fast for me to process. "What's he doing?"

Shiva has gone mad. It wants to fulfill its destiny.

"Its destiny?"

Jeni looked up at the swirling clouds that were quickly disappearing into a black void at the center. In a solemn voice that carried over the sounds of gunfire and the rising maelstrom, she said, "He is the Destroyer of Worlds, Daddy."

Oh shit.

LOST IN TIME AND SPACE

I stood up and ran to the still bodies lying on the cold ground. The Micawbers—father and daughter—lay near one another, their forms a twisted ruin. It looked like the forceful blast had shattered every bone in their bodies. Cybil's chest had collapsed into a wet, concave hole, and her pale blue eyes stared lifelessly at the sky. The colonel's body was also on its back, with its limbs splayed and twisted unnaturally; however, his head was turned in the opposite direction, face down in the dirt.

I gazed down at the body of the man who had been my commander, mentor, nemesis, and like it or not, even a bit of a father figure. I muttered, "You lose, asshole." I searched for the field-disrupting rifle that Cybil had fired at us. I found it not far away, smashed to pieces.

Peering down the hill toward the orchard, the two armies were still fighting each other, but a few on both sides recognized the danger Shiva/Mort presented and were trying to bring the one-man spider army out of the sky. The clouds were being sucked into the spinning vortex in the sky, and a strong wind was whipping through the farm.

"Daphne, what's he doing?"

If I had to guess, he's using the Lens to refocus the earth's magnetic field. He's magnifying it, trying to manifest a quantum mechanical black hole.

"A black hole?"

A micro-black hole. But one that's more than sufficient to destroy Earth and fulfill Shiva's desire.

Well, there's something you don't see every day.

I reflected that might be a bit of an understatement. "Can he do that? How do we stop it?"

A small target light lit up on the HUD across my eyes. It was indicating something only a few feet away. I searched and found the remaining collar, its lights still gleaming dully. I picked it up and looked into the sky. Shiva/Mort was only a tiny dot, high above the ground.

"You're joking. How are we supposed to get this on him?"

We have help.

I felt a small hand grab mine, and I looked down at Jeni. She was no longer glowing: she looked like a beautiful but ordinary little girl who was up past her bedtime. My disquiet fled at the sight of her. She was just a little girl, not the incubating demigoddess I had imagined. Not yet, anyhow.

"We will help Daddy. We are strong together."

I remembered what Mort had said in the restaurant. 'Two strong together, apart...weak.'

Are you ready, sugar?

I nodded.

Jeni tugged on my hand and pulled me down to her. She wrapped her arms around my neck and buried her face into my shoulder.

Jeni and Alice will remain on the ground to anchor us. We may not return.

I understood and hugged Jeni to me.

"I love you big as the sky, baby."

"Me too, Daddy."

She stepped back, and the glow around her grew again. The sheathed machete was on the ground, so I picked it up and strapped it back on.

Wrong weapon, sugar.

I hung the collar from the belt, securing the machete.

"Call it a security blanket. Let's do this."

I stared at the rotating vortex above my head. The swirl of clouds stretched across the river to the north, into Washington State, past Mount St. Helens, and it looked like it had spread as far west as Portland. With our enhanced vision, I could just make out Shiva/Mort's form rotating in time with the vortex far above us.

"They are not exactly going to just meekly bow their head and let us put this on them," I said over the sound of the whipping wind.

Shiva cannot fight us and maintain the buildup of gravity through the field sufficient to power the black hole simultaneously. They must choose to fight and survive or try to continue their mad quest.

I checked the HUD. The field-disruption rifle had emptied our stored sonic energy, and the eye-con was flat.

"Okay," I said as I looked up, "how do we get him down here?"

We don't.

I groaned.

"This would have been much easier if you hadn't freed them."

I gave my word. We didn't have a choice.

I grumbled, "I didn't like it then, I don't like it now, but I get it."

The sound of gunfire had dropped from a steady staccato thunder to occasional pops, like popcorn that had almost finished cooking. I looked down the hill and could see black-clad Section operatives with their hands raised as FBI reinforcements arrived.

I looked behind me at Jeni just in time to see her wave as she faded from view. She had activated her LightCam. Being invisible should keep her safe from the two armies below while we tried to take out Shiva/Mort.

"The kids have enough juice to get us up there?"

In answer, I felt my feet leave the ground as I rose into the air.

"Have I mentioned that I hate flying?" I yelled as we sped higher and faster. The cold wind had grown stronger as we left the ground. I looked down below and instantly regretted it—the farm was a dwindling anthill beneath our feet. Two of the armies had stopped fighting; it was time for the three war machines to go at it.

Mt. Hood was a lonely shadow against the night sky at our backs as we picked up speed and rocketed toward Shiva/Mort and the spreading patch of black at the center of the maelstrom.

The wind howled louder as we rose higher, and it pulled at us as it swept toward the center of the spinning mass of blue-black clouds.

Daphne, we have no power. How are we going to fight them?

I barely had time to finish the thought as we picked up even more speed, rocketing into Spider/Mort and sending them spinning away.

Ramming speed! Daphne crowed in my head.

The wind dropped, and the spinning of the clouds above us slowed.

We can't just keep knocking them around. We need an endgame, I thought.

Wait for it.

Lightning lit up the sky around us, and I grinned. "Oh! You good with this now?" I yelled.

The power eye-con filled, and we exploded with light.

I'm ready this time. I am more; WE are more.

Shiva/Mort came speeding toward us. His howl of rage thundered as he crossed the sky in a blur. They collided with us as we hurtled across the sky, and their long-articulated legs tried to wrap around us as they did at the restaurant. The dark line of the Columbia River appeared below us as we twisted and spun through the air.

There wasn't time to pull the collar out before I heard Daphne's command.

Now.

The lightning launched out of our Lens field, aimed at Shiva/Mort. I expected to smell barbecued spider, but his field absorbed our power, and the wind howled louder as they threw us downward to the ground, laughing madly.

I had time to convey to Daphne: *I think that made him stronger!*

There was a supporting push from the ground, and I knew Alice/Jeni were sending us what strength they had to keep us aloft. Our descent slowed, and we hung in midair below the vortex. Shiva/Mort had resumed his position and was spinning in time with the clouds again.

Again, we rocketed upward. This time, I pulled out the collar and was ready. Before we could get close, Shiva/Mort pointed toward us, and there was a crushing weight from above us like he had dropped a mountain on our heads—despite there being nothing there.

We were thrown to the ground again, landing in an empty field abutting the forest with a terrific *thud!* In the explosion of dirt and rocks, a deep crater was formed. Our field absorbed the blow, and the kinetic force filled our power eye-con.

His power has grown beyond what should be possible, Daphne whispered in our mind.

"Force isn't going to work. Can't you access the power he's using?"

I am trying, but they are intercepting every attempt I make.

"You are saying they're cock-blocking us?"

Essentially.

I looked down at the collar in my hand. "We have another problem," I said.

The collar had broken during the fall. I still held a half-crescent of metal; the other half was nowhere to be seen. As I searched around, a long-dead tree nearby was shaking and quaking as it was pulled out of the ground. Its massive roots trailed behind it as it twirled away into the maddened sky. Dirt and small bushes followed as they too were pulled out of the ground and catapulted into the heavens.

"Now what?" I yelled over the howling wind.

We need a power source as great as Shiva's, but there is nothing to compare to that. We have failed.

The ground shook and vibrated as additional objects were hurtled skyward. More trees and bushes were uprooted; even fences and parts of buildings rose and spun upward. The terrified lowing of a cow caught my ears, and I watched as the large animal was raised aloft.

"We need to get Jeni to safety!" I yelled.

I have already alerted them. They have taken shelter in the bunker.

The earth shook again, and we fell to the ground. Our teeth chattered in time with the vibrations from deep within the ground, and we knew it wouldn't be long before everything around us became grist for the mill in the sky. We climbed out of the crater only to fall against the trunk of an enormous live oak. The living wood quivered madly from the vibrations.

Vibrations.

I thought back to what Chuckie had told me as we sat in his living room. *Energy, man. Everything in the universe—all matter—is just energy vibrating at different frequencies. Tap into that shit, and you're in touch with God, man.*

Now that our minds were no longer separated by biology, the surprise that welled up from Daphne at my thoughts caught me off-guard. We were a unit, a single entity now.

There was a change in the Lens.

"What's happening?" I yelled.

Calibrating.

Before I had time to question, the oak beneath my hands shook faster and faster. As the vibrations grew in intensity, the tree suddenly grew insubstantial, thinning in mass as it faded from view before drifting into nothingness.

The power meter on our eye-con filled.

Surprise and a chaser shot of glee went through me; It wasn't me—it was all Daphne.

We dropped to our knees and placed our hands on the earth. The Lens field hummed with power around us as the ground and everything in our sight for a hundred yards shook and grew insubstantial.

The power meter went from green to violet to a powerful, pulsing scarlet. The night disappeared as we glowed with the light of a small sun.

We rose into the air once more, leaving a hundred-yard crater in the earth behind us. We pulled more and more power into us as the forest and fields surrounding us faded away.

Our body shook with power: it dripped out of our skin like sweat and fell away as we sped upward toward Shiva/Mort. Time stretched again. I pulled the machete from its sheath and pointed it in front of us as we left a sonic boom behind. An extra surge of strength rose from the earth as Alice/Jeni sent their extra power and resolve to us. The machete glowed like a diamond in the sun, refracting a rainbow radiance that spread scattershot across the chaotic, dark sky.

Shiva/Mort had no time to act. One moment we were on the ground; the next, we had punched into them. The brilliantly glowing blade of the machete passed effortlessly through their field and penetrated their midsection, exiting through the back.

We continued to shoot upward toward the vortex as Shiva/Mort screamed in agony. The energy we had collected shot out ahead of us in a coherent, solid beam of multi-colored light, headed to the center of the dark mass. Its impact rocked us through the Lens.

I had a moment to think to Daphne. *What are you doing?*

We're going down the rabbit hole and pulling it in after us.

Debris flew around us. Daphne had hardened the Lens around us into a protective field, protecting us from impacts and absorbing the kinetic energy. Parts of buildings, trees, and cars swept past us on their way to the vortex.

What does that mean? I asked.

It's too late to shut down the gravity well, so I'm altering it.

To what?

An Einstein-Rosen bridge.

What?

Daphne flashed the information across my mind, and I only had time to understand one thing.

It was a wormhole.

Daphne, that's a one-way trip! We won't survive!

I'll try to keep the bridge from collapsing, but it's time to leave the party, hon.

Shiva/Mort screamed on the end of our blade, but he was stuck like a bug on a pin. Lightning flickered and flashed as we passed through the clouds and the inky black spot sucked in everything, even light, into the center of the swirling clouds. Across the HUD, I saw flares of radiation spewing from the sides of the hole.

Jeni!

Alice will care for her. She understands she must hide Jeni. Given enough time, no force on earth will harm her. Jeni will be safe with Alice.

A powerful sadness passed through me. I had only just gotten Jeni back.

Shiva is too dangerous. We are too dangerous. We can't stay—we would be hunted forever.

No one else knows about Jeni and Alice. What did your friend Mrs. Taniguchi write to you? Ren, sugar. You have to let go.

She was right, but that didn't make it any easier. I wished I could tell Jeni how much I loved her. I wished that I could say goodbye. I hoped she understood that I never wanted to leave her. At the same time, I was filled with fear at the possibility of what she might become without me.

Transmitting.

A waterfall of emotion cascaded through me—every moment I had felt love for Jeni, plus all my hopes and dreams for her. Everything I had ever felt for her ran through my mind and then passed out of me in a tight beam as Daphne sent it down to earth. The hole's edge grew in our vision as everything slowed and stretched. Shiva/Mort howled in fury but could not stop our rush. The hole had us all, and we couldn't escape now even if we wanted to.

Receiving.

It hit me as we rocketed into the dark...the sweet, uncomplicated trust and love of my little girl sent up by Alice. It wrapped around me, expanded within, and filled me. The fear disappeared, my anger drained from me, and I felt a peace I had never known.

I let go. I was ready.

The powerful tidal pull of the gravity distortion grabbed us tighter. We went ever faster—no longer going upward but falling downward. The horizon approached, and Shiva/Mort stretched out into a straight line in front of us, sucked off the end of the glowing machete as they disappeared into the wormhole.

The world around us was a spinning kaleidoscopic vortex that held me in awe.

Scared, sugar?

No. I'm not afraid because I'm not alone.

Never again. You have me, and I have you—we are one. Ready?

Always know when to leave the party.

I smiled as we passed the edge of the wormhole. The world at our back disappeared as the hole snapped shut behind us. We stretched out to infinity, and I gave a rebel yell of pure delight.

What a ride.

ABOUT THE AUTHOR

Gregory Peterson is a SoCal native and graduate of the University of California, Berkeley, where he studied writing and Chinese studies. After graduation, he was employed as a magazine editor in Los Angeles. He is married and the father of two children who know him as That Guy Who Works In Our Kitchen. An avid surf and snow fiend, he also enjoys playing the guitar and sneaking out in the morning to pursue his lifelong obsession with picking up heavy things and putting them back down again. He lives in Denver, Colorado. You can reach him at SixStringWordSmith@gmail.com or on Threads @6StringWord.